Deadly Redemption

Candle Sutton

Prologue

Rain battered the windshield. The wipers whipped water from the glass, but couldn't keep up with the onslaught.

Brody gripped the wheel. The storm outside paled compared to the one raging within.

He'd found a traitor.

Even now, with irrefutable proof, he could hardly believe it. That Judas had been in their midst for weeks; how could none of them have seen it?

Tim would be furious.

Headlights bore down in his rearview mirror. Brody didn't need to see the car to know who it was. That treacherous leach would do anything to stop him from telling Tim the truth.

Because once Tim knew, he'd take care of the problem. He always did.

The car drew closer. Brody squashed the accelerator.

The Hemi in his truck responded with a power that usually thrilled him.

But not tonight.

Wind threw rainwater against his truck in waves. Going this fast was foolish, but what choice did he have? He had to get back to headquarters before they could stop him.

If only his phone hadn't gotten crushed in the struggle. Then he could've called Tim and wouldn't be driving in the storm like some kind of maniac.

The wind increased as his truck crossed the threshold to

the Wappoo Creek Bridge.

Flashing lights glimmered through his rain-spattered windshield. An accident?

He slammed the brakes. The wheels screamed on the flooded asphalt, the truck's bed whipping like a pendulum.

The guardrail filled his vision.

The crunch of metal, the tinkle of glass, and the lurch of sudden impact registered a second before he felt himself freefalling into darkness.

The truck hit the water with a jolt.

The airbag exploded against his chest and face. He twisted to the side to see around it. Then he wished he hadn't. Liquid blackness encased him.

Water rushed in.

The cold shocked his limbs. He couldn't move. All he could do was stare at the black liquid as it filled the floorboards and crawled up his legs.

Do something!

He punched the airbag out of the way as he felt the truck lazily tip backward.

His fingers fumbled with the seatbelt release. Jammed!

Jerking at the strap did no good. The accident had locked it up.

He strained for the glove box and the knife he kept inside.

The water reached the bottom of his ribcage, plastering his t-shirt against his stomach. Shivers rocked his body.

Cool metal met his searching fingers. He flipped the blade open.

The vehicle pivoted. His body fell forward, the seatbelt cutting into his chest and stomach.

He was headed to the bottom. Fast.

Water splashed his face. He turned his head and sucked in a breath. The water level climbed higher.

He couldn't see, but he put the knife against the seatbelt and sawed.

Fire engulfed his lungs. His movements slowed.

It was no use.

He couldn't hold his breath any longer. But he'd have to or he'd drown. Even as he commanded his body to obey, his mouth opened and sucked in a lungful of liquid salt.

He coughed, but only drew in more saltwater.

Blackness lurked at the edges of his mind.

He'd failed. And his friends would pay the price.

One

"You 'fraid ta take me on?"

Nate Miller stared at the pipsqueak in front of him. The kid stood at least six inches shorter and a good fifty pounds lighter. From the looks of things, he had more ego than muscle.

"Just walk away."

A handful of guys noticed the tension in the kid's stance and came over, probably smelling a fight.

The things that passed for entertainment in the yard.

The kid fisted his fingers and stepped forward. "Whatsa matter, old man?"

Old? Okay, so he had twenty years on the kid. Forty-three hardly made him old.

Well, so much for the fresh air. Nate pushed himself up. Sometimes it was easier to just stay in his cell, no matter how nice the sun felt on his face.

"Not so tough without Stevens watchin' your back, are you?"

Nate paused and turned, spearing the kid with his eyes. "Who do you think taught him to shoot?"

Okay, so maybe the kid wasn't the only one whose ego got the better of him sometimes.

Silence descended as Nate strode away.

No wonder. He'd never told anyone that piece of information before. Completely true, but not something he was particularly proud of, especially considering the body count Stevens had accumulated with the training Nate had given him.

That blood was on his hands.

Nate crossed to an empty bench and sank down, scanning the yard. Orange jumpsuits and razor wire as far as the eye could see. Some days it seemed unbelievable that his life had come to this.

Several furtive glances angled his direction.

Yep, the rumor mill was active and healthy. By the end of the day, what he'd said would probably be exaggerated to the point that everyone would believe he'd not only trained Stevens, but that he *was* Stevens.

Funny how being associated with Stevens had given him instant street cred in this place.

It had also made him a target for the new guys looking to prove something. Like the kid who'd tried to get in his face just a few minutes ago.

He leaned his head back and stared at the storm clouds building overhead.

The sky might open up any time. In fact, he could smell the rain on the wind.

"Miller."

Now what?

Nate turned his head to find not an inmate, but a guard, walking toward him. "Hey Abrams. What's up?"

"You got a visitor."

Weird. Lana was the only one who ever came to see him and she only came on Saturdays. Never on a Tuesday afternoon.

Unless something was wrong.

He rose from the bench and followed Abrams inside. The former Marine fell into step beside him as the door closed.

"Know who it is?"

"Negative." Abrams' voice contained its usual note of steel. "But don't get too excited. It wasn't that hot deputy friend of yours."

Darn. Although a part of him was glad since a break in her routine would signify trouble.

"You ask me, the guy looked like one of those cookie-cutter Fed types."

A Fed? Even weirder.

Well, he'd find out soon enough.

Nate angled his eyes toward Abrams. "How were your days off?"

"Too short. But I caught the game so it wasn't a total waste."

"How're the Jags looking this season?" The season had only started, but from everything he'd heard, the team was strong this year.

Abrams shrugged. "Okay. But I'm a Cowboys fan, myself."

"Traitor."

"Hey, I may live here, but I'll always be a Texan at heart."

Movement caught Nate's attention and he glanced over to find Kirk, the newest guard on the team, leaning against a door with his arms crossed over his chest. The kid said nothing, but he didn't have to. His look said more than enough.

Well, at least he was keeping his snide remarks to himself. For once.

As the newest and youngest guard, the kid displayed his superiority complex as proudly as he did his badge.

Abrams opened the door to the private visitation room and waved Nate inside. An abused wooden table sat in the center of the room, all four legs bolted to the floor. On either side of the table, wooden chairs faced off.

The room's lone occupant looked up as Nate approached the table.

Drawn features, piercing eyes, and short brown hair gave the man a hawk-like appearance. The gray pinstriped suit, white shirt, and gray tie screamed federal agent. Or public defender, but since Nate had no need of a defense, that seemed unlikely. A cheap briefcase sat closed on the corner of the table.

Pale eyes stared out of an equally pale face. The man's pinched eyebrows lowered and his mouth looked like he'd just crunched a Granny Smith apple.

Obviously coming here to talk to him hadn't been this guy's first choice.

Yeah, buddy? Well, that makes two of us.

Nate pulled out the chair across from the agent and eased down.

The man cleared his throat. "Nate Miller?"

What, he thought the guards would bring back the wrong man? "Yeah."

"Agent Underwood, FBI."

In spite of the curiosity roiling inside him, Nate remained silent. This meeting was Underwood's idea; let him get it started.

"Tell me about yourself." A condescending tone colored the demand.

Other than arching his eyebrow, Nate didn't move. No way had this Fed driven all the way down here just to get to know him. Something was up. "You've got my file."

"It doesn't say why you turned yourself in."

So that was it. He should've known.

"Freedom was boring. Thought I'd see what life was like on the inside."

Underwood leaned in, his hands clenching. "I cleared my day for this. I'm not leaving until I get some answers."

"Suit yourself. I'm not going anywhere."

Underwood stared him down.

Nate bit back a chuckle. Did this pinstriped pipsqueak really think he could intimidate him?

A minute passed before Underwood spoke, his tone cold. "Look, you wanna know why I'm here, right? Level with me and I'll tell you."

Something compelled him to honesty. Experience told

Nate it was probably the Holy Spirit. "I had to. There were some people in my life who deserved to know the truth."

"So they suspected you."

"No, but I had to..." Breath hissed from between Nate's teeth. "I don't expect you to understand. But when you hear God telling-"

"Aw, man. Don't tell me you're one of those who found God while locked inside."

"I found Him before."

"Sure you did."

Ignoring the sarcasm, Nate kept his eyes locked on Underwood. "Believe me or not, I don't care, but I held up my end. Tell me why you're here."

Underwood leaned his elbows on the table, interlaced his fingers, and ground out words that he apparently would have rather kept locked away. "You're being given a chance to serve your country."

"Think I'm a little too old to join the Army."

A muscle in Underwood's jaw twitched.

"A killer with a sense of humor. Great."

"I've never killed anyone."

"In the law's eyes, you did. Accomplice to murder is the same as pulling the trigger." He didn't wait for Nate to respond before pushing forward. "We need your help."

Out of the scenarios Nate could have imagined, this one never would've crossed his mind. "The FBI?"

A curt nod answered his question. "We need you to infiltrate a militant group."

"You want me to do undercover work for the FBI?" The absurdity of the request almost made him laugh. "Whose sick idea of a joke is this?"

An abrupt chuckle burst from Underwood's lips. "Don't I wish. It's no joke."

If it wasn't a joke, then it was some kind of trap. There was no way the FBI wanted him on their payroll. "Well, gee. Thanks for asking me to join J. Edgar Hoover's finest, but I'll pass. I'm not exactly FBI material."

"You wouldn't be joining. Think of it more as consulting."

Unbelievable. "Why me?"

"They just lost their system's expert in a car accident."

So he was good with computers and had hacked many high-level systems in order to get into places that he shouldn't. He wasn't the only one who could do that. "Come on. The FBI has their own computer geeks. People better than me, I'm sure."

"None with your reputation. It'd take too long to get one of our agents correctly positioned. You're already well known in certain circles. Plus you're acquainted with one of this group's members."

Really? He couldn't think of anyone he knew who was part of a militia. "Who?"

"Edward Carson."

Edward Carson? Nate racked his memory to place the name. It didn't sound familiar...

"Also goes by Eddie. He's in here with you right now."

An image of the twenty-something guy with a shaved head and plugs in his ears flashed through Nate's mind. The guy had been here about six months and had attached himself to Nate for some reason that Nate had yet to figure out. They'd talked a bit, but had Eddie ever mentioned being in a militia? If so, Nate had missed that detail. "What group is he with?"

"They call themselves White Fire. They're well-funded, well-armed, and growing more deadly."

White Fire. Sounded like an acid rock band from the '80s. But with a name like that, they had to be a white supremacist group. "What are they into?"

"Lots of things. They've been around for years, but have escalated in the last few months."

"Into what?"

"Most recently, bio-toxins. They've already killed forty people with it and our intel tells us they have a lot more where that came from."

"Where do you get your intel?"

Underwood hesitated. "I'm not at liberty to say, but I can tell you it's accurate."

Sure it was. Because snitches never gave bad information. "I don't know what you think I can do from in here."

"You wouldn't be in here." Underwood opened the briefcase, removed a stack of papers, and slid them across the table. "You're being offered a full pardon and a new identity for your assistance in bringing these guys to justice."

No way.

In spite of his reservations, Nate couldn't help skimming the letter attached to the top of the stack. The signature at the bottom snagged his attention.

The president. Of the United States.

Man, this was big.

"All you have to do is help us dismantle the group from the inside. We want everyone involved with them behind bars. After that, you're a free man."

Free. No more being treated like the second-class citizen he was.

He'd be able to see his kids.

Better yet, he'd be able to see Lana. Any time he wanted.

An ache settled deep in his chest. No matter how much he looked forward to them, weekly visits weren't enough.

But to get there, he'd have to return to a life he'd sworn to leave behind forever. "And if they want me to hack into someplace important? Like the FBI's database or the Pentagon? What if they expect me to steal several million credit card numbers? What then?"

"String them along. Fake the information. Whatever you have to do. We want them stopped."

"So what, the ends justify the means?"

Underwood's silence provided all the confirmation he needed.

Freedom.

What he wouldn't give to be out of this place. But at what cost? What if he gained freedom only to imprison his soul?

He shoved the papers back across the table. "I can't."

"You got any idea how lucky you are? Things like this are *never* handed out, especially not to scum like you. Why the heck wouldn't you do it?"

"I left that life behind. I won't go back to being a criminal."

"It may not come to that. All we need is an in, then we can take them down."

"And if I can't get what you need without breaking the law? What then?"

Underwood's snort sounded loud in the barren room. "You've gotta be kidding me. All the laws you've broken and you're worried about one more?"

"I'm not the guy I used to be."

Pushing back his chair, Underwood stood. "Fine. Sit here in your little cell and rot."

Nate never moved as Underwood tossed the file into a briefcase and stalked by him.

He'd just turned down a one-way ticket out of here. He must be absolutely crazy.

Tim Williams watched the casket lower into the ground.

Beside him, his sister Amanda sniffled.

They'd miss Brody. He'd been a good friend. Without equal when it came to loyalty.

If only he'd done more to talk Brody out of buying that stupid truck. Most vehicles would've just hit the guardrail on that bridge, but Brody's truck – with the lift kit and monster tires – had flipped right over it.

"What was he even doing in that part of town?" Anguish

added a husky quality to Amanda's voice.

"I don't know." They probably never would.

So many unanswered questions. Like why Brody was on that bridge. Why he'd been driving like a fool in such heavy rain. Why he'd been out so late in the first place.

Sure, he'd had Brody plant a device earlier in the day, but it'd been in a different part of town and had been completed hours before the crash. Where Brody had gone after that was a mystery. Everyone he'd asked claimed to have not seen Brody.

Someone had to know. If so, he'd track them down and learn the truth.

That device would be Brody's legacy. The victims walked among the living now, but soon they would exhibit symptoms.

Then it would be too late.

A shovelful of dirt landed on Brody's coffin.

A sob broke from Amanda and Tim wrapped an arm around her shoulders. His burning throat begged him to share in her grief, but he wouldn't give in.

He clenched his jaw.

Overhead, storm clouds growled as if commiserating with his misery.

Twenty years of friendship meant something.

Whatever had happened, wherever Brody had been, whatever he'd been doing, and whomever he'd been with, Tim would find out. And if anyone had anything to do with Brody's accident, he'd see to it that they paid for killing his friend.

Two

What an idiot! A big, stupid, freakin' idiot.

And the FBI was almost as stupid for wanting to turn a psycho like that loose in society.

On the fifty-seven minute drive back to the Federal building, Underwood alternated between berating the FBI and badmouthing the criminal on which he'd wasted so much of his day.

The plum clouds overhead dumped oceans of rain, thunder growled, and lightning flashed.

Seriously. If he'd had to blow a whole day on this ridiculous assignment, it could've at least been sunny.

Underwood pulled into the secured parking garage, climbed out of the government-issued car, and slammed the door. Going to prison to ask an inmate for help. Disgusting.

Who'd he cross to get saddled with such a revolting job?

At least Miller had turned them down. There had to be a better option than begging a convict to bail them out.

But Special Agent in Charge Reyes wasn't going to be happy about this.

Underwood went through the security checkpoint, got into the elevator, and pushed the button for the eighth floor. No matter how much he wanted to avoid Reyes, there was no point in putting it off.

The doors dinged open and he headed down the all-too-familiar hallway. Reyes had the office at the northeast corner.

Reaching the open door, he drew a lungful of air and

stepped inside. Reyes' curvy redheaded secretary gave him a forced obligatory smile. "Can I help you?"

Like she didn't remember him. It'd been less than three hours since he'd been in here.

"Agent Underwood here to see SAC Reyes."

"I'll let him know you're here. Have a seat."

It was the last thing he wanted to do, but Underwood found himself sitting in one of the uncomfortable chairs upholstered in a drab gray canvas. Had the chair always been this hard?

The door to Reyes' office opened a minute later and Reyes waved him in.

A navy double-breasted suit accented Reyes' trim build and a gold watch flashed from his wrist. His full head of black hair was perfectly styled and looked like it could withstand hurricane–force winds.

"Agent Underwood, have a seat."

What a schmuck. Underwood sat anyway.

Reyes wasted no time with pleasantries. "So, is Mr. Miller on board with our plan?"

"Uh, not exactly."

"Your orders were to secure his cooperation. Did you offer him the pardon?"

"He turned it down."

Eyes narrowed, Reyes studied him. "Explain."

Underwood recapped the conversation. "The scum wouldn't budge."

"Scum. And I suppose you let him know your opinion of him. No wonder he said no."

"What'd you expect me to do? Compliment his choice in friends?"

"Let me explain how this works. I give you an order and you follow it. End of story. And my order was to do whatever it took to get a man condemned to life in prison to switch loyalties and work with us. Too difficult for you?"

Might as well put his opinion out there. What could it

hurt? "To be honest, sir, I don't see why we need this guy's help. We've already got someone on the inside."

"Who has been unable to penetrate to the higher ranks of this group. We need someone with credibility in their eyes."

"So have someone pretend to be him. Or Stevens. Or any other lowlife that they might trust."

"And if someone in the group has met one of them, what then? What if they press him for details about some of his past jobs? We don't have time to train an agent to believably pass for Miller."

What a bunch of....

"But turning a criminal loose? We spent years hunting this guy down and now you want to put him back on the street?"

"When you're running the agency, you can do what you want. For now, your job is to follow orders."

"If you think it's so easy, then maybe you should go and convince him yourself."

Dang.

Reyes was sure to write him up for that one. For insubordination, if nothing else.

If Reyes noticed his tone, he didn't respond to it. "Maybe I should."

Good. Let Reyes deal with Miller. See for himself it wasn't fun. At least it was no longer Underwood's concern.

Reyes' voice slapped him. "Be back here in two hours. You're going with me."

And the day just kept going from bad to worse.

Reyes wasn't done. "I want all the information we have on Nate Miller. The name of his attorney, any known family or friends, former co-workers, doctors, priests, the whole deal."

Underwood snapped open the briefcase and pulled out the thinner of the two files inside. It hit the desk with a sharp slap. "That's all we've got."

"Get me prison records. I want to know if he's called anyone in the time he's been inside, who's writing to him, if anyone visits him."

Teeth clenched, Underwood nodded. "Anything else?"

"Yes. I want that information on my desk within the hour."

U.S. Marshal Milana Tanner shut down the computer and reached for her purse. It had been the longest of days. Between working with a witness who was angry at everyone and another who wouldn't stop crying, she was drained.

All she wanted to do was go home, change into her running clothes, and go for an hour-long run.

Just her, God, and the fresh air. It didn't get much better than that.

The phone on her desk shrilled.

Man, she should've been five minutes faster getting out of this place. Of course, she could ignore it.

She reached for it anyway. "Tanner."

"I'm looking for Deputy Milana Tanner."

The silky male voice was too smooth to be trusted. "You found her."

"Deputy, this is SAC Manuel Reyes, FBI. I'm glad I caught you."

Yeah. Me, too.

She managed to keep the irritation out of her tone. "You almost didn't. I'm on my way out the door."

"I'll make this short. We need your help with a simple matter. Shouldn't take more than an hour of your time. Would you be available to meet with us?"

The FBI wanted her help?

The request itself was strange, but what really struck her was that the request hadn't come through Barker, her superior.

To top it all off, the Special Agent in Charge himself had called to request it. Contacting her hadn't been delegated to a secretary or field agent, but he'd handled it himself. The Special Agent in Charge. How had she even gotten on his radar?

"What matter?"

"I'd really rather not discuss it now. I'll explain everything in person."

"When were you thinking?"

A slight pause. "Within the hour, if you're available."

Within the hour? What could possibly be so urgent that it had to be handled tonight?

She bit back her curiosity. "All interagency requests have to go through the proper channels. You know that."

Silence punctuated his momentary hesitation. "This isn't actually an interagency matter. More of a personal one."

Personal?

She'd never met Reyes. And it had been a while since she'd worked with anyone from the FBI, so a connection there was unlikely.

Rejection swelled on her tongue, but refused to leave her mouth.

If she refused, the curiosity would keep her awake all night.

Nothing terribly pressing awaited her attention tonight. And while she'd be forfeiting her run, cooperating with other agencies often paid off in unexpected favors.

What could it hurt to hear them out? "Where did you want to meet?"

"Florida State Penitentiary."

Paul. Nate. His names flickered through her head, but the face tied to them remained the same.

It couldn't be a coincidence that the FBI wanted to meet her at the same prison in which he had spent the last two and a half years. "You don't need me if you want to talk to Nate Miller. What's this about?"

"Can I count on you being there? Say, around seven?"

Obviously he didn't intend to tell her anything more over the phone. Part of her wanted to tell him to forget it, but curiosity gnawed her into agreement. "I'll be there."

Lana opened her door as the silver four-door sedan approached. The asphalt beneath her feet bounced the sun's heat back up at her. The rain from earlier in the day had turned into humidity that smothered her like a heavy quilt.

The car parked two spaces away. Two men sat inside, one a shrewd-eyed man in a gray suit, the other a black haired man in pinstriped suit and pumpkin orange tie.

The passenger door swung open and the pumpkin-tied man stepped out. His dark eyes locked on her.

"Deputy Tanner?" Surprise tinged his tone, telling her she wasn't at all what he'd expected.

Not surprising. It had taken her less than six months on the job to realize that when people saw her petite build, long hair, and young-looking face, they thought of anything but law enforcement.

She would've made a good undercover agent. Maybe.

After locking the door, she covered the distance between them. "You must be SAC Reyes."

He offered his hand.

Sad; his nails looked better than hers did. But she had more important things to do than visit the salon every ten days to have her nails done.

In spite of his well-manicured hands, his grip was firm and confident. "Thank you for meeting us here."

"Of course. But I must admit, I'd like to know why you wanted me to drive all the way out here." Her eyes drifted toward the other agent, but his blank face revealed nothing.

Reyes flashed a charming smile that might fool witnesses but didn't work on her. He retrieved a brown leather briefcase from the back seat. "I'm sure you would. Is it all right if we head inside first?"

Without waiting for a reply, he led the way toward the prison.

Looked like she didn't have much choice but to go along with Reyes' agenda, whatever that might be.

Stale air greeted her as she stepped inside. Welcome to Florida State Pen.

They signed in and surrendered their weapons. Ten minutes later, they sat in the visitation room, waiting for Nate to arrive.

Lana cleared her throat.

"SAC Reyes. I'd really appreciate an explanation." She tried to keep the exasperation out of her voice, but wasn't able to completely hide it.

A nod acknowledged her request. "Naturally. But first I must have your word that none of what you hear today will leave this room. Can I count on you to keep this private?"

Sirens blared in her head, telling her to not agree to anything. After all, *he'd* asked her to be here. She owed him nothing. "I guess it depends on what I hear."

"Understandable, but unless you'll give me your word, I'm afraid you wasted a trip out here."

Unbelievable. Did the man think the world revolved around him?

She should get up and walk out. Have no part of this mess.

But it involved a friend and she didn't trust this oh-so-smooth Special Agent in Charge. She had to know what was going on, which meant she'd have to play by Reyes' rules.

Ignoring the instincts screaming to run the other way, she managed a tight nod.

"Very good. Earlier today, Agent Underwood," he indicated the light haired man next to him, "Came to visit with Mr. Miller. You see, a situation has come up and we need his help. But Mr. Miller was, how shall we say, less than cooperative. I'm hoping you may get further with him than we were able to."

"Wait a second. You asked me to give up my evening, drive all the way out here, so you could *use* me to further your own agenda?"

The congenial smile on Reyes' face never faltered in spite of the anger lacing her tone. "Of course not. I'm simply hoping you can help convince Mr. Miller to see beyond himself. He can help us save lives."

"How? What can he possibly do from in–"

"Lana?"

She swiveled in her chair to find Nate approaching. "Hey, Paul."

It didn't matter that Paul wasn't his real name. It was what she'd always called him, what he himself had asked her to call him.

His hair hung past his ears and seemed to have more gray in it every time she saw him. A thick mustache and beard encircled his mouth and shared the salt and pepper coloring. The shaggy appearance was a far cry from how he'd looked prior to being incarcerated.

His eyes flicked from her to the two agents sitting on the other side of the table and back again, his smile growing slightly strained. "They dragged you into this, too, huh?"

"I still don't know what 'this' is." She turned and leveled a look at Reyes.

"Mr. Miller. Nice to meet you. I'm Special Agent in Charge Reyes." The smile on Reyes' face was as fake as his friendliness. "I was just about to tell Deputy Tanner about the very generous offer we extended earlier."

Nate took the chair next to her. "I already told you no. Bringing her into this won't make a bit of difference."

"I understand. However, I had hoped her presence might convince you that we have no hidden agenda. We only want to save lives."

Though Reyes' tone was sincere, something about the way he spoke made Lana want to gag.

No wonder Nate hadn't bought into this super-secretive scheme of theirs.

"Guys, I rearranged my evening to be here. If you don't mind, I'd like to at least know why."

Nate spoke before either agent said a word. "They want me to infiltrate some militia group."

"What?" She whipped her head to find Reyes watching, a serious expression on his face.

"Not just infiltrate, bring to justice. In exchange we're offering Mr. Miller his freedom and a clean slate."

Unprecedented.

In all her time as a deputy, she'd never heard of such an offer. She could hardly believe she was hearing it now. "Why him?"

"We need someone who can infiltrate this group quickly and with his reputation we feel he is our best option. He's also become acquainted with one of the men from this group during his time here."

"What group?"

"A supremacist group calling themselves White Fire."

White Fire. Something about that tugged at her memory... wait. "Wasn't that the group that killed all those kids? Infected them with something?"

A single nod. "You can see why we're anxious to stop them."

"Groups like this pop up all the time. What's so special about this one?" Yes, they had killed forty some people, but still... releasing a man from prison usually took more than forty deaths.

"I'm afraid that's privileged information." Reyes folded his hands in front of him.

"Not good enough." Nate leaned his elbows on the table. "You're asking me to stick my neck out there. I have a right to know everything you do."

A stiff smile sprang to Reyes' face. "Upon agreement, I'm authorized to reveal more details, but for now, you have no rights at all."

This was ridiculous. They expected Nate to help them without even knowing why?

"Soooo..." Lana scrutinized Reyes' eyes. "Has the group made any threats? Demands? Anything to indicate that something bad is coming?"

"That's information that I'm unable to release. You understand."

Just because she understood didn't mean she had to accept it. Lana tapped her finger slowly on the table. "Who authorized this deal?"

"The president."

"Really?" How had Nate's name even made it on the president's radar?

"Sometimes extreme circumstances require alternative methods of resolution."

A tightening of Underwood's lips told her he wasn't at all in favor of these alternative methods, but the man was smart enough to not openly contradict his superior.

She forced a level tone. "I'm surprised you guys would trust someone with Paul, um, Nate's background. It wasn't that long ago you were hunting him yourself."

"If you'll forgive my bluntness, we've been left with no other viable options. Besides, Mr. Miller has a number of things working in his favor."

"I'd like to hear those things. If you don't mind." It registered in her mind that she'd crossed into her protect and attack mode, but she wasn't about to back off.

In spite of his past, Nate had become a good friend.

He'd even done what he could to try to make atonement.

Reyes counted off on his fingers. "One, he turned himself in when the law had all but given up looking for him. Two, the warden and the guards all vouch for him. And three, he has a contact in the U.S. Marshal's office," a slight nod angled her direction, "who by all appearances is a close friend of his, regardless of his past crimes."

"Look, this has all been entertaining," Nate leaned forward slightly, "But you guys wasted your time coming down here. My answer's the same as it was earlier. I can't help you."

"You mean won't, don't you?" Challenge laced Underwood's tone.

The two regarded each other silently for a second before Lana stepped in. "It sounds like you have your answer."

Reyes swiveled to face her. "Deputy Tanner, would you give us a minute alone with Mr. Miller?"

What the...?

First they wanted her to drive all the way down here and now they wanted her out? What did they plan to do? Beat him into cooperating?

"Please, only for a moment. We aren't here to use violence or deception to coerce Mr. Miller into helping us. In fact, you may wait right outside the room if that will satisfy you. I'd just like a moment to outline his options."

"I think anything you want to say to him, you can say with me in the room."

The smile on Reyes' face indicated he was amused by her response. "I don't believe I can. If I may be so bold, you seem to be controlling Mr. Miller's end of the conversation. He needs to be able to think and respond for himself."

How dare he! Accusing her of being a control freak....

Arguing would only reinforce the point in his mind.

Without a word, she rose and headed for the door. She stepped into the hall and shut the door behind her with a little more force than she'd intended.

The two guards standing nearby stopped talking and stared at her. They turned away as she held their gaze.

Pressing her back flat against the wall next to the door, she crossed her arms over her chest. Just because he was an

SAC, Reyes thought he could order anyone to do anything.

News flash, buddy. I don't have to listen to you or take your orders.

But Nate hadn't really said much since the time he'd been led into the room, had he?

Oh, man, she *had* been controlling.

Just like Reyes said.

The anger evaporated and she leaned her head against the wall. Her thoughts drifted to inside the room. Now that she was out of the way, what was going on in there?

Three

Nate flinched as the door slammed shut.

These guys had no clue who they were messing with here. Lana was not going to be happy when she re-entered the room.

The real question was why Reyes wanted to get rid of Lana. If not for the fact Lana and the guards were nearby, he might've been worried that Reyes would have Underwood beat him into cooperating.

Not that Underwood stood a chance of winning if Nate decided to fight back.

"Quite a woman, your friend."

What was he up to? Suspicion lodged in Nate's mind as he regarded Reyes.

Reyes leaned back in his chair, crossing his ankle over his knee. "Before you turned yourself in, you two were friends, right? I heard you ran a group home and she used to help out. You probably saw her what, at least three, four times a week?"

Pain sliced through the suspicion.

Man, did he miss those days. They were truly the best days of his life.

He tried to keep his emotions off his face. "What of it?"

With eyes as sharp as a snake's fangs, Reyes continued, "If you were released, you could see her as often as you wanted. I'm sure you'd like that. I just met her and I'd like to see her again."

Who was this guy kidding? Nate released a small snort. "I

doubt that."

Uncrossing his legs, Reyes leaned forward. "Why do you say that?"

Nate pointed at Reyes' left hand. "The tan line on your finger tells me you're married. Probably took the ring off in the car before coming inside, right? I bet it's in the center console. Unless you put it in your pocket."

Surprise darted across Reyes' face and he chuckled. "Very observant."

"That's not all I observed. Your eyes tell me you aren't attracted to her, unlike your lackey behind you."

Crimson exploded across Underwood's face and his lips moved but no words came out. The glimmer of a smile on Reyes' face expanded into a full grin.

"I underestimated you, Mr. Miller. You're a very sharp man."

"When you have as much time on your hands as I do, you do a lot of reading. I've been studying human psychology." He shifted his mind back to the issue at hand. "But what I'm really trying to understand is why you're asking me to do this. Aren't you afraid I'll disappear?"

"My feelings on that issue are irrelevant. The Director has requested your release. That's all I need to know."

"So in other words, you agree with your agent, there. That I should never see daylight again." Why it mattered, he was unsure, but the question detoured the conversation and delayed his answer a bit longer.

"I used to. But after speaking with you and meeting Deputy Tanner, I doubt you'd run." Reyes paused, his gaze roving Nate's face. "A successful outcome on this matter is of great personal importance to the president. You would have the gratitude and respect of the most powerful man in the country."

Now probably wasn't the time to mention that he would've voted for the president's opponent in the last election. If he'd been able to vote, that is. "Much as I'd love to get out of this place, I won't be played. Find someone else."

Bending, Reyes picked up the briefcase sitting next to his feet, plopped it on the table, and removed a manila envelope. He undid the clasp and slid out the contents.

"Before I show you these, I need to make something perfectly clear. You are not to discuss our conversation with anyone. Not even Deputy Tanner–"

"Hey, you brought her into this."

"That I did. But this doesn't concern her and she doesn't need to be aware of all the details of this mission. Am I understood?"

Perfectly. But that didn't mean Nate owed Reyes blind obedience. "If I agree to this, I will tell Lana."

Displeasure glimmered in Reyes' eyes and for a moment, Nate was certain the Special Agent in Charge would stuff everything back into the briefcase and storm out of the room.

Finally, Reyes allowed a small sigh. "That would be acceptable. With her current line of work, I trust she knows how to keep confidences."

Reyes slid the contents of the envelope across the table.

Pictures.

Of some kind of industrial equipment? A large tank. Hooked up to what appeared to be an air conditioning system.

He looked up at Reyes.

"That was the delivery system. If you'll keep going...."

Nate turned to the next picture.

An African-American girl, who couldn't have been any older than six, slept in a sea of white linens. More tubes than anyone should have to endure ran from her nose, her mouth, her arms.

"That's Amelia. She died a day after that was taken. She was five years old."

All moisture evaporated from his mouth.

Would the next picture be like this one? He didn't want to look, but found himself pushing the picture of Amelia aside.

Another child, a boy this time, also still as death. Unlike

Amelia, he wasn't in a hospital bed, but on a gurney. His mouth hung slack and his eyes stared wide.

"Jamal. He was the first victim."

Although several photos remained, Nate couldn't take any more.

He shoved the stack aside and met Reyes' eyes. "What happened?"

"White Fire. They released a toxic gas at a preschool. All forty children, as well as the six adults working there, died within a week."

"What gas?"

"Some new bio-toxin. We don't know what it is, nor do we have a cure at this point. It causes respiratory and heart failure. It seems to have a five-day incubation period. Once symptoms present, death usually occurs within twenty-four to forty-eight hours."

"How do you know this wasn't a targeted attack? The danger might be past."

"This attack was a trial run for something much bigger."

"How do you know?"

"I'm not at liberty to discuss that. Suffice it to say, we have solid intel."

That's right. Their source. "So if your source knows all that, how come he can't tell you when or where that attack is going to happen?"

"Our source isn't privy to the details. That's why we need your help."

They were placing way too much stock in his meager connection with Eddie and his past reputation. "A group like this doesn't let just anyone in on their plans. They probably won't even let me get close."

"They might if you helped Edward Carson escape from prison."

"So let me get this straight. The best plan you could come up with was releasing not one, but *two* men from prison?" Didn't inspire much confidence in law enforcement.

Reyes' smile grew strained. "As I said, sometimes extreme–"

"Yeah, I got that."

"Carson is a low-level offender. In spite of his connection to White Fire, he's never been convicted of a violent crime–"

"Yet."

"Yet. And we'd be trusting you to keep it that way. Besides, we'd be arresting him along with the rest of White Fire." Reyes leaned forward, intensity burning in his eyes. "As you can see, we have a great deal of confidence in you, confidence I believe is well-placed. What's your answer, Mr. Miller? In or out?"

No more stalling. He had the information he needed to make a decision.

Help or mind his own business?

It could be a kamikaze mission. Tangling with a supremacist group who'd already taken a number of lives was always risky.

Risk was a part of life. Heck, he faced risk in here every day.

Time to stop thinking about himself. If he had the opportunity to save lives, didn't he also have the obligation to accept?

"I'd like to talk to Lana. Alone." His voice croaked through a scratchy throat.

Triumph highlighted Reyes' face before he could mask it. "Of course."

Snapping open the briefcase, Reyes withdrew a small stack of papers and set it on the table. "Knowing how thorough Deputy Tanner is, I'm sure she will be interested in reading this herself."

Underwood followed on Reyes' heels as the SAC headed for the door. Pausing at the threshold, Reyes added, "We'll be right outside when you're done discussing the matter. But please remember, Mr. Miller, that this group has already killed forty children. Their next target might take out even more."

Muted voices drifted in and then Lana was there, sitting across from him, concern sketched in her eyes. "Paul, you can't do this."

What? He'd thought Lana would be all for saving lives.

Then again, she didn't know that lives were even at stake.

He glanced at the closed door behind him before returning his attention to her. "What makes you say that?"

"The only reason they're offering you this deal is because they don't think you'll survive."

Was Lana right?

While he understood the risks, neither Reyes nor Underwood had mentioned this being a suicide mission. Not that they'd likely advertise that fact.

It didn't matter. Dying wouldn't be so bad if he knew it saved many other lives.

"I think I have to do this."

"No, you don't. Whatever they want, they have other options."

"I'm not sure that they do." He picked up the photographs of the dead children and slid it across the table.

The lines around Lana's eyes deepened. "Are these the children who died in White Fire's last attack?"

"And the next attack is supposed to be worse. If I have a chance to stop this from happening, I've got to do it."

"Just do me one favor. Ask for twenty-four hours so you can pray this over."

In all the craziness, he hadn't even thought to pray about it. What would he do without Lana to keep him grounded? "You got it."

She snatched up the documents. "Let me take a look at this deal to make sure there are no loopholes in it."

Good idea. He'd have no clue what to look for, but Lana probably knew.

Minutes ticked by as she pored over the pages.

"It looks okay, but I'd like to have a lawyer go over it to

make sure." She set the papers aside. "I really don't feel good about this."

"And I don't feel like I have a choice."

A sigh slipped from her soft-looking lips. Papers in hand, she pushed back from the table. "I'll see if I can take this. Hopefully I can get someone to look them over today."

"Your brother?" Her brother Reilly worked for the prosecutor's office and would be the perfect person to examine the documents.

She shook her head. "He's out of town until tomorrow night. Some kind of conference."

"Did you keep in touch with the Pools? I bet Jason would check it out." Although Jason's specialty was wills and estate planning, he should still be able to decipher all the legal mumbo-jumbo.

The Pools, Jason and Stefani, had adopted a couple of his kids right after he turned himself in. He heard from them regularly and although they kept him up to speed on what was happening with the kids, they'd never mentioned Lana.

She nodded. "I see them at church. I'll call him as soon as I leave here."

"Thanks."

The smile she gave him looked forced. "I'll talk to you tomorrow."

She was coming back? While he knew it shouldn't surprise him, it did.

His eyes lingered on the doorway as she stepped out of sight. Soft voices drifted in from the hallway and a moment later, Reyes' polished appearance filled his vision. Nate turned around in his chair and waited for the two agents to sit opposite him.

"Do we have a deal? We're prepared to get you out today."

"I need a day to think things through."

Underwood's scowl deepened. "You realize lives are at stake here, right?"

"One more day won't change that fact."

Reyes didn't look particularly pleased at the delay, but Nate was beyond caring.

"I understand." Reyes' tone belied his words. "We'll be here at eight a.m. for your answer."

Eight... Nate wasn't sure what time Lana intended to talk to him, but it might be better to give her a little more time. "Make it ten."

The smile – fake or otherwise – disappeared from Reyes' features. "Fine. We'll see you in the morning."

It was late, but this had to be done tonight.

Lana turned onto the street Paul used to live on, drove toward the house he used to occupy. A house currently owned by Dale and Annie Webber, the couple who had taken over his group home when he'd turned himself in.

Although the Pools didn't live at the same house, they stopped by at least once a week to visit with the other kids and let the kids they'd adopted play with their friends. Tonight was one of those nights.

The clock read eight fifty-two when she glided to a stop in front of the old mansion.

The Pools' car was parked in the driveway, next to a gleaming silver BMW convertible.

Nice. A potential parent perhaps? Looked like they could probably afford to help a child in need. Maybe more than one.

Although it was awfully late at night for a potential parent to visit.

Killing the engine, Lana stepped from her car. Rain pelted the top of her head as she jogged up the front path. She hugged the file folder containing Paul's pardon close to her chest to keep it dry.

Not that the FBI would begrudge her a few water spots.

"You can't stop me from seeing her."

The growled words stalled her steps. She looked up, caught sight of two figures on the covered porch that ran the length of the house.

How she'd missed them before was a mystery.

"As long as she lives here, I–"

"She won't be here much longer."

"Don't kid yourself. You'll never get custody."

She was too far away to see faces, but one of the voices was Dale's. The porch light backlit the two men, throwing them both into shadow, but not hiding the tension stiffening their bodies.

She moved closer.

The man closest to her stepped forward, hands fisted by his sides. "You really think you can keep her from me?"

Now that she was closer, she could make out the firm set of Dale's face. "I'm sure as heck not letting you get anywhere near her. Now get lost. I want you off my property."

Her foot hit the bottom step.

A muscle in the stranger's jaw twitched. His fist jerked.

It was slight, but enough to convince her to intervene before this thing exploded to blows.

She reached the landing. "Okay, guys. Break it up."

Neither man moved.

Dale's gaze brushed her momentarily, but returned almost immediately to the scrawny black-haired man standing a few feet away from him.

Pushing between them, she put a hand on the stranger's chest and forced him back a few paces.

She flashed her badge just long enough for him to see it.

"I believe Mr. Webber asked you to vacate the premises. You'd be wise to do so now."

Dark irises blended with his pupils, making his eyes look black. Those black orbs surveyed her. Saying nothing, he held his ground.

"If you aren't off this property in the next five seconds, I'll arrest you for trespassing."

The soulless eyes locked with hers. "I'm going. But this isn't over."

Dale's voice drifted over her shoulder. "I don't want to see you on my property again."

"I'll do what I want. It's a free country."

"But this is private property." Lana forced a relaxed posture that she didn't feel, her senses attuned to any sign of impending attack. "If you come here again, you'll discover what it's like to lose your freedoms. Are we understood?"

The corners of his lips twitched downward and his eyes narrowed into slits. Without uttering a word, he whirled and stalked down the steps.

Lana didn't move, her attention never wavering from his gangly form. Her hand rested gently on the butt of her Glock, ready to pull it if he so much as looked like he might reach for a weapon.

Reaching the BMW, he jerked open the door, dropped inside, and slammed the door shut. Tires screamed as he reversed out of the driveway; gears ground as he put the vehicle in drive.

She watched until his car was little more than a speck in the distance, then turned to face Dale. "Who was that?"

"Maria's uncle. Richie Ochoa."

What? Not possible. The man had nearly destroyed that child's life and he had the gall to show up here? "What did he want?"

"To see her. He's trying to get custody."

"After what he did to her?"

"That's the problem. There's not really much information about what went on inside that house."

She could hardly believe they were having this conversation. "It was bad enough that CPS removed her."

"I know, right? You'd think that'd be enough, but I'm concerned it won't be. If there's one thing I've learned from working at the school, it's that people who lie and manipulate are good at it."

Experience had taught her the same thing.

She pushed her damp hair behind her ear. "Well, at least Jason knows some good lawyers."

"Yeah. And first thing tomorrow I'll be looking into a restraining order."

"Good."

Richie's glare haunted her memory. Something she'd seen there, although she couldn't nail down exactly what, didn't settle well with her. She'd looked in the face of evil too many times to not recognize it.

Maria couldn't go to live with that man. It might destroy the child who'd already lived through more horrors than a girl her age should know.

It wouldn't happen. Lana wouldn't let it. One way or another, she'd find a way to stop him.

Four

"Miller. Visitor."

Nate looked up as Kirk signaled someone at the end of the hall. A visitor could be Lana. Or someone from the FBI.

Leave it to Kirk to not tell him which one.

The door to Nate's cell buzzed and Kirk opened the door. Crossing to where Kirk stood, Nate stepped into the hallway. The cell door clanged shut behind him.

Kirk's hand smacked between Nate's shoulder blades and propelled him forward.

Stinkin' Kirk.

Would it kill him to show the slightest bit of consideration for others?

The walk to the visitation room was made in silence. Nate felt the stares of other inmates as he passed by their cells. Probably wondering what made him so special as to receive visitors outside of the normal visiting hours.

Good thing he wasn't going to be sticking around much longer. He'd really take heat over this one.

Lana glanced up as he stepped into the room. A folder sat on the table in front of her.

Neither of them said a word until Kirk strode out, closing the door with a bit more force than necessary. Lana shook her head. "That must be the new guy you told me about. Mr. Personality."

"You got it."

Man, she looked good. Her long black hair was in a

ponytail and the black dress pants and tailored jacket she wore highlighted her slim figure. "You must have court."

She smiled but didn't answer, confirming the suspicion.

"What'd you decide?" An impassive mask covered her face, preventing him from seeing her thoughts. But he knew how she'd feel about his answer.

"I'm going for it."

"I thought you'd say that. You know there's a good chance you won't survive." Anger underscored her mostly flat tone.

"At least I'll die trying to help people."

Serious dark eyes traveled across his face, undoubtedly trying to gauge his sincerity. Probably looking for the slightest trace of doubt to see if she could talk him out of it. But she wouldn't find any. This was the right thing to do.

"I talked to Jason last night. He looked over the letter of pardon and said it all looks legit."

"What about the rest of it? The contract or whatever they're calling it."

"You think the FBI would let me take highly classified documents? I'm lucky they let me take anything. Jason said to read every word and don't sign unless you understand it all. Of course he also recommended having your attorney present, but something tells me that won't be an option."

As secretive as Reyes had been? Probably not. Which didn't feel entirely legal, but he wasn't going to push the issue. "They should be here any time. Are you sticking around?"

"I have a ton of work waiting for me."

As much as he wanted to beg her to stay, he simply nodded. He stared at her, trying to absorb as much as possible. Hard to say when he'd see her again.

If he'd see her again.

No. He'd come through this okay, assuming he hadn't lost his touch. And if he had, well, he'd have to fake it a little.

Lines marred her forehead and her thumb tapped silently

against the table. Did her eyes look suspiciously damp?

They did. She was upset about something.

This couldn't just be about him. Something else had happened.

Stretching his hand across the table, he rested it on top of hers. "Hey. What's wrong?"

"What isn't wrong? You're walking into a deathtrap–"

"That's not it. There's something else."

Her hand tensed. The air around him solidified and he struggled to draw it in. What could be so awful?

"Are you okay? Your family? Did someone die?"

Wait, she'd come from seeing Jason. Who was still highly connected to his home and the Webbers.

His kids.

"Something happened to one of my kids." What little air he had remaining slipped out in a rush.

"Calm down. Everyone's fine." Her eyes slid shut for a second before opening. The grim resolve he saw there belied her words.

"Just tell me."

"It's Maria. Her uncle is trying to regain custody."

Maria's uncle. Richie.

Fire flashed through his body. His muscles tensed and his teeth clenched tight enough to make his jaw hurt.

"Richie wants her back?" He ground the words through stiff lips.

A slight nod provided all the answer he needed.

That dirty, worthless...

What, stealing Maria's childhood hadn't been enough? Now he wanted to destroy her teenage years, too?

Not that she was a teenager yet, but she'd turn nine this year. Her teen years weren't too far off.

"How... what...?" Pulling his hand back, he slammed his palm down. "*Why?*"

Elbow propped on the table, she rested her temple against her fingers. "He gave some song and dance about changing, realizing what's important in life, blah, blah, blah."

"I don't buy it."

"Me either. And I'll tell you what, Dale's ready to do battle. No way Richie will get her without some very lengthy and costly court proceedings. Jason's right there with him, helping as much as he can."

The fact that Jason was a lawyer brought a small measure of relief. "Good."

Now more than ever, Paul knew he had to accept the FBI's offer. With any luck, he could shut down this White Fire group in a few days and head home to protect Maria from the man who'd nearly ruined her life.

"Does she know? Maria?"

Lana hesitated. "I don't think so. But Richie did stop by the house. I guess just seeing him scared her half to death."

Man, what he wouldn't give for five minutes alone with that coward! He'd teach him not to abuse a child.

Why did Richie want her?

The question gnawed him like acid. He had to learn the real reason, not the politically correct, family-friendly answer Richie had given.

Maybe he wanted to sell her to the highest bidder.

Child labor. Prostitution. Drug smuggling.

The list of options went on, but he pushed the thoughts aside. "The court wouldn't actually give her back to him, would they?"

"I–I don't know. He's claiming the abuse came from his ex-wife and he didn't know about it. They've been divorced for a few years now, so she's no longer in the picture."

"What a joke. He practically tortured her! And you said she's scared of him. That oughta count for something."

"She never officially went on record blaming him–"

"She told me. I'll testify. Tell them what a wreck she was when she first came to my home. How it's taken years for her to be able to function."

"Look where you are. A good lawyer will discredit

anything you say before it's left your mouth." Delivered gently, her words contained no trace of censure.

She was right.

Even a first-year law student would be able to discredit a con in prison. Especially one who'd lived a lie so convincingly for so long.

"There has to be something we can do to stop him."

"Paul." Lana reached for his hand. "You need to calm down. God has the matter in His hands and there's no better place to leave it."

A sigh bubbled from his mouth. So easy to say, but not as simple to do. "CPS will at least investigate Richie, right?"

"Absolutely."

She studied him for a second. Contemplation shone in her eyes, like she was debating how much to tell him. While there were a number of secrets she held closely, mostly related to her work, he rarely saw this guarded side of her.

He didn't like it. Not at all.

After a few more seconds, she straightened, folding her hands on the table in front of her. "More than that, I plan to do some investigating of my own."

Good. He knew few people who would pursue truth like Lana.

But Richie was a violent loser. The idea of Lana tangling with a guy like that didn't settle well. Never mind that she probably dealt with men like Richie on a regular basis.

"Just be careful, okay?"

"I always am."

Sure, she was. That was why she'd had more brushes with death than anyone else he knew. "Do me a favor and be about a hundred times more careful than you normally are."

"You're the one I'm worried about." Her eyes darkened. "Promise me you'll watch your back. No unnecessary risks. Get in, do what you have to do, and get out. These militia types usually take out anyone who gets in their way."

He conjured up a smile he didn't feel. "Hey, I'll be fine.

I've dealt with worse clowns than these guys before."

"You were never working undercover for the FBI before. That changes everything."

Words stuck in his throat and created a painful knot he couldn't dislodge. The shift in conversation told him she was about to leave.

He'd never learned to say good-bye. At least not in a meaningful way.

Lana spoke first. "I expect you to call me as soon as all this is over."

"Call you? I'm likely to show up."

A tight smile crossed her lips. "I'll hold you to that."

All he could think as she pushed her chair back and rose was that this might be the last time he saw her. Pressure built in his chest and the air thickened.

What was he thinking?

He could still back out. Hadn't signed anything yet. And while seeing her inside this dump wasn't the same as getting to spend real time with her, it was better than nothing.

Amelia's face drifted into his mind, followed by Jamal's. If he didn't do this, other children would die. Children like his own kids. Heck, it might even be his own kids. No telling where a group like this would strike next.

Not to mention that he couldn't protect Maria from inside these stone walls.

He had to do this.

Lana had just rounded the table when he stood and lightly caught her arm. Drawing her to himself, he held her tightly.

A shudder rocked from her body to his; a rare show of emotion from someone who always kept everything locked deep inside. Tension slowly drained from her as she returned the hug.

Everything in him wanted to kiss her, but he held it back. Not only was it not fair to her, it would only make this whole mess harder than it already was.

"Pray for me?"

"I always do." Her voice muffled into his shirt, but he caught the words.

Man, God had blessed him by bringing her into his life. He didn't deserve her friendship. Just like he didn't deserve God's goodness and mercy.

He released her, treasured the forced smile she gave, and watched her walk to the door. Sinking back into the chair, he kept his body turned so he could see her until she stepped into the hall and out of sight.

Kirk filled his vision a moment later. "Come on."

Nate stepped into the hallway, unable to resist looking at Lana's retreating form.

A vise clamped onto his arm. Kirk jerked him around, dragging him down the hallway.

"Never understood why women like the bad boys." Irritation laced Kirk's tone.

"What do you mean?"

"On the outside, a girl like that'd never give you the time of day. But slap some cuffs on you and give you a rap sheet and boom. Instant groupie."

"Right. Like a U.S. Marshal's gonna be an inmate groupie."

Kirk's head whipped toward him. "She's a Marshal?"

"And a pastor's daughter. Not the bad boy type."

They reached Nate's cell and Kirk shoved him inside. "Well, she's sure a bad judge of character."

Without waiting for a reply, Kirk stalked out of the cell, slamming the door behind him.

Man, that guy ticked him off!

Seriously. How hard was it to be civil?

And the bummer was that Kirk would probably be the one to collect him when the Feds arrived.

"Sure like to teach that jerk a lesson," Nate's cellmate muttered.

"He's not worth the trouble."

His cellmate surveyed him for a second. "So how'd you

get so lucky as to have visitors now?"

The less the guys in here knew about Lana, the better. Nate shrugged. "The Feds think I know something about something and are trying to get me to talk."

Close enough to the truth.

Although technically a half-truth was still a lie.

"Do you?"

"I know about a lot of things that they don't need to know."

His cellmate chuckled. "Let 'em chase their own shadows, huh?"

Nate dropped onto his cot.

This mess with Maria and Richie, the knowledge that lives were in his hands, and the enormity of his decision hung over him like the ebony clouds before a hurricane.

So much could go wrong. And if things started to fall apart, it would likely happen too quickly for him to do anything to stop it.

A bullet to the head would be all he had to show for his efforts then.

Nate's stomach constricted around the breakfast he'd choked down earlier, threatening a repeat visit.

Was he absolutely sure he wanted to do this?

The cell door buzzed again. Kirk didn't look any happier now than he had five minutes ago.

Nate trudged down the hall and back to the visitation room. Reyes and Underwood looked up as he entered.

Once Kirk had stepped out and shut the door behind him, Reyes took charge. "What is your decision?"

"What's your plan?"

Reyes leaned forward, dropping his voice a few notches. "We release you, you infiltrate White Fire using whatever connections you might have, find out their plan, and loop us in. We'll take it from there and you'll be a free man."

They made it sound so simple. Unbelievably so.

"You mentioned busting Eddie from prison. How do you

plan to do that?"

"We'll arrange to have a few of you transferred from this facility to another one. You'll slip out of your handcuffs en route, attack the guards, then take Carson with you when you escape. All staged, of course, but we can make Carson think it's real."

"So, just because I help Eddie escape, you think he'll ask me to join his militia?"

"I'm sure you can persuade him. From everything I hear, you're a bit of a legend in here anyway."

Only because of his past association with Stevens.

Nate ran the plan through his head. Crazy as it sounded, it just might work. The trickiest part would be to get Eddie to lead him to White Fire.

"So, in or out Mr. Miller?"

Last chance to save himself....

"I'll do it." The words were out before he could allow doubt to stop them.

"Excellent! All I need is your signature–"

"But only on my terms."

The smile faded from Reyes' face. "And what might those be?"

Nate leaned back in his chair. "No tracking devices, no bugs, no tails."

Underwood snorted. "Who're you kidding? You think–"

A look from Reyes silenced further comment. Reyes picked up where Underwood left off. "We need some way to monitor your activities. How else will we know if it's time to move in?"

"I'll get word to you. But if these guys are as paranoid as I think they are, they'll be able to spot a tracking device from miles away. Then they'll kill me and you'll be no closer to the truth."

Dark eyes bored into him. After a moment, Reyes spoke, his tone flat. "So essentially, you expect me to release two convicts from prison, let you join up with a group of known criminals, with no way of monitoring your activities. You see why I might have a problem with that?"

"Believe me, I get it. But see, you have a choice. Either you trust me enough to let me do this, or you don't. Only one of those options will help stop White Fire."

All traces of civility slipped from Reyes' voice. "Fine. But make no mistake. If you renege on our deal, disappear on me, or even look like you're thinking about returning to your old ways, I will make life miserable for everyone you know. Starting with your friend Deputy Tanner and the people running your group home. Am I understood?"

"Perfectly."

Papers slid across the table. A pen followed.

Nate picked up the papers, thoroughly read every word, and reached for the pen. The pen scratched across the paper, the noise sounding loud in the silent room.

And then it was done.

As Reyes collected the papers and slid them back into the file folder, dread gnawed on Nate's nerves.

Life as he knew it was about to get a whole lot more complicated.

"The first victim was just admitted."

Tim looked up as Amanda leaned against the door to his study, still in her pink floral printed scrubs. "Excellent. Have the doctors figured out what they're dealing with?"

"Not yet." Amanda crossed the plush carpet and sank into the chair opposite him. "I'm betting it will take one or two more cases for them to connect it all together."

Not that it mattered. The hospitals didn't have access to the antitoxin anyway.

Brody would've been pleased to know his final mission

was a success.

"What's next?" Mild curiosity lingered on Amanda's question, similar to what he might hear when she asked what sounded good for dinner.

"Doug's putting together the next device and says it'll be ready in a few days. I'm still working on how to access the target." That'd been Brody's area of expertise. Tim sighed. "I need a new hacker."

Amanda arched an eyebrow. "Surely one of your guys knows his way around a computer."

If only. "None of them are that good. Brody would've had the system breached by now."

Without Brody, they might have to switch to an easier target.

The idea burned him. He didn't want to switch targets. The big one had been carefully selected.

Amanda stood and stretched. "Well, I'm sure you'll figure it out. I'm going to go soak in the hot tub."

Naturally. That way all his men could ogle her in the scraps of fabric she called a bikini.

Whatever. He had more pressing concerns.

Like how to track down another hacker. Changing their targets wasn't an option. He wouldn't compromise and he wouldn't be stopped.

Five

The transport truck rocked side to side on the narrow two-lane road.

Nate flexed his fingers and kept his eyes on the road. It should be any minute now.

Three other prisoners, one of them Eddie, sat around him. Shackles on hands and feet, connected by a chain looped around his waist and locked to a loop on the floor of the transport vehicle, ensured each man remained secure.

What none of the other prisoners knew was that Nate had been slipped a lock pick. The restraints around his wrists were now just for show.

A sign advertising plantation tours caught his eye.

This was it. Reyes had told him to attack as soon as he saw the sign.

The guards had seated Nate closest to the front of the truck so he'd be able to reach the guard with his feet shackled to the floor.

He caught the guard's gaze and the almost imperceptible nod.

Okay. Now or never.

He drew a deep breath and lunged.

The chain around his waist pulled taught, cutting into his gut with enough force to bruise. His fingers circled around the guard's gun.

The guard yelled. Nate raised the gun to chest level and pulled the trigger.

The shot reverberated off the metal walls of the vehicle and rang through his head.

Red blossomed on the guard's uniform. He slumped to the side.

Nate whirled to the driver and passenger, squeezed off two more shots.

Blood spattered the windshield.

The driver slumped against the steering wheel. The truck veered off the shoulder of the road and bumped down an embankment.

Nate planted his legs, but the rough ride threw him against the wall of the truck.

The truck crunched to a sudden stop. He crashed against the floor.

For a second, the only sound in the vehicle was the engine pinging and hissing. Ragged breathing from the other prisoners reminded him that the show wasn't over. He pushed himself to his knees and shook his head slowly.

Okay, couldn't screw this up now.

His hands shook as he fit the lock pick into the keyhole on the shackles. It took a few tries to get free from the rest of his restraints, but he managed.

The guard in the passenger seat groaned.

Just as expected. Nate stepped up to the mesh and pushed the gun against the man's head. "Open the door. Or you'll join your friends."

The guard rolled his head to look at him, clutching a shoulder oozing blood. "Go to–"

"Now!"

The man groaned again as he reached forward and pushed a button on a control panel.

The sliding door to Nate's right clicked. Nate stepped back, started toward the door, then turned and pulled the trigger. Had to make it look like it was an afterthought or the guys might wonder why he hadn't shot the guard in the head.

One of the inmates, he thought the man's name might be

Ramon, jerked at his own restraints. "Hey, dude, get us outta here!"

"You're on your own, man."

"Come on, Miller, help us out, yo." Eddie's voice contained a hint of desperation. "I'd do the same for you."

Nate laughed. "Yeah, right."

"Seriously. I always liked you, man."

Nate pushed open the door.

"Yo, you got a plan? I can help you!"

Nate paused, then turned to look at Eddie. "What're you talking about?"

"You need a place to go, right? Some money? I got friends who'll help you out. We could use a guy with your skills."

Nate pretended to consider it. "Forget it. I don't take orders."

"Naw, man. Ain't like that. Tim's a good guy. You'll be treated as an equal."

"Don't know that I'm lookin' for work."

"Just hear him out, yo. You don't like the sounds of it, you can walk. Just get me outta here."

Nate glanced around as if expecting trouble then lunged for Eddie and picked the locks on his restraints. The chains rattled to the floor of the truck. "Let's go."

The other two inmates pleaded, cursed, yelled, but Nate ignored them as he jumped from the vehicle to the ground.

Eddie's feet thudded to the soft earth beside him.

Nate glanced around. It looked like they were in a ditch of some sort. Probably a rainwater runoff. As long as it didn't suddenly start pouring, they should be good here.

Chains rattled, the sound mingling with the inmates' incensed cursing. Nate slammed the door shut. Using his body to shield his actions from Eddie, he tossed the gun under the van. If Eddie got his hands on it, he'd notice it was only loaded with blanks and the jig would be up.

He grabbed Eddie's arm and jerked him forward. "Come on. I saw a sign for a plantation up ahead. Bet there'll be a car we can jack to get us outta here."

Jogging side by side, they made their way down the gully.

Eddie didn't try to carry on a conversation and Nate didn't force it. There'd be time to get more information later. For now, they just needed to put as many miles between them and the crash site as possible.

It wouldn't be long before the transport was missed. Then a search would ensue.

Reyes had told him that the search would be real. Only a very limited number of people would know the truth. The manhunt would be massive and intense.

Getting caught before they even got started would help no one.

An engine growled on the road above their heads. Nate ducked, pulling Eddie down with him. The tall grasses scratched his cheek as the engine grew louder, then passed without slowing down.

The last thing they needed was a motorist reporting two men dressed as carrots jogging by the road.

Moving as one, they pushed up and continued forward.

Sweat streamed down his back, plastering the cotton jumpsuit against his skin.

He couldn't believe he'd pulled it off. The blood had looked so real. Everything had looked real.

Then again, that was the whole point.

Okay, so the first order of business would be to find some new clothes. Prison orange wasn't exactly a good way to blend in. Unless it was Halloween, and even then it was questionable.

Then transportation.

Fortunately, he knew they'd luck out on both counts at the plantation. One thing he had to give Reyes – the man knew how to put together a good con.

Up ahead, a split-rail fence appeared on the top of the rise to their left.

That had to be the plantation.

They jogged a little further before the gully shallowed and sloped up to a driveway.

Nate scrambled up far enough to check out the terrain.

A parking lot and brick house to their left. The empty road to their right. No sign of any people hanging around.

The parking lot contained four cars. A Corvette convertible, a black SUV, a silver sedan, and a blue minivan.

Reyes had told him to take the sedan.

They scurried out of the gully and sprinted toward the closest vehicle, the SUV.

Eddie reached for the door handle, but Nate stopped him. "Not this one."

"Yeah? And why's that?"

Nate nodded at the emblem toward the front of the vehicle. "It's a Lexus. Probably has GPS. They'll be able to track us as soon as it's reported stolen."

They crept around the front and bypassed the Corvette.

He stopped by the sedan. "This one."

Eddie nodded.

Nate knelt by the driver's door and picked the lock. The car was at least ten years old and looked like a base model. Probably didn't even have an alarm.

He hoped it didn't have an alarm.

Although Reyes had planted it here for them, so even if it did, surely the SAC wouldn't have armed it.

He tried the handle. The door opened and he climbed inside, hitting the button to unlock the passenger door. Eddie slid in.

Man, it'd been years since he'd boosted a car. Hopefully it was as easy as riding a bike.

He ripped off the panel under the dash and grabbed the wires. A few tries and the engine roared to life.

Okay. Now to get out of here before anyone saw them.

He put the car into reverse and backed out, then pulled away from the plantation.

Eddie released a shaky sigh and cranked the air

conditioner. "Man, it's good to be free."

"Yeah, well we're not out of the woods yet."

"Yo, why you gotta go rain on my parade, huh? We made it this far."

Nate nodded. "I figure we'll drive a ways, then see if we can't find someplace to pull off and search the vehicle."

Of course he already knew what they'd find in the trunk. Three suitcases, two with children's clothes and one with both men and women's clothing, as well as a backpack with toys and books. Reyes had said the car would be staged as belonging to a family of four on vacation.

"Sounds like a plan. Thanks, man. I owe you."

"You hook me up with some cash and we'll call it even."

"No sweat. Like I said, my group can use a guy like you. And there's plenty of cash involved. Trust me."

Trust Eddie? Not likely.

He trusted Eddie even less than he trusted the FBI.

Speaking of which, they'd want to ditch the vehicle before too long, just in case Reyes had planted some kind of tracking device after all.

"So, uh..." Eddie cleared his throat. "That really true what you said? 'Bout you teaching Stevens to shoot?"

Where had that come from? Nate glanced at Eddie, whose breaths seemed to be coming a little too quickly. "Yeah. Matt was good, but I helped him hone his skills."

Not that it had taken long. Matt had always been a quick study.

"So why didn't you go into the biz like your buddy, huh?"

"I didn't have the stomach for killing. It's why I got out of the military." No point in mentioning that he'd faked an injury to get medically discharged, unlike Matt, who had been dishonorably discharged.

"Guess you're past all that now, huh?"

Nate swallowed the denial that lingered on his tongue. As much as he wanted to set things straight, he had to let Eddie believe he'd just killed three men in cold blood.

A metallic taste filled his mouth and he swallowed hard. "Sometimes you do what you have to do."

What could Richie Ochoa possibly want with a nine-year-old girl?

No matter how many times Lana tried to push the question from her mind, it kept intruding. Not a good thing when she was supposed to be working.

Still, she could think of several reasons. None of them good.

Child prostitution, human trafficking, drug smuggling, pornography....

She halted the tirade. If she thought about those things much longer, it'd make her sick.

She wouldn't let Maria fall into that monster's hands. No matter what it took, she'd protect Maria from whatever harm Ochoa had intended.

A file smacked down in front of her.

She blinked Micah Rawlings' face into focus.

"Hope that scowl wasn't directed at me."

She flashed him a smile. "No. Just thinking about something that happened yesterday."

"Obviously not something good."

Tell him or keep it private? It had nothing to do with work, but Micah was a friend. And it would help to let it out. "This guy's trying to get custody of his niece, but he's not a good guy."

"How so?"

"Think scum of the earth who likes to hurt children."

He cocked his head to the side. "Don't have a high view of this guy, do you?"

"He just about killed her the last time."

Serious brown eyes locked on her. "How am I just now hearing about this? Is it one of our current cases?"

"No. It's personal." Maybe she shouldn't have brought it up. Not like there was anything he could do about it anyway. "Forget I mentioned it."

"Okay. Well, if there's anything I can do...."

"I'm sure it'll work itself out. There are a lot of people praying about this."

"No better response than that." Silence descended for a second and he shifted his weight. "I stopped by to see how court went this morning."

"Good. I was a little concerned the witness would change her story, but she pulled through."

"That really frustrated me when I was a cop. You build a solid case, line up some credible witnesses, and make a good arrest, but sometimes the punk still walked because the witness would lie on the stand."

"That's life in law enforcement."

"It still stinks." He stuffed his hands into his pockets. "So. How about dinner tonight?"

Whoa. Where had that come from? He'd worked in the office for over a month now and every interaction had been completely professional.

"I-I...." All words escaped her.

A warm laugh surrounded her. "I think this is the first time that you haven't known what to say."

Oh, she knew what to say all right.

That she didn't date law enforcement. Especially co-workers. That a part of her was still very much hung up on someone with whom she could logically have no future.

But none of those reasons made it from her mind to her mouth. "That's probably not a good idea."

His smile dimmed a shade but didn't disappear. "I disagree. It sounds like a great idea."

"Fraternization–"

"–is discouraged. I know." Planting his palms on her desk,

he leaned forward. "Come on, Tanner. It's just dinner. You have to eat, you know."

"Thanks. I appreciate the offer, but I'm going to have to decline. I never date co-workers."

Although for this one, she might be tempted to break her own rules. Not only was he fun, he was a Christian.

And not bad to look at either.

Black curls covered his head, long enough to avoid looking frizzy but not so long as to look messy. A skin tone that suggested Hispanic heritage, not that his name hinted at any such thing. About five foot ten, solid and chiseled, with a strong jaw line, cocker spaniel eyes, a ready smile showing lots of straight white teeth – a girl could get used to looking at someone like that.

But not this girl.

"Maybe I should go back to being a cop." He shook his head, smile still in place. "Okay, I get the message. No dating. But friends can still hang out over dinner."

"Not tonight. There's something I have to do."

While she'd tried to keep the comment casual, something in her tone must've given her away. Micah straightened, his smile flattening out. "Anything I can do to help?"

What if he knew something about Ochoa? Or knew someone who had information about Ochoa? If the man was half the crook she thought he was, he ought to be on the radar of a lot of cops.

And it might not be a bad idea to have someone to cover her back tonight when she staked out Ochoa's place.

Especially someone of Micah's size.

No. She just turned down his dinner invitation. No way would she ask him to sacrifice his time off to go on an unofficial stakeout.

But asking a few questions wouldn't hurt anything.

"You used to work VICE, right?"

He dragged a chair up to her desk. "Nah. I was patrol. But I know a few of the guys in VICE."

"Think you could get any information on a Richie Ochoa?"

"I'll ask around. He got something to do with one of your cases?"

"No. It's unofficial."

"That personal matter you mentioned? Mind if I ask what's going on?"

Should she reveal any details? Why not? It wouldn't hurt anything.

"A friend of mine owns a group home. One of the kids there is Ochoa's niece and he's petitioning for custody. I want to know if he's still neck deep in drugs and prostitution."

He nodded. "I'll find out. Anything else I can do?"

"Not unless you want to give up your evening for a stakeout." Dang it. Why had she said that? The words had slipped out before she'd even thought them through.

Too bad Alex wasn't here. Alex was always game for whatever. But being on maternity leave was a pretty good reason to avoid helping with a stakeout.

Especially an unsanctioned one.

Narrowed eyes locked on her. "You were planning to go alone?"

She lifted her shoulders slightly and tried not to squirm under his scrutiny. "Like you said, it's personal. I couldn't exactly ask Barker to send someone to back me up."

"I'm beginning to see how you got yourself shot. And captured by a serial killer."

"How the heck do you know about that?"

"You're kidding, right? It was one of the biggest cases to hit this town."

"But it's been over two years. No one remembers the names of... the people involved." Strange how, even now, she couldn't bring herself to say "victim".

He shrugged. "Alex. Before she left, she pulled me aside and lectured me on how I have to watch your back while she's gone and how you're good at getting into trouble and how you have more guts than common sense sometimes."

Yeah. That sounded like Alex, all right. "The Ripper wasn't my fault."

Crossing his arms over his chest, he smirked. "Uh-huh. That's not what I heard. I heard you left your car and pursued him on foot."

"Not even close. He faked a car accident to draw me out. I didn't know it was him until he had me penned in."

"Well, if you think I'm letting you go it alone again, you're nuts. What time?"

"Maybe about nine? I want to see what happens when the sun goes down."

"When do you want to meet?" He hesitated, but didn't give her a chance to reply before continuing, "How about seven? At the Sistine House of Pasta?"

"How did you know that's one of my favorite restaurants?"

A grin spread across his face. "I do my research."

"Alex."

"Guilty as charged. So what do you say?"

Well, she did have to eat. "As friends?"

"Absolutely." It was almost convincing.

"Okay."

"Good. Now I'll have all evening to change your mind."

Nate stuffed the orange jumpsuits in the trunk and slammed the lid.

True to his word, Reyes had put some men's clothes in one of the suitcases. Too bad none of them actually fit.

Probably would've been too suspicious if they had.

The shirt was as snug as a bodybuilder's and the shorts a closer fit than he liked. But at least it didn't look like prison garb.

Eddie's problem was exactly the opposite. The clothes hung off Eddie's scrawny frame, giving him a 90's grunge vibe.

The sooner they could get some cash and make it to a store, the better.

At least the old farmhouse with the overgrown lawn and crooked "for sale" sign in the front yard had afforded the level of privacy they'd needed to search the vehicle and change clothes.

There'd been no cash or credit cards in the luggage, though. Then again, that probably would've been too obvious.

Eddie slid into the passenger seat and dug in the glove compartment. Nothing but the car's registration and manual.

Next, he opened the center console. A few country CDs; couldn't Reyes have at least had the courtesy to put in something good? He flipped open the lid to the ashtray and found a dozen quarters scattered inside. Eddie scooped them out with a grin. "Let's find a pay phone, yo."

"We should also think about ditching this car."

Surprise momentarily darted across Eddie's face, but then he nodded. "Yeah, I guess. It was pretty close to where we crashed, huh?"

"Too close. Won't be long before every cop in the state is looking for it."

They got back on the road and drove for a while before seeing a sign for the Interstate. Nate merged with the moderate traffic, keeping his eyes open for directional signs to let him know where they were.

A sign for Daytona Beach came into view.

Good enough. Not only should there be a pay phone at the beach, but it should be populated enough that they could blend in.

Assuming their pictures hadn't already been plastered all over the TV and Internet.

Probably not a safe assumption.

Nate rubbed his shaggy beard. A haircut and shave would have to be at the top of his agenda as soon as he got his hands on some money. Until then, hopefully the baseball cap he'd found in the trunk would be enough to disguise his appearance.

It'd have to be. Lives depended upon him.

Six

"Tanner! My office. Now."

Lana jerked her head up from the file she'd been reading as Barker's voice lashed her ears. Yikes. That didn't sound good at all.

Pushing herself up from her chair, she followed him across the workspace, trying to ignore the stares from the deputies she passed along the way. As they crossed the threshold to his office, he paused. "Close the door."

Nope. Definitely not good.

She did as commanded and sank into one of the chairs opposite him.

Everything in her wanted to ask what was going on, but she bit the questions back. He was the one who'd called her in here. He'd be the one to break the silence.

"Have you heard? About your buddy Miller?"

He knew? The FBI had sworn her to secrecy but then filled in her supervisor? "Heard...?"

"He escaped. Killed the three guards transporting him and released another prisoner."

What? Paul had killed three guards? "There must be some mistake. He's not a killer."

"No mistake. Check out the BOLO if you don't believe me."

Just because the police had issued a "be on the lookout" didn't make him guilty. She didn't release the words. Barker was hot enough already. No point riling him further. She pulled in a breath. "Are they sure he killed the guards? Maybe it was the other prisoner."

"The two prisoners he left behind confirmed the story. They found the gun with his prints all over it. It was him, Tanner."

Impossible. Wasn't it?

This had to all be part of Reyes' plan. It was the only explanation that made any sense.

Why the heck hadn't she pushed for more details?

Because Reyes likely would've refused to give them to her, that's why. Besides, the less she knew the better, especially since she'd been told not to say anything to anyone.

"Sir, I had no idea. And frankly, I'm not sure what it has to do with–"

"You're listed as his last visitor. Just this morning, in fact."

Because, of course, the FBI would've had their visit with him kept off the record.

And now she couldn't even say anything to defend herself. "It was a personal matter. I swear to you that he never mentioned any of this."

"You also visited him last night." Barker's dark eyes glittered in his face. "You can see how this looks."

"I know."

"I'm going to have to insist that you tell me why you visited him. Personal or not."

What should she do? She'd given her word that she wouldn't tell anyone.

And she tried to always keep her word.

"I can't."

His eyebrows burrowed into his eyes. "What do you mean can't?"

She may have promised Reyes she wouldn't tell anyone, but she had no problem pushing this whole mess back on him. "I was ordered by SAC Reyes to remain silent."

"What's the FBI got to do with this?"

"You'd have to ask him."

"Oh, I intend to. In the meantime, you don't answer to him. I'm ordering you to tell me."

Oxygen lodged in her lungs. What should she do?

God, I could really use some help here.

No answer was forthcoming. But a promise was a promise. "Sir, a man's life is at stake. Please, just call Reyes."

"I will, but unless you answer me, I'll be forced to place you on administrative leave, pending an investigation."

Administrative leave. The words bulldozed her.

She'd never so much as had a warning; now she was on a leave pending investigation! How could things go so wrong so quickly?

"Please. SAC Reyes will clear this whole mess up–"

"Sorry, Tanner. You're the one who maintained a relationship with a convicted felon. Until I know more about what's going on, I can't risk having anyone question your level of involvement."

She should just tell him. She owed Reyes nothing. Especially not her loyalty.

But Paul was a different story. What if revealing what she knew endangered his life?

Tears burned. "If I promise to steer clear of the manhunt...?"

Barker shook his head. "Sorry. I have to protect this office. You can pass your current caseload off to Rawlings."

Great.

So not only was she on a mandatory leave, she'd have to let others know by handing off her cases.

"I'll need your badge and service weapon."

A tremor shook her hand as she reached for them.

Fog filled her mind. This couldn't be happening.

The badge staring at her from Barker's desk told her that it was. A tear escaped, trailing a hot streak down her cheek.

Barker picked up her badge and weapon and locked them in a drawer before retrieving a tissue box. "Look, kid, you think I like doing this? You're one of my best, but there are protocols. So unless you're gonna tell me what's going on...."

"I can't." The words broke from her in a sigh.

"Then I've got no choice. I'll call SAC Reyes, hopefully get you back in here right away."

It didn't matter if this was cleared up by day's end. Her reputation would be shot. Everyone would think she was dirty. Even when she was exonerated, the rumors and damage would linger.

She had to tell him. It took too long to build a reputation in this business.

Especially for a woman.

The words wouldn't come. Instead, her legs carried her toward the door.

It felt like every eye was on her as she strode across the office. Reaching her desk, she sank into her chair and forced a deep breath.

She could hardly believe that'd happened.

There had to be something she could do to reverse this. Something that didn't compromise the safety of her friend.

If there was a good option, she couldn't see it right now.

No point in prolonging this.

She unlocked her desk and pulled out several file folders, then headed for Micah's desk.

He looked up as she approached, flashing a smile that faded as she drew closer. "What's wrong?"

She dropped the files on his desk. "I need to be out of the office for a while. Barker told me to give my cases to you."

Black eyebrows knit together. "What's going on? Is this about that custody thing we talked about earlier?"

If only it were that simple. "I can't talk about it."

He absorbed that with a simple nod. "Okay. Well, are we still a go for tonight?"

"You still want to help?"

"Sure. Why not?"

Yeah, why not? He didn't know she'd been accused of being an accomplice in a triple homicide.

But maybe she should tell him to forget it.

Bad enough that her reputation was shot; she didn't need to drag him down, too.

"Look, maybe we should bag the idea–"

"So you're not going to stake out this guy's house tonight?"

She clamped her lips together.

"That's what I thought. You're not going alone."

"Thanks." At least someone was on her side. "I need to get going."

"Okay. Seven p.m., right?"

She nodded before returning to her desk to gather her purse and keys.

The walk to the elevator seemed twice as long as usual and the elevator took forever to reach the underground parking garage. At least no one else was in it. She didn't want to see or deal with anyone right now.

Suspended! And for what? Protecting Paul.

It was a good thing she didn't know where he was right now, or she'd give him a piece of her mind. And probably say some things she'd later regret.

But seriously. This whole mess was his fault. How could he do this to her?

No. Paul was a pawn in this, just like she was. Reyes was the chess master. He was the one commanding the moves, the one orchestrating the game. If anyone was to blame, it was him.

And she did know where to find him.

Maybe it was time to pay him a visit and demand answers. She'd been compliant for long enough.

He'd always hated flying without a plan.

In his former life, it would've been suicide. It still kind of felt that way.

Nate shut the door of the stolen car behind him and looked around the restaurant parking lot. Cracks webbed the asphalt, which was littered with enough broken glass to fill a suitcase. Several other vehicles sat like sentinels in the parking lot, each with at least one broken window.

Traffic moved at a steady clip on the four lane street in front of him. Foot traffic was almost as heavy and diverse, ranging from professionals in three-piece suits to prostitutes in next to nothing. Warehouses and office buildings sat side-by-side with motels that advertised hourly rates.

How'd he wind up here, anyway?

But he knew how. And why.

The pay phone tucked against the side of the restaurant had beckoned with a siren's song.

"Wait here, yo." Eddie tugged up his baggy pants and sauntered toward the phone.

Here? Right. He'd never attract any attention just standing in the middle of a parking lot.

Besides, he wanted to hear what Eddie had to say.

He headed for the building and leaned against the wall, careful to make sure he was far enough away that it didn't look like he was eavesdropping on Eddie's conversation.

Which, of course, he was. Although he couldn't be too obvious about it.

"Yo, man, it's me."

Eddie was obviously trying to be quiet, but fortunately for Nate, quiet wasn't a part of Eddie's vocabulary.

"Yeah, man. He busted me out. I thought we could use a guy like him."

What he wouldn't give to hear both ends of the conversation, instead of just Eddie's. What if this guy didn't want anything to do with him? The FBI would toss him back in prison and this time he'd have a new reputation – snitch.

Not a great nickname on the inside.

"Nah, he's cool. Taught a hit man how to shoot, yo. And he's got computer skills. Thought he might be able to help Brody and Zoe out, you know?"

On the sidewalk, two girls with high heels, short skirts, and lipstick that could stop a raging bull watched him.

Just walk on his mind begged.

He looked away.

"Dude. I'm sorry. I know you guys were tight, yo."

Hmmm. That sounded interesting. He'd have to find out more about that later.

"Yo, Miller."

Nate turned to look at Eddie, who had covered the mouthpiece on the phone with his hand.

"Supposed to ask you what your handle was."

"Black Vapor."

Obviously White Fire planned to check him out. It'd been so long since he'd been active in the online community, he just hoped someone remembered him.

Eddie's conversation lasted a few seconds longer before he sauntered over to where Nate waited.

"You see those chicks checkin' us out? That blonde was hot, yo."

"They were prostitutes."

"So what? Hot is hot."

Figured Eddie would go for that kind of thing.

Watch it. He couldn't allow his disdain for Eddie or White Fire to be apparent. Doing so would buy him an immediate ticket to eternity.

"So what's the plan?"

"Tim's sendin' Zoe to pick us up but it won't be 'til tomorrow."

"And what're we supposed to do until then?"

"Lay low."

Great. So they had no money, no food, and no place to sleep.

Did they risk keeping the car? Maybe if they switched out

the plates…

Not an easy task without tools.

Okay, so maybe they drove out of town, found a remote place to park for the night. Or maybe they could find a homeless shelter. Using a shelter's limited resources wasn't something he especially liked, but their options were pretty limited.

And technically, they were homeless.

Still, it felt like taking help away from people who needed it a lot more than he did.

"Okay, so what if we drive out of town and find some bushes or trees to park the car in for the night?"

"Or we could crash at somebody's house, yo. Find a place for sale that nobody's livin' in and break in. Let you show off your skills."

He could already feel the criminal charges piling up. First breaking and entering, then what? Murder?

But something about the way Eddie said it made it sound like a test. If he didn't go along with it, it might end this whole idea of working with White Fire.

Well, Reyes had pretty much told him to do what he needed to do.

And really, this was a victimless crime. They wouldn't damage anything, just sleep there.

"You know, I think we passed a vacant storefront not too far back. Maybe we could check that out." Even as the words left his mouth, he wished he could pull them back. This was a road he'd vowed never to walk again. What was he doing?

He was selling it. Just like Reyes had told him to.

"Now you're talkin', yo."

"But we leave the car. Don't want it parked outside the place we're holed up, right?"

"True dat."

They headed up the street. A police car cruised past, but didn't slow.

The sooner they got out of sight, the better.

Especially since the black clouds rolling in looked anything but empty. If he were a betting man, he'd say they were in for one heck of a thunderstorm before long.

They passed the "For Lease" sign in the front window. Faded lettering, some of which had been scratched off, still boasted the largest inventory of refrigerators, stoves, and ovens in town.

The main room of the building yawned beyond the glass. The counter running along the back wall provided the only cover in the entire room.

But that was okay. He didn't plan to hang out in the front room any more than he planned to enter via the main doors. There had to be a service entrance around back or on the side. That was their entry point.

He just hoped the alarms weren't still active.

He turned down the alley running between the empty store and the bar next door.

A girl wearing tight jeans and an even tighter t-shirt started as they stepped into the alley. She glanced at the door propped open behind her, then at the cigarette pinched between her fingers. The lure of the nicotine beat out the safety of the bar as she put the cigarette between her lips and inhaled, her eyes never leaving them.

Nate met her eyes and offered a tight smile before continuing down the alley, walking on the opposite side. The last thing they needed was for her to perceive them as a threat and call for help.

"'Sup." Eddie's voice sounded behind him.

Idiot. What was he doing calling extra attention to himself like that?

The girl fixed narrowed eyes on him. "Not interested."

Nate kept his eyes forward as he strode past her. His gaze slid to a steel door on the empty building as he passed, but he didn't pause or draw any attention to it.

He could feel her glare following them down the alley.

They rounded the corner into another alley, this one

empty. A roll-up door dominated the back of the vacant building.

He glanced up the alley. No sign of anyone.

Approaching the roll-up door, he tested it. It didn't budge.

Not that he'd expected it to. Hoped, maybe, but not expected. Looked like the entrance they'd passed in the previous alley was their best option.

He turned to Eddie and spoke in low tones. "Okay, we wait for her to go back inside, then I'll jimmy the lock."

Eddie nodded. "She was hotter than those hoes, huh?"

Seriously? They were on the run from the cops and all Eddie could think about was women?

Nate leaned against the building. "I'm guessing she won't be out here too long. Maybe a few minutes. Then we'll be in the clear."

A horn blared from the street a block away and the faint hum of traffic bounced between the buildings. Thunder growled. At least he thought it was thunder; his stomach had been rumbling for the last hour.

And would continue to rumble. They didn't have any money to buy food.

He looked at Eddie. "Don't think I've heard much about White Fire. What're you guys into?"

"Cleansing, man. We're cleanin' this country up one mission at a time."

Eddie made killing children sound like such a noble cause.

Let them think that. They'd soon realize the truth. There was nothing noble about killing people.

A raindrop splashed against his head. Followed by a second and a third.

Great. Just what they needed.

He peeked around the corner. The restaurant door was closed. No sign of anyone around.

Good enough. Now to see if he still had what it took to break inside.

"Tim."

Tim glanced up from the deposition in front of him as his secretary stuck her head in the office.

"Your sister's on line two. She says it's important."

Of course it was. With Amanda, it was always important, even when it wasn't. He held back a sigh.

"I'll get it. Thanks, Gretchen." Once the door was closed, he picked up the phone. "Amanda?"

"You didn't answer your phone!"

What, like he had to explain himself to his little sister? "I'm at work. And busy. Whatever it is–"

"You've gotta get back here right now! Oh my... it's bad. It's so bad."

Okay, so maybe this was a big deal. First time for everything. "Amanda! Calm down."

She drew a deep breath. "There's been an accident."

"What kind of accident?"

"One of the vials. Ben dropped it." The words tumbled through the phone. "They're all exposed. Doug. Adam. Jack."

Jack? No, not Jack. "Are you sure?"

A sob broke from her. "Yes. He told me himself."

Jack was more than just an older brother. He'd stepped in and taken care of both him and Amanda after their parents had died. Made sure they got an education. Fixed whatever problems came up.

Now Jack needed something fixed. And he'd do everything he could to fix it.

"You've gotta contact your guy." Panic drove Amanda's voice up an octave. "Get him to bring some of the antitoxin."

If only it were that easy. But after keeping the man locked up in the storm cellar beneath the barn, he wouldn't likely retrieve the antitoxin. "He's not an option."

"He has to be! What else are we gonna do?"

"I'll take care of it. Just calm down and stick with the plan."

"And what about Jack?"

"They should be able to continue with what they were doing. Just don't let anyone else go in there. And tell them not to worry. I've got this."

He hung up the phone and stared at the file in front of him without really seeing it.

Jack. Exposed to the same bio-toxin that they'd used to cleanse various parts of the city. Which meant he had seven days to live, tops.

He slammed his clenched fist on the top of his desk.

No. They'd get that antitoxin. No matter what it took, they'd have that antitoxin in hand before the toxin took effect.

Too bad he hadn't paid the guy to smuggle out the antitoxin as well.

That left one option. The hacker and thief who'd broken Eddie out of prison. If he was as good as Eddie claimed, breaking into this lab should be a simple matter.

He hated having to rely so heavily upon a man he'd never met.

This guy better be good. Or Jack wouldn't be the only one to die.

Seven

"SAC Reyes, please."

The red-headed secretary eyed Lana, her lips curled in a forced smile. "Do you have an appointment."

Not a question. Probably because the secretary already knew the answer.

"No. But he'll see me. Tell him Deputy Milana Tanner is here."

"I'm sorry, but the Special Agent in Charge is a very busy man. You'll need to make an appointment."

Right. So he could squeeze her in the day after never. "This is important."

"It always is." The secretary's tone was even more condescending than her smile. "I'm sorry, but I have orders to not disturb him right now."

Maybe she should march past this woman and let herself into Reyes' office. But that would only get her kicked out. And possibly put another disciplinary mark on her record, this time one that she deserved.

"I'll wait. Thanks to him, I have nowhere else to be right now."

"He'll be in meetings–"

"I'm not leaving until I've spoken to him." Lana turned and settled onto a gray chair that had less padding than a skeleton.

The secretary's overpainted lips pressed into a firm line but she said nothing.

Lana let her gaze rove the office. Institutional white on the walls, dust colored carpet, chairs in a slightly darker shade of dust. Even the picture on the wall was a grayscale shot of still water.

The goal had probably been tranquility, but it was more likely to put someone into a coma.

And since she was the one sitting in here, possibly for hours, she'd be the comatose one by the end of the day.

She talked a tough game, but she really hoped she wouldn't have to wait too long.

Maybe she could hurry things along a bit.

Folding her hands in her lap, she stared at the receptionist. Every movement, every action, followed by her eyes. The receptionist's eyes darted up, met her gaze, then returned to the computer screen in front of her.

The receptionist's acrylic nails clicked across the keyboard.

Every few minutes, the receptionist's eyes would find hers, then quickly avert.

It shouldn't be long now.

The receptionist reached for a coffee cup on the corner of the desk. Her hand bumped it, sending black liquid sloshing across a stack of papers.

Hopefully those weren't important.

A soft curse slipped from the receptionist as she grabbed a handful of tissues from the box on her desk.

Several minutes passed before the secretary got everything mopped up and wiped down, but the second the tissues hit he garbage can, the woman fixed a narrowed gaze on her. "You can't just sit here. I have work to do."

"I'm not keeping you from it."

"I'm calling security to escort you from the premises."

"Go ahead. But if you do, you get to tell SAC Reyes that I will *not* be keeping quiet about that matter we discussed earlier today."

Pink washed the woman's cheeks. She pushed herself up

from her chair and swung around her desk. With her chin in the air and shoulders back, the woman strode toward Reyes' closed office door and knocked twice before letting herself in. The door closed with enough force to rattle the pictures hanging on the wall.

Okay, so maybe harassing the secretary wasn't the nicest move she could've made. After all, the woman was just doing her job. But seriously. Would it have killed her to at least pick up the phone?

The door opened a moment later and the secretary reappeared.

"He said he can spare five minutes." No hint of a smile this time, nor any trace of civility in her tone. In fact, she almost sounded hostile.

Lana offered a smile anyway. "Thank you."

She stepped into Reyes' office and closed the door behind her. "Thank you for seeing me."

"Doesn't sound like you left me much choice." Reyes looked up from the papers spread across his desk. "But this is really not a good time. I'm sure you can appreciate the pressures of work."

In spite of his not-so-subtle dismissal, she made herself comfortable on the chair opposite him.

"Actually, at the moment, I can't. Thanks to you, I'm on administrative leave." She did nothing to mask her anger. "All because you dragged me into this mess and made me promise not to say anything."

Setting his pen aside, Reyes folded his hands on the desk in front of him. "I apologize. It was never my intent to cause you trouble."

"No, just manipulate me."

He opened his mouth as if to argue, then simply nodded. "I can see how it might seem that way."

More than just seem. She let it slide.

"So, Deputy Tanner, what is it you want from me?"

"Call my superior. Tell him what's going on so he can

drop this ridiculous suspension."

Reyes stared at her, his face impassive. Hopefully he was considering the idea, because if he wouldn't loop Barker in, she would. Coming here had given her enough clarity to do that.

"I suppose that would be okay. I'll call him when we're done here."

Thank God. She'd half expected a battle.

She pulled one of Barker's cards from her pocket and passed it across the desk.

Amusement lit in his eyes as he glanced at the card. "Pretty confident I'd say yes, weren't you?"

She was much less amused by this than he was. "Well, it is the reasonable response. And if you'd refused, I would've told him myself."

"Rest assured that I will phone him myself this afternoon."

That would have to be good enough, even though she wanted him to pick up the phone and do it now. "Thank you."

As she turned to leave, she remembered Barker's words about Paul. "By the way, what really happened in the escape earlier?"

"What do you mean?"

"We both know Pa–uh, Nate, didn't kill anyone. So what really happened?"

Several seconds of silence lingered.

Oh, come on. Seriously? As much as she already knew and he was debating whether or not to tell her anything further?

"The guards are three of my agents." He folded his hands on the desk in front of him. "The whole thing was staged to convince the public that Miller is a dangerous criminal. Only a handful of us know otherwise."

She knew Paul hadn't killed anyone.

But it was still nice to hear the truth firsthand.

"And you'll tell Barker that, too?"

"I'll tell him what he needs to know. Nothing more."

Not what she wanted to hear, but Reyes had been pretty agreeable so far. No point in pushing her luck.

"Now if that's all, Deputy Tanner, I have a lot of work to do. And a phone call to make."

"Of course. Thank you." Lana opened the office door and stepped into the receptionist's area. The temperature dropped about ten degrees thanks to the chill radiating from the redhead.

Lana tossed a quick smile before crossing the carpet.

Once Reyes called Barker, she should be back in business. Hopefully this would go down as the shortest, most undeserved suspension in history.

What was that?

Nate sat up, his ears trained to the silence around him.

Nothing. But he'd heard something, hadn't he?

Maybe it was just Eddie. He could barely make out the younger man's outline in the dim light filtering through the room's sole window.

What time was it, anyway? It wasn't completely dark outside, but definitely after sunset.

"Hey, you hear that?" He kept his voice a low whisper, so low that Eddie didn't stir.

How he could sleep on this scratchy, threadbare carpet was a mystery.

At least they'd found a room with carpet. There wasn't a single piece of furniture in this whole building and, hard as this floor was, bare concrete or tile would be even worse. The window was a bonus since the electricity wasn't on.

Okay then. He must've been hearing things...

There! A rattling from the main room of the shop.

His booby trap. Eddie had razzed him about grabbing a few beer bottles from the dumpster and putting them in front of the doors, but it'd paid off.

A beam of light moved in the main room.

A man's voice murmured.

He jumped up and eased the door closed. The click of the lock as he pushed it echoed in the stillness.

Kneeling next to Eddie, he shook his shoulder. "Come on. We've gotta go."

"Wha–"

"Police! Show yourself." The voice boomed from the main room.

Cops. He knew it. How'd they find them?

Not important. What mattered was getting out of here before they were caught.

He hurried to the window.

It was barely big enough for them to fit through, but it didn't open. They'd have to bust it.

At least the window was as old as the building. Shouldn't be too hard to bust out.

He ripped off his shirt, wrapped it around his arm, and drove his elbow out with all the force he could.

The glass shattered.

His arm burned, settling into a dull throb almost instantly. Blood streaked the windowsill, but he couldn't worry about his injuries right now.

Feet pounded from the outer room. The doorknob rattled.

Something banged against the door. "Open up!"

Right.

Brushing the glass off the sill, he climbed through the opening. Rain splatted his head.

Eddie landed beside him.

They tore down the alley, headed toward the back of the building. It wouldn't be long before the cops busted down that cheap door and pursued them.

Or just went out the side door.

They reached the alley at the back of the building.

Nate glanced both directions. A light bounced in the alley on the other side of the building. Headed their way.

"Come on."

He raced the opposite direction. If they could just reach the street, maybe make it across and find another alley. Or find a crowd to blend with, anything. Of course, a guy running with no shirt on was kind of obvious, especially in the rain.

But the greater concern was the blood streaking down his arm.

He wrapped his shirt around his arm. The move slowed him down a little, but it was better than leaving a trail of blood drops.

"Stop right there!"

They reached the corner and pulled a hard right. His shoes slipped on the wet pavement, but he didn't go down.

Sirens started behind him, spurred his muscles to move faster.

They cut across the street, bolted down an alley, burst onto another street. Zig-zagged around pedestrians. Dodged umbrellas and lampposts and utility poles. Vaulted fire hydrants.

The yelling had stopped and city noise drowned out any sound of pursuing footsteps, but the sirens blared from every side. Drew nearer. Closed in.

Darting into traffic, he narrowly avoided a convertible that resembled a tomato on wheels. Horns protested as drivers slammed on their brakes.

They reached the sidewalk and entered the gloom of an alley. A nearly empty, two lane side street intersected the alley. They made a hard right, raced down the block, crossed the street, turned left into another alley.

Eddie's labored breathing sounded right behind him. At least he hadn't lost his meal ticket.

The sirens seemed louder than ever.

His lungs screamed for mercy, his legs wobbled like toothpicks, and his heart felt on the verge of collapse. No way could he go on like this much longer.

Halfway down the alley, a rickety fire escape clung to an ancient brick wall. A peeling green dumpster hugged the wall a few feet from the escape. Maybe, just maybe…

He glanced over his shoulder, saw no one in pursuit.

But they were back there. Somewhere.

He smacked Eddie's arm. "Over here."

Closing the lid on the dumpster, he hauled himself up. The fire escape's railing was five feet from the far edge of the dumpster. He pushed his muscles into motion, dashed across the lid of the dumpster, and launched himself toward the escape.

The rusted railing loomed as he arced through the air. He felt gravity pulling him down, stretched his hands out–

Slap!

His palms made contact with the metal. He curled his fingers around the pole, felt his hands slipping.

Stupid rain.

A grunt formed in his throat.

He gritted his teeth and pulled his body up, inch by slow, painful inch, until he could swing his leg up onto the rough metal surface. Rolling onto the grate-like flooring, he collapsed onto his back, chest heaving, muscles quivering, sweat rolling down his face.

"Dude, I'll never make that jump!" Panic tinged Eddie's words.

He rolled to his stomach and draped his arms over the edge. "Come on!"

Eddie clambered on top of the dumpster and sprinted across the surface. Arms and legs flailed as he flew through the air.

The rough metal surface dug into Nate's chest and stomach.

Eddie's palms slapped against his forearms. He fisted his

hands around Eddie's arms.

The weight dragged him forward several inches. Fresh pain assailed him as the metal grated his skin.

Eddie's body jerked to a halt.

Planting his knees against the rough surface, Nate arched his back and pulled. Eddie's hands latched onto the edge.

Nate released him and fell back, a hand going to his chest. Stickiness met his fingers. Several long scratches oozed blood.

Great. More evidence for the police to find.

Thank God for the rain. Maybe it would wash it all away.

Eddie collapsed on the landing beside him.

Every fiber of his being wanted to remain where he was, but he pushed himself to his feet. Get to the roof, then he could rest.

"Come on."

Moving as silently as he could, he climbed the steps, Eddie right behind him.

The sirens sounded louder than ever.

He paused at the second landing to listen. Male voices bounced between the buildings. Not below them, but definitely getting closer.

Glancing back the way they came, he saw several lights bouncing toward the alley, the beams stark against the darkness that had descended in the last five minutes.

He looked up. Three flights to go.

It was too far.

No matter how hard they tried to be quiet, the fire escape still rattled with every step.

He plastered his back against the brick behind him. With a nod toward the street, he pushed Eddie against the wall and waited, barely daring to breathe.

The lights rounded the corner.

Footsteps pounded the alley, the sound reverberating in his ears.

All they had to do was shine their lights up and this whole thing would be over.

Please, God. Make them keep going.

Several of the cops ran past. Two stopped by the dumpster.

Uh-oh. This was it. Busted.

One opened the lid while the other trained his gun on the chipped metal exterior. The first cop looked inside, then shook his head. The second cop glanced up at the fire escape.

Dang. Any second now–

"Hey!" The shout came from the direction the other police officers had gone.

The cop jerked his head toward the opposite end of the alley as another shout sounded. "Hold it!"

The two took off in the direction of the yelling.

A breath exploded from his chest. He hadn't even realized he'd been holding it in.

They waited a few more seconds for all the police to exit the alley before moving, climbing as cautiously as they could.

Who the police were chasing now didn't matter. At least it wasn't them.

Thank you, Lord.

By the time he hauled himself onto the roof, his body felt like it was shutting down. He doubted he could go any further.

Not even if his life depended on it.

He sprawled on the roof, pain coursing through every cell in his body. His legs shook like an epileptic having a seizure.

Eddie dropped down beside him.

Sirens passed their location, so close the wail burned his ears, but they didn't stop.

The area would be crawling with cops for hours as they scoured every business that was still open, every parking lot, every dumpster, in an effort to find them. Waiting here would be the best option.

As long as they didn't check the rooftops.

Or bring out a helicopter.

Rain poured on top of him, washing away the sweat and

the blood. A breeze tickled his face, and shivers ravaged his body.

Eddie slugged his shoulder gently. "That was awesome, yo. Just like in the movies."

He was too exhausted to be irritated.

Besides, in many ways, Eddie was right. The cops swarming around them, the narrow escape, the rain and sirens.

He was even bare-chested and bloody.

One thing those action heroes forgot to mention was how much it hurt. And how cold it was.

"So what now, yo?"

He rolled his head to look at Eddie and whisked the water from his eyes. "We wait. Once the heat is off, we'll get the heck out of here."

"Cool."

Seriously? Eddie sounded more like a teenager than some criminal. "Where're we supposed to meet our ride?"

"The beach."

Well, at least that was good news. He'd blend in okay without a shirt. Because putting his bloody shirt back on wasn't an option.

"How'd they find us, yo?"

Nate sat up. The same question had been bugging him, too, and he'd only come up with two options. "It had to be that chick in the alley. She must've seen us break in."

Unless they'd tripped a silent alarm when they broke in. But wouldn't the police have gotten there a lot faster if they had?

Besides, that took electricity and the building had none. An alternate energy supply was always possible, especially for an alarm, but he'd checked for alarms and come up empty.

And why would someone pay to alarm an empty building, anyway?

He settled onto his back with a small groan.

His body felt like it'd been put through a meat grinder.

Maybe he could catch a few hours' sleep before they headed for their morning rendezvous.

He just hoped he didn't wake up to find a flashlight in his face and handcuffs on his wrists.

Eight

Lana adjusted her seat for what seemed like the tenth time in the last hour. The new position felt moderately better on her tailbone, but she held no hopes that the slight comfort would last more than a few minutes.

Stakeouts. Ugh.

Why had she thought this would be a good idea?

And she didn't even have anything promising to show for it. She just hoped this night didn't end up being a complete waste of time.

In the three hours they'd been sitting out here, not a single car had come or gone, no one had approached the front door or stood in front of a window. The only indicator anyone was even home were the lights that clicked on and off in various rooms.

Although, really, that could all be controlled by timer.

She glanced over at the passenger seat to find Micah slouched down, his eyes staring vacantly at the house. Probably wishing he hadn't wasted his time by agreeing to join her. "I'm thinking if we don't see any activity by 12:30, it'll be time to call it a night."

"Sounds good. This is why I never made the move to detective. Too much waiting around." Shifting, he leaned against the passenger door so he could see both her and the house. "What happened today?"

"What do you mean?" Like she didn't know. He wanted to know about her hasty exit, the way she'd had to dump her workload on his desk.

"You, uh, said you'd be out for a while. Are we talking a day, a week, longer? Anything I can help with?"

Too bad it wasn't that easy. "It's not something I can really talk about, but I hope it won't be for more than a day or two."

Frankly, she was surprised she hadn't heard from Barker earlier today. Reyes had said he'd call right away, so the whole mess should've already been cleared up by now.

Unless Reyes hadn't followed through.

She'd give it through tomorrow, then camp out in his office again until she saw him with the phone in his hand.

"Well, if you need anything...."

"Thanks. I appreciate the offer."

"All right, I can take a hint." Micah straightened. "We've got movement at three o'clock."

Lana trained her gaze on the two shadowy figures stealing across the overgrown lawn. Though the darkness obscured any details, it appeared to be a man and a woman.

Dang. She knew she should've gotten her hands on some night vision goggles.

The two passed under a large tree. The smaller figure – the woman, if Lana's guess was correct – stumbled, only to be jerked along by her companion.

They approached the dark porch.

The door opened before they reached it. Framed by the light inside, Ochoa glanced around before stepping out of sight.

The woman entered first.

The meager light was enough for Lana to make out the barest of details. Blonde hair with a dark color capping the tips, jeans, fitted pink shirt.

Looked young. It was hard to tell for sure from this distance, but the thin frame and hesitancy in her step brought to mind a teenager rather than an adult.

Or maybe it was just the contrast between her size and

that of the man with her.

The girl faltered just inside the door, but a hand to her back propelled her forward.

The man following two steps behind her had a bouncer's build. Knee length shorts, white top, shaved head. Something dark snaked up the man's neck onto the back of his head.

A tattoo, more than likely.

The closing of the door kept her from seeing anything further.

She glanced at Micah. "What do you think? Prostitute and pimp?"

"Dealer and drug mule? Or maybe your friendly neighborhood Mormons?"

A laugh slipped from her lips. "The last one. Definitely."

The lit windows showed no sign of movement, not even a silhouette, much less something incriminating. "It'd be nice to have x-ray vision right about now."

"If I suddenly developed x-ray vision, would you go out with me?"

She couldn't stop the smile that his teasing tone provoked. "If you could see inside that house, I'd probably marry you."

White teeth gleamed in the dark. "Well in that case, sit tight."

He reached for the door handle.

Whoa, whoa, whoa! "Hold up. I was only kidding!"

"I know and I won't hold you to it. But we've been sitting here all night and I'm sure as heck not leaving until we've got something concrete to go on."

"You can't go up there."

As he turned toward her, she noticed that determination had replaced the humor. "I'm just going to take a peek." "It's illegal."

"I'm willing to bet that whatever they're doing in there is too."

"That's what they do. But *we're* the good guys." She held his eyes with her own. "I want this guy, but it has to be something that will stand up in court or it's of no use. Anything we see spying in his window will get tossed out."

Easing back against the seat, he sighed. "Yeah, you're right. I ever mention how much I hate stakeouts? Especially when we're muzzled by legalities."

"Me, too." A thought flashed into her mind. "Was it just me or did that woman look like she might be under duress?"

"You know, I thought that, too. She might even be in mortal danger." He studied her briefly. "I like the way you think."

"Let's go, then."

"No."

Whipping her head around, she stared at him. "What do you mean, no? You were the one all gung-ho to do this a minute ago."

"It's twice as likely we'll be spotted if we both go. I'll check it out. You wait here."

Who did he think he was? Not only could she handle herself, the macho protect-the-girl attitude was something she encountered way too often with men in law enforcement. "Then I'll go. This is my battle, not yours."

She reached for the door handle.

A hand gently caught her arm. "Hey. I didn't mean it like that. But you said this guy has seen you, right? So if you're caught, he'll know what we're up to. If I'm caught, I can claim to be looking for my cat or something."

"You really think he'd buy that?"

"Maybe, maybe not. But he'd never buy it from you."

He was right. And she had completely overreacted. This whole suspension fmust have really messed with her perspective. "Point made. I'll stay here."

"I won't be long."

She nodded at the glove box. "I have a flashlight in there. You can use it to signal me if you need backup."

After retrieving the flashlight, he stepped from the vehicle. He didn't turn on the beam, not that she had expected him to. With his black hair and dark clothes, he blended into the night surrounding him, but she was able to make out his figure crossing the lawn.

He moved gracefully. Kind of like a dancer or martial arts expert.

What was she thinking?

Shaking her head, she pushed the thoughts aside. He was the kind of guy with whom she could imagine getting involved, but she couldn't do it. Not as long as they worked together.

Never mind the fact that Micah had proven himself to be exceptionally good company tonight. Funny, deep-thinking, cute....

Stop it!

She blinked and forced her attention back to the house in front of her. Or more specifically, the silhouette sneaking up to one of the lit windows.

Standing to the right of the window, he edged toward it. Peeked inside.

Several seconds passed before he inched down the side of the house to the next window.

This was ridiculous. Why had she even suggested it?

The curtains covering the windows appeared to be thin, but even so, how much could he really see?

Then again, he hadn't moved from the second window, which meant he'd found something or someone worth watching.

After several minutes, he turned and hurried back to the car.

She barely waited for the door to close. "Well? What'd you see?"

"Not enough to hang him." He returned the flashlight to the glove box and swiveled to face her. "That girl looked sick. And young. Maybe sixteen. "

"Did you see anyone else?"

"No, but the way she was holding her stomach, I'd guess

she was on the verge of throwing up."

"And Ochoa? What was he doing?"

"Both Ochoa and the muscle ignored her. Looked like they were talking about something more important."

Not exactly the blaring alarm she'd hoped to find. Still, the fact that this girl was in his house, sick, and he didn't care, should count for something.

She wanted to call for backup. Get a warrant and raid the house.

But this snippet of information was so ambiguous that no judge would move on it. No probable cause. They hadn't witnessed any physical abuse to the girl, nor had a gun or any other weapon been exposed; in fact, there'd be no indication that anything illegal was going on.

Unfortunately.

The front door opened and the big guy exited alone. He stole across the lawn, disappearing into the dark.

One by one, the lights went out in the house.

Probably no point in hanging out any longer. Lana cranked the key.

"So what's next?" Micah articulated the question plaguing her mind.

"I'm not sure."

A horn blared.

Nate jerked upright. The full moon overhead cast a ghostly glow across the rooftop.

What was he doing here? And in wet clothes? Why did he hurt all over?

Memories cascaded over him.

The staged escape. Driving the planted car. The hookers. The cops. Escaping for real.

A breeze swept the roof, sending a shiver up his body. Wet clothes, wind, and darkness were a horrible combination.

At least the rain had stopped.

He looked down at the scratches on his chest. Raw and angry, with blood congealed around the edges.

So much for blending in.

He couldn't walk around like this. Everyone who saw him would be calling the cops about some guy walking around with blood all over his chest.

The throbbing in his elbow reminded him that his chest wasn't even his biggest concern, but he couldn't see the damage there.

Maybe he was making too big a deal about it.

Then again, maybe not.

So he had some injuries. How many people would really get involved?

Either way, it was a chance he couldn't afford to take. It'd be best to stay out of sight, which meant making it down to the beach before the sun came up.

What he wouldn't give to have a watch. A phone. Anything to tell time.

He glanced up at the moon. Straight overhead. Did that mean it was around midnight? Two a.m.?

Stiff muscles protested as he pushed to his feet and walked to the edge of the roof.

The street below was empty. A few parked cars, but hardly any traffic. And no visible cops.

He should wake Eddie. They could head down to the beach now, before anyone was out to notice them.

From driving around earlier, he knew the beach was about a dozen blocks away. Shouldn't take too long to walk there.

He nudged Eddie with his shoe. "Hey, wake up."

Eddie groaned. "Yo, man. What gives?"

"We need to get moving."

"It's the middle of the night, yo."

"Exactly. We're less likely to be seen."

Eddie cussed and rolled to his knees. "This is messed up."

He wanted to tell the punk to quit whining, but bit back the words. No matter what he wanted, he had to keep Eddie on his side.

For now.

If all went according to plan, he wouldn't have to worry about it for too long.

But the bad thing about plans was that it took very little to send them careening into chaos.

Ugh. Morning had come way too soon after such a late night.

And, idiot that she was, she'd decided to return to Ochoa's house before he was even awake to watch for any sign of the girl she and Micah had witnessed last night.

At least she didn't have to worry about being late for work.

Although she wasn't really sure that was a good thing.

She took a swig of the triple-shot espresso sitting in the cup holder. The iced liquid, chocked full of caffeine and calories, barely took the edge off her fatigue.

Twenty minutes and so far, no activity at the house across the street. What was going on in there? And what had happened to the blonde girl? Was she even still there?

Movement at one of the windows caught her attention.

Hmm. It was the window Micah had looked in last night. Coincidence? Possible, but not likely.

She straightened in her seat.

Subtlety wasn't her aim today. Heck, she had parked directly across the street from his front door.

No, she wanted him to see her. Know that she was

watching. Sweat a little.

And maybe slip up.

The front door opened and Richie Ochoa stepped onto the porch, wearing only brightly colored boxers and flip-flops. Hair dotted his bony chest.

Well. She could've lived her whole life without seeing *that*.

In his hands, he hauled a large plastic trash bag.

What if it contained the body of that girl she'd seen last night?

No, it was too light to contain a body. While it might have incriminating evidence, she could safely assume there wasn't a corpse inside.

He deposited it in the trash can before wheeling the can down his driveway and setting it on the curb.

As he turned to head back to the house, his gaze passed over her. He took one step toward the house, paused, and whipped around.

Their eyes locked.

His jaw slackened and for several seconds he seemed incapable of movement.

Even from across the street, she knew the instant the shock wore off. Color flooded his face and he stormed into the street.

She opened her door and met him at the center line of the street that, thankfully, saw very little traffic.

"You! What do you think you're doing?" Spittle flew with his words.

Crossing her arms over her chest, she offered a smile. "Just enjoying my coffee. This looked like a nice place to park for a while."

"You think I'm an idiot?"

Ooh, he had no idea how badly she wanted to answer that one.

Evidently he didn't expect an answer because he plowed on. "Why're you followin' me?"

"Who says I am?"

If any more blood rushed to his head, it'd probably explode. Which, admittedly, wouldn't solve all her problems but would take care of one of them.

"I'm gonna call my lawyer. Get him to write up a restraining order." Whirling, he began to stomp away.

"Go ahead. I'll just tell the judge about the questionable activities occurring at your house after dark. By the way, what happened to the blonde girl last night?"

He turned back to her. The color ebbed from his face. "I don't know what you're talkin' 'bout."

"Oh, please. I sat here and watched a young blonde girl get pushed inside your house by a guy that's bigger than both of us combined. A little while later, that guy came out. Alone."

"So? I got friends."

"You and I both know she's not a friend. That meeting I saw last night was business."

"Good luck provin' it."

"Give me time."

He stomped toward her until he stood less than a foot away. Glared down at her with both hands fisted at his sides.

Did he honestly think he could intimidate her just because he was a few inches taller?

"What agency you work for again?"

"U.S. Marshal's office." At least she hoped she still did.

If the information scared him, he didn't show it. "Uh-huh. Was you out here on official business?"

"I told you. This is a nice place to park."

He pointed a finger at her but stopped short of actually jabbing her with it. "This is harassment. I'm gonna file a complaint."

"Do whatever you want. What you fail to understand is that the street is public property. I can come and go as I please. And if I want to sit here and watch your house every single night until this custody issue is settled, that's my right."

Dark eyes narrowed into black slits and words hissed

through tightly pressed lips. "Fine. But I'm tellin' ya, it ain't safe for a woman to sit in her car at night. This is a rough neighborhood."

"Is that a threat?"

"Call it friendly concern."

Without another word, he turned and marched toward the house. Reaching the front door, he paused to send one final glare her way before slamming the door behind him.

If that was friendly concern, she'd hate to see what hostility looked like.

She returned to her car and slid behind the wheel. Eased out a breath.

For a minute there, she'd been certain Ochoa would pull out a weapon. He couldn't have been packing, not with just his boxer shorts on, but he could've had a knife. If nothing else, he had his fists.

Part of her wished he had hit her. Then she could've filed charges.

Which would've ruined any chance he might have of gaining custody of Maria.

At least now he'd be looking over his shoulder all the time. With pressure like that, it was only a matter of time before that wanna-be chameleon showed his true colors.

Slight movement at one of the curtains drew her attention.

A smile tickled her lips.

She hoped he was sweating.

Realistically, he had legitimate grounds for a harassment complaint, but she didn't think he'd pursue that. It would draw too much attention from law enforcement and, if last night was any indication, that was the last thing he wanted.

If he did file one, though, it'd make her look bad, something that was especially undesirable given everything else going on.

She'd have to be careful. Unpredictable.

Her phone rang. A gasp slid from her and she jumped, smacking her leg against the steering wheel.

Stupid phone.

She looked at the number.

It was the office. Maybe it was Barker calling with good news.

Please, oh, please, be Barker calling with good news. "This is Lana."

"Got a call from Reyes. When can you get here?"

Yes! It sounded like she was back. "Well, I'm across town right now, so it'll probably take me about an hour."

"See me when you get in."

She set her phone aside and started the car. Had she been reinstated? Barker hadn't really said. But if Reyes had called, she should be in the clear.

Unless Reyes had given some kind of cover story. Heck, he could've even lied and made things worse.

No. What reason would he have to do such a thing?

Still, it was going to be a really long drive.

Nine

"You'll never believe what he did. He actually had the gall to say it was my fault!"

A woman's voice drifted through the dark.

"No way. Who does he think he is?" Another woman.

Shoes tapped a rhythm, coming closer.

Nate's eyelids flipped open. Veiled sunlight hurt his eyes and he squeezed them shut again.

The footsteps passed his location. The voices faded.

Ugh.

He felt half-dead. Grit scratched his eyes, the scrapes on his chest burned, and his elbow ached.

Not to mention how uncomfortable too-tight shorts were when slightly damp.

At least he was alive. And free. Things could be a lot worse.

He eased his eyes open.

Filmy clouds muted the sun's brightness. Moisture laced the air, creating a damp blanket that enveloped him in its sticky embrace. Between the sunlight and the mugginess, it was somewhat amazing he'd slept as long as he had.

The ground beneath him rocked slowly. So soothing.

He jerked upright.

They were on a boat! How could he have forgotten?

A snort drew his attention to the cushions on the other side. With an arm draped across his eyes, Eddie slept on his back, his mouth gaping open.

Nate looked around. No sign of anyone else, not on this boat or the neighboring ones. Not even anyone walking along the pier.

That could change any second. And this boat didn't belong to them.

Why had he let Eddie talk him into crashing on some stranger's boat overnight?

No matter how much he'd like to put the whole thing on Eddie, it hadn't taken much convincing. The boat sat high enough that the risk of being seen from the pier was minimal. It provided an out-of-sight place to wait for their ride. The cushions lining the bench seats on either side of the boat had only sealed the deal. Even now, he had to admit that he'd slept a heck of a lot better than he would have on the hard ground.

But that was then. Now the sun was up and they needed to get the heck off this vessel. Before the owners or someone who knew the owners showed up and saw them here.

He crossed the deck. "Eddie. Wake up, man."

"Dude. I'm sleepin, yo."

"The sun's up. We need to get moving."

"Seriously, dude. You need ta lighten up."

What part of being a fugitive didn't Eddie understand? "You can tell the cops that when they catch you."

With a sigh, Eddie slid off the cushions. "S'pose we should be watchin' for Zoe."

Gee, you think? "Who's Zoe, anyway?"

"She's this hot little piece of flesh who works for Tim. Got some hacking skills. She 'n Brody used to be a thing, but now that Brody's dead...." Eddie rolled his shoulders in a limp shrug.

Didn't seem to be any love lost for this Brody guy. "Where's she meeting us?"

Eddie jumped to the pier before pointing out to sea. "Out there."

"We're going by boat?"

A grin stretched Eddie's face. "Can you think of a better way to avoid the cops?"

He had a point. Too bad the Coast Guard would also be looking for two fugitives on the run. Even so, he liked their odds on the water better than on land, especially after last night's escapade.

"So where do we board?"

"End of the pier."

They were basically at the end of the pier already. Nate looked at the half dozen boats docked in front of them. "Which one?"

"She ain't here yet." Eddie sat on the dock and leaned against a post. "Tim said she'd be here sometime this morning. I'll know the boat when I see it, yo."

Great. So now they waited.

He blew out a breath.

He hated waiting.

But, oh did that sun feel great. A light breeze carried the scent of the saltwater to him. Even the fishy stench in the air didn't bother him.

The gentle slap of the waves hitting the hulls of the surrounding boats had a comforting effect.

His eyes felt heavy. Might as well sneak a small nap while they were waiting.

No. He needed to stay awake, be alert, watch out for signs of trouble.

Didn't matter. He felt himself drifting off.

"Yo, there she is."

Nate jerked awake. How long had he been asleep?

Not important. He pushed himself to his feet and watched a sleek speedboat approach. Sunlight glinted off the shiny chrome trim. A throaty rumble drifted across the waters.

Eddie jumped up and waved his arms.

The boat slowed as it glided down the channel. The name *Freedom Fighter* was painted in glittery letters across the bow.

Appropriate.

There were no slips open. Where was she planning to dock?

She eased the boat to a stop behind two small vessels, stepped away from the wheel, and approached the edge of the boat. A shock of hair the color of the ocean brushed her shoulders and looked especially bright contrasted against her white sweatshirt.

Eddie gently backhanded Nate's chest. "Okay, dude. Let's go."

Problem was, forty feet of water separated them from the boat. "We're swimming?"

"You got a problem with that?" Eddie studied him for a second. "You can swim, right?"

"Yeah. Just a little sick of being wet."

"There'll be dry clothes on the boat." Eddie kicked his shoes into the ocean.

Well, that was something. But with all the cuts on his body, that saltwater was gonna sting like heck.

Eddie jumped in.

Several drops of water splashed Nate's face, the coolness refreshing against the humidity surrounding him.

He pulled off his socks and shoes and dove in.

Cool water enveloped him. Hundreds of needles pricked his chest and elbow and he clenched his jaw against the pain.

Ironic how the water could feel so good and so horrible at the same time.

Just make it to the boat.

Usually he liked swimming, but not today. Each stroke lengthened the ache in his elbow and the salt burned like acid.

Almost there.

He flopped his wet shoes on the swim platform at the rear of the boat and hauled himself up. Water ran down into his eyes and he swiped it away.

The blue-haired woman stood on the deck, lanky arms crossed over her chest, a bored expression on her face. "There're towels up here if you want 'em."

"Sweet." Eddie stripped off his drenched shirt and dropped it on the deck before reaching for a towel.

After squeezing the excess water from his hair, Nate stepped on board the boat and grabbed the other towel. He rubbed the towel over his hair, wiped his face and neck, and gently patted down his chest.

The blue-haired woman appraised him with serious eyes. "Those are some nasty looking scratches."

He managed a smile. "Don't feel so hot, either."

"I bet." A Jersey accent colored her words. She cocked her head to the side. "I'm Zoe."

"Nate Miller."

"Amanda can patch you up when we get to headquarters. For now, I think there's a first aid kit around here somewhere."

He wasn't sure who Amanda was, but unless she had medical training, he didn't think he wanted her touching him. Truth be told, he didn't really want anyone from this group touching him, although it wouldn't benefit him to voice his thoughts. "Thanks."

Eddie draped his towel around his neck. "Sorry to hear 'bout Brody, yo."

A small shrug lifted her slight shoulders. Zoe pressed her lips together and averted her gaze. "Thanks. But I don't really talk about it."

While Zoe had the bony build of a chronic drug abuser, her eyes were clear, her speech crisp and intentional. Probably mid-twenties, with pale skin, big eyes, prominent cheekbones, and well-proportioned curves.

Too young and scrawny for his tastes, but he could see why Eddie would call her hot.

"We better get going." Zoe turned toward the captain's chair. "Dry clothes under the bench."

"What about something to eat? I'm starvin'." Eddie rubbed his stomach.

"I think Tom's got stuff in there. You'd have to check."

The boat surged forward. Nate braced himself against the sudden movement, waiting a few seconds before following Eddie toward the bench seat along the edge of the boat. The unfamiliar motion made him feel drunk as he swayed from side to side, but he made it to the bench without falling overboard.

Thank God. It wouldn't take long for him to be left behind at the speed they were going.

Assuming they'd even try to save him.

At this point, it'd be just as easy for them to toss him into the ocean and leave him behind.

He knelt to the deck as Eddie pulled out a pair of shorts and glanced at the size before shoving them toward him.

"Think this is more your size, yo."

They'd be a little large, but better than the too-small size he'd been wearing the last twenty-four hours.

A shirt flew his direction. Again, too big, but at least it wasn't an orange jumpsuit.

Eddie stripped out of his wet clothes and pulled on some cargo shorts.

Okay, so they changed out here, huh? Nate glanced over at Zoe, who had her attention fixed forward.

Naturally. Two guys getting dressed was probably at the low end of things she wanted to see today.

He peeled off the wet shorts and slid on the others. Wearing them over wet underwear kind of defeated the purpose, but the only other option was going commando and that had never been his favorite thing.

Besides, it'd all dry soon enough.

Several pairs of flip flops sat in the bottom of the cabinet. He grabbed the largest pair, which were still a touch too small, and slid them on. They were cheap and felt like walking on plywood, but they'd do.

Eddie pulled out a few small bags of chips and some candy bars.

Not exactly quality food, but it was better than nothing.

His stomach rumbled as Eddie opened the bag and the barbeque smell wafted over. Grabbing a bag of cheese flavored chips, he ripped into it.

Once the chips were gone, he scarfed one of the candy bars.

Had peanut butter cups ever tasted that good?

He looked up to find Zoe watching the two of them.

"How long's it been since you guys ate?" Her words, practically yelled, carried on the wind.

"Not since breakfast yesterday."

She nodded. "We'll pick up some real food once we dock."

Real food. Now that sounded good.

He just hoped it didn't wind up being his last meal.

He was headed straight into enemy territory. One wrong move and they'd make sure his body was never found.

"Welcome back."

Lana smiled as Micah stopped by her desk. "Thanks. And thanks again for backing me up last night. It was nice to have someone to talk to."

"No sweat. Let me know if you plan another stakeout."

"Well, I'll have to be more strategic from now on. Richie made some threats–"

"Wait, when did this happen?" His smile vanished.

"This morning. I decided to try a direct approach and parked right across the street. I'm not really worried about his pathetic little threats, but I don't want to get hit with a harassment complaint, either."

He planted his hands on her desk and leaned forward. "Dang it, Lana, you should've told me."

"It was spur of the moment."

"You still could've called me." Narrowed eyes regarded her carefully. "And you should be concerned about his threats. Especially if he's involved in anything shady. What'd he say?"

She shrugged. "Basically that he didn't want me hanging around–"

"Exact words."

"I don't remember. Something about it not being safe to hang out in a car by myself."

"That all?"

For crying out loud. She felt like a suspect in interrogation.

"Unless you count him threatening to file a complaint and slap me with a restraining order, yes." Irritation laced her words, but she didn't care.

Straightening, he eased into the closest chair. "You take too many unnecessary risks."

"It's none of your business what I do." The words slipped out before she'd thought them through.

Yikes, that sounded horrible. She was a jerk. The guy sacrificed his evening to back her up, showed concern for her safety, and all she did was bite his head off.

"Look, I'm sorry. Your concern is noted, but I'm capable of taking care of myself."

"Really. Do tell."

"I'm an excellent shot. Aside from that, I have belts in Karate, Ju-Jitsu, and Tai Kwon Do."

"You have…" He pulled back and stared at her. "Really?"

"Really."

"What, were you training to be a human weapon?"

"Hey, us short girls have to know how to protect ourselves."

"The real reason have anything to do with the scar on your forehead?"

Her fingers flew up to the faded mark along her hairline. It did, but he didn't need to know about her past. Telling him she'd been abducted as a child would only make her seem more weak and helpless, something which he'd obviously already convinced himself to be true.

"An old childhood injury. Let's just say I decided never to be the victim again."

"Oh yeah? And how's that working out for you? From what I've heard, you step into trouble all the time."

He was right, but she wasn't about to admit that to him. Instead, she studied the serious set to his eyebrows, the stubborn locking of his jaw.

This argument wouldn't be won by either of them. Time for a truce.

She shook her head slightly. "Alex taught you well."

"Huh?"

"I don't know how many times Alex and I have had similar... conversations."

"Maybe it's time you started listening."

Maybe it was. While she was skilled at taking care of herself, the last few years had taught her that she wasn't invincible.

She'd had too many brushes with death. Way more than her fair share. Next time might not end well.

Ten

The SUV bounced on the traffic-worn road but the leather seats cushioned the bulk of the impact.

"You can take that thing off. We're just about there."

Nate ripped off the blindfold he'd had to wear for the last half hour and blinked in the sunlight. It was about time.

The blindfold had been tossed his direction as they'd left the city limits of Charleston. While the fact they'd wanted to keep the location of their headquarters a secret indicated that they didn't intend to kill him, having to wear the blindfold was irritating.

His gaze drifted to the side mirror and, more specifically, the stranger he saw staring back at him. Gone was the shaggy, gray streaked hair he'd sported only two hours earlier. In its place, short reddish-brown hair – auburn, the stylist had called it – framed his face in a messy, tousled style.

It was weird to see that face in the mirror.

The overall effect made him look about ten years younger. Whether it was the color, the cut, or some combination of the two, he wasn't sure, but he liked it.

And even better, he was once again clean-shaven. Facial hair had never been his thing.

Lana probably wouldn't even recognize him.

At least he no longer looked like America's most wanted man.

Things were definitely looking up. They'd stopped for burgers and fries, bought a few articles of clothing that actually fit, picked up some toiletries, and were almost to headquarters, wherever that was.

Eddie was sprawled across the back seat, mouth open, snoring softly.

Classic rock drifted through the speakers, but Zoe drove in silence.

Now. She'd spent the first part of the drive grilling him about his time as a hacker, asking about jobs he'd pulled, how he'd beat certain firewalls, broken into various systems, even throwing in a few places he hadn't accessed. All a test, no doubt. After all, they'd want to make sure he really was who he claimed to be.

Since she hadn't pulled over and left him at the side of the road, he could only assume he'd passed the test.

For now, anyway. No doubt Tim would have more questions and tests.

Nothing he couldn't handle. He may be undercover, but at least he wasn't pretending to be someone else. No one knew more about his past than he did.

Well, this might be a good time to try to get more information.

"How long you been with White Fire?"

Zoe never removed her eyes from the road. "A few months. Brody recruited me."

"So you're one of their systems experts?"

"Yes."

Not exactly talkative when it came to herself, was she? "So if they've got you, why do they need my help?"

"You'll have to ask Tim that one."

"What're they currently working on?"

"Again, you'll have to ask Tim."

"Because you don't know or because you won't tell me?"

A pause. "A little of both. I'm low level, so I'm not in on everything that's going on."

So White Fire operated on an informational hierarchy system. Where would he fall in the pyramid?

Probably not high enough to get the information Reyes wanted. After all, they didn't know him; why would they trust him? He wouldn't trust him if their positions were reversed.

Since Zoe obviously wasn't feeling very conversational any longer, he allowed the silence to resume.

No sign of the city. They were traveling down a two lane country road. Rolling fields, plantation-style homes, and working farms lined either side. How long they'd been in the car, he wasn't sure, but it had been at least an hour.

He wasn't even sure they were still in Charleston.

Acid burned in his stomach. This was extremely isolated. If he ran into trouble, it'd likely be hours before he'd get any kind of assistance.

The vehicle slowed and she made a right onto a long magnolia-lined driveway.

As they left the canopy of trees, a house came into view.

Not just a house, a true southern mansion. The brick building rose majestically before him, standing two, maybe three, stories tall. Four white pillars graced the front.

Felt like he'd crossed the boundaries of time and stepped back into the days of horse-drawn carriages and family-owned plantations. Of course the very modern SUV provided clear proof of reality.

Zoe swung the SUV around the semicircular drive and parked in front of the wide stairs leading to the veranda.

He followed Zoe and Eddie as they climbed the stairs.

Antique two-person bench to his right, wrought iron table and chairs to his left. Directly ahead, an ornately-carved set of double doors that appeared to be solid oak.

Pausing at the top step, he turned and took in the panoramic view of manicured lawns and blooming trees.

Not exactly the fenced-in, heavily-fortified compound he'd been expecting.

Zoe pushed open the front door and crossed the threshold. He and Eddie followed.

A chime sounded, the ring echoing through the cavernous entry way.

An elaborate crystal chandelier dangled above a vast, high-ceilinged room that had probably been used as a ballroom in more genteel times. Straight in front of them, toward the back of the room, a wide staircase ascended to the second floor. About halfway up it crested, splitting into two new staircases, one going right, the other left.

The FBI had it wrong. This group wasn't just well-funded, it was stinkin' rich.

"Welcome to Stonefield Manor."

Nate turned toward the deep male voice. A trim man with blond hair and a plastic smile crossed from a hallway on their left.

"Tim! Yo, man, good ta see ya." Eddie hurried toward the blond man and pumped his arm.

Tim's smile shifted to genuine. "Likewise. Welcome back."

"Owe it all to this guy here." Eddie gestured at Nate.

That was his cue. He stepped closer and extended his hand. "Nate Miller."

Tim's grip was cool and firm, his hands free of calluses. Obviously he wasn't the one who did the extensive maintenance required to keep this place looking as good as it did. "You have quite a reputation."

How should he respond to that? He lifted his shoulders in a small shrug, then glanced around him. "Nice place you've got here."

"It's been in the family for years. One of a dwindling number of plantations that are still owned by the original family." Pride laced the words.

Old money. That explained a lot.

"Well. I'm sure you'd both like a few minutes to clean up and settle in before we get down to business. I've had a few of the guest rooms prepared. Come on." Tim led the way up the stairs.

When the stairway split, Tim headed left.

"So do most of your, uh, members live here?"

Tim glanced back at Nate, his lips quirked, amusement lingering in his eyes. "Most of them have their own places in town. A couple of my guys stay here, but for the most part we're all normal people with lives and jobs and families, doing what we can to make this country a better place."

Yeah, one terrorist activity at a time.

These people sure had an interesting definition of better.

Tim didn't seem to expect any kind of response. "But since the two of you don't have anywhere else to stay and need a place to lay low for a while, I thought putting you up here was the best option."

Not to mention it allowed Tim to keep a close eye on them.

No matter. It served Nate's purposes, for the time being, anyhow.

"Thanks." He'd had enough running and sleeping in the elements to last the rest of his life.

They reached the top of the stairs. A hallway stretched before them. Four doors opened into the hallway, two on either side.

"Camo is my right-hand man. You'll meet him in a bit, but he has that room." Tim gestured to the only closed door. "He's a light sleeper so if you need anything, just let him know. There's a shared bathroom between the bedroom you'll be using and his."

The unspoken message came through clearly. Everything he did would be seen by someone so he better watch his step.

Passing Camo's room, Tim stopped outside the other door on the left. "Here's your room. Eddie, you're across the hall."

No coincidence that he'd have to pass both Camo and Eddie when he left his room.

Tim checked the shiny white-gold watch on his wrist. "Get settled. We'll meet in thirty minutes in the sitting room to discuss our plans."

"And the sitting room would be...?"

"Take a right at the bottom of the stairs. Eddie can show you."

"Yeah, man, got you covered."

As Tim turned to leave, Nate stepped into the bedroom. A patchwork quilt topped the queen bed to his right. Windows covered by sheer curtains lined the wall straight ahead, flooding the room with filtered light.

To his left, two closed doors. Closet and the bathroom, no doubt.

Well, he had a half hour. Might as well check things out.

The first door opened to reveal a closet that contained nothing but a few hangers. The second door opened into a full bathroom, complete with a pedestal sink and claw-foot bathtub/shower combo.

Even the toilet looked expensive.

Returning to the room, his gaze traveled the vintage cherry-wood headboard, dresser, and bedside table. A wingback chair and small table sat next to one of the windows.

Okay. Well, that took two of his thirty minutes.

He really wanted to collapse on the bed and take a nap, but thirty minutes wouldn't be nearly long enough.

But it was enough time for a quick shower. For now, that'd have to do.

"Are you ready?" Lana leaned forward and gently touched the shoulder of the woman sitting across from her.

Tamara's chin trembled as she nodded. Wide eyes locked on Lana. "Y–you're sure he can't hurt me?"

Poor Tamara. It was bad enough that she'd had to witness her fiancé stab someone, but to learn that it wasn't the first person he'd killed, not to mention that she'd made his personal hit list, had to be about as easy as swimming through quicksand.

"Absolutely. Now just remember, when you get in there, look at the lawyers, the judge, me, anywhere but him. He's going to try his best to intimidate you, but he can only do that if you let him."

Pushing up from her chair, Tamara paced the confines of the small room on shaky legs. "I can't believe I'm doin' this. I mean, what was I thinkin'?"

Pre-trial jitters were the worst.

Not only did it put the witness on edge, it also worried the prosecution – and all members of law enforcement assigned to the case – that the witness would take the stand and change their story.

Lana leaned back in her chair. "You were thinking that your girls need their mother. That if you didn't enter WITSEC, if you didn't testify, that Robbie would kill you and raise your girls."

A shudder shook Tamara's heavy frame. "I shoulda talked to him. He wouldn'ta killed me. Not if I promised not to tell."

Great.

She'd moved beyond jitters to full denial. "He's killed for less. And even if he didn't kill you, there are a lot of people in his gang. One of them would have."

"Maybe not." She sounded less convinced than she had a second ago.

"You know they would have. They might've even killed your girls. That boy you saw him stab? He was only fifteen. His name was Jorge. And he has a mother who loved him every bit as much as you love your daughters."

Moisture rushed Tamara's eyes and her face crinkled.

Lana softened her voice. "Tamara, he didn't leave you a choice. You did what you had to do to protect yourself and your children."

"I know." The words were half-spoken, half-wailed, as

tears streaked down her cheeks. Tamara crumpled against the wall and slid down to her knees. "I just wi–wish he hadn't done it."

Kneeling next to her, Lana put her arm around the woman's shoulders. "I know. I wish he hadn't, too."

Tamara clung to Lana, sobbing for several minutes before pulling away to try to regain her composure. The tears may have lasted only a few minutes, but Lana was drained. She hated these emotional cases. Life would be so much easier if she could be cold and heartless.

Inside her pocket, Lana's cell phone vibrated. She reached for it.

The display read "Paul – home."

But of course it wasn't Paul, it was one of the Webbers. She'd never gotten around to changing it in her phone's memory.

Or maybe she'd just never wanted to.

A glance at Tamara found her eyes puffy and mascara running, but no fresh tears.

With a hand on her shoulder, Lana offered a small smile. "Are you okay?"

"Yeah. Thanks."

"Good. Why don't you go ahead and freshen up while I take this?" Lana accepted the call as she rose from the floor and moved away. "This is Lana."

"The judge denied the restraining order." Frustration laced Dale's tone.

"What?" Ooh, that'd been loud. Lana dropped her voice. "Why?"

"Richie's lawyer beat us to the punch. They've filed for visitation. The judge wouldn't even consider a restraining order."

Lana glanced over her shoulder at Tamara, who leafed through a magazine but obviously wasn't reading a word. "The judge hasn't granted it, right? The visitation?"

"I haven't seen any paperwork, but I bet he will."

"But Maria's terrified of him!"

"He's still a blood relative. That weighs heavily with the courts." Dale expelled a breath. "Look, I'm not giving up on this. I'll fight it with everything I am. But it could get real ugly."

A knock sounded on the door next to her. They were up.

"Hey, I have to go. I'll call you later."

She slid her phone into her pocket and turned to Tamara. She had to keep her focus here, but how could she? Maria was being pursued by a jackal and there might not be a single thing she could do to stop it.

"So what's your take?" Tim leaned against the desk and studied Zoe, who sat in the chair opposite him.

"I think he's legit." She pushed her ridiculous blue hair behind her ear. "I grilled him like you asked and he knows his stuff. Plus, he was able to tell me about some of his hacks. If he's a fake, he's super good."

They didn't have time for him to be a fake. Jack didn't have time. "Did you learn anything useful?"

She summarized some of the things they'd discussed, then paused.

Hesitation was never a good thing. "What?"

"Well..." she leaned back in the chair and crossed her legs. "He was pretty closed off when I asked about prison. I think he's hiding something."

Okay, so not a flaming red flag. There could be any number of things he'd want to hide about prison for any number of reasons.

Still, it warranted further conversation. "Anything else?"

"Well, he cut himself up pretty good. I thought maybe Amanda could patch him up."

"Okay." Really, he couldn't care less about that. "There's nothing else I should know though, right?"

"I don't think so."

Good. He needed Miller to be the real deal. "Thanks. This will really help further our cause."

"Glad to do it." She straightened. "Besides, it was super cool to meet him. I mean, this guy's a legend in the online world. I can't wait to see him in action."

That made two of them.

Miller had better live up to the hype. Because if he didn't, the only thing he'd get out of this arrangement was a bullet to the brain.

Eleven

Judge, jury, and executioner.

The thought refused to budge from Nate's mind as he stared at the men in front of him.

Tim sat directly across from him, ready to lead the proceedings.

He was flanked by men much larger than himself, one of whom was built enough to have stepped straight out of any professional wrestling ring in the world. The man had to be at least two hundred and fifty pounds of solid muscle. Tim introduced him simply as Camo. Probably a nickname, but it fit him.

The other man, Jimmy, was marginally smaller and had a mop of shaggy brown hair.

While not as large as Camo, Nate immediately pegged him as the executioner. Something about the man's eyes reminded Nate of a shark. Wide-set, under thin eyebrows, they contained a cold aloofness that gave Jimmy a predatory appearance.

Tim and Camo sat in matching wingback chairs; Jimmy leaned against the wall to Tim's left. Seated on an antique sofa to the right of Camo's location sat Zoe and Eddie.

Kind of felt like he was the main attraction at the circus.

"So tell me about prison."

Prison? What the heck. "Why?"

The stare Tim leveled at Nate revealed none of the man's thoughts. "Humor me."

"Well, let's see. It had bars." Sarcasm might not have been the wisest response, but Nate did nothing to temper it.

Silence ensued for several seconds before Tim spoke again, his voice even. "There are some gaps in the story when it comes to your incarceration. Before I loop you in, I need to know I can trust you."

"Course you can, man. I wouldn' ta brought him here if you couldn't, yo." Anxiety highlighted Eddie's words.

"I want to hear the story from him." Tim leveled a look at Eddie that warned him not to speak again.

He should've seen this coming. "If there's something on your mind, just ask."

"I had Zoe do some digging and we learned a few things. That you'd gone dark, for one. That the FBI never would've caught up to you. That you turned yourself in."

Play it straight or lie? Tim sounded pretty sure about those things; if he lied, it might cast unnecessary suspicion on him.

But admitting to turning himself in could be fatal.

"All true. Except for the bit about turning myself in."

"So you want me to believe Zoe made that up."

"No, but you know how things are online." He slanted a glance toward Zoe. "Rumors spread faster than the truth."

Tim looked at Zoe for confirmation.

She shrugged. "Possible."

"Then how'd you get–"

Heels tapped a brisk pace toward them.

A tall blonde woman strode into the room, a purse hanging over her arm. Her generous curves filled out floral nurse's scrubs that looked to be a size too small.

Her eyes passed over everyone in the room and locked on him. A slow smile curled her painted lips. Swinging her hips as if in time to some unheard beat, she approached the group.

"Sorry I'm late. Traffic was a bear."

Nate glanced at Tim, then back at her. No missing the family resemblance here. Brother and sister, if he had to wager a guess. She was likely a few inches shorter than Tim, but had the same curly blonde hair, blue eyes, and high cheekbones.

"We were just getting started." Tim gestured at the woman. "Meet my sister Amanda. Amanda, Nate Miller."

"Well don't you make a good first impression. And what should *I* call you?"

The open flirtation in her tone stole his words.

How long had it been since someone had flirted with him?

A very, very long time. Even before prison, the only woman he'd really spent much time around was Lana. And Lana wasn't one to flirt.

The coy smile on her face steadily grew.

Come on, dude. Pull it together.

"Nate." Was that the best he could do? Real smooth.

She sat on the edge of the sofa nearest his chair, crossed her long legs at the ankles with her bent knees angled his direction, and leaned toward him. "Maybe I oughta give you a nickname, hmm?"

"Nate's good."

"So formal? I was hoping we could be more casually acquainted–"

"Knock it off, Amanda. He's here to do a job, not be your newest toy."

"Who says he can't do both?" Although the words were directed at Tim, Amanda's gaze never left Nate.

"Professional distance, Amanda." Tim's expression mirrored the warning.

A sigh burst from her lips as she swiveled to face her brother. "Honestly, Tim. You're such a buzzkill."

"And you're a bit of a..." Tim pressed his lips together. "Never mind."

"I just like to have a good time. You could stand to loosen up a little, you know."

Hmmm. Nate glanced between the two. Talk about interesting family dynamics. Tim, clearly older, had obviously mastered the role of protective big brother.

And Amanda? Well, she acted more like an irresponsible child who refused to grow up.

"Let's talk about this later." Turning back to Nate, Tim cleared his throat. "I'm still waiting to hear how you ended up in prison."

"Look, I screwed up, okay? Fell for the wrong woman, who learned the truth and turned me in."

Silence. He stared at Tim, but couldn't tell if the man bought the story or not.

It was close to the truth.

What he'd failed to mention was that he'd purposely told Lana and asked her to turn him in.

"How'd she learn about your past?"

"I slipped up. She–" He caught himself before revealing Lana's profession. "She's good at reading people and really inquisitive. She figured it out."

"I'll need to check out your story. What's her name?"

"No."

Tim's eyebrows lowered. "What do you mean, no?"

"You can either take my word for it or forget the whole thing." A risky play, given that he really didn't have anything to bargain with, but there was no way he would point them to Lana.

"I don't know you. Why should I believe a thing you say?"

"You probably shouldn't, but I'm not dragging her into this."

"She turned you in and you're still protecting her? That's gotta be the sweetest thing I've ever heard." A glance at Amanda found her once again leaning his direction. The intensity in her smile unnerved him.

A little flirting might be harmless, but there could be serious trouble if she tried to take things any further than that. He didn't know what worried him more: the reaction Tim would have if Amanda showed interest or what Tim might do when he rejected Amanda.

Tim appeared to ignore his sister's romantic overtures. "If you want to make it out of here alive, you'll give me her name. Now."

Nate's heart battered his ribs.

Jimmy flexed his fingers and slowly crossed his arms over his chest. Yep, definitely the executioner in the room.

In his mind, he could hear Lana telling him to cooperate fully, that she could take care of herself, to not take any stupid risks. But telling them would put Lana on their radar.

Which was an unacceptable risk.

"No."

A small gasp came from Amanda's direction. "You'd die for her?"

"If I had to."

Stillness permeated the air. Any second now, Tim would pull a gun, put a slug through his chest.

No. A pretty-boy like Tim might not even know how to load a gun, much less use one effectively. Even if he did, he didn't seem the type to get his hands dirty.

He'd have Jimmy do it. Or Camo. But he wouldn't do it himself.

And he probably wouldn't do it inside his house. Blood didn't match the décor.

"Why would you stick your neck out for her? She betrayed you." Tim's voice was flat, giving no evidence as to his state of mind.

"You want to get technical, I betrayed her first. I lied about who I was. Besides, she didn't want to. It tore her up."

"Then why'd she do it?"

"She's a Christian and she has principles. I knew that when I met her. It's one of the things that drew me to her."

"You still love her." A hint of scorn underscored Amanda's words.

It was that obvious? He glanced at her before turning his attention back to Tim. "We're still friends. She visited me in prison."

Dang. Maybe he shouldn't have said that part. They might have a way to look at the visitation records and get her name that way.

No. Those records wouldn't be available for public viewing. Would they?

Too late now. Either way, he didn't have to give them anything further. "I'm done talking about this. You aren't getting her name."

Silence descended like a storm, so complete that he could hear the hands on the ancient grandfather clock scraping past the seconds.

Tim's nod broke the stalemate. "It's admirable to find such loyalty."

Great. He'd earned the approval of a racist militant. "Anything else you want to know?"

"How does ten thousand in cash sound to you?"

Wow. Just throw that right out there, why don't you?

Eddie had hinted at financial compensation. From the sounds of things, they'd meant it. "Depends. What's the job?"

"We'll get to that."

"Well, given that I just got out of prison and only have the clothes you bought, ten k sounds pretty darn good."

"I'd like to know more about what you did for Stevens. I would've expected him to work alone."

"He did, for the most part." Nate scanned Tim's face. How much did this guy want to hear, anyway? "Look, I was a hacker and a thief. Pretty good at both, too. I knew how to get around security systems, pick locks, crack safes, bypass firewalls, you name it. Sometimes Matt, uh, Stevens, needed to get inside more secure places to take down his target and he'd have me help him with the logistics."

"How'd you get mixed up with him in the first place?"

"We grew up together. Matt was the closest thing to a brother that I had."

Tim studied him. "So if one of his jobs required access to a highly secured facility..."

"I'd have likely had a hand at getting him inside." Unfortunately. It was one of those things that Nate wished he could take back.

Tim steepled his fingers. "We need you to retrieve something for us."

He'd figured as much. "Where?"

"A lab in Sardinia. Not many people know of its existence, but we have a contact who told us how to get inside. Ever done any scuba diving?"

Where was this lab? A submarine? "Once or twice, but it's been a while."

"You're about to get a refresher."

"What's the score?"

"An antitoxin. My brother and a few of my guys were exposed."

His brother. So failure wasn't an option. "Have you already scoped this place out?"

"I have intel from my source. It's located beneath a prison, about four stories underground. The emergency exit is through an underground cavern, which supposedly has an underwater access point."

Cave diving? He'd never actually done that. And from everything he'd heard, it was difficult and dangerous.

The whole thing sounded like something out of a spy movie.

Also sounded a bit far-fetched. "What kind of emergency exit requires dive gear?"

"The exit runs through the cavern and has a trapdoor that opens above ground, but my source didn't know how to access it from there. Diving is our best option."

"Why not just con your way in?"

"Not an option. The lab can only be accessed by an elevator hidden in an unused wing of the prison. The warden doesn't even know its location and receives a nice chunk of change to keep it that way. The elevator itself can only be operated from a control room in the lab and there are armed guards and bullet–proof glass to greet everyone who steps off it."

There had to be an easier way than diving in. "What about false identities? I could whip up some pretty believable trails online that would sell us as lab techs or something."

"We don't have that kind of time. Besides, this place won't let just anyone in. You have to know someone."

What, his contact couldn't pull a few strings? "You do."

"My contact stole the bio-toxin. He's not exactly on their good list."

"Why not just buy it? Looks to me like you can afford it."

"You think I didn't try that first? Everyone I spoke to denied any knowledge." Tim's jaw tensed. "You have a problem with this?"

Yeah, he had a problem with it. A big one. But saying as much could end with a gun in his face. "My diving was all pretty basic. Cave diving is advanced. Besides, the last time I went down, I was with an inexperienced diver who nearly killed us both so no, I'm not anxious to jump back in."

"You don't gotta worry about that last one." Camo puffed out his chest like a rooster. "Navy Seal for twenty years. Try not to slow me down."

"We'll supply you with everything you need. All you have to do is get in, find the antitoxin, and get out. If it goes well, there might even be a place for you here. I could use a guy with your skills in my inner circle."

The inner circle. Which was exactly what the FBI wanted him to infiltrate.

"You'll be on the next flight out. Zoe, prepare some passports."

So. That's what Zoe brought to this operation. She was a forger.

Camo cleared his throat. "Tim, there's one thing you oughta know. Can't fly for at least twenty-four hours after diving."

"That'd put you guys back what, Sunday?"

"At the earliest." Camo's tone was somber. "Might be later if we can't break in on the first attempt or the flights aren't what we need them to be."

The next question Tim directed at Amanda. "What will that mean for Jack?"

Lines creased her forehead and her blue eyes glistened. "Sunday is day four. I don't think we can take the chance."

Tim swore softly.

"I'll go!"

The enthusiasm lacing Amanda's words concerned Nate. Not that he could pin down exactly why. He kept the concerns bottled as she continued speaking.

"It's perfect, really. I can stay on the boat, keep people away, verify the antitoxin when they bring it to me, fly it home and administer it."

"I'll send someone else."

"No." Amanda pushed up from the sofa. "I'm the most logical choice and you know it. I'm going."

"Fine. Get packed." Tim glanced between Nate and Camo. "One more thing. I want you to grab every last drop of antitoxin they have. Then I want that place destroyed."

Destroyed?

Before Nate could form any words, Camo asked, "Explosives?"

"Whatever's easiest. Just as long as it's history."

"Why?" Nate couldn't stop the word from escaping.

"Then no one else will have the bio-toxin or antitoxin. Gives us unlimited bargaining power."

Somehow he doubted Tim intended to use his power for bargaining.

No way. He didn't sign on for this.

He'd already been a passive participant in more murders than he cared to think about; he was done.

But if he didn't go along with it, lots of innocent people would die.

This group had to be stopped.

Wasn't sacrificing a few lives worth saving hundreds or thousands? Especially since the lives that would be lost were the people who'd created such a terrible toxin to begin with. That ranked them right up with terrorists, didn't it?

Funny how that justification didn't make him feel any better.

Tim didn't seem interested in his response anyway. "We're done here. Zoe, get to work on those passports and book the next flight out. Tonight, if possible."

So much for sleeping.

Maybe he'd be able to sleep on the plane. It'd be a first, but he'd never been this exhausted before either.

Nate knew a dismissal when he heard one. Rising, he turned to go, well aware of the way the others followed suit.

Behind him, he heard murmuring.

"Oh, Amanda? I guess Nate needs some medical attention."

"I can handle that." She shot a glance at Tim before turning to Nate. A slow grin spread across her face. "Let's get those clothes off you."

"Amanda."

She tossed her head back and laughed. "Seriously, Tim, I'm just messing with you. You are so easy."

Lips tightening, Tim stared at Nate. No words were needed for Tim to convey his message.

Hands off. Or else.

"Come on, Nate. I've got a first aid kit in the bathroom down the hall."

He followed her across the room. As they crossed the threshold into the hallway, he heard Tim's voice behind him.

"Jimmy. Hang back for a minute."

Hmmm. Tim wanted to talk to Jimmy alone. And Nate would bet his life that he knew who they would be discussing.

No matter. They needed him, so for now, he was safe.

Once they breached the lab and retrieved the antitoxin, well, he knew better than to turn his back on any of them at that point.

They passed several doors in silence before she stepped into a room and flicked the switch. Light flooded a bathroom that was almost as big as his cell back at prison.

As she opened a cabinet beneath the counter, he caught sight of boxes of gauze, medical tape, and wraps, as well as multiple bottles of what appeared to be rubbing alcohol and hydrogen peroxide.

Geez. How many injuries did she have to patch up here?

She set some supplies on the counter and turned to him. "So, let's see the damage."

He twisted his arm for her to see his elbow.

Eyes narrowed, she stepped closer and grasped his arm. "How'd this happen?"

"Eddie and I were cornered. Had to bust out a window."

"And you thought your arm was the best option?"

"I didn't really have a lot of options."

She looked up at him. "This it?"

The scrapes on his chest weren't too bad, but it might not be a bad idea to have them disinfected. After all, that fire escape likely wasn't the cleanest surface in the city.

But he didn't really like the idea of taking off any article of clothing, not the way she'd been acting. Especially not after what she'd said to rile Tim.

"That's the worst one."

She arched a thin, light eyebrow. "If there are others, let's get them all taken care of. Better than dealing with an infection later on, right?"

She had a point.

Without a word, he peeled off his shirt.

Her gaze traveled his chest with a boldness that made his ears burn. "Ooh, prison was good to you."

A woman hadn't looked at him like that in... actually, he didn't think he'd ever had a woman look at him like that. Funny thing was, she didn't even have to look up that much to meet his eyes. She was probably only about a half foot shorter than him. Much taller than Lana. Curvier, too. Had the figure of a model and was not afraid to flaunt it.

But he didn't want, or need, someone made of plastic.

No matter what anyone else might say, he found Lana more attractive in every way possible.

Amanda stepped closer. A musky floral scent tickled his senses. "I'm sure looking forward to spending more time together."

Time to put a stop to this now. "Like your brother said, professional."

"Tim just needs to get out more."

"Sorry. Not interested. Can you patch me up or should I grab a few bandages and be on my way?"

Sighing, she stepped back. "Hop on the counter."

He sat on the counter, but found it impossible to relax the tension tightening his muscles.

As she dabbed at the scratches with something that stung worse than a dozen wasps, she angled her eyes up at him. "What's your deal, anyway? I'm not suggesting we get married or anything."

"Tim made his stance on that pretty clear."

"Tim doesn't control me. Or you."

Maybe she'd back off if he told her the real reason. "You want the truth? It's like you said earlier. I'm still hung up on someone else."

"Oh, come on. You're a fugitive on the run. She's the first place the cops are going to look. There's no future there and you know it."

"I'm not ready to let her go."

She made no further argument. Instead, she finished bandaging his chest and stomach and turned her attention to his elbow. "This really should've had stitches."

He'd figured as much. "Well, that's not an option, is it?"

"We'll need to change the bandage regularly. Are you current on your tetanus shot?"

"Wasn't exactly a high priority when I was rotting in

prison."

"You might want to make it a priority when we get back."

While he knew he should be concerned about tetanus, his only priority was getting whatever information he needed to bring this group down so he could have his freedom and return to the people who mattered most to him.

Something told him Amanda could jeopardize all that. She obviously wasn't used to hearing no.

That was all she'd hear from him, though. He just hoped she didn't do anything to cause him trouble.

"What's up?" Jimmy pushed off the wall and joined Tim in the center of the room.

Tim buried his hands in the pockets on his khakis. "What do you think?"

"I don't trust him." Unshaven, with shaggy hair that perpetually stank of cigarettes, Jimmy's appearance contrasted sharply with his cultured, British-accented voice.

"What don't you trust?"

Positioning himself so he could see into the hall, Tim divided his attention between the doorway and Jimmy.

"The bloke is an unpredictable one. I think he might disappear."

"Precisely why Camo's going along. Did you see his face when I said to destroy the lab?"

"I expected him to walk out. I think what's needed here is a personal motivator to cooperate." Jimmy stroked the tattoo of a blood dipped dagger dominating his bicep.

"So the question is, how can we make this personal?" It wasn't a question, not really, more just thinking out loud. An idea had already formed and Tim was mentally making the plans to carry it out. "His girl."

Jimmy's eyebrows shot up. "And you think you can figure out her identity in time for her to be of use, do you?"

"I'm sure my contact inside Florida State Pen can get the information. If she visited like Nate said she did, there'd be records. All I need is the name and we can take it from there."

Tim glanced at his watch. Not quite six p.m. With any luck, Kirk would still be on duty. "Okay, here's how this works. Once the three of them are in the air, you and I will secure Miller's full participation."

"Are you sure you want to push that bloke's buttons? Unpredictable, you know." Jimmy crossed his tattooed arms over his solid chest.

"I'm not scared of him. He crosses a line, he's going to meet the unfriendly end of my gun."

Twelve

Nate leaned on the railing of their rented yacht and surveyed the rugged coastline. The prison perched on the edge of a short bluff, like a lighthouse directing people which way *not* to go. No other sign of civilization was in sight.

A breeze whipped through his sweatshirt, chilling the skin underneath.

He didn't think a cold wind had ever felt so welcome. It'd been two days since his escape and he wondered how he'd managed to retain his sanity trapped inside those walls. Part of him thought he could stay outside forever, regardless of the location or the weather.

The telltale tap-tap of Amanda's heels came up behind him.

So much for his peace and quiet.

He turned to find her standing a few feet away, rubbing her sweater-clad arms. "Camo wants to go over the details."

With barely a nod, he followed her into the boat's main cabin. The yacht was old and could use some updates – including a few coats of paint – but it offered them a level of convenience and privacy that a hotel would lack.

It would also take them to the precise place they needed to dive.

He glanced at the dive gear stacked in the corner of the room. Half a dozen tanks, two wetsuits, regulators, fins, masks, snorkels, weights; the gear took up an obscene amount of space in an already cramped room.

Sinking onto the cushions of a green and gold floral print chair, he met Camo's gaze. "What's the plan?"

Camo leaned forward with his elbows on his knees and his fingers laced. "I've been studying the layout. The lab's divided into two sections. You've got the actual lab on one end and living quarters on the other, with a hallway connecting them. We come in at the living quarter end of the hall. The lab will be off to our right."

"And the guards? Where are they in relation to all of this?"

"The other side of the living quarters." Camo pulled a folded piece of paper from his pocket and smoothed it on the table. "So if you were using the elevator, you'd encounter the guards, then the living quarters, down the hallway, past the door we'll be using, to the lab."

"Did your guy tell you what the door is like? How easy it'll be to break in?"

A low growl came from Camo's throat. "He claimed he'd never really paid attention. Makes our job a lot harder. I don't even know what kind of gear we'll need to take."

"Face it. We can't really haul a lot anyway."

Camo studied him with narrowed eyes. "Good thing I got a world-renowned thief with me 'cause I hate going in without a plan."

Yeah, Camo struck him as the type that didn't do things half-cocked.

Camo pushed himself to his feet. "Let's do this."

Now? So what, no plan meant you threw all strategy out the window? "Actually, I think going in early morning would be our best bet."

That the idea hadn't even occurred to Camo before was evidenced by the way he mulled the idea over. "Yeah. Try to catch 'em while they're sleeping. I like it."

"We breach security, wait for the first geek to enter the lab, then force him to give us the antitoxin." Sounded simple. Then why couldn't he shake the feeling that it wouldn't be nearly that easy?

"What time?"

"Four a.m.? Should put us down there before five, then we'll have an hour or so to work on the door before everyone's up and around." Assuming the people living underground kept a normal schedule. Without the usual concerns of daylight hours or keeping appointments, it was hard to say what they'd encounter in the early morning hours.

A nod confirmed Camo's approval. "Let's do a recon dive now. Make sure we know where we're goin', see how long it's gonna take, that kinda thing."

Not a bad idea. They'd never been down there before and all they had were some vague directions given by a guy who'd never dived there either.

"Will that give us enough time between dives?"

"It'll be fine. 'Sides, we're on a pretty tight timeline."

He tried to remember the consequences of not leaving enough time between dives, but the possible risks eluded him.

However, from what he remembered, not following all the proper procedures always ended badly.

Well, Camo was the former SEAL. Hopefully he knew what he was doing.

"I've also been thinking exit strategy." Nate rested his elbows on his knees and leaned in. "Tim wants the place in ashes, right? You rig the place to blow, we pull the fire alarm, and file out with the rest of the people evacuating. No one's the wiser."

"You don't think people would get suspicious when they don't recognize us?"

"We'll come up with a cover story. Besides, it'll be so crazy with people trying to get out that they probably won't think anything of it."

"Except that Tim wants the people responsible to fry, too."

Nate shook his head. "Forget it."

"You don't got much choice in the matter."

"Oh, yeah? I can refuse to help you break in."

"And I can kill you now and drop your body into the drink." Camo's bushy eyebrows dropped over his eyes. "What's your problem?"

"I don't kill."

"Oh, yeah? What about those guards when you broke out?"

Dang. He needed to keep his story straight or he'd blow the whole thing. "That was different. Self-preservation."

"So's this."

Nate snorted. "Not even close."

"Well, it'll be the explosion or fire killing them so your conscience will be clear."

"Set by us."

"Set by me. Really no different from when you were helpin' your buddy Stevens."

"I'm not the same guy I was then."

"Drop the act, will you?" Narrowed eyes gleamed from Camo's face. "We're doin' the world a favor. They're terrorists. They've got this one coming."

"It's not my place to judge." He stood and turned for the door.

Moving with the agility of a cheetah, Camo rose and stepped in front of Nate. He leaned so close that Nate could smell the peanut butter on the man's breath. "If you're not with me, you're against me. Make your choice."

"I'm with you." Maybe a different strategy was needed here. "Look, evacuating with a group is our best option. If we're the only two who come out, we'll draw attention to ourselves."

"We'll go out the way we came in. Underwater."

"Will we have enough oxygen?"

"We'll make it work."

"You know as well as I do that the emergency exit will be the best option. The antitoxin will be easier to transport that way."

Camo appeared to consider that. "I'll keep that open as Plan B. Now let's suit up."

Nate's light cut through the black water. Where was that stinkin' cave?

Twice now he thought he'd found it, only to discover that it was just a small cave that didn't lead anywhere, much less to an underground cavern. That was twice they'd had to backtrack.

A glance at his gauges revealed that he didn't have much oxygen left. They'd have to begin their ascent in the next few minutes.

A fish darted out of the rock just ahead of him. No, not out of the rock. Out of yet another cave.

Go in? He checked his oxygen again.

A few minutes would be okay. It'd be cutting it close, but at least he'd know if this was the right one.

The cave went back further than any of the others. The rock wall at the back of the cave had a narrow opening.

He shined his light through.

The light was quickly swallowed up by the black water, but it appeared that this cave continued back a ways. This might be it.

But they had no time to find out right now.

Turning, he found Camo right behind him. Nate pointed at his gauges, then pointed up. After a glance at his own gauges, Camo nodded.

They exited the cave and Nate referenced his compass so he'd be able to swim straight to the cave next time. Once he'd made a mental note as to the cave's relative location, he adjusted his course toward the boat.

Halfway there, he consulted his gauges once again. Ooh,

not good.

He touched Camo's arm and pointed upward. Regardless of the fact that they still had a ways to go, they'd have to surface now.

Or face the decompression chamber later.

The controlled ascent felt like it took ages and by the time Nate's head broke the surface, he was straining for every breath.

He spit out the regulator and drew in a deep breath. A wave splashed his face, filling his mouth with salt water.

Gagging, he spewed the water back into the ocean and reached for his snorkel.

It took him a few seconds to realize that Camo was already swimming toward the boat. Nate put his head into the water and followed.

Five minutes later, he hauled himself aboard the boat, dropped his tank on the deck, and ripped off his hood, mask, and fins. He looked up to find Camo studying him. "Think that was it?"

"I'd guess so. It looked like it went back a ways. And it's in the right location."

Hopefully there weren't other caves that did the same.

"That opening didn't look very big. I don't think diving with two tanks will be an option." Camo consulted the clock on the wall. "Six hours until we head back down and do this thing for real."

Nate clenched his jaw. He could hardly wait.

"What's taking so bloody long?"

Tim ignored the irritation in Jimmy's rantings. "He'll be here. He's probably stuck in traffic."

The marina bustled around them. People of all types

moved through their field of vision. From the rusty old fisherman to the trust-fund baby in designer clothes and everything in between, there appeared to be no shortage of people who had no better place to be on a Thursday afternoon.

Except Kirk. As of yet, there was no trace of Kirk's little white Camaro.

"I bloody hope you can trust this bloke." Jimmy's mutterings were just loud enough to hear.

"Simmer down. He's one of us."

Another five minutes slogged by before a shiny white Camaro with ghost flames on the hood whipped around the corner and into the parking lot.

Tim shot a glance toward Jimmy. "Keep the engine running. I'll handle this."

Not waiting for a reply, Tim pushed open the door and stepped into the sticky afternoon air.

The Camaro eased into a nearby parking spot and Kirk emerged from the driver's side. Tim met him by the car's trunk.

"You brought the picture?"

Silence lingered for a few seconds before Kirk crossed his well-defined biceps over his chest. "Look, man, I've been thinking. I don't want no part in anythin' to do with cops."

What was Kirk babbling about? "Who said anything about cops?"

"The chick you asked about. The one who turned Miller in. She's a U.S. Marshal."

What? Miller had forgotten to mention that little detail. "Really. And she visited him in prison?"

"Like clockwork."

Okay. That was an unexpected twist that would take time to process, but it didn't change the fact that he needed leverage on Miller. "What's your point?"

A sigh gusted from Kirk, who deflated like a popped balloon. He rubbed his hand over his shaved head. "I dunno, man. It's a loyalty thing. It'd be like me turnin' one of the guys I work with loose in a room full of cons. I can't have nothin' to do with her bein' killed."

Simpleton.

But Tim knew from past experience that Kirk was also easily manipulated. "I don't plan to kill her."

Skepticism glimmered in Kirk's narrowed eyes. "Then what's this about?"

"I don't trust Miller. I need him solidly on my side for this op–"

"Wait." Red flashed across Kirk's face. "You're workin' with this guy?"

Uh-oh. Time to do some damage control or Kirk wouldn't give him anything. "Temporarily. We need him to get us into a secured facility."

"He killed three guards!"

"He's also my best shot at getting into this place. My brother's life is on the line here." He was losing Kirk. The hardness in the man's eyes told the truth. "Come on. You can see why I need the info, can't you? Miller can't be trusted. She's my insurance policy."

"I dunno."

Okay, time to take off the gloves. Tim lowered his voice to barely above a hiss. "I've got a thousand dollars in my pocket with your name on it and you're *hesitating*? You've never had a problem taking my money before."

"Never been 'bout a cop before!"

"Pipe down." Tim glanced around, but saw no one close enough to have overheard. "You knew what you'd signed up for when you aligned yourself with White Fire. If we go down, so do you."

"You threatenin' me?" Blood flooded Kirk's cheeks and the man took a step forward, invading Tim's personal space.

It might've been intimidating, had Kirk been about six inches taller. And had Tim not been fully aware that Jimmy sat in the Escalade behind him, a 9 mil sitting on his lap.

Putting a hand on Kirk's shoulder, Tim gave the stocky man a firm shove backward. "More of a guarantee."

Kirk's narrowed eyes shifted behind Tim and back again. "This is it. After this, we're done."

Without waiting for a reply, Kirk dug a folded piece of paper from his pocket and thrust it toward Tim. Tim unfolded the paper.

The image was crisp and clear. Surprising, since it had come from a security camera.

A dark-haired woman who looked tiny compared to the guard walking next to her commanded his attention. She was a Marshal?

Sliding his gaze from the picture, he locked it on Kirk. "And you're sure this is her."

"Course I'm sure. I'm not an idiot."

No point in arguing that. "Her name?"

"Milana Tanner."

Tim pulled an envelope from his pocket, which Kirk snatched the second it was offered.

As Kirk opened the door of his Camaro, Tim returned to the Escalade.

"So the bloke came through." Jimmy sounded moderately surprised. "He give you some trouble?"

Tires squealed as the Camaro zipped out of the lot.

"Let's say his loyalties are divided." Betrayal always began with divided loyalty. Tim shifted to face Jimmy. "I think we're done working with Kirk."

"Want me to take care of him?"

"I'm still deciding." It wasn't like Kirk could turn on them, not without implicating himself. But Kirk was a loose end and he'd never liked loose ends.

Nodding at the paper Tim held in his hand, Jimmy grunted. "Lemme see."

The paper crinkled as Jimmy unfolded it. "She's no match for your sister, but not bad."

Tim's nails dug into his hand and he bit back the words

threatening to spill out. To have Amanda compared with anyone so casually was an insult. That it came from someone with whom Amanda had a history made it even worse.

Of course, neither Amanda nor Jimmy knew that Tim was aware of their history.

"Going to pick her up now, are we?"

Tim blinked at Jimmy. "You want to abduct a U.S. Marshal? Are you nuts?"

"She's a fed?"

"Yes."

"Knew something was off about Miller's story." Jimmy handed the picture back. "You wanted leverage. Let's grab her."

"There are better ways." Tim stared down at the picture in his hands. "Let's get a picture of her, maybe in her own home. It'll prove to Miller that we know who she is and how to find her. That ought to be enough to convince him to play this straight."

"And if it's not?"

"Then we'll go back and kill her."

He really hoped it wouldn't come to that. It'd be nice to have Miller join them willingly, long-term.

Aside from that, the bigger concern was Camo's reaction to the murder of a U.S. Marshal. Camo had done a lot for both him and White Fire. The only thing he'd ever asked in return was that they leave law enforcement alone as much as possible.

Loyalty mattered. They'd abduct or kill her only as a last resort.

"I think our best bet is to get to the courthouse before she leaves work, then follow her home." They'd better hurry. It was already well into the afternoon, so she could leave work any time.

At that point, tracking her down would be considerably more difficult.

Only fifteen minutes until Micah picked her up. When he'd heard her plans to return to Ochoa's house tonight, he'd insisted on joining her.

As much as it felt like he was only coming out of some macho instinct to protect her, she had to admit that the company would be nice.

Lana rinsed her dish in the sink before plunking it into the dishwasher.

Click.

She stilled. That noise had been both unexpected and foreign.

Silence ruled the night.

Several seconds passed. The quiet had a presence all its own.

Closing the dishwasher, she moved toward the living room. She flipped down the light switch on her way past, darkening the kitchen in the dim light of dusk.

Light bled in from the living room.

No further sounds reached her ears. Nor did she see any shifting shadows to indicate trouble.

This whole Richie Ochoa thing had really put her on edge. Now she was hearing things–

She turned the corner into the living room and smacked into something big.

Something dark. Something hard.

Not something.

Someone.

A hand slapped over her mouth. A well-defined bicep crushed her neck and slammed her against the wall.

She locked on the blue eyes staring out of a brown ski mask.

Those eyes stripped her body, resting in all the wrong

places. "You 'n me, we could 'ave some fun."

Never.

She tried to push the words past the fingers smothering her lips, but all that came out was a muffled "mmpf".

"You got somethin' to say, do ya, now?" The hand slipped away.

"Try anything and you'll be picking yourself up from the floor." A bold statement, given that her feet barely met the carpet at the moment. At least his current position offered him little opportunity to make good on his threat either.

A low chuckle slid from lips curled up in a sinister sneer. "Luv, when I come for you, you won't 'ave a choice."

When. Not if.

She couldn't completely suppress the shudder that quivered her limbs.

If he thought she would be some easy victim, he was dead wrong. As long as oxygen flowed through her lungs, she had a choice.

Rolling her eyes back in her head, she let her legs go limp.

The pressure on her throat increased as her body sagged against the arm pinning her to the wall. Her windpipe felt like it was collapsing. Misery fogged her mind, but she refused to give in.

This man had to believe she'd passed out or his guard would never drop enough for her to have a chance.

The arm loosened.

She ripped away. Fisted her hand and smashed it against his temple with as much strength as she could muster.

The man's head barely moved.

Lashing out in her best judo kick, her foot connected solidly with his groin.

A growl filtered through the mask as he doubled over.

Had to get to her gun! She'd left it next to her purse on the table.

Whirling, she raced into the kitchen. Skirted the island, crossed the darkened room, into the dining room. Almost there.

Her fingers curled around the grip.

Movement to her right! Her peripheral caught something sailing toward her head.

Pain pounded in her temple. Bells echoed between her ears.

A leather-gloved hand closed over the gun's barrel. Jerked it from her grasp. The gun clattered on the tile somewhere behind them.

She dropped to the floor and swung her leg toward him.

The blow caught him behind the ankles. He teetered. She pushed herself up, embedded her shoulder into his chest.

They toppled to the floor. A grunt emanated from a face hidden behind a blue mask.

Blue?

A second attacker. Not as large as the first, but still a good head taller than she.

God, I need help here!

She rolled off him, scrambled to her feet. Had to find the gun.

Footsteps pounded toward her as Brown Mask charged.

A knife flashed. Fire erupted across her upper arm, the blood tickling down to her fingers.

Her leg lashed out in a kick that would've made her former sensei wince.

The blade kissed her calf; a cry slid from her lips. She aimed another kick toward the hand holding the knife and sent the weapon flying.

Her gun. Where was her gun?

There, by the fridge! She limped toward it.

Feet shuffled behind her. An arm snaked around her arms and chest.

Pinned to the hot body behind her, she could hardly move.

She slid the foot of her uninjured leg back until it bumped something solid. The man's foot, with any luck.

She stomped her foot down.

Profanity blasted her ears. The man's grasp loosened enough for her to twist away.

She was close to her gun. Only a few more feet and she'd have it.

Something smashed into her with the force of an atomic bomb. For a second she was airborne, until her head slammed into the island with bone-jarring force.

Her vision dimmed.

She smacked against the cool tile floor. The breath whooshed from her lungs and she struggled to draw in more.

Come on.

She fought to hang onto consciousness. Pain ricocheted through her torso.

A body covered hers, pinned her to the floor. Made it nearly impossible to breathe. Stale cigarette smoke tainted what little air she managed to draw in.

She blinked. Once. Twice. Again and again until her vision cleared.

Had to break free. She jammed the heel of her hand into Brown Mask's nose.

More obscenities spilled into the air. A gloved hand went to his nose as he fell back.

Behind him, she caught a glimpse of the blue-masked man approaching, knife in hand.

She rolled to her side and pushed herself to her knees. The gun was barely out of reach–

Brown Mask roared.

A flying fist barely registered before agony exploded across her head. Her vision darkened.

As she fell, voices filtered in the background. Two men. One, the accented voice of the brown masked man. The other, definitely American. Arguing, maybe.

She struggled to bring the words into focus, but couldn't even clear her vision.

Iron weighted her eyes. A moan slipped from her lips.

The voices stilled.

Hands grabbed her arms and jerked her upright. If her head had been swimming before, it was drowning now.

The blackness consumed her like a riptide.

Thirteen

Tim jerked the woman up. A few mumbled words that he couldn't make out slid from her lips before she went limp.

"I'm tellin' you, she's too much bloody trouble. Slit her throat and be done with her."

Idiot. Tim shot a glare Jimmy's direction, but the Brit was too focused on murder to notice. "She's not leverage if she's dead."

Tossing her unconscious body to the tile, Tim pulled his cell phone from his pocket and snapped a few shots.

Time to go.

He slid his phone back into his pocket. "Let's get out of here."

"I think she broke my freakin' nose." Hatred still burned in Jimmy's eyes as he ripped off his mask. Blood smeared his upper lip and continued to trickle from both nostrils.

"Hey! Be careful you don't leave blood for forensics to find."

This whole thing had already been messy enough.

The cops would likely find some trace evidence as it was. No need to make it any easier to identify them.

If only she'd had her blinds open, they could've snapped pictures from the outside as originally planned.

But the blinds had been closed and she'd heard them breaking in. At least he'd had the presence of mind to grab the masks.

Jimmy blotted his lip with the ski mask, then held it under

his nose.

With a few more words that Tim had no inclination to decipher, Jimmy turned toward the front door.

As much as Tim wanted to remove the hot ski mask sticking to his head, he left it in place. The possibility existed that a neighbor could see them and while Jimmy might be stupid enough to show his face, Tim wasn't willing to take that risk.

He followed Jimmy to the car and slid into the driver's seat. On the other side of the vehicle, Jimmy reclined his seat and leaned his head back, clutching the ski mask underneath his already swelling nose.

As Tim put the car in gear and pulled onto the street, he tore the mask from his head and speared Jimmy with a look. "What the heck were you thinking? Attacking her like that."

A snort answered the question. "She's still alive. What more do you bloody want from me?"

"I want you to use your head. How do you think Miller is going to react when he sees that picture of her?"

Jimmy shot Tim a sideways glance. "Thought you weren't scared of him."

"You poke a dog with a stick and sooner or later, that dog's going to attack. Miller will only put up with so much before he reacts." And with Amanda in striking distance, making Miller mad was the last thing he wanted to do.

Why the heck had he let Amanda go?

At least Camo was there. He could keep an eye on Amanda. And keep Miller in line, if need be.

All he had to do was make one thing completely clear. If Miller touched Amanda, Milana Tanner would be the one to pay.

Micah pulled to a stop at the curb in front of Lana's house. It still surprised him that she had agreed to being picked up rather than meeting at some neutral location, but he'd take it as a sign of developing trust.

He checked his teeth in the rearview mirror. Good. No traces of the double cheeseburger he'd just wolfed down.

Not a date, dude.

The reminder did little to stem the nerves jumping in his stomach. This may not be a date, but if he had his way, it could be the precursor to one. Cheeseburger in the teeth was not a great way to make a good impression.

And now he'd lingered in the car just long enough to seem creepy. Great.

He pushed open the door to his '68 Mustang and climbed out. Rounding the car, he approached the modest, single-story house in front of him.

Grass brushed his ankles as he crossed the lawn. Mowing had obviously been at the low end of her priority list lately.

Maybe she'd like the name of that kid at his church with a lawn-mowing business.

Lights glowed through the windows, but the porch was dark. Strange that she wouldn't have turned on the light when she knew he was coming.

He rang the doorbell. Chimes echoed inside and he stuffed his hands into his pockets to wait.

Seconds passed. No sounds came from within.

Huh. Maybe she was in the bathroom–

Wait. Was that light seeping around the door? He gently tapped on the door, which swung open under his hand.

Alarm pounded through him. Lana was much too cautious to leave the front door open.

Maybe she'd started to step outside and had turned back to grab something.

Without turning on the porch light? Not a chance. Maybe Ochoa had made good on his threat.

Go in or respect her privacy?

He listened. Prayed for her to step into the living room and laugh because she hadn't shut the door.

An unnatural stillness cloaked the house.

This wasn't right.

He pulled the gun holstered at his hip and sidestepped inside. Keeping the gun pointed slightly downward, he edged forward, ready to bring the weapon up at the first sign of trouble.

The living room opened up on his right. A hallway on his left.

He stuck his head around the corner, but the hall and all the rooms off of it were dark.

He refocused on the living room.

Neutral-colored furniture met his eyes. Unopened mail piled on the coffee table. Condensation from a half-full glass of water wept on an end table. Nothing appeared out of place.

He crept across the carpet. Into the kitchen.

A large island occupied the center of the room. Fridge and sink to his right, cabinets and pantry to his left. Straight ahead, a dining room and back door.

A Glock lay on the tile in front of the fridge. He edged around the island.

Blood smeared the floor in several places. The sight of the blood froze his muscles.

The kitchen narrowed around him. Not enough blood to make him think someone had died in this room, but more than Lana would've gotten from a simple kitchen accident.

Add to that the discarded gun and it told a story that was neither peaceful nor attractive.

He fought the urge to run through the house yelling her name. If there had been an altercation, as the scene suggested, the attacker could still be here. No point in making himself an easy target.

Couldn't go this way. He might contaminate the scene even further.

Backtracking, he rounded the island on the other side.

Wait… was that a foot?

Lana!

Crumpled against the island, her neck craned at an unnatural angle.

He stooped beside her, his fingers going to her neck.

A strong pulse vibrated. Thank you, God.

He ripped out his cell phone and called 911. After relaying his badge number, the address, and a request for medical and police services, he ignored the dispatcher's request that he stay on the line and dropped the phone back into his pocket.

There were more important things than talking to the dispatcher. Like making sure that whoever did this wasn't waiting to take him down, too.

Easing to his feet, he continued through the kitchen.

Past the empty dining room.

Down a short hallway that connected to the one off the living room.

It took less than a minute to search the house and determine that no one had stuck around.

Except an unresponsive Lana.

He eased out a breath. Now that he knew he was in the clear, he had one last call to make. A call he distinctly did *not* want to place, but not doing so would be even worse. He pulled out his phone and dialed Barker's cell.

"Barker."

"Lana's been attacked."

"She okay?" The clipped words carried a note of concern.

"I think so. She's out cold–"

"Where are you?"

"Her place." Ugh. That sounded pretty sketchy. He was going to have some explaining to do when Barker got here. "EMS is on the way."

"So am I. Stay put."

A click signaled the end of the call. He slid the phone into his pocket and crossed to flip on the light.

Careful to avoid the blood, he knelt beside her. "Lana?

Hey, come on. Time to wake up."

She didn't move.

"You better open your eyes before I call Alex and tell her you've done it again." He tried to keep his tone light, but couldn't pull it off.

Of course she was in no condition to notice.

He wanted to put his fist through a wall. Or better yet, the head of the guy responsible for her condition. If he ever got his hands on the jerk who did this....

Sirens wailed in the distance.

For the first time, he stopped to assess the damage. No visible blood on her head, that was good. But there was some weird discoloration on her neck that concerned him. The goose-egg forming on her temple explained her comatose state.

And of course the blood coating her arm and leg couldn't be a good thing.

At least that explained the smears on the floor. Some of which were still moist.

This was recent. He might've even passed the person responsible on the drive here.

Not that he could remember any of the vehicles.

Coincidence that this happened the exact same day Richie Ochoa threatened her? Not likely. It had to be connected to that rotten lowlife.

The sirens cut off abruptly.

He headed toward the living room. Two EMTs pushed through the still-ajar front door just before he reached it.

More sirens howled nearby.

The police, no doubt. They'd probably be here in a matter of seconds.

He led the EMTs into the kitchen and stepped back to watch them work.

"Rawlings? You the one who phoned this in?"

He glanced up to find Detective Sam Arnett approaching. A second officer, one Micah didn't recognize, trailed Sam by half a step. "Yeah. You know me. Where you find trouble–"

"–you find Micah Rawlings. Believe me, I remember." Sam introduced Micah to his partner before pulling a notepad from his pocket. "Run through what happened here."

"I don't really know. I got here to pick her up and found the door open and this." Micah gestured to the scene around them.

"Girlfriend?" Sam lightly punched his arm. "Not bad, Rawlings. Don't know what she sees in you–"

"No. Just a friend from work."

Sam swiveled to look at her. "She's a deputy?"

"Pretty well-known one, too. She helped bring down the Ripper a few years back."

"Huh. Guess that explains why you're around. You look for trouble, she attracts it." Sam shook his head. "Okay, you said the door was open?"

"Barely. I pushed it open, got *that* feeling, and came in."

"And there was no sign of whoever did this?"

"No. Just the gun," he pointed toward the fridge, "and her. I swept the house–"

"Rawlings!" Barker's voice sliced across the room. "What the heck happened here?"

Before he could answer, a startled expletive came from behind Micah. He turned to find one of the EMTs rubbing his jaw. The other was trying to catch Lana's flailing hands while simultaneously avoiding being struck by them.

Barker adjusted his route and crouched next to the EMT. "Tanner. Hey, kid, cool it. They're just trying to help."

Micah approached in time to see the last traces of panic fade from her eyes. The disorientation lingered a second longer as her eyes moved from Barker to the EMT and finally to him.

"Tanner, you okay?" Rare gentleness traced Barker's words.

Her eyes flicked back to Barker.

"I think so." She started to sit up, but only managed a few

inches before a gasp slid from her mouth and her eyes pinched. "Maybe I'll stay put."

Pushing up to his full six foot height, Barker nodded. "You do that. And let these men do their job."

The EMTs eased her onto the gurney.

"Deputy Tanner." Sam stepped forward. "Why don't you tell us what happened."

"Later." The growled word from Barker froze Sam's movements. "You can talk to her at the hospital."

"It's okay." The words, barely above a whisper, scratched from Lana's mouth. "I can–"

"After they've patched her up." Narrowed eyes sliced Lana's direction. Barker's look dared her to disagree.

A part of him expected Lana to argue the point, stubborn as she was.

But she remained silent. Unlike Sam. "The more time that passes, the more likely her memory–"

"I know the statistics." The gurney rattled as the EMTs wheeled it out of the room, but Barker never turned. "Now you listen to me. That woman is a deputy for the U.S. Marshal's office. A darn good one. Her memory will be as sharp in two hours as it is now. Maybe more so."

Lips tight, Sam closed his notepad and slid it into his pocket. "You this protective of all your deputies or is there somethin' special about her?"

Ooh. Time to smooth this over before accusations really started to fly. "It's everyone."

Sam's eyes shifted to Micah, obviously trying to weigh the truth in his words. "Really."

"Yeah. It's probably why openings don't come up in his office very often." It was one of the things that had drawn Micah to the job. Barker's reputation for fierce loyalty was hardly a secret.

While he didn't know exactly what had happened here tonight, he knew one thing for certain. Barker would pursue the truth with the tenacity of a pit bull.

Pain still roared inside her head.

Lana had barely felt the prick of the IV when the nurse jabbed her earlier. But that had been over an hour ago. Shouldn't the morphine drip have done something to help?

Even the soft lighting hurt. Keeping her eyes closed, she tried to focus on something other than the pain.

Which only brought her mind back to the question of the hour: what could those men have wanted?

"I think she's asleep." Micah's softly spoken words drifted across the room.

"Let's go. I'm not letting you wake her up." Barker. Looking out for her, as usual.

"I'm awake." The words scratched from her throat in a barely audible whisper. "Just fighting a headache."

Ooh. She wouldn't have thought it possible for anything to hurt worse than her head, but her throat won the prize.

That jerk had probably almost crushed her larynx.

She forced her eyes open to find Micah and Barker standing inside the doorway to her private room.

Behind them stood two other men she didn't recognize.

Wait. Hadn't they been at her house?

She couldn't remember. Beyond the attack, the rest of the evening blurred.

The men approached. One of the men, a stocky blond carrying at least forty extra pounds, introduced himself as Detective Sam Arnett. The almost cocky swagger in his step, not to mention the way the rookie trailed him, clearly marked him as the lead on this case. "Can you give me a rundown of what happened earlier?"

She recapped what she remembered, using as few words as possible. Between her raw throat, the pounding in her head, and the narcotics dulling her mind, she had trouble focusing.

"And you got no clue why these guys busted in?" Arnett's sharp eyes locked on her.

"No. And his voice wasn't familiar."

"One of them spoke to you?"

Hadn't she told him that? "He had a British accent."

And a foul mouth. But his coarse language wouldn't help them catch him.

She felt her eyes slipping closed. Any residual adrenaline had long since faded. Should she be this tired? Maybe they'd put something in her IV.

"Deputy Tanner." Arnett's voice sounded closer.

After struggling to open her eyes, it took her a few seconds to focus them on the detective now standing directly next to her bed.

"I know you've been through a lot, but the first forty-eight hours are critical."

"I–" She cleared her throat. "I know. Sorry, I'm... tired." And hurting, but she doubted he really cared about that detail.

"What did the man say? Word for word, if you can."

The fog wrapped around her brain did nothing to keep the words from flooding back. The vulgarity of the man's intentions twisted her stomach like a twig in a hurricane. " 'You and me, we could have some fun.' "

Silence oppressed the room for several long seconds. Arnett shifted his weight. "But he, uh, didn't follow through?"

"Got the feeling it was said to scare me." Unfortunately, the tactic had worked all too well. "I think they were there for some other reason."

"But you don't know what that was."

"No."

"Are you kidding?" Micah stepped closer. "Does the name Richie Ochoa ring a bell?"

Had that just been this morning? It felt like so long ago.

"Who's this Ochoa character?" Arnett glanced between

her and Micah.

"A lowlife with a criminal record. Lana was looking into him and he threatened her. This morning."

"Not much of a threat." She nearly choked on the words. Fire scorched her throat; pressure built behind her eyes from tears she didn't think she could hide much longer. "I'm beat. Can we continue tomorrow?"

Barker didn't give Arnett time to respond. "She's right. Let's get out of here."

Without waiting for a reply, Barker clapped one of his mammoth hands on Arnett's shoulder and forcibly turned him around. Arnett glanced back at her as Barker propelled him toward the door. Bushy eyebrows dropped over Arnett's eyes and his already thin lips pressed flat.

To his credit, he gave no argument. Didn't even resist.

Before stepping from the room, Barker paused and fixed her with a look that shot fire. "You. Sleep. We've got a guard on you, so don't worry about them coming back."

She nodded. The door clicked shut softly behind the men.

Honestly, worry was about the furthest thing from her mind at the moment. Questions, however, wouldn't stop flooding her thoughts.

Her eyes slid closed, but her brain didn't shut down nearly as quickly.

Two men. In her house. Why?

And would they return?

Fourteen

"Hey, Miller."

Nate looked away from the stupid romantic comedy Amanda was watching as Camo approached. Stiffness lined Camo's shoulders and his jaw muscles twitched like a strung out meth-head.

A black phone was clenched in Camo's white-knuckled hand. Camo thrust the device in Nate's face. "Tim wanted you to see this."

He took the phone. An image dominated the small display. His mind rebelled at what his eyes clearly saw.

Lana. Unconscious.

Or dead.

The room seemed to squeeze around him. Every breath burned past the mountain lodged in his throat.

"Take it that's your girl." Camo's words registered – barely – but Nate couldn't formulate a response.

He didn't want to look at the photo. Yet he couldn't take his eyes off it.

Faked. Had to be.

It would take more than a clown like Tim to bring Lana down. Somehow Tim had gotten a picture of Lana and transposed her face over whoever it was that lay on the floor.

If only.

He recognized the tile under her still body, the wood on the island behind her. Even the light blue shirt she wore was familiar.

It *was* Lana and the picture had been taken inside her kitchen.

Blood smeared the floor around her. A small pool stained the tile under her torso; more colored one leg of her jeans.

Before any words could form, the phone rang. The display read "Tim calling."

Didn't matter that it wasn't his phone, Nate accepted the call. "You're a dead man."

A pause greeted him. "Cool down. She's all right."

Satisfaction flitted through Nate at the hesitation in Tim's voice. The preppy snob should be scared; heck, he should be terrified. To think that he could kill Lana and get away–

Wait. What had Tim said? "She's alive?"

"For now."

The image of Lana lying in her own blood seared his memory. This could be a bluff. "I don't believe you. She looked pretty dead to me."

"Let's just say she fought back more than Jimmy expected and he got rough. As long as you do what we say, she'll recover."

"You're a fool. You've probably got every member of law enforcement on the East Coast looking for you right about now. You can't attack a Marshal and get away with it."

"That's nothing compared to what we'll do if you don't get me that antitoxin in time."

Unable to sit any longer, Nate sprung from the chair and paced outside into the dank night air. "You touch her again, there won't be a place on this earth you can hide from me."

"You think I'm scared by your pathetic little threats?"

Nate conjured up a tone he hadn't used since, well, frankly, *he'd* never used it. But he'd heard Matt use it on more than one occasion. The cool, controlled tone had always worked well in the past. And he'd quickly discovered that a softly spoken threat was more effective than a screamed one. "I'll destroy everyone you care about. Starting with your sister."

Not that he had any intention of doing such a thing. Amanda was as much a victim here as Lana.

Almost.

Anger exploded across the line. "You touch my sister and you'll pay for it."

Now there was a pathetic little threat. Nate had hidden from people much worse than Tim.

How did he know Lana was really okay?

Sure, Tim said she was, but he doubted Tim would tell him that she was dead, not when they needed his help. "I'm going to call her."

"So you can tell her who we are? Not a chance."

"I'm not helping you unless I know she's okay."

"You don't do as I say and I'll send Jimmy back to finish the job. Now let me talk to Camo."

Nate stormed back into the living room to find Amanda and Camo both watching him. Without a word, he passed the phone to Camo and dropped into a chair.

Nausea stampeded through his stomach.

All he saw, everywhere he looked, was Lana. Bloody and still.

He'd seen her like that once before and it had changed his life. He couldn't shake the feeling that this time would be no different.

Camo's voice filtered through the image imbedded in his head. "Tim. What's this about the U.S. Marshals?"

Something in Camo's voice snagged Nate's attention. A glance at the man found his lips set in a thin line, creases wrinkling the brow above his narrowed eyes.

Why would Camo be upset about this situation with Lana?

Nate didn't know, but one way or another, he was going to find out.

Camo's voice softened and his monosyllabic answers revealed nothing.

Muttering something about needing air, Nate strode from

the room. The cool breeze blowing off the ocean cut through his shirt, but did nothing to squelch the fire coursing through him.

Salt water misted his face.

He closed his eyes, but all he saw was the photo. If ripping out his eyes would remove the image, he thought he might do it. But the picture had seared his mind.

Those meatheads had attacked her. In her home.

He wanted to beat Tim to a bloody pulp.

No. He wanted to kill him.

It wouldn't be hard. Supremacist groups typically had more guns than some police departments. All he had to do was find their weapons cache' and he could take them all down.

It is mine to avenge. I will repay.

That Bible verse always surfaced at the worst times.

Nate stamped it down. Sometimes God's vengeance didn't come soon enough. Other times it felt like God's mercy overrode His justice.

Heels clicked along the deck behind him.

Great. Just who he didn't want to deal with right now.

Amanda leaned one arm on the railing next to him. After a glance her direction, he returned his attention to the tumultuous water.

"So that's her, huh?"

"Stay out of it."

"Stay out of it? In case you didn't notice, this involves all of us."

He couldn't find a response.

"Personally, I expected better."

He whirled to face her. "Meaning?"

"She's just so plain. I guess I thought she'd be something special. I mean, really. You rejected this-" She waved a well-manicured hand down her body, "-for *that*?"

Of all the....

Fingernails cut into his palms. He worked to keep his

voice level. "There's nothing to compare."

"She turned you in!"

"And visited me every week."

Narrowed eyes regarded him and a scowl twisted her lips. "What makes her so special? She's not even white. She's a mutt!"

He leaned over her, his face inches from hers. "Don't you *ever* talk about her like that again."

Fear danced in her suddenly widened eyes. She took a small step back. "But it's true. She's, what, part Hispanic?" The words, spoken softly, contained a slight tremor.

"Greek-Italian. But so what? Why's skin color such a big deal to you guys?"

Hands on her hips, she jutted her chin toward him. "God reached perfection when He created white skin."

"All of a sudden you want to talk about God?"

"I never said I didn't believe in God."

"So you believe what? That all the other colors were God's screw-ups?"

"Experimentation."

Unbelievable. He'd had enough. "You don't know the first thing about God."

If she had a reply, he had no desire to hear it.

Far more disturbing than her theories on skin color was the fact that she considered Lana to be inferior. And if she thought that, no doubt Tim thought the same thing.

Would that make Lana more expendable in their eyes? Like all those kids they'd already killed?

The answers to those questions were too disturbing to dwell on for long. He shifted from the questions to finding a solution.

Unlikely as it seemed, Camo might be his best ally.

He didn't know what Camo's hang-up was with law enforcement, but he was going to find out. If his reasons were strong enough, Nate might be able to flip Camo to his side. And he had to do it before Tim – or Amanda – decided Lana wasn't white enough to live.

The first two glasses of Jack Daniels hadn't seemed to faze him. The third put a buzz in his ears. Nate pushed away his nearly empty glass.

Enough. It'd been a long time since he'd had alcohol. The three glasses had already taken a toll on him.

Camo took a swig from his own glass and reached for the bottle. "So here we were, taking heavy fire, and one of my men gets the big idea to charge the ship. 'Course the freakin' idiot got himself shot, then I had to clean up his mess."

By the second glass of whiskey, Camo's tongue had loosened sufficiently for him to start relaying war stories. If all the stories could be believed, Camo had been quite the accomplished soldier.

Amanda tossed back another shot of tequila. The vacant look in her eyes told him she either couldn't care less about Camo's war stories or had heard them all before. Or maybe she'd just had too much to drink.

Could be a little of each.

He'd lost track of how many shots she'd had, but it'd been a lot. More than he'd expected someone of her size to be able to handle.

Nate focused back in on Camo's story, not that the ex-soldier seemed to notice the lack of response. "So did the kid survive? The wannabe hero?"

A snort accompanied Camo's nod. "Yeah, he made it. Lost one of his legs, but he's alive."

Conversation lulled. Might be a good time to try to gain some intel.

"So how'd you get hooked up with White Fire? Someone from your unit?"

"Nah. Met Tim at a firing range. He was firing this antique musket that belonged to his great granddad or someone."

Nate tried to imagine how the conversation had gone but couldn't quite make it work. No way Tim would have said "Hey, you look like a racist. Wanna join my militia?"

But somehow the issue of their personal prejudices must have come up. "So he asked you to join?"

"Eventually. I worked at the range so I saw him all the time."

"You still at the firing range?"

"Nah, that was a short term gig. Now I'm a Navy recruiter."

Somehow, he had a hard time imagining Camo schmoozing high school and college kids into joining the military.

Camo polished off another glass. "Tim would come to the range a couple of times a week. We got to talkin and before I knew it, I was in."

"So, about today. Does Tim do things like this often?"

With the glass inches from his lips, Camo paused. "What?"

"Cut you out of the loop."

"Tim doesn't answer to me any more than I answer to him." The nonchalant answer was as genuine as a three-headed zombie. Camo emptied his glass, refilled, and offered Nate the bottle. Nate declined.

Silence descended as Camo seemed to ponder his drink.

The subtle approach obviously hadn't worked. Looked like he'd have to be more direct. "So what's your deal with cops, anyway?"

Narrowed eyes flitted his way. "What do you mean?"

"Come on. You weren't happy with Tim for attacking a cop."

"You listened in on my conversation?"

"You weren't exactly being quiet."

Camo tossed back the last of the whiskey and stared at Nate. Weighed him. Nate maintained eye contact.

The irritation lining Camo's face slowly loosened. He sighed. "I come from a family of cops. My grandpa, dad, brother, all cops. Heck, even my mom worked in dispatch. My great-grandpa was a Texas Ranger, killed in the line of duty."

"Why didn't you become one?"

"I did. After the Seals, I joined the force for several years."

Did he quit? Or was he fired for his prejudice? The open way he'd said it made Nate think the decision to leave had been Camo's. "Why'd you quit?"

"Too much bureaucratic red tape. You just about gotta get a warrant to breathe these days." Camo poured more Jack Daniels into his glass. "This way I can still exact justice, but without all the politics."

"Too bad Tim doesn't value you enough to respect your feelings."

"It's got nothin' to do with that! The kid's focused on his agenda. Don't see anythin' else." Three swigs demolished the whiskey in Camo's glass. "Besides, he's not gonna do anything to her."

"Too late. You saw the picture."

"What I hear, she asked for that. Tim said if you get the antitoxin, he'll leave her alone."

"Really? And if he told you the world was gonna end tomorrow, I suppose you'd believe that, too." Slamming his hand on the table, Nate leaned in. "Wake up. Tim tells you what you want to hear. You don't find it coincidental that he waited until you were out of the country before attacking a U.S. Marshal?"

"A situation came up and he made a judgment call."

"Well, his judgment call impacts more than just him. You said you don't answer to him, so that'd make you guys partners. And that's how the law will see you if they catch him. You'll go down as an accessory after the fact. Trust me. I know."

"Tim knows how to deal with the law." Camo's crossed his arms over his broad chest. "Besides, it's done. Nothin' I can do 'bout it."

Nate lowered his voice. "Let me warn her."

"Won't go against Tim like that."

"I won't tell them anything that could point to you guys. I'll just let them know that she's been targeted." No matter how hard he tried to hold it back, desperation seeped into his voice. "That way Tim can't do something you'll regret. Look, I'm keeping my end of the bargain here. He'll get the stupid antitoxin. Let me remove her from the equation."

After surveying him for a second, Camo shook his head. "Lighten up. We get that antitoxin tomorrow and he'll leave her alone."

"And if he doesn't?"

"Tim and me, we're tight. He wouldn't lie to me."

Was that doubt in Camo's voice? "Just like he wouldn't do something you're completely opposed to? Like put a U.S. Marshal in the hospital?"

Camo downed the rest of his drink. "We'd better get some sleep. Got a big day ahead."

He was right. It was already after two a.m. and they were planning on going down around four.

Obviously they hadn't adjusted to the time difference yet.

Movement to his left caught his attention.

Dang. Amanda had been so quiet that he'd forgotten she was here. Would she report what he'd said to Tim?

Amanda threw back another shot, then set her glass on the table. "Well, that's 'bout as interestin' as watchin' mold grow. I'm much int'rested 'n Nate."

Leaning across the small table, she snagged his hand.

Great. A sober Amanda was bad enough, but a drunk one?

He jerked his hand away. "Knock it off, Amanda."

She straightened. Arms crossed over her chest, her lips curled into a pout. "You can't 'ell me what to do. Not a child."

"Then stop acting like one!" Irritation lined Camo's words.

Pushing up from her chair, she staggered a few steps before finding her way to the head. The door slammed behind her.

Camo shook his head slowly. "Tim says she wasn't always like this. He says she went to college a sweet kid and came back a tramp."

Somehow, he had trouble seeing Amanda as a sweet kid.

Amanda stepped from the small bathroom and made her way on unsteady feet back to her chair. Pink rimmed her bloodshot eyes and her splotchy face was pale.

Had she been crying? Over what? Camo's comment about behaving like a child?

Collecting his now-empty glass, Camo rose. "I'm turnin' in."

It'd probably be wise for him to do the same. Especially with the state Amanda was in. Nate rinsed his glass in the sink and moved toward the back of the room.

With his hand on the doorknob, he paused. Glanced back.

Amanda stared at some distant spot on the wall.

Man. She looked lost.

And completely wasted.

No matter how much his brain told him to leave, that she'd brought this misery upon herself, he heard himself asking, "You okay?"

She blinked, focused on him, and swiped at a tear. "Yeah. Sure. Why wouldn't I be?"

"I don't know. You just seemed, I don't know."

"What's so bad 'bout havin' fun?" Fresh tears pooled in her eyes.

Several steps brought him back into the room. He leaned against the wall across from her. "Are you really having fun?"

Nice. Like he was a good one to offer advice.

"N'body understands."

He pulled out the chair directly opposite her, careful to

leave the table in between them. "Understands what?"

She stared at him for a few seconds. Maybe considering her answer. Or maybe just zoning out. She'd downed a lot of alcohol.

Finally, she gave an exaggerated shake of her head.

"Ne'er mind. Don't wanna talk 'bout this 'ny more." She pushed back from the table and rose to her feet. Swayed. "Ooh. Water's rough."

There was no point in telling her that the boat hadn't moved.

A few more teetering steps put her in the center of the room. After wavering for a second, she toppled to the floor.

Dang. If he didn't help her, she might do some serious damage.

So what? She'd done this to herself. No one had been pouring the alcohol down her throat. Let her drag herself back to her cabin if that's what she had to do.

He turned to go, but didn't make it more than two steps.

Helping her was the right thing to do. Even if she didn't deserve it.

Besides, what if she hurt herself and told Tim that he'd done something to her? Or worse, fell overboard? While he wasn't scared of Tim alone, he was seriously outnumbered with Tim and his group of gun-happy militants.

Not to mention what might happen to Lana.

Fine. He'd help her. But just to the door of her cabin. No further. This was Amanda, after all.

She hadn't risen from the floor. Passed out? Even better.

Then he heard the muffled sobs.

Ugh. He didn't want to feel sorry for her. Arrogant Amanda he could handle. Flirty Amanda he was learning to deal with, but he had no clue how to respond to a teary Amanda.

Kneeling beside her, he put a hand on her shoulder. "You okay?"

"Never be okay."

"Come on, let me help you up."

Once on her feet, she leaned heavily on him as he led her down the narrow passageway to the staterooms. Opening her door, he guided her inside, but stopped only two steps into the room.

Not only did he not want to give Amanda the wrong idea, he didn't want to risk having Camo catch him in here.

Turning her around, he tilted her chin up to look in her eyes. "I'm gonna let go now. You get some sleep and this'll all look better in the morning."

"You nice guy." The slurred words were barely discernable.

He took a small step back, only to have her fall toward him. His hands shot out, caught her arms, and steadied her on her feet once again.

This was getting ridiculous. Tomorrow he'd have to hide the alcohol.

She pulled her arms free and threw them around his neck.

Suddenly she was in his face, her lips on his. His mind blanked. His body froze. His thoughts battled.

Fingers ran up the back of his scalp. Perfume, part sweet, part musk, teased his senses. Tension seeped from his shoulders.

His mind screamed at him to pull back. But his body rooted to the spot.

What was he doing?

Who cared?

It was nice to be touched. Almost of its own volition, his hand landed on her back. The other cradled her neck.

It'd been so long since he'd been this close to a woman. Too long. Not since he'd kissed Lana more than two years ago....

Lana.

He jerked Amanda's arms from his neck and stepped back so suddenly that she stumbled forward.

Hurt and confusion mingled in her eyes. "Just little fun."

It sounded so logical coming from her lips.

Why not? It wasn't like he and Lana had a future together anyway. She was way too good for him and with her career, well, he doubted the U.S. Marshal's office would smile on one of their own marrying a former criminal.

Which meant he either spent the rest of his life alone or took love where he could find it. And Amanda was more than available.

He looked at her.

Large blue eyes stared back at him. Blonde curls tousled around her pale face and full pink lips.

Between her looks, her mannerisms, and her personality, she was different from Lana in practically every way imaginable.

Lana's face flashed into his mind. The memory of how good she'd felt in his arms flooded him.

He could still hear her laugh.

See her quick smile.

Smell the fruity intoxication of her perfume.

Future or no future, he wanted no one else. Especially not someone who probably didn't know the meaning of the word monogamous.

Pressure on his chest caused him to look down. Her long-fingered hand rested in the center of his ribcage.

"Stay." The word half-slurred, half-purred from her lips.

He brushed her hand from his chest and took a step backward. "I can't."

Red stained her cheeks as her eyes narrowed. "Whatsa matter? Think too good fer me?"

Alarms rang in his head. All he needed was for her to call her brother in tears saying he'd attacked her or used her or something. He had to tread carefully. "No. But you deserve better than all this."

"Tha's sweet, but don't want better. Want you."

Now what? He couldn't risk setting her off. Maybe in a situation like this, nothing was safer than the truth.

"I'm sorry, but I..." His shoulders lifted in a small shrug. "I love her."

"What's she got that's so special?"

There was no safe way to answer that. He grabbed the door knob and stepped into the hall, pulling the door closed behind him.

It was almost shut when he heard two words murmured from within.

"Love me."

Whether or not she'd intended him to hear, he couldn't be sure. But responding to something he shouldn't have heard could invite her wrath. Or tears. Neither one of which he felt equipped to handle.

The latch clicked softly.

Easing a sigh, he hurried down the hall to his own cabin and shut the door behind him. The lock scraped into place and his heart rate slowly declined.

His legs quaked as he collapsed on the bed.

That'd been close. Too close. What had he been thinking?

Lana had been through a nightmare today because of him and here he was kissing another woman. It didn't matter that he and Lana weren't dating and probably never would, he should've kept himself in check.

He was a jerk. An idiot. One who didn't deserve Lana, even if he could one day have a shot with her.

Heaviness blanketed his heart. He hated Amanda's forwardness, her fixation with him.

But he'd loved the contact. And craved more.

Rolling to his stomach, he slid from the bed and landed on his knees.

Four o'clock was going to come awfully early, but first he had to spend some time in prayer. Or next time, he may not escape the temptation. Next time, he might do something he'd really regret.

Fifteen

Jimmy lifted the .357 magnum and unloaded it into the target ten yards away. The target practice did nothing to alleviate the rage boiling inside him.

Not even killing that whiny little bloke Kirk had helped. No, the only one who would suffice was Miller's little chick herself.

He could see his bloody nose!

Not only was it swollen to twice its normal size, that wretched little witch had busted it. He couldn't remember the last time he'd wanted to kill someone so badly.

That did it. He was gonna make himself another trip down there and finish her.

Slowly.

He stalked toward the target. Holes dotted the outer rings, but shied away from the bulls-eye.

Dang it! Not only had she injured him in places he didn't care to discuss, he was so distracted that he couldn't even aim properly.

He ripped off the target and slammed his fist against the plywood behind it. Pain rippled up his arm, but the release felt good.

He did it again. The bullet-scarred wood splintered under his fist.

A snap came from behind him. He whirled, bringing the gun up and focusing on the silhouette moving toward him.

From several yards away, Tim held up his hands. "Point

that thing somewhere else, will you?"

The gun lowered.

"Little late for target practice, isn't it?"

What did he care what bloody hour it was? "Had to blow off some steam."

Tim nodded at the now broken target. "Did it help?"

With the gun hanging limply at his side, Jimmy glared at Tim. "She's mine. I'm gonna finish her."

"No. We've gotta keep Camo on our side. With all his contacts, he's too valuable to risk alienating."

"Well, it wasn't Camo's nose she broke now, was it?"

"Come on, Jimmy. You do anything to her and you'll have the whole East Coast looking for you. She's not worth it."

"I'll be the judge of that." Brushing past Tim, he stomped across the field toward the house.

Easy for Tim to take the bloody high road. The scuffle hadn't left a mark on him.

If Tim thought he could order Jimmy around, the bloke was delusional.

Jimmy threw open the back door and clomped across the kitchen. Nobody controlled him. He'd do what he wanted, when he wanted. If he wanted to put a bullet between someone's eyes, no one could stop him.

And right now, a scrawny, dark-haired U.S. Marshal topped his list.

Lightning cracked the black sky. Fat raindrops splashed the already wet deck. Nate stared at the whitecaps that rocked the boat beneath his feet. Diving under these conditions was not a good plan.

He turned to face Camo and raised his voice to carry above the storm. "We shouldn't go down in this weather."

"You don't have a choice." Amanda's voice sliced from behind him. "My brother doesn't have time to wait for good weather."

Whirling, he found her standing only a few feet away. In spite of the darkness, sunken eyes squinted at him and she appeared to have aged twenty years in the last two hours. Too much alcohol and too little sleep were obviously not a winning combination. "If we drown, he'll die anyway. At least by waiting, we stand a shot at getting what he needs."

Her eyes slid to Camo. "You can do this, can't you?"

A tight nod answered her. "When I was in the Seals, I dove in worse conditions than this."

Great. Nate bit back his irritation.

Between Amanda, who didn't know the first thing about scuba diving, and Camo, whose ego overrode common sense, they were going to make sure he drowned.

Amanda stepped forward, her face just inches from his own. "Do it. Or I'll call Jimmy and tell him to pay a visit to your friend. Alone. Without Tim around, Jimmy won't be nearly so nice."

If that last visit had been Jimmy being nice, he'd hate to see what happened when Jimmy's mean streak came to the forefront.

Without another word, Nate pulled on his dive hood and reached for the rest of his gear.

Once they were both suited up, he hooked a buddy line to his weight belt and handed Camo the other end. Conditions down there were likely to be murky, at least until they reached deeper levels. The last thing they could afford to do was waste time looking for each other.

Half of him expected Camo to argue, but the all-capable former Seal just clipped the line in place. They each grabbed their waterproof bags, approached the edge of the boat, and wrestled on their fins.

A minute later they were in the water. The roughness of the sea made swimming at the surface impossible.

They dove.

Nate clicked on his dive light. The high-powered beam filtered through the dark, swirling water. He glanced over, but couldn't see Camo through the murk.

A look at his gauges told him he was only at twenty-five feet. He kept going lower.

The temperature in the water around him plummeted. Cold bit into the small amount of exposed skin on his face. The water cleared slightly.

He paused to reference his compass. The buddy line pulled taut.

Well, at least he knew Camo was still with him.

After finding his heading, Nate pressed on. The cliff came into view. No cave in sight.

He checked his depth. Ninety-seven feet. It should be right here.

Aiming the light to his left, he looked for the tell-tale rock outcropping. No sign of it. Not that he could see very far. He checked to his right. Still nothing.

They didn't have the oxygen to hunt for long. Which way?

Camo slugged his shoulder and pointed insistently to the left.

Why not? It wasn't like he had any better ideas. Nodding, he swam that direction.

They hadn't gone far before their lights picked up a familiar cluster of rocks.

Huh. Maybe Camo was good for something after all.

Rounding the rocks, Nate paused to unfasten the buddy line before leading the way inside the cave.

A school of fish burst out at him.

He started. The flashlight slipped from his gloved hand, but didn't go further than a few inches thanks to the strap looped securely around his arm.

After retrieving the light, he continued on.

The walls narrowed around him, the ceiling lowered above him, the floor rose up to meet him. Directly in front of him was the jagged opening that hopefully would lead to the cavern and the lab.

He shined the light through the opening. It was small. Too small.

Getting through wouldn't be easy. The trick would be to angle his body just right.

The waterproof bag went through first. With his arms over his head, he eased through the opening, wriggling his shoulders through the narrow gap.

Rock scraped down his sides and clanged against his tank.

Placing his hands on the wall on either side of the entrance, he tried to push himself through. He kicked furiously, but didn't budge.

Maybe he could go back and try this from a different angle. He planted his knees against the rock and tried to pull back into the cavern where Camo waited.

Nothing. Not even an inch.

He was stuck.

He glanced at his gauges. Under half a tank.

They were going to die down here.

No matter how hard he tried to control his breathing, he gulped in air as he thrashed against the rock restraining him.

Pressure against his feet. Camo must be pushing.

Not that such an action would be terribly effective under water, but he'd take whatever help he could get.

He writhed, squirmed, twisted. Moved inch by painful inch.

And then he was in.

Shaking blitzed his limbs. He'd made it. He didn't know how he was going to get back out, but for now, he was glad to be free.

Camo's arms and head popped through the opening, followed by the top of his shoulders. The rocks prevented him from getting much further.

A burst of bubbles – that Nate imagined would be profanity-laced if Camo could speak – exploded from the regulator.

Following Nate's lead, Camo pushed against the rock and twisted. He didn't move.

Nate grabbed Camo's upper arms and pulled. What he wouldn't give to have the proper leverage.

Of course, he could leave Camo down here.

Nobody would have to know. He could say there'd been a tragic accident, that Camo really wasn't the accomplished diver he'd claimed to be.

No one could refute him.

It'd even the odds a tiny bit.

No. Out of all of them, Camo was the only potential ally he had.

Besides, leaving Camo to die was the same as killing him. And he didn't want to go down that road.

Repositioning his hold on Camo's arms, he tried swimming away. Nothing.

He reached for his light and examined the hole in which Camo was wedged, hoping to see something, anything, that kept him from slipping free.

Nothing specific presented itself as the problem. Camo was simply too large to fit through the opening.

Nate glanced at his equipment. The water resistant timepiece told him they'd been at this depth for seventeen minutes. The maximum recommended time was only twenty-five minutes.

If they didn't ascend soon, their chances of suffering decompression sickness skyrocketed.

Bubbles exploded from Camo's regulator as he thrashed against his stone prison. He twisted a few degrees and slid forward almost six inches.

Nate grabbed his arms and pulled.

A few more inches.

The tank grated against stone, the sound searing Nate's eardrums. But Camo continued to inch forward.

With a final scrape, Camo popped free.

Bubbles spurted upward. Lots of bubbles. Camo spit out his regulator and drew his hand in a line across his throat.

The universal signal for no air.

Nate grabbed his backup regulator and passed it to Camo. As he did, he checked his submersible pressure gauge.

Less than a quarter of a tank left. For two of them. Not good.

How far would they have to go to get to the cavern? Assuming they were even in the right place.

Nate pointed upward and inflated his buoyancy compensator to begin his controlled ascent. Eighty feet. Then sixty.

Almost out of air.

If they died down here, would anyone ever find their bodies?

Fifty feet. Forty. Thirty.

Would Lana know how much he loved her? Would she think that he'd taken off rather than risk going back to prison?

Oh no. Would Tim think he'd taken off? Would he kill Lana as retribution?

Twenty feet.

Was the air feeling thicker?

Fifteen feet.

The air was gone. He abandoned all control and released his weight belt. Man, did he hope they were in the right place. And that the cave ceiling was high enough that he wouldn't hit his head when he surfaced.

His head broke the surface and he sucked in air like a junkie needing a fix. Beside him, he heard Camo doing the same.

The darkness that surrounded them was as absolute as it had been underwater. Lifting his light, Nate illuminated Camo.

"You good?"

Camo cussed. "Yeah. That stupid rock ripped my hose."

That explained all the bubbles. Nate shifted his light from

Camo to the area around them.

The cavern was larger than he'd imagined. Not even the powerful light in his hands could reach the furthest corners.

How would they ever find the entrance to the lab in such a big, dark place?

Well, one thing was for certain. They wouldn't find the entrance bobbing here in the middle of the room.

He swam to his left, pausing every few yards to scan the area with his light.

His light landed on a sheer rock wall. At least he had a reference point now.

Swimming parallel to the wall, he kept going.

What if this wasn't the right cavern? What if there was no way out except the way they came in?

They could hook his regulator up to Camo's tank. And pray that there was enough oxygen to get both of them out of here.

But as hard as it had been to get through that opening one time, he doubted they could do it again. Especially on such a limited oxygen supply.

Not to mention he'd dropped his weight belt and he suspected Camo had, too.

No, going back down wouldn't be an option.

Come on, God. I need a little hope here.

His light caught something ahead of him about the same time that one of his fins connected with something solid.

Shallow water. And up ahead, solid ground. Or more accurately, rock.

He pulled off his fins, planted his feet underneath him, and braced a hand on the wall. A few seconds later, he left the water behind and stood dripping on the uneven, rocky ground.

In front of him, the ground rose about a dozen more feet before leveling off.

Without exchanging a word, he and Camo trudged up the incline. His legs ached by the time he reached the top.

Evidently it didn't matter how toned he was; lugging the extra weight from the tank and all his gear wasn't easy.

The area in front of them was about the size of a basketball court and reasonably level. Beyond that, a series of stairs switchbacked to a solid metal door.

He let his light trace the wall.

The beam picked up a metal catwalk and stair combo that followed the wall and steadily led to the ceiling.

The emergency exit. And probably their only way out of this place.

Kneeling, he shrugged out of his buoyancy compensator and let it and his tank fall to the rock behind him. The dull clunk echoed through the chamber.

"They have tanks inside?" Camo's voice echoed through the cavernous space.

"No clue. I think Plan B is our only option."

"You talking about that evacuation idea you had?"

"Yeah. We get one of the lab geeks to implement emergency lockdown procedures. The guards and people who aren't in the lab will evacuate through the elevator while those of us in the lab will take this route. You'll have rigged the lab to blow, which should buy us time to get away."

Narrowed eyes surveyed him. "Should? I don't like should."

"You got a better plan?"

While Camo clearly wasn't pleased, he didn't argue any further. Instead he opened up his waterproof bag and pulled out a wicked looking Bowie knife.

Nate opened his own bag and removed the street clothes packed inside.

Good thing they'd thought to bring these. Hard to blend into a crowd wearing a wetsuit.

He stripped out of his wetsuit and swim trunks and pulled on the dry clothes.

Camo finished dressing about the same time. "We'll have to leave our gear."

Must be nice to have that kind of money to throw around. Diving equipment wasn't cheap. And the dive shop where they'd rented everything would no doubt add a hefty charge to Camo's credit card when it wasn't returned.

From what he'd seen, it wouldn't even dent this group's finances.

Gathering the gear, he followed Camo toward a cluster of rocks in one of the furthest corners of the cavern. They crammed the wetsuits, tanks, buoyancy compensators, fins, and regulators around the rocks.

Unless someone really explored this space, no one would ever find their cast-offs.

Now the only evidence remaining of their dip in the water was wet hair and the dive boots on their feet.

Without a word, they approached the stairs leading up to the metal door. The closer he got, the more Nate could see that this wasn't going to be easy.

The door appeared solid. No visible hinges or latches of any kind.

Once he stood in front of it, he could see that it didn't even swing open. It slid. Short of some C4, a blowtorch, or a really large can opener, he saw no way to get through it.

Camo evidently felt the same way. "Now what, genius?"

Good question.

Lana's life hinged on his ability to get past this door.

He danced the light across the dull steel. Up the walls on either side. The beam passed over a floodlight mounted on the wall beside the door.

Huh.

He kept the beam moving. Around the platform on which they stood.

The rectangular platform looked like it belonged on any number of fire escapes. Vented surface beneath them, thin railing. It even had a folding metal chair and ashtray–

Wait a second.

There was only one reason for a chair and ashtray to be

out here.

"Looks like there's at least one smoker inside."

Not waiting for Camo's reply, Nate approached the ashtray and glanced at the contents. Several different brands of cigarette butts littered the area.

Most likely more than one smoker.

He turned to Camo. "We'll wait for someone to come out and ambush them."

Angling his light at his watch, he saw it was after five a.m. It probably wouldn't be long before someone opened that door.

If they were going to operate a successful ambush, they needed to find a place to hide. And this platform offered them nothing with which to work.

"We better get outta sight." Camo's voice bounced off the rock surrounding them.

Returning to the stairs, they went down about half a dozen steps and sat. As much as he dreaded doing it, Nate clicked off the light.

Blackness swallowed them.

Amanda paced the confines of the cabin.

The boat swayed beneath her feet, her stomach lurching with every roll. Ugh. She really should've cut herself off sooner last night. This morning. Whatever. Bile burned her throat and she barely made it to the head before emptying her stomach.

She sank to her knees by the toilet, dropping her throbbing head into her hands.

Rain pummeled the deck and pinged off the roof, but the storm berating the boat took a backseat to the one raging inside her.

No matter how hard she tried, she couldn't erase the image from her mind. The look on Nate's face when she'd threatened to send Jimmy after that black-haired slut with whom Nate seemed infatuated.

Not infatuated.

He loved her. He'd said so himself.

What did he see in that mixed breed anyway?

It didn't matter. She wanted it.

Out of all the guys she'd been with, all the ones who claimed they'd do anything for her, she knew not one of them would risk his life to protect her. For years she'd enjoyed the casual relationships, but she was ready for more.

She'd pulled out all the stops. But as long as the competition was in the way, it looked like she didn't stand a chance.

What if the competition was eliminated?

Jimmy.

She could talk him into almost anything. She knew it. And if what Camo said was true, if that chick really had left Jimmy with a broken nose and bruises, Jimmy's pride would demand vengeance.

Once she was out of the way, then Amanda could move in. Nothing healed a broken heart like another woman's arms, right?

Making him forget all about that other woman would be simple.

Amanda turned from the toilet and staggered back to her cabin. She snatched up the phone and dialed Jimmy's cell. As the first ring filled her ear, it dawned on her that it was almost midnight back home.

Oh well. If she woke Jimmy up, he'd get over it. She had to complete this call before Nate and Camo returned. And who knew how long they'd be gone.

The ringing stopped and Jimmy's voice mumbled unintelligibly across the line.

"Jimmy? Wake up."

"Who's this?"

Seriously. Like her number wasn't programmed into his cell phone. "Amanda."

" 'Ello, luv." A yawn. "You got any idear what bloody time it is?"

"This couldn't wait." Hmmm. How to begin? She couldn't just ask if he was feeling murderous at the moment. "I wanted to talk to you about this girl."

"Girl?"

"Nate's girl." It killed her to say that. "I hear she almost got the better of you."

He snorted. "That's a load of–"

"I hear you have a broken nose."

"Look, she's a scrappy one, she is. That what you wanna hear?" He swore. All traces of sleep disappeared from his tone. "I'm hanging up. Can't believe you woke me up to talk about this."

Dang. She'd better get to the point. "How'd you like to even the score?"

Dead air. Had she lost him?

No. She could hear him breathing.

"Whaddya mean?" Caution lined his words.

"I mean go back and finish the job. I want her dead."

"Why?"

"None of your business."

"You think I'll kill her on your say-so?"

"Why not? You want her dead."

"Ya think so, do you?"

A laugh slipped from her lips. "I know you. You're itching to go back and show her who really has the power."

A pause. Jimmy's breathing thickened.

Perfect. She had him.

"Come on, Jimmy. You can't tell me you haven't at least thought about it."

A low chuckle sent chills crawling up her back. "Oh, I've done more than just think on it. I'm planning a trip south in a few days."

"Do it today. Before we get stateside."

"What's the rush, luv?"

The rush was that she wanted it done. Now. While Nate only had her and Camo for solace.

Because heaven knew he wouldn't turn to Camo. Which only left him one option.

Her.

But she couldn't tell Jimmy that. "Because if we get back there and Nate hears she's dead and then realizes you weren't around at the time, he might kill you."

"You worried about my safety, is that it?"

Sure. Whatever. "Of course."

Honestly, she couldn't care less about Jimmy's safety. Their brief fling had taught her Jimmy was nothing but a thug with a charming accent.

"I'm thinkin' it's a good day to visit my new friend."

A shiver tickled across her skin at the casual way Jimmy referred to murder. "I'll let you get back to sleep."

After a brief good-bye, she terminated the call.

An odd numbness buzzed through her mind.

She'd ordered someone's death.

While her brother had done it on a number of occasions, this was the first time she'd made such a call. It was strange how much that thought unsettled her.

And exhilarated her.

By this time tomorrow, Nate Miller's little crush would be a thing of the past.

Sixteen

Cold metal stairs had to be about the most uncomfortable seat imaginable. Nate shifted slightly, not that it helped much. By the time this was over, he'd probably have a permanent indentation across his butt.

Movement nearby told him Camo was just as uncomfortable.

"How long do you think it's been?" Camo's whisper seemed loud in the blackness.

"I don't know. Maybe an hour."

A grunt. "Woulda thought we'd have seen someone by now."

"Let's hope they didn't kick the habit." Of course, multiple brands indicated multiple smokers, but those cigarette butts could be months old.

Quiet descended once again, but didn't last long before Camo's voice sliced through. "So your friend, she good at what she does?"

Friend. She. Camo could only be referring to Lana. "What, you mean being a U.S. Marshal?"

"Yeah."

Why was he asking? And more importantly, how would Nate's answer impact Lana? Tell the truth or lie?

Camo was speaking before he reached a decision. "See, I'm thinking she's dirty."

Of all the....

If Nate could see enough to do it, he'd probably plant his

fist in Camo's nose. "Not even close. She's one of the best."

"Oh yeah? Then what's she doing hanging out with a guy like you?"

"You think I told her? By the time she found out, we were already friends."

A low chuckle emanated from somewhere to Nate's right. "I bet that was a fun conversation. 'Hey, by the way, I used to hang with an international assassin. Helped him out a time or two.' She freak out?"

The day flashed through his head. Lana's living room, the way her face had gone from friendly to guarded, the anger lacing her words. "She handled it better than I would've."

"Where'd you meet a U.S. Marshal, anyway?"

"On a beach. I didn't know it at the time, but she was protecting the man Matt had been hired to kill."

Who just happened to be her brother. More fun stories.

"So she finds out you helped the guy who iced one of her witnesses and still visits you in prison? Sounds like a dirty cop to me."

"Matt didn't kill the guy. I talked him into retiring."

A pause. Camo cleared his throat. "This I gotta hear."

"Matt and I were like brothers. When he'd take a job, I'd usually go along. Not on the hit, but to wherever the target lived. Anyway, he was on a job when I met her. I knew she was something special and I told him all about this chick I met, well, what I knew anyway. Then one day, we were out running around and we ran into her. When Matt goes to take down the mark, she was there. Guess she put up a fight, getting between him and his mark. Normally he would've taken her down, too, but he knew how much she meant to me."

"See, I still have a problem with the fact she didn't arrest you."

"She didn't know. Matt wore a mask and I sure as heck wasn't going to tell her the truth."

The memories assailed him as if they'd just happened.

Matt storming into the rental house.

The yelling.

Matt punching him when he wouldn't get out of the way.

But most of all, the heartache of realizing he and the woman he loved were on opposite sides of the law.

"Another hit man was hired. A guy named Young." It took a moment for him to realize he'd said the words aloud. "After she shot Young to save her witness, he went after her. He almost killed her."

"Sounds like she should learn to aim better."

"She saved my life." Guilt that he hadn't felt in a long time bubbled up inside him. "Young thought I was Stevens and tried to kill me, but she took the bullet."

The silence held Nate in a cold embrace.

He couldn't repress a shiver. Whether just from the cool dampness of the cavern or from the memories battling in his mind, he wasn't sure, but he was suddenly freezing.

"Let me get this straight." A hard edge lined Camo's words. "She thought you were Stevens and still protected you?"

"That's who she is. She always puts herself between the threat and everyone else. She would've arrested me, but getting shot kinda put a stop to that. I left before she recovered."

Stillness took over for several seconds before Camo broke it. "I hate dirty cops. Always have."

What, so suddenly Camo had these high moral standards? Nate refrained from pointing out the hypocrisy and remained mute.

"A dirty cop almost killed my brother."

Nate looked toward the sound of Camo's voice. "What happened?"

"Oh, my brother caught the cop pocketing some meth. The guy reached for his gun. My brother's a faster draw."

"Glad he's okay." Lame. Was that the best he could come up with?

"Listen, this doesn't leave this room, but as soon as we get back to the boat, you can call your girl. Let her know that now's a good time for a vacation. But no names or locations, got it?"

Really? Man, he wished he could see Camo's face so he'd know if Camo was serious. "You're going to let me warn her?"

"Soon as we get outta this hole."

Camo sounded serious, but he'd also said he wouldn't cross Tim. "You're not just messing with me, are you? What about Tim?"

"Look, this morning with Amanda, when she said... I've been around long enough to know that she usually gets what she wants. She tells Tim she wants your friend outta the way and Tim'll probably end up doing it. I don't want any part of that."

Praise God. He could warn Lana. Give her a chance to hide.

Although if he knew Lana, she'd set some kind of trap using herself as bait.

Couldn't let that happen. He'd have to be really convincing.

"Thanks. I owe you one."

Camo snorted. "You helped me out of a jam down there. We'll call it even."

The blackness surrounding them didn't seem as cold as it had a minute ago. Ridiculous, because Nate knew that the temperature hadn't changed. Amazing what a little shift in perspective could accomplish.

Too bad it didn't help the time pass any faster though.

If anything, the anticipation of making sure Lana would be well-protected made the wait seem longer. He didn't know if they'd been waiting for minutes or hours.

All he knew was that he was sick to death of sitting on hard metal.

Light flooded the space above them.

He squinted at the sudden brightness and flattened himself against the stairs. A glance at Camo found him in the same position.

A screech ripped through his eardrums and filled the cavern. Footsteps sounded on the metal platform above them. A lighter click-click-clicked to life.

Lifting his head slightly, Nate risked a glance. A blond man – who didn't look like the scrawny nerd Nate had expected – leaned against the railing, his attention focused on the water and rocks below.

Behind him, the door to the lab cracked open.

Camo jumped to his feet, vaulted onto the landing, and rushed the blond, who turned just in time to find a knife pressed against his throat. "You say a word and you won't live to regret it."

The cigarette slid from the man's fingers.

When the man had paled several shades, Camo eased the weapon back a few inches and spoke in a low, controlled tone. "A new toxin disappeared from your lab recently. I want the antitoxin."

"I-I don't h-have anything–"

Camo pushed the point of the knife into the man's neck with enough force to draw a speck of blood. "You sure you wanna waste my time?"

"No, really! I'm a chemist in a different department."

"Then you're of no use to me."

"I-I know who you need to talk to. Sam O'Conner."

Camo stepped back and gestured with the knife. "Lead the way. And don't try anything stupid."

As they approached the door, Nate spoke up for the first time. "If anyone asks, we're investors taking a look around, got it?"

The chemist nodded.

Once at the door, Camo grabbed the man's arm. "Check to see if all's clear. And don't think you can pull anything over on me."

He didn't relinquish his hold on the man, but instead shoved him toward the opening. The man leaned inside and scanned both directions before nodding. "We're good."

While the man's shoes squeaked against the vinyl flooring, the dive boots were silent. The short corridor they traveled intersected with another, where they headed to the right.

Ahead, two doors, one on either side of the hall. Nate glanced behind him. Same setup. At both ends of the hall, a red button, protected by a plastic box and surrounded by black and yellow hazard tape, caught his attention. A sign above the cover read "Emergency Fire Suppression".

They stopped outside a door simply labeled as Lab two.

The man glanced at the two of them and slowly pushed the door open.

A petite woman with short rust-colored curls didn't look up from the series of test tubes in front of her.

"George, you must come see this. It's positively fascinat–" The brogue-crusted words died in her mouth as she turned. "Bradley. What are you doing here?"

Camo kicked the door closed and twisted the lock.

With a hand between the blond man's shoulder blades, Camo propelled him toward her. "I thought you were taking us to Sam O'Conner."

The woman stood up straighter and narrowed her eyes. "*Doctor* O'Conner."

Spunky. Unlike her trembling counterpart beside her. The knife didn't even seem to faze her.

"You're Sam?" Doubt colored Camo's words.

Pink flushed her cheeks. "*Doctor* Samantha O'Conner. Now kindly get out of my lab."

Nate almost wanted to laugh. It reminded him of another fiery and fearless woman he knew. A woman who was close to the same size as the not-so-good doctor.

Of course the similarities stopped there.

Lana would never make something that could cause so

much sickness and death.

The waterproof bag Camo carried hit the floor with a soft thump as he made no move to obey her demand.

"Hard of hearing, are you? I said leave."

"Can't do it, doc. See, your little experiment there was stolen and some friends of mine were infected. I want the antitoxin. All of it."

"Do you now? I'd like a private island in the tropics, but I don't see that happening either."

Camo nodded at the knife in his hand. "I have no problem using this."

Crossing her arms over her chest, she laughed. "I grew up in Dublin. Caught between the IRA and anyone who would cross them. You think you can scare me?"

Camo twirled the knife. "I don't care if you're scared. You don't give me what I want and you'll pay the price."

The smile slid from her lips. "You'll never make it out of this facility alive."

"Let me worry about that. The antitoxin. Now."

"No."

Camo twirled the knife and stepped closer.

A smirk twisted her lips. "You kill me and your friends are dead."

"They've never been close friends."

"Of course not. That's why you broke into a top secret lab to steal the antitoxin."

Camo nodded at a door on the far wall. The keypad next to the door screamed restricted access. "Look, I know it's in there. Just grab it for me and we'll get out of your hair."

"Forget it."

Camo grabbed her arm, jerked her toward him, and shoved the flat edge of the blade under her chin. "Last chance. Is it worth dying for?"

"You won't kill me."

Was it his imagination or did she sound slightly less confident than she had a moment ago?

Nate studied her, caught a barely perceptible quiver as it traveled down her body. One more push ought to do it.

He grabbed a beaker off a counter near him and smashed it against the tile beneath his feet. Knelt to pick up a large piece of broken glass. Slowly examined the jagged edge leading to a malicious looking point.

Sliding his gaze up, he found the hostages watching him. The blond man looked scared enough to wet himself and a gray pallor tinged O'Conner's face.

Perfect. He had their attention.

"Maybe we won't kill you." His tone, low and impassive, contained an edge he hadn't used in years. "But believe me when I tell you that a few well-placed slices," he pointed the piece of glass at her, "will have you begging for death."

If her face lost any more color, it'd match the walls surrounding them. Her gaze darted from Nate to Camo before resting on the chunk of glass held lightly between his fingers.

After several shallow breaths, she let out a curse. "Fine."

Camo released her and shoved her backward.

Whirling, she stomped toward the door, arms rigid and hands fisted at her sides.

Camo handed Nate the knife and knelt by the bag at his feet. He opened the bag and pulled out a wrench, his dive hood, and goggles. "Go. I've got work to do."

Right. The explosion.

Whether he liked it or not, he was completely committed to seeing this through. Setting the piece of glass on the counter, Nate gestured to the man O'Conner had called Bradley. "Move."

Bradley scurried after O'Conner, sending frequent backward glances at Nate as though afraid to let him out of his sight.

At the door, O'Conner hit a series of buttons. The door opened with a click, florescent lights blinked on, and she stepped inside.

Nate caught the door before she could pull it closed

behind her.

A twitch moved her jaw and her eyes narrowed, but she didn't say a word as she marched into a white-walled room large enough to hold a cargo van. Shelves lined three of the walls, each shelf containing dozens of vials filled with a cloudy liquid.

The fourth wall, the one housing the door through which he'd just passed, held shelves full of brown tinted vials.

Most likely the antitoxin. It didn't take a genius to realize that they would likely produce more toxin than antitoxin. Terrorists were really only interested in the product that would kill, not the one that would save.

O'Conner stopped in the center of the room and whipped around to face him. "Good luck getting all of this out of here unnoticed."

She was right, of course. There were probably more than a hundred vials of antitoxin here. And at least five times as many vials of the toxin itself.

They'd just have to carry what they could and leave the rest.

The destruction of the lab might be a good thing. It would keep more of this junk from ending up in the wrong hands. Until O'Conner set up another lab and created more, anyway.

He gestured with the knife to the brown tinted vials. "That the antitoxin?"

A sneer curled her lips. "Why don't you drink one and find out?"

Using his free hand, he snatched a vial and tossed it to her. "You drink it."

Wide eyes and jerky movements indicated her surprise. She barely caught it before it hit her in the stomach. "You can't be serious."

"If it's the toxin, you have the antitoxin right behind you. If it's the antitoxin, it shouldn't do anything to you."

"I'm not drinking anything."

"You're drinking one of them if I have to have that guy,"

he nodded at Bradley, "sit on you and pour it down your throat."

"Fine! It's the antitoxin. Is that what you want to hear?" The brogue coloring her words thickened.

"Only if it's true."

"It is."

He couldn't just take her word for it. If they brought the wrong vial back to Tim and Tim's brother died... he didn't even want to think about what Tim might do in response.

"Prove it."

"How do you–"

A noise came from the lab behind him. Reacting on instinct, Nate sidestepped to the left, well out of sight from anyone in the main lab.

And chided himself for his paranoia.

It had to be Camo, right? No one would be able to come inside without Camo's notice. Aside from that, Camo had locked the door.

"Sam?" A man's voice, strong and crisp.

Definitely not Camo.

"Why was the door locked?" Footsteps echoed, drew closer.

For the first time since he and Camo had entered the lab, panic lit O'Conner's eyes. So. She wasn't afraid for herself, but this guy meant something to her. A definite advantage.

"Act natural or you both die."

The glare she shot him confirmed she'd heard the whispered threat.

Scurrying. Followed by the same voice. "Who the...?"

The words died abruptly. Probably spotted Camo.

A second later, the man stumbled into the room, Camo only a few steps behind him. After a quick assessment, Camo disappeared from sight.

Nate pointed with the knife. "Over there. By your friends."

"Wha–what's going on?" The man's gaze never left the

weapon as he shifted toward the middle of the room. He stopped with his back to O'Conner, strategically placing himself between her and the blade.

Brave. Especially considering the tremors attacking the man's hands.

"What's in the vial?"

"Vial?"

"In her hands. What is she holding?"

He didn't even glance back. "The br-brown vials contain the antitoxin for the cl-cl-clear vials."

Good enough.

The man was too scared to lie. Now to find out how many vials he needed to take.

"And if someone had been exposed to the clear vials, how much antitoxin would he need to survive?"

George shook his head. "It's not that simple. There are variables, like the level of exposure, what stage the toxin is in, the person's size and weight."

Okay, now to test his memory. "I think exposure was about three days ago and it was a pretty hefty dose. Can't tell you the guy's size or weight, but probably a little smaller than me."

George hesitated. "I'd really not want to make–"

"Unless you're planning to come and personally nurse this guy back to health, I suggest you break it down."

"Start with one whole vial. If you don't see marked improvement in four hours, give him another."

"And if we overdose him with the stuff?" That would be all he needed; to give Amanda instructions that unintentionally killed her brother.

"He'll experience severe abdominal cramps until he's purged his system, but he'll survive."

At least it was better than the alternative.

Movements cautious and deliberate, Nate backed into the lab. "Okay, I want all of you out here. Nice and slow."

George appeared first, followed by O'Conner, and finally

Bradley.

Lips curled in a snarl, O'Conner crossed her arms over her chest. "Now what? You slit our throats and make a break for it?"

"Now we wait for my associate." Nate waved them toward a small desk on the opposite side of the room from the door before risking a glance at Camo.

Who was nowhere in sight.

A large vial filled with a clear liquid evidenced that Camo had done something, but the man himself wasn't around.

Great. Now what?

No option but to wait. And hope no one else decided to enter the lab.

Seventeen

How would they transport the vials without breaking them? The lab was sure to have padded boxes or briefcases of some sort designed specifically for that purpose, but it would look suspicious for them to evacuate carrying such an item.

They'd probably just have to stuff their pockets and be careful how they moved. Which could prove tricky if they had to make a break for it.

Well, Camo was the mastermind of this mission. Let him figure it out.

The door opened a minute later and Camo slipped inside, dive mask, goggles, and wrench in hand. Camo looked at him. "You got it?"

"The brown vials."

Camo crossed to the storage room and returned a second later, a clear vial in his hands. The stopper had been removed.

The thought barely registered in Nate's mind before Camo approached O'Conner and tossed the full contents of the vial in her face.

Silence cloaked the room for several long seconds.

"You… you imbecile!" O'Conner reached up to wipe the liquid from her face. She pushed past George and scurried across the lab.

"Not another step!" Camo's voice lashed across the room.

"You going to have your buddy toss that knife at me? Go ahead. If I don't get that antitoxin, I'm dead anyway."

So George had been telling the truth.

The revelation didn't surprise Nate, but it was good to know his instincts were spot on. Now as long as they got the antitoxin stateside before Tim and Amanda's brother croaked, he was home free.

He refused to think about the consequences of it arriving too late.

Nate shifted slightly to keep an eye on O'Conner as she snagged a vial of the brown liquid and pulled a syringe from an unmarked cardboard box. Ripping out the stopper, she tossed it to the ground, filled the syringe, and jabbed it into her arm.

When she turned and met his eyes, he motioned for her to rejoin her friends.

She silently complied.

Apparently satisfied, Camo went back to the storage room and reappeared a minute later with odd bulges in his pockets. Several brown vials filled his hands and he passed the vials to Nate.

Nate stuffed them in his own pockets. At least his pants were a loose cut and had lots of pockets.

Probably still looked ridiculous.

Camo approached a yellow metal box against the far wall. Signs screamed warnings of flammable contents.

Another sign warned of silane. What the heck was silane?

Camo opened the cabinet and used the wrench to remove something from the top of the tank, but Nate couldn't see exactly what.

"What're you doing?" O'Conner's voice rose an octave. "Do you know what's in that tank? It's silane. It's highly toxic!"

"I know." Returning to the group, Camo crossed his arms over his chest and assessed the hostages. "Okay, if you wanna survive the day, here's how this plays out. You're gonna trigger emergency lockdown and evacuation procedures. We'll all file out of here nice and neat. You three keep your heads down and your mouths shut and I'll let you live. You try to tip anyone off or give us up and you'll end up with your throat slashed. Got it?"

Two tight nods responded; O'Conner simply glared at them.

Camo locked his eyes firmly on her. "Got. It?"

"You can't honestly believe you can walk away from here."

"You should be more concerned about getting out of this place before it blows."

"An explosion?" Her head jerked toward the vial sitting on the counter. "You can't blow up this lab. You'll destroy all our samples!"

"Good."

"It's years' worth of work! No. No. Just leave. We won't–"

Camo stepped forward, his fist already in motion. It connected with O'Conner's left temple with a solid thunk and she crumpled without a word.

"Sam!" George knelt by her side.

Camo turned his attention to Bradley. "Emergency lockdown and evacuation. Now. Or we leave you here to die."

Bradley scurried toward an alarm panel next to the room's main door and punched a couple of buttons.

Camo pulled on the dive hood and goggles.

Emergency lights kicked on.

Alarms blared, almost masking a mechanized voice directing everyone to evacuate the building via the nearest emergency exit.

Camo twisted the valve on the tank.

If the alarms weren't so loud, Nate would probably hear the hissing of the gas as it filled the room.

Camo snatched up the beaker and set it on the hot plate. Cranked the plate up to high.

Time to go.

Nate nodded at George. "Pick her up and let's get out of here."

George grunted as he struggled to lift his lightweight

partner.

They didn't have time for this. Nate didn't know how long it would take for this place to blow, but he wasn't sticking around to find out.

"You." He pointed the knife at Bradley. "Help him."

Each taking one of her arms, the two scientists hauled her to her feet.

Camo ripped off the mask and goggles, discarded them on the floor, then plucked the knife from Nate's hand. "Lead the way. I'll bring up the rear."

The empty hallway evidenced the fact that everyone else had already exited the facility. He hoped.

Retracing their earlier steps, Nate found the cavern door ajar, evidence that at least someone had already come this way.

The damp cave air seeped through his clothes.

Emergency lights hung from a cable suspended above the walkway, providing almost adequate lighting for their escape route.

Their feet pounded on the catwalk as they rushed toward the exit, but they appeared to be the only ones currently evacuating. Echoes from the walls around them made it sound like a small army rather than only a few people.

How much time did they have left? What would happen if the lab blew before they got out?

He glanced behind him. Red faces and shallow breathing told him that George and Bradley were struggling with O'Conner's dead weight, but they hadn't fallen behind.

No one was visible behind Camo.

Hopefully that meant that everyone else had already evacuated. If not, they couldn't say they weren't appropriately warned. His ears still rang from the alarms.

Ahead, a shaft of daylight beckoned.

Seeing it brought a burst of energy. He picked up speed.

Judging by the noises behind him, he wasn't the only one.

A boom echoed through the cavern; the walkway vibrated

like a skyscraper in an earthquake.

"Move, move!"

Camo didn't have to tell him twice. Jogging the last few feet, Nate put his foot on the bottom rung and scaled the eight foot ladder to the surface above. Fresh air assaulted his senses.

Never thought he'd be glad to see an overcast sky, but the sight was more welcome than almost any other.

Even if the light did hurt his eyes.

Rocky ground surrounded him. About twenty yards to the east, the razor-wire topped chain-link fence confirmed they were outside the prison grounds. A small cluster of people hovered nearby, murmuring and glancing his direction. Probably the rest of the people who had escaped what would soon be an underground inferno.

He knelt next to the opening and reached down. "Hand her up."

O'Conner's head hung limply as her body swayed closer. Snagging her twiggy biceps, Nate planted his feet beneath him and pulled.

Dang. She was heavy for such a small thing.

A grunt slid from his lips. He locked his knees and slowly straightened, feeling the strain course up his arms, across his shoulder blades, and throughout his back.

Okay. Torso clear. Now for the rest of her.

He used his body weight and gave a final tug.

She popped out of the hole and fell toward him, knocked him to the ground. Man, did he hope she hadn't busted the vials of antitoxin in his pockets.

A soft moan revealed that she was coming around.

Figured. It would've been nice if she'd been alert enough to get herself out of the cave.

Pushing her off him, he rose to his feet as George exited. Bradley appeared next, followed by Camo. While the knife was nowhere in sight, Nate had little doubt it was close by, probably in a sheath at Camo's waist.

"Who're you?"

The question drew Nate's attention to the group of evacuees. The speaker, a fifty-ish man with a round belly and thinning hair, stared at him with eyes that resembled the rocks beneath their feet.

"Investors. We were seeing the fruits of our investment when the alarms went off."

"Hmm." The word dripped with skepticism, but the man's attention shifted to O'Conner. "What happened to her?"

Nate tried to work up a concerned tone. "I think maybe she inhaled some fumes. All I know is one minute she's telling me about her current project and the next she's hitting her head on the counter on her way down."

"Does anyone have first aid training?" Kneeling next to her, George gently brushed her hair back from the knot forming on her head.

"I do." A gangly woman stepped forward and joined George at O'Conner's side.

As the rest of the group gathered around, Nate slowly backed away. A barely perceptible jerk of Camo's head sent a clear message. No time like the present to put some distance between them and the chaos they'd created.

They kept a brisk pace, cutting a wide swath around the front of the prison and meeting up with the road.

Rock formations lined them on either side. Not a single vehicle was in sight.

Camo broke the silence. "I figure we've got five minutes, ten tops, before they send guards after us."

Ahead, the road curved sharply to the left. Rocks obscured any view of where it led after that.

"Where are we going?"

Camo shot a look his direction. "There's a fishing village a few miles up the road. Soon as we're around this corner, we break from the road and go the rest of the way back country."

Ugh. She felt like she'd been hit by a Zamboni.

Memories of the big Brit who'd invaded her home assaulted her. Maybe Zamboni wasn't too far off.

She eased her eyes open.

Shades covered the window, filtering the morning sunlight. Most of the lights in the room were turned off, but what little remained still hurt her head.

At least the pain had decreased to a manageable level.

A dull ache settled between her temples, but it was better than the migraine level pain she remembered from last night.

Rustling came from the corner. A gasp slipped from her lips as a shadow moved.

Someone was there! A man, judging from the size, slouched in a chair.

She blinked a few times, but the man didn't move again. As she studied the figure, she was able to make out more details. Including dark, curly hair.

Micah? What would he be doing sacked out in the chair in her hospital room?

"Oh good. You're awake."

She turned her head to find a tall nurse entering the room.

The nurse clicked on the light above Lana's bed, grabbed a chart, and made a few notations. "How're you feeling?"

Lana blinked like a mole seeing sunlight for the first time. "Better."

While the word rasped through a throat that felt drier than sunburned skin, it didn't hurt nearly as much as the words she'd forced out last night.

"Any pain?"

Was she kidding? "All over."

"Do you need more pain killers?"

"I'll be okay."

Evidently she hadn't made nearly the progress she'd

initially thought. Her throat still punished her with every word. And if that wasn't bad enough, it sounded like her voice might go out.

"If you change your mind, let me know." The nurse asked a few questions, referenced the equipment next to the bed, and jotted a few more things on the chart in her hands. "Well, you have a concussion, multiple contusions and abrasions, and two lacerations that required stitches."

The way those two thugs had gone at her, it could've been much worse. Actually, she was surprised broken bones hadn't been a part of the diagnosis.

The nurse left, promising to return soon with breakfast.

Probably soggy oatmeal, stale toast, and rubber eggs. Now there was something she could look forward to.

"Hey." Micah's voice, husky with sleep, drew her attention back to the other side of the bed. With stiff movements, he approached. "How're you doing?"

"Tell me you didn't stay here all night."

Yawning, he ruffled his curls. "Hey, you were attacked. What if those guys came back for more?"

"I'm in a hospital. Which has security."

He snorted. "Minimal."

"Barker said someone would be outside my room."

"The guy's shift ended. I volunteered."

Great. So now they were treating her like some damsel in distress.

No. It was worse than that.

They were treating her like a witness.

Just a few hours – most of which had been spent in sleep – and she already knew she hated it. The hardest part was that she'd have done the same thing had their positions been reversed.

"And you didn't answer my question. You told the nurse you still have pain?"

"Big surprise." She had picked a fight with a guy almost twice her size.

"What hurts?"

"Throat's the worst. Hurts to talk."

"Anything I can do?"

"Go home and get some sleep."

He shook his head. "Not gonna happen. Until we figure this thing out and those guys are in prison, you can consider me your shadow."

"Micah." Her voice failed on the tail end of his name. Clearing her throat brought tears to her eyes, which she quickly blinked away. "You can't camp out on my doorstep."

"True. Because you can't go home."

Can't go home? Of course she could.

Dang. He was right. Her house was an active crime scene.

But even if it wasn't, she didn't know that she wanted to go back. It no longer felt like a safe haven.

Where else could she go?

Ordinarily, her parents or Reilly's house would be a good alternative, but she wasn't going near her family until she figured out why those men had been in her house last night. Even though her parents were on vacation, the last thing she wanted was to draw those men to where her parents lived.

Alex or the Webbers would also welcome her, but again, she refused to put anyone else in harm's way.

Looked like she'd be living out of a motel for a while.

Or maybe one of the local safe houses wasn't in use. That would be a good alternative. They'd even have increased security measures in place.

"Look, while you may not be under official protection, I'm keeping a close eye on you until this thing blows over. Barker's orders." Micah dragged a chair close to her bed and collapsed onto it.

"Not necess–"

"Don't argue. Your throat hurts, remember?" A quick grin stole across his face.

Part of her wanted to laugh. Part of her wanted to cry. And part of her was annoyed that they were making such a big deal about this.

"I don't need a bodyguard. If there hadn't been two of them, I would've taken that guy down."

Micah leaned forward, intensity darkening his eyes. "But there were two of them. And after the fight you put up, there might be four of them next time."

"If they return." Her throat burned too badly to continue arguing. Besides, he was right. If they came back, she might find herself up against twice as many assailants.

"Hey. Look who's awake. How's the patient?"

"Obstinate as ever," Micah piped up before she could answer.

Swiveling her head, she saw Barker walking toward her. "Forensics find anything?"

"Still working on it. But there's a promising blood smear on the front door."

"Got in a few good blows. Might've drawn some blood." The words cost her, but if that blood could help identify one of the attackers, it would be worth the pain.

"They're running the DNA. They've also got a lot of hair and fibers, most of which I imagine will be yours."

Probably. "Working theory?"

"Isn't one. They're thinking it might be a robbery gone bad, but most likely it'll connect to one of your recent cases." Barker leaned against the wall across from her bed. "Rawlings filled me in on the Richie Ochoa angle. We're looking into that one as well."

As convenient as that would be, she didn't think this would connect to Ochoa. It was more of a gut feeling than anything else, but she'd learned long ago to trust her gut.

Wind buffeted them as the boat bounced over the choppy

waves.

The shoreline behind them had long since faded from faint to nonexistent as Camo steered the stolen speedboat further out to sea.

The rented yacht came into view. As they approached, Nate could make out a figure standing on deck. The blonde curls blowing in the wind identified her long before he could make out her features.

Camo eased back on the throttle and steered toward the yacht's stern. He cut the engine.

"Did you get it?" Amanda's question greeted them as soon as the motor silenced.

"Sure did." Camo leaned from the speedboat, grabbed the railing on the yacht, and hauled himself aboard. Nate followed, the cut at his elbow protesting his weight.

"And you're sure it's the right one." Camo stared down at her. "You think I'd leave anything to chance with Jack's life on the line?"

"Good." She pulled out her phone and brought up a number. "Zoe? I'm coming home. Book me the first flight out."

A pause.

"Yeah. Get the guys on something tomorrow or the next day."

She ended the call and slid the phone back into her pocket. No "thanks", "see you soon", or any kind of pleasantry.

Instead, she turned her attention to Camo. "Let's get to shore. I hope to be out of this miserable place by the end of the day."

Lana swung her legs over the edge of the bed. Blackness

swept her vision and she waited for it to pass before sliding from the mattress.

Pain throbbed dully in her injured leg, but not badly enough to stop her from taking a few small steps. The nurse had removed the IV about five minutes ago and encouraged her to get up and move around. She was only too happy to get out of the bed.

Aside from that, the sooner she proved she was doing okay, the sooner the nurse would return with discharge papers.

Not that she could go home.

The knowledge dimmed her anticipation a little. Aside from the fact that her house was an active crime scene, she had a suspicion that Micah – if not Barker himself – was about to smother her with protection. Whether she wanted it or not.

"Are you supposed to be out of bed?"

Her heart stuttered and she jolted so badly that her weak legs threatened to dump her on the floor. Stupid, especially since she'd heard that voice all her life. It was Reilly, the best brother she could ask for, even if he was a tad overprotective at times.

Before she could even turn, a hand was under her elbow, guiding her back to the bed.

"Ri, I'm fine. You just startled me."

Reilly didn't stop until she was seated on the edge of the bed. "You didn't answer my question. Does the doctor know you're walking around?"

"Yes. The nurse told me to."

A frown curled Reilly's mouth as he studied her. Light blue eyes traveled her face, examined her neck, and landed on the bandage on her arm. Good thing he hadn't noticed the one on her leg.

A sigh slid from her lips. "It's not as bad as it looks."

"Really. Because from where I stand, it looks pretty darn bad."

"I'll live." She hesitated. "You didn't tell Mom and Dad,

did you?"

The firm set to his clean-shaven jaw told her that he hadn't and he wasn't pleased about it. "I should. You know how upset they're going to be when they find out you kept this from them?"

"I'll tell them later. I don't want them to cut their trip short." It wasn't often that their parents got away on a real vacation and she didn't want to do anything to ruin that for them.

"You're going to make me old, you know that?" He pulled up a chair and collapsed into it. "How're you holding up?"

"I've been better." Reilly was one of the few people in the world to whom she could admit the truth locked inside. "I'm scared. I don't even want to go home."

"I'd be worried if you weren't scared. And I'm glad you don't want to go home." He shook his head slowly. "A part of me was afraid you'd want to just to convince everyone that you're okay."

Yeah, that sounded like something she'd do. Normally.

But not this time.

Maybe she was getting old. Some might say she was growing wiser. Or maybe she'd just had too many brushes with death in the last few years to foolishly rush toward another one.

Reilly reached for the bag at his feet. "I brought the things you asked for. I had Des pick them out."

Taking the bag, Lana pulled out a pair of lightweight gray and green yoga pants, a green short sleeve v-neck, and a package of socks. Desiree, Reilly's wife, had picked them out all right; everything matched. Including the undergarments she opted to leave at the bottom of the bag. "Thanks. How much?"

"Don't worry about it."

"Sorry to take you from work." The prosecutor's office was so busy, she couldn't believe he'd managed to get away.

He arched an eyebrow. "How hard did you hit your head, anyway? It's Saturday."

Of course it was. Last night had been the worst Friday night on record. "Well, I still appreciate it."

Elbows on his knees, he leaned toward her. "Once you're released, we can pick up whatever else you need. Then I'll get you settled in the guest room and whip up some of my famous chicken fettuccini alfredo."

"I can't stay with you."

"You can and you will. We already covered the not going home bit, remember?"

Ooh, she'd gotten the big brother tone. And look.

Lucky for her, years of dealing with it had made her immune. "Until I know why this happened, I have to work under the assumption it could happen again. I won't jeopardize your safety."

"We have an alarm system. Speaking of which, how'd those guys get past your system?"

Not a question she really wanted to answer. "I'm going to a safe house."

"You're dodging my question."

It didn't sound like he was planning to let this go. Man, she was going to hear about it for this one. "It was my own stupid fault. I knew I was headed out again soon, so I didn't set the alarm."

"That doesn't sound like you."

"Actually..." She sighed. "It's not that unusual. I guess I've grown complacent lately."

The lecture she was sure lingered beneath the surface didn't manifest. Instead, he reached out and placed one of his long-fingered hands over her own. "Forget the safe house. Stay with us."

"I couldn't handle it if something happened to you guys because I was there. Besides, it's just for a few days. Once they're done processing my house, I'll be going back."

"They're not putting you in protective custody?"

"We don't know for sure that I'm in any danger."

"Those guys broke into your house and roughed you up. What, do they have to kill you before the threat's taken seriously?"

"That's just it. They could've killed me, but they didn't. They didn't threaten me, try to get information, or leave any kind of warning. It could've been as simple as a home invasion gone bad."

"You don't believe that any more than I do."

"No, I don't. But again, they didn't give any of the typical indicators that this was anything personal."

"Did they take anything?"

"I won't know until I've had a chance to look around, but the TV and computer are still there, so probably not."

"Then it's likely personal, right?"

"Possibly. Which is why a safe house is my best option."

"A safe house." Distaste lined his words. "So you'll be locked inside at all times, right?"

"Except when I'm at work, yeah."

His scowl deepened. "They're making you go to work?"

"Making me? I had to fight to be able to return."

She refused to allow those two jerks who'd attacked her to completely disrupt her life. Barker had initially been adamant about her taking a few days off, but he'd finally caved.

"I'll be back to work Monday." Probably best to refrain from mentioning that she'd be driving her own car in, too.

"I don't like this. Any of it."

"I'm not surprised." She ripped the tags off the clothing. "I'll take you up on the ride home to grab my things, if that's okay."

"No problem."

Movements slow, she pushed herself to her feet. The dizziness passed even more quickly this time. Aside from the pain in her throat and the fear scratching at the back of her mind, she was beginning to feel like herself again.

Gathering the bag, she headed into the bathroom to

change.

"They've at least assigned someone to watch your back, right?" Reilly's question greeted her as she stepped back into the room.

"Not officially. Although I think I have an unofficial bodyguard."

"The amount of trouble you get into? You should probably have a whole fleet."

Eighteen

"Gotta hand it to you. Not many men tell Amanda no."

Nate's finger stopped dancing through the condensation on his still-full glass of bourbon and looked up at Camo. What was this about? And, more importantly, how did Camo expect him to respond?

Reaching for the bottle, Camo poured himself what had to be his fourth glass. "You want more?"

Right. He hadn't wanted the glass that sat in front of him right now, but Camo had poured it anyway.

Not that pointing out such a thing would do him any good. "Nah, I'm full up."

The yacht was moored at a marina. Amanda had left hours ago to catch her flight, leaving the two of them to kill time until they could safely fly tomorrow afternoon.

Camo took a swig. "The kid's used to having guys fall at her feet. Pulled out all the stops with you, probably 'cause you didn't."

"I told you. There's this girl–"

"Didn't stop you from kissing her."

The air spurted from Nate's lungs. How did... there was no way Camo could know about that! "What're you talking about?"

"Her cabin. Last night." A grin – that more closely resembled a sneer – smothered his face. "No point denyin' it. I saw you."

Dang it!

What would Tim do when Camo told him? Or had Camo already told him? "Then you also saw me cut it off. And walk away."

Silence. Camo slowly lifted his glass and took a long drink.

"Hey, she initiated it. I was helping her to her room so she wouldn't fall overboard and she kissed me." Pushing the glass aside, he rested his elbows on the table and leaned forward. "Tim doesn't need to know about this because *nothing happened.*"

"I'm not tellin' Tim. 'Sides, I get it." Unfocused eyes stared straight ahead. "Believe me, I get it."

The last words, muttered softly, probably hadn't been meant for anyone to hear, but Nate heard them. Camo and Amanda? Really?

He bet Tim didn't know about that one.

Probably be best if he pretended he didn't either. "It was late, it'd been a long time since I'd had a drink so I was a little out of it. Once I realized what was going on, I got out of there. How'd you know?"

"Little tip 'bout these boats: walls are toothpick thin. I heard everything." Camo drained his glass and shoved it aside. "Tim told me to keep an eye on the two of you, so when it got quiet, I went to check it out. You know what I saw."

Yeah. Camo saw him almost throw away any possibility with Lana for someone he could never love that deeply.

The memory of how close he'd come to giving in still cut him. Alcohol or no alcohol, how could he have ever entertained the idea in the first place?

He felt completely unfaithful. Unworthy.

Lana deserved better.

"Takes a lotta strength to walk away."

"It was the right thing to do."

"Well, I respect that." Camo fished a phone from the pocket of his shorts. "Five minutes. No more. Tell her nothing about us or I shoot you myself."

Nate took the cell phone from Camo's outstretched hand. Simply amazing. "Thanks, man. You've got no idea how much I appreciate this."

"Just remember. Be careful what you say."

Now to see if he could remember her number. It'd been a long time since he'd actually dialed it, but he thought he knew what it was. He punched in the number.

It rang once. Twice. What time was it back in Jacksonville, anyway?

"H-hello?"

The voice was scratchy. Between that and the hesitation, it sounded nothing like Lana.

But he was pretty sure it was her. "Lana?"

"Paul?"

"Yeah, it's Nate." Maybe that little correction would raise her suspicions. In spite of the fact that Nate was his real name, she always referred to him as Paul. "Are you okay?"

"I will be."

"What's going on?"

A breath eased across the line. "A couple guys broke into my house last night."

Even though he knew all about it, hearing her say the words wrenched his gut. "Are you all right? Did they hurt you?"

What a fraud. He already knew the answer to that question.

"It's nothing that won't heal. And I got in a few good hits of my own."

As well trained as Lana was, he had no doubt she'd gotten in a few *very* good hits. He hoped Jimmy was in serious pain. "Are you sure you're okay?"

"I'll be good as new by the time you get back. How's the assignment going, anyway?"

"I'm good." Didn't really answer her question, but he couldn't. Not with Camo sitting so close. He had to get the focus back on her. "Uh, hey listen. Um, that, uh, wasn't a random break in."

Silence blanketed the line for several seconds.

"What do you mean?" Her voice was calm and controlled. Too controlled.

She'd slipped into work mode, where she hid her emotions so well no one could read her.

Least of all him.

Normally, he hated it. Today, he was glad for it. She'd be more likely to process this as a deputy than as a victim.

"I mean that they showed up as a warning. To me. I'm sorry."

"A warning?" The pitch of her words rose slightly and her voice tightened. "How the heck do they even know about – you know what, never mind. Will they be back?"

"I don't know. But I want you to get out of there. Use some of that vacation time you've got built up or something."

"You expect me to run?"

"Just until I know it's safe to come back."

"No."

No? That she'd refuse hadn't even occurred to him.

But it should have. She was the most stubborn person he knew. "Please. You don't know these guys–"

Camo shot him a warning look.

"If anything happened... I can't lose you."

"You won't." Her voice sounded stronger. And angrier, but he'd take that over the fear and weakness he'd heard earlier. "Now that I know what's going on, I'll be ready for them if they come back. They won't get the drop on me a second time."

Camo pointed at his watch.

Time was up. And he hadn't done a good enough job of convincing Lana to enlist help.

"Hey, I gotta go. Roaming charges are murder." In spite of Nate's light tone, Camo's eyes narrowed in a glare. "Just get out of town or go into witness protection or something, okay?"

"Don't worry about me. I'll be fine. You be careful and come home in one piece, got it?"

The concern in her voice soothed his frazzled nerves. It didn't sound like she was angry with him. He should've known better than to think she would be. "Yeah. See you soon."

Terminating the call, Nate handed the phone back to Camo.

"So, she heading for a tropical island or something?"

Didn't he wish.

Nate shook his head. "I doubt it. Knowing her, she'll try to set some kind of trap for them if they come back."

Dang. He probably shouldn't have said that.

Camo would likely tell Tim, who would up the ante the next time around.

"Then her blood's on her own head." Camo pushed away from the table, grabbed the empty bourbon bottle and tossed it in the trash on his way out of the room.

He should've called someone other than Lana.

Her supervisor. Or Reyes. Someone who would take the threat seriously enough to act on it.

But he'd needed to hear her voice, needed to know she was really alive.

Numbness fogged Nate's mind. Lana had sounded funny. And he'd definitely heard pain in her voice. The very fact that she hadn't been able to mask it proved how much pain she was really in.

If given half a chance, he'd make sure Jimmy and Tim paid for picking on a woman half their size. And God help him, he didn't even care if he killed them.

Lana tapped the end call button. The phone trembled in

her hand.

It was confirmed. She *had* been targeted. And it had something to do with Paul and whatever he was doing with this militia group.

Which had absolutely nothing to do with her.

Her fingers tightened on the hard plastic phone.

She'd told him not to get mixed up in this! But did he listen? Oh, no. Big macho guy thought he could handle whatever was thrown at him.

Only *he* hadn't been the one flattened by someone twice his size.

It'd happened to her!

How the heck had she gotten involved in this mess? Those guys shouldn't even know her name, much less where to find her. How had they learned of her connection to him?

Paul must have let it slip.

The thought no more than crossed her mind before she rejected it. With his past, there was no way he'd have been careless enough to mention her name. But what other option was there?

Not a question she could dwell on at this point in time. Regardless of how they'd found her, this whole thing was clearly Paul's fault.

She wanted to deck him. How could he do this to her?

Anger wouldn't do her any good right now.

She measured out a breath.

Fact: no matter what those guys should or should not know, they knew what she looked like and where to find her.

So what did she do now?

If she told Barker, like Paul wanted her to, he'd probably lock her up in some remote safe house on the other side of the country until all of this wrapped up. Micah or Reilly would push for the same.

Looked like she was on her own.

A knock sounded on her closed bedroom door. "Lana? Everything okay?"

Taking a second to compose her features, she opened the door. "Sorry. I had to take that call."

Reilly's scrutiny was worse than being under interrogation. Intense eyes analyzed her face. "Work?"

"I can't talk about it. Would you mind grabbing my suitcase for me?" Not that it was heavy, but the doctor had warned her against doing much with her injured arm.

He didn't move.

"Try not to worry, okay? Once I get packed, we'll meet up with Micah and I'll be hiding out in some safe house. Probably being guarded like a dignitary."

"You'd tell me if it was something I needed to know, right?"

No matter how much she wanted to reassure him, she wouldn't lie. "If it was something you could help with, yes."

A frown deepened the creases around his eyes. He opened his mouth, but the doorbell rang before any words could come out.

They were back!

They must've been watching the place and when they saw her and Reilly come in, they called for backup and were here to finish the job.

And rang the doorbell to announce their arrival?

Maybe it was to create a false sense of security. After all, who would expect them to ring the doorbell?

She'd open the door and bam! Bullet to the heart.

Reilly's hand landed on her shoulder. "Relax. It's probably one of your neighbors checking on you."

She slowly released the breath that had caught in her chest. The tension in her muscles refused to dissipate so easily. "I'm sure you're right."

To be honest, she was sure of no such thing.

Crossing to the bed, she retrieved the gun she kept in a hidden panel on her headboard. The doorbell rang again, followed by some loud pounding.

She slipped down the hallway, keeping her back against

the wall.

The pounding grew louder.

Reilly stepped in front of her. "I got this."

Not a chance. Not only was Reilly unarmed, he lacked the necessary training to wield a gun effectively.

"No." She lifted her gun for emphasis. "I do."

As she reached the living room, she heard someone calling her name through the door.

A voice she recognized. Micah.

She eased to the door and peered through the peep hole. Micah's face, distorted by the curved glass, looked uneasily at the door.

After twisting the deadbolt, unlatching the chain, and popping the lock, she opened the door.

Relief washed his face.

Maybe she should tell Micah about the phone call after all.

Without waiting for an invitation, he stepped inside and pushed the door closed behind him. "You shouldn't be here alone. Why didn't you call me?"

"Reilly's here."

"Reilly?"

"My brother."

"Is he carrying?"

Her silence answered the question.

"Then he doesn't count." Micah looked over her shoulder. "No offense."

Glancing behind her, she found Reilly leaning against the wall. "Hey, I'm the one who told her she should have her own personal security team."

Forget telling either one of them about that phone call.

If she did, they'd have her under so much protection that it'd be years before she saw the light of day. "Would you guys knock it off?"

She whirled and headed down the hallway.

If Reilly hadn't grabbed her suitcase, she'd do it herself. Right now she didn't feel like asking either of them for anything.

The suitcase lay open on her bed.

Going to the closet, she grabbed several shirts, a few pairs of dress pants, and a couple of jackets. The weight of the garments caused her arm to throb, which only fueled her irritation.

It was bad enough that her private space had been invaded, but now those two were treating her like some sort of child. For crying out loud, she had more martial arts training than the two of them combined!

She stuffed the clothes into the suitcase and returned for her dress shoes. After slamming the shoes on top of the clothes, she headed for the dresser.

Footsteps, muffled by the carpet, approached. She didn't have to look to know it would be Reilly.

"You know, twenty years ago I would've told you to take a chill pill."

Wow. There was a phrase she hadn't heard in ages.

Funny how she hadn't missed hearing it either.

"We're worried about you, that's all."

She whirled to find Reilly standing alone.

Of course. Micah was probably booby-trapping the doors.

"You're being overprotective and overbearing. I know how to lay low just fine on my own."

He leaned against the doorframe. "You also know how to get into trouble."

"I've been advising witnesses for years! I know what I'm doing."

"You're not cautious enough when it comes to your own safety."

"I take every precaution!"

"And sometimes it's not enough." Reilly raked his fingers through his neatly trimmed hair. "Seriously, Lana. If our positions were reversed, what would you do?"

"I've been in your position, remember?"

Like either of them could forget the weeks he'd been

under the Marshals' protection after witnessing a murder. No matter how many years had passed, it was one memory time would never erase.

And if it happened again, she'd respond exactly as she had the last time.

She'd force Reilly into protective custody, lock him in a windowless room if she had to. She'd be ten times worse than he was right now.

"Then you know how I feel." Reilly's gentle words broke into her thoughts. "Except you were in a position to actually help me. There's not a thing I can do for you except hover, so here I am."

Why did he have to be so logical? The tension drained from her body.

A sigh broke free. "You've made your point. But could you back off a little? It's bad enough that I have Micah and Barker freaking out about this. I don't need it from you, too."

Tears bubbled unexpectedly.

She clenched her jaw and dug her nails into her palm to hold them off.

Reilly pushed off the doorframe, took one look at her face, and wrapped his arms around her. "I'm sorry."

The whispered words shattered any semblance of control. Harsh sobs burned her throat, making her cry harder.

She wasn't even sure why she was crying.

Fear, pain, frustration, anger; it could even be some strange combination of the emotions.

The reason didn't matter; the tears kept coming.

Several minutes passed before she pulled back. Wiping the moisture from her cheeks, she tried to offer a smile. "Sorry about the salt water bath."

"Don't worry about it. It's a side effect of the job."

A headache pulsed behind her eyes. "Job?"

"Bet you didn't know that the big brother gig comes with a job description." He stepped toward the suitcase and tucked in a few sleeves hanging over the edges. "Now we better finish getting you packed before Micah comes in and cracks the whip."

He was right. And so was Micah.

It wasn't safe here.

But as she grabbed some things from her dresser and added them to the suitcase, she resolved one thing. She wouldn't sit idly by and wait for the threat to pass.

The only way to get her life back was to flip the tables. The hunted was going after the hunter.

Nate slipped from his cabin and headed down the hallway. In spite of the long day, sleep had been elusive.

All he could think about was Lana.

The danger she was in.

He couldn't just sit here and hope for the best.

But could he really sneak off the boat, find a pay phone, and make a call without Camo knowing? Assuming he could find one, would pay phones even make international calls?

Wait. He could use a computer to call Reyes.

There'd been an internet café next to the pub where he and Camo had grabbed dinner. Maybe they hadn't closed yet.

He paused by the door. Listened.

Tim had warned him that Camo was a light sleeper, but so far there was no sign that his movements had disturbed Camo. With the amount of alcohol the man had ingested, he should sleep solidly until morning.

He hoped. Either way, this was a risk he had to take.

The door opened silently and Nate stepped into the damp night air.

He walked as lightly as he could, sending frequent glances over his shoulder but never seeing any sign of light or movement from the yacht. When he was a fair distance down the boardwalk, he broke into a jog.

Had to hurry. In case Camo woke up.

It only took a few minutes to reach the pub and café, both of which were still open.

He entered the café, which was surprisingly busy for eleven at night, and headed toward the front counter.

Thank God he had a little money left over from what Camo had given him to buy dinner earlier. He only hoped it was enough.

Pulling the money from his pocket, he plopped it on the counter. "Hi. I need to use a computer for a few minutes."

The kid stared at him blankly.

Aw, man. The kid didn't speak English. Probably only Italian or Spanish or whatever people in this part of the world spoke.

None of which Nate knew.

"Uh, do you speak English?"

The kid rattled something off but Nate couldn't understand any of it.

He didn't have time for this! Camo could wake up any second and things would get ugly if he found out Nate wasn't there.

The kid shook his head, dragged the money across the counter, clicked a few things on his own computer, then pointed to a computer in the corner.

Okay. Well, hopefully this would work.

He headed for the indicated machine. It took him a minute to log in, bring up the website and download the app he needed, but then he was in business.

Turning on the cheap combination webcam/microphone, he dialed the number Reyes had given him. Hopefully Reyes had been telling the truth when he'd said it was his cell number, but if this directed him to another agent, he could still stress the importance of getting the message to Reyes immediately.

It was the best he could do.

It rang once.

What time was it back in Florida, anyway? And would Reyes even answer his cell on a Saturday?

The other end rang a second time, then a third.

What would he do if Reyes didn't answer? He didn't have the phone number for Reilly or anyone in Lana's family. Maybe he could find the number for the U.S. Marshals' office and call her superior that way–

"Manuel Reyes."

Yes! Thank you, God.

"This is Nate Miller." He didn't wait for the Special Agent in Charge to respond before plowing ahead. "A credible threat has been made against Deputy Milana Tanner's life. You need to put her in protective custody."

"A threat. From whom?"

The ultra-calm air to Reyes' voice spiked Nate's anger. "Who do you think? Look, if you don't protect her, the guy who attacked her yesterday will finish what he started."

"She was attacked? Why?"

"Because of me."

"She was attacked because of your current, uh, situation?"

Finally, a hint of alarm in the man's tone. "Yes. Call her supervisor. Tell him what I told you. He'll take care of the rest."

From what Lana had told him about her supervisor, the man would make sure she was safe. Nate hoped Lana would be hidden somewhere remote. Maybe the middle of the Alaskan wilderness with several dozen agents protecting her.

"I'll pass the message along."

"Right away?"

"As soon as we hang up the phone." A tinge of urgency invaded Reyes' tone. "We won't let anything happen to her."

"I'm gonna hold you to that."

"Any progress on the other matter we discussed?"

Other matter? Reyes must mean White Fire's plans. "I'm still trying to infiltrate the inner circle."

"I see."

"I've gotta go before I'm missed, but I'll keep you posted." Nate terminated the call and closed out the program.

Now to get back to the boat before Camo noticed he wasn't on it.

The boat was still dark when he approached.

He boarded, stopping briefly in the galley for a bottle of water. Just in case Camo woke up and asked what he was doing.

Heading down the hallway, he watched for light under Camo's door. Nothing.

No sound either. Just the soft creaking of the yacht rocking in the waves, his muffled footsteps on the floorboards, and the impossibly loud pounding of his heart.

None of which seemed to have awakened Camo.

He reached his cabin without incident and closed the door behind him.

He'd made it.

Stripping down to his boxers, he climbed into bed and stared into the darkness.

Now as long as Lana didn't convince Reyes to do things her way, everything should be fine. Reyes didn't strike him as a man who could be pushed around, but Lana could be pretty persuasive.

She wouldn't be happy with him for going over her head like that, but as long as she came through this without further injury, he could deal with her wrath.

Nineteen

Lana closed the lid of her laptop as the sound of a key in the lock reached her ears. Fingers circling around her Glock, she eased from her seat.

Pain spiked up her body at the simple movement.

She clenched her teeth and drew in a breath. The pounding of her heart echoed in her ears. A tremor shook down her arm even as heat roared through her body.

Stay calm.

So someone was here. It was probably Barker or Micah. Or someone else from work.

It's not like the safe house's location was public knowledge.

The person had a key.

None of the arguments made her feel any better.

It was nearly seven p.m. Barker, Micah, everyone from the office, they should all be at home, not here checking up on her.

She eased around the table, put the fridge between herself and the door.

Ordinarily the safe house would have multiple layers of protection, everything from a security system to deputies guarding the doors, but since she wasn't officially in protective custody, she was on her own.

The deadbolt scraped open.

She adjusted her grip on the Glock.

The person outside moved on to the next deadbolt.

Scrape.

Two down; only the knob remained. And the chain. Would the intruder force the door?

If they did, she'd be ready for them.

The knob jiggled.

She angled the gun toward the floor.

The lock on the doorknob popped.

Should've called for help before getting into position. Her gaze darted to the table. The phone wasn't there. Must've left it in the bedroom.

The door opened. The chain snapped taut.

Her fingers tightened around the gun.

"Tanner, open up."

Barker.

She relaxed her grip on the gun, but didn't put the weapon away. Why hadn't he just called her? Or at least knocked on the door rather than trying to force his way in?

"Tanner?" Urgency laced the word.

"Just a moment."

Something felt off. It was definitely Barker's voice, but he shouldn't be here.

She pushed the door closed, stretched up to look through the peep hole. A distorted view of Barker's face filled her vision. Behind him, another man, someone familiar. Recognition flashed.

SAC Reyes.

Something had happened. To Nate.

But she'd just talked to him a few hours ago. He'd been fine.

Then. Too bad he could go from fine to dead in a matter of seconds.

An iron fist slammed into her chest. A task as simple as breathing became a struggle with the burning coal lodged in her throat.

She stretched shaking fingers toward the chain.

Stop borrowing trouble.

For all she knew they were here to tell her they'd arrested

the people involved. That Nate was coming home and she was out of danger.

She slid the chain and opened the door.

If the news were that simple, they would've called. Only bad news had to be delivered in person.

Not to mention that both men looked grim.

Funny how she no longer cared that it was Nate's fault she was stuck in this house. Her injuries, fear, and paranoia faded at the idea that he might be gone.

Barker closed the door behind Reyes and secured every lock.

The thin smile Reyes offered looked forced. "Deputy Tanner. Good to see you again."

She didn't have the patience for false pleasantries. "What happened?"

"There's been a development."

Barker wasted no time with pretense. "Why don't we have a seat."

Not a suggestion. She took it for the order it was, forced her legs to carry her to the table, and sank down into the chair she'd vacated not three minutes earlier.

The two men sat opposite her.

As much as she was dying for answers, she forced her lips to remain together.

Reyes cleared his throat. "Your friend Nate Miller contacted me this afternoon. He was very concerned–"

"You've been targeted."

Nate was okay.

A breath slid from her and she tried not to laugh at how worked up she'd gotten. And for what? Nothing.

"Tanner?" A slight frown curved Barker's mouth. "Did you hear me?"

Her relief must've been evident on her face. They probably thought she'd lost it.

"I was targeted," she repeated calmly. "Big deal. We already knew that."

Both men stared at her.

Realization slammed her seconds later. No, they hadn't known that. She knew, because Nate had already told her, but she'd chosen not to share that piece of information with anyone.

"You knew?" Barker's flat words belied the tightening of his lips.

No point in denying it any longer.

"Nate called me earlier today. He mentioned that the attack was related to what you have him working on." She nodded at Reyes.

Red flashed across Barker's cheeks and his nostrils flared ever so slightly.

Uh-oh. She'd witnessed the look enough times to know what it meant. She was in for it now.

"You didn't think it was important to maybe, I don't know, fill your *supervisor* in on that little detail?"

"Hey, I'm here, aren't I? I didn't stay at home where I'd be an easy mark."

"You also purposely withheld information."

"And what would you have done if I'd told you?"

"I'd have put a team with you."

Crossing her arms on the table in front of her, she leaned in. "Precisely why I didn't tell you. There was no proof that I was even in any danger."

"So he didn't say you were still a target?"

"He said that it was possible."

"Darn it, Tanner!" His fist slammed against the top of the table with a loud thud. "I oughta arrest you for hindering an investigation."

She knew an empty threat when she heard one, but it was time to run some damage control. "Look, I'm sorry. I knew that if I told you, you'd overreact."

Like you are right now.

Such a comment would likely only land her in deeper trouble.

"Putting you under protection when there's an active threat against you is not overreacting." Barker forced a few long breaths and when he spoke, his tone was markedly quieter. "Miller indicated the guy is coming back for round two."

Lust-filled blue eyes staring out of a brown ski mask invaded her mind. As did the implications of another run-in with him.

The air in her lungs thickened and her breath came in quick bursts. Running into that guy again, whether in her home or a dark alley or a busy police station, was near the top of a list of things she never wanted to do.

But this could be the perfect opportunity to put him behind bars. Using herself as bait.

Could she face him again?

She wanted to say no. As much as she wanted the guy in custody, she didn't want to get anywhere near him without solid steel bars separating them.

Maybe not even then.

But it might be her only chance to regain her freedom and – hopefully – her sense of security. It had to be done.

Drawing a deep breath, she transferred her gaze between Barker and Reyes. "Let's set a trap."

"Way ahead of you." Reyes checked his elegant gold watch. "My team should be setting up in that foreclosed house across the street from yours as we speak. The second he makes an appearance, we'll have him."

"And if he sneaks in the back?"

"I plan to put an agent on the inside."

"So he can look in a window, see someone who clearly isn't me, and walk away?" No matter how much she didn't like the idea, there was really only one way to ensure they got this guy. "You need to put me on the inside."

"Forget it, Tanner." Barker spat the words. "You're in no condition to take on this guy again."

She bit back the urge to argue the truth in his words. "It

wouldn't come to that, would it? The FBI will be right there to arrest him the second he breaks in."

Assuming they saw him. She didn't have a lot of faith in the across-the-street-surveillance idea.

"This is not open for debate. You're staying put."

"For how long?" Lana shifted to persuasion mode. "Sir, it's me this guy is after. What happens if he decides to wait us out? I can't stay here indefinitely."

Okay, so she'd only been here a few hours.

Still, the idea of living here, in this strange house with only a suitcase-worth of her things, was anything but appealing.

The scowl never left Barker's face, but a subtle shift in his eyes spoke volumes.

Her words were having the desired effect.

"Send me in. Bug the house, put an agent or two in the garage, and we'll have him before he gets within five feet of me."

"We'll send in a double."

That would be the ideal option, but it'd also take time. "So you have someone in mind."

Both men stared at her.

"I didn't think so. It has to be me."

Barker rubbed the back of his neck and released a gusty sigh. "Fine. But I want Rawlings stationed inside the house." His gaze cut to Reyes. "And agents in the garage. The U.S. Marshals won't be losing a deputy on my watch, got it?"

"Nor on mine." Reyes held the look with his own.

She turned away from the nonverbal power struggle.

Micah. She could think of few people she would rather have covering her back than him. Of course, he'd have to remain hidden or they'd lose the element of surprise, but knowing he'd be close provided a slight measure of peace.

Very slight.

She was going home.

No warmth or joy accompanied the thought. Home no

longer felt like the sanctuary it once had been. In fact, at the moment she hardly cared if she ever set foot inside again.

How long would it take to regain the independence that had been so harshly stripped away?

There she was.

Jimmy watched his black-haired target limp toward her front door, escorted by two suits who were obvious feds.

Had the little witch just now been released from the hospital? Maybe he'd done more damage than he thought.

The idea brought a glimmer of satisfaction.

He shifted positions and stretched. Redirected his attention to the knothole through which he'd surveyed the neighborhood for way too many hours.

Hiding in someone's back yard was a bit risky, even with the six-foot privacy fence surrounding him. But it had been the best of his options. There were no windows close to his location and the neighbor's single story house didn't pose much threat, either. Best of all, the hole provided clear line of sight to his target's home.

Several interesting facts had become clear during the hours he'd spent in hiding.

Like the fact that the one house on the block with a realtor's sign in the front yard was currently being used by the feds to monitor his target.

A vain attempt to keep her safe, no doubt.

More than that, he'd witnessed a man entering the target's house about an hour earlier. The man had yet to leave.

A bodyguard, perhaps.

Or maybe a boyfriend. Yeah, that option seemed the more likely of the two.

The man had possessed a key, after all. Besides, the role of a bodyguard was to remain *with* the target, not hang out at her house without her.

A smirk tweaked his lips. Did Miller know his chick was steppin' out on him?

Unlikely. He suspected Miller's loyalty might waver if he knew the truth.

The two suits exited the house and climbed into the gray SUV they'd arrived in only minutes before. There was no sign of the mystery man or the target.

As the SUV pulled away, he settled in to wait.

With the FBI watching and an unknown person in the house, he'd be better served using darkness for cover. It would make for a long evening, but it was a small price to pay to exact his revenge.

The television chattered softly in the background, but Lana had no idea what was on. She'd simply wanted to give the appearance of relaxing in case *they* were watching.

Blackness lurked beyond her windows. They could strike any time.

Assuming they were even coming today.

Or at all. At this point, all they had were a few vague threats and Nate's paranoia.

Something she intended to address when this thing was all over.

How dare he go behind her back like that? He should've trusted her to handle things like she'd said she would, not turned to the FBI.

Of course she knew why he'd done things the way he had, but that didn't make it okay.

She didn't need him to protect her.

Contrary to what everyone obviously thought, she could

take care of herself. And she could certainly make sound decisions regarding matters of her own personal safety.

A glance at the clock showed it was nearing eleven. The last time they'd attacked, it had been earlier than this.

Much earlier.

Did that mean they weren't coming? Or that they were waiting for her to go to bed?

The throbbing between her temples continued to increase until it was too much to ignore. No doubt had something to do with the tension stiffening her neck and spine.

She rolled her head from side to side in an attempt to loosen the muscles, but it didn't work. Not even rubbing her neck helped. No, the only way to get any relief would be to see the men who had attacked her being led away in handcuffs.

But a couple of aspirin couldn't hurt.

A yawn snuck up on her. The stress, not to mention the lack of sleep the night before, was starting to get to her.

Too bad sleeping in her own bed would bring nothing but nightmares.

"You should take something for that headache."

She started, her attention whipping around to the hallway, where Micah laughed softly.

A glimmer of irritation lit through her, although she couldn't tell if it was directed at him or herself. "Don't do that."

Although the shadows mostly hid his face, she saw him try to smother his amusement. "Sorry."

Okay, so maybe it was kind of funny. "No you're not."

"I am a little." His grin faded and he studied her. "On second thought, why don't you head to bed? You look wiped."

"I don't think I'll be able to sleep until we catch this guy, but that doesn't mean you need to stay up." She nodded behind him. "The sheets on the guest bed are clean."

"Forget it." He stared at her with a look that dared her to

argue. "Barker tasked me with looking out for you. How am I gonna do that with my eyes closed?"

"You'll be close enough to hear if anything happens. Besides, he'll trip the alarm if he comes in." They'd set the alarm to silent and given the alarm company the contact information for the lead agent watching the house. The house would be swarming with agents in seconds if the perimeter were breached.

"I'm good. It's not the first time I've gone without sleep and we both know it won't be the last."

Not even a pause to consider the option.

Big surprise. It hadn't taken her long to see that Micah rivaled her in stubbornness.

"I think I'll take something and at least lay down." She rose from the sofa, went to the windows, and lowered the shades that she'd left open in case the men returned.

With a glass of water in her hand, she headed for her bedroom.

Pausing in the doorway, she turned back to Micah. "If you change your mind, the guest room's just down the hall."

"I won't, but do you mind if I watch TV?"

Now that the shades were drawn, it'd be safe enough for Micah to go out into the open. "Go for it."

She eased her door closed and turned on the lamp beside her bed. Soft light banished the shadows to the room's furthest corners.

First some pain pills. Then she'd climb into bed and see if she couldn't get rid of this killer headache.

Blimey, didn't she ever go to bed?

Jimmy rose from his position behind the knothole and stretched. Stepping a few feet away, he emptied his bladder on the lawn again before resuming his watch of the house.

Light still glowed from the windows. Who'd have guessed the tramp was such a night owl?

Movement at one of the windows caught his eye. The distance made it impossible to make out any features, but the slight build of the silhouette told him all he needed to know. It was her.

Shades dropped over the window, effectively cutting off his line of sight.

He pushed the button on his watch and checked the time. 11:15.

Maybe she was finally going to bed. Or maybe she'd be too scared to close her eyes. Either way, he was done waiting.

He could practically feel the soft flesh of her neck beneath his fingers. If she thought their last encounter was bad, just wait. It'd pale in comparison to what he had planned for tonight.

Only the darkness witnessed his leer. He flexed his fingers and released the latch on the gate.

There were still complications.

The Feds watching the house, for example. The mystery man who'd never left. The fact that she was undoubtedly armed and, unlike a lot of people who owned a gun, well trained on how to use it.

Nothing he couldn't handle.

Circling the block and approaching from the rear would shield him from the Feds. Careful entry and a search of the house would help him take care of the man. And a surprise attack would rob her of the time she'd need to brandish and use her weapon.

He probably should've brought a gun of his own, rather than the hunting knife he had strapped to his calf. But he was looking forward to killing her with his bare hands.

After having a little fun with her, of course.

Besides, guns were noisy and with the feds watching, it was probably for the best that he didn't have one. He was just as efficient with his knife as with a firearm, maybe more so.

After circling the block, he counted off the houses.

One. Two. Three. Four.

Should be right here. He strode between two darkened houses. Through grass so tall it brushed his ankles. Skirted a child's swing set. Approached a six foot privacy fence that he instantly recognized as the one encircling her back yard.

Now to figure out what to do about the man in the house.

Killing him was the logical solution. But a part of him liked the idea of letting this guy find her body. Not to mention the adrenaline rush that would accompany knowing her boyfriend lay unconscious in the next room while she slowly bled to death.

That settled it. Given the choice, he'd take down the other guy. Rough him up, but not kill him.

He scaled the fence and landed with a soft thump.

Pausing, he listened to the night surrounding him.

The hum of a nearby air conditioner. A dog barking down the block. The distant rumble of a truck a few blocks away.

No voices or movement or any sign that he'd been spotted.

He eased along the fence, down the side of the detached garage, more fence, then finally, the house.

Time to make her pay.

Twenty

Had she heard something?

Lana sat up and listened. Silence. Not even any noise from the TV. Maybe Micah had never turned it on.

Either way, she was jumping at shadows. Again.

Easing back down, she rested her cheek on the pillow. Her eyes locked on the bedroom door.

Maybe she should block it.

Put a chair under the knob or slide the dresser in front of it or something. Anything that would keep an intruder out.

If she did that, the men would probably come through the window. With the door blocked, Micah wouldn't even be able to back her up. And she wouldn't be able to make a quick escape should the need arise.

She rolled over, her gaze fixing on the shade-covered window.

Actually, that seemed a more likely point of entry. If she was going to break into someone's house to murder them, that's how she'd choose to do it.

She stared at the window. Expected it to open any second.

Stop it!

Not only was her worry counterproductive, it gave solid proof to a shaky trust in God. God had brought her through a fire and being kidnapped as a child, encounters with two assassins, a brush with a serial killer, and this most recent attack in her home. Hadn't He proven Himself to her time and again?

She should stop worrying and start trusting.

Besides, the men were probably miles away. Really. What were the odds they'd return her first night back in her house?

Unless they'd been watching it, waiting for her to return.

The ice lodged in her ribcage refused to melt. Chills tingled through her veins.

If they'd been watching, they knew she wasn't alone. And while the one guy was bigger than Micah, she doubted they'd be stupid enough to think they could take on two armed federal agents.

But whoever said they were smart?

In fact, they'd shown a great degree of recklessness the last time they'd been here. Common sense might not be their forte.

If they did come, the bed would be the first place they'd look for her.

She slid from beneath the covers, her feet landing silently on the soft carpet. Snagging two of her pillows from the head of the bed, she stuffed them under the blanket.

And berated herself for giving in to the fear and paranoia.

Regardless, she inspected the makeshift body in her bed. While close scrutiny would reveal the ruse to anyone with eyes, it should sidetrack them long enough for her to gain control of the situation.

If they came. Which they probably wouldn't.

Gun in hand, she crossed the room, skirting the bed and passing the door, to settle in the shadowy corner. She sank to the carpet and leaned her head back against the wall.

A small measure of peace settled swelled inside her. She felt safer than she had since the attack.

This corner was one of the furthest points from the window and provided a good view of both it and the door. From here, she'd see anyone entering the room long before he saw her.

A yawn surprised her. She was more tired than she thought.

While the aspirin had taken the edge off the headache, a dull throb still pulsed through her temples. She placed her gun on the floor next to her hip and let her eyes glide closed.

Maybe she could catch a short nap. One uninterrupted by nightmares.

Micah suppressed a yawn. Okay, so maybe he was a little more zapped than he'd led Lana to believe.

Not like he'd gotten any decent sleep in that hospital chair last night.

But it didn't matter.

Sleeping wasn't an option. He was the last line of defense between Lana and whoever wanted her dead.

Snagging the sugar-loaded, heavily-caffeinated energy drink from the end table beside him, he took a long swig. A few more hours and the sun would be up, Barker or someone else could take over his post, and he could crash so he was rested enough to do this all over again tomorrow night.

Closed captioning flashed across the bottom of the muted TV, but his eyes felt too grainy to read it.

A crackle came through his earpiece. "Rawlings, alarm company is registering an open window. Confirm all is okay."

He pushed the button on the communicator. "Give me a minute to check it out. They say which window?"

"Negative."

"I'll keep you updated."

Could someone have gotten in without his hearing? It seemed impossible.

Maybe he should call in reinforcements.

But having the team storm the house would alert anyone who might be monitoring the place.

He'd check on Lana first.

While he couldn't see her opening a window under the present circumstances, he wanted to rule it out before calling for backup.

He stood, cradled his gun lightly in both hands. Eased around the coffee table.

With his back to the wall, he slid toward the hallway leading to the bedrooms.

The unnatural silence felt alive.

He paused at the mouth of the hallway to let his eyes adjust to the darkness.

Movement! He jerked back.

Not fast enough. Something crashed against the side of his head. Spots filled his vision.

No.

He blinked. Couldn't pass out.

Pain erupted across his face. He staggered backward, tripping over his own feet.

Something smashed into his face. Again and again.

A fist.

The thought sparked like faulty wiring before the darkness engulfed him.

Lana jerked. Blinked as she stared across the inky room.

How long had she been asleep? The weight of her eyelids and the grit underneath them confirmed it hadn't been long enough.

The bedroom door stood open. A shadow moved.

The oxygen in her lungs turned to tar. A scream backed up in her throat.

Maybe it was Micah.

The darkness prevented her from positively identifying him.

But she knew in her heart it wasn't Micah. He wouldn't come into her room. Especially without knocking or somehow identifying himself.

Someone was in the house. She didn't have to see him to know who.

The figure approached the bed.

Her muscles were about as flexible as the wall at her back.

A low chuckle drifted on the dead air. She forgot how to breathe.

"Wake up, luv."

That voice! She'd never forget that voice.

Commands flashed in her brain.

Move. Grab the gun. Empty the magazine into the man who'd haunted her thoughts the past twenty-four hours.

Her body rebelled.

She couldn't move. Not even to pull the trigger.

All she could do was sit like some kind of stupid statue and watch the shadow move closer to her bed.

The bedside lamp clicked on.

Big guy; white face, shaggy brown hair, tattooed arms the size of tree trunks.

No mask.

"What the bloody...?"

She lunged for her gun. Shaking fingers slammed into the grip, sent the weapon spinning into the center of the room.

Scrambling after it, she glanced up in time to see his bulk flying toward her. She wrenched left.

Away from her gun.

The floor vibrated as the man landed hard.

"Micah!" How could he not have heard all this?

"That the bloke's name?" The man laughed. "Hate to break it to ya, *luv*, but Micah won't be comin' to the rescue anytime soon."

Micah, dead?

No gunshot. Meant this man had stabbed, strangled, or slit Micah's throat.

A hand clamped over her right ankle. It squeezed hard and tugged her backward.

She snagged the leg of her bed.

Pain shot up her arm as the man jerked her toward him, but she didn't let go.

The hand moved up to her calf.

She glanced back, assessed, rolled to her side and swung her left leg around with as much force as she could. Her foot connected with his skull.

A roar echoed through the room; his grip loosened.

If her stinging foot was any indication, he should be battling one heck of a headache.

Too bad she hadn't been wearing steel-toed boots. Or stilettos. Neither of which she owned.

She scurried out of his reach and leapt to her feet. Darted around the end of the bed.

Where was her backup? What was the point of FBI surveillance if they weren't going to help?

The man pushed himself to his feet, one hand gingerly pressing on his head near his left ear. "You're gonna pay for that."

"What did you do to Micah?"

"Luv, you oughta be worryin' 'bout yourself."

Though her eyes never left his face, her mind raced around the room.

Had to be a way out.

The window wasn't far from her back. But she'd never get it open before he caught up to her.

She could go through it.

And hope the glass didn't do any serious damage. Although slitting her own throat diving through the window sounded preferable to whatever this man had planned.

Maybe under the bed? No way this meathead would be able to follow her.

But he'd probably just lift the whole bed.

He launched himself across the mattress.

The tips of his fingers brushed her arm as she sidestepped his reach. She raced around the bed, her gaze sweeping the floor.

Where was her gun?

"You wouldn't be lookin' for this now, would you, luv?"

He stood on the other side of the bed, lifting his shirt enough to reveal the Glock tucked into his waistband. Her Glock.

She ran for the door.

Movement sounded behind her, but she refused to look back. The door slammed closed as she reached for it.

She grabbed the knob, twisted it, and jerked.

The door didn't budge. An arm stretched above her head, palm flat against the door.

A vise seized her shoulder.

It ripped her backward and whirled her around. His face was only a foot from hers, close enough for her to gag on the stale cigarette smoke, to feel puffs of hot breath against her forehead.

The grip shifted to her upper arm as he slammed her against the wall beside the door.

The knife wound from their last encounter burned underneath his oppressive grip. A cry spilled from her lips.

Satisfaction lit his eyes.

He lifted her a few inches. Just enough to force her to her toes.

Black tinged her vision; revulsion twisted her stomach. She lacked the leverage required to land a good kick.

She needed reinforcements to arrive.

Too much time had passed. If they were going to come, they would've gotten here by now. She was on her own.

Rage glistened in his blue eyes. "You're gonna wish I'd killed you last time, luv."

Had to break free. There must be something she could use.

On the nightstand. To her left.

Her hand shot out, fisted around the lamp, and swung it toward his head. Darkness enveloped them as the cord ripped from the wall.

Even without light, she knew the blow was solid. The impact jarred down her arm.

The pressure on her shoulder vanished.

A low moan, accompanied by a string of indiscernible words that she doubted she wanted to understand, drifted from in front of her. She reached behind her and flipped a switch. The ceiling light illuminated the room.

The man knelt in front of her, one hand cradling the side of his head. Blood seeped through his fingers.

It took everything in her to keep from kicking him in the gut.

She darted close enough to snag the gun from his waistband, then took several steps backward to put some distance between them. "On your stomach."

If he heard her, he chose not to respond. Much less obey.

He shook his head slowly as if trying to clear it, then lifted his gaze and locked hate-filled eyes on her once again.

"Down. Now."

A smirk twisted his lips. "You won't shoot me."

"You wouldn't be the first man I've killed." She sighted on his head. "And I'm well within my rights to do so now. Go ahead, push your luck."

Part of her hoped he would.

After all he'd done, the fear she now had in her own home, the pain and bruises and stiches, not to mention whatever he'd done to Micah, she wanted a reason to shoot him.

He stared at her a few seconds longer before easing to his stomach.

"Hands behind your head. Fingers laced together."

She veered around him as he silently obeyed.

No matter how much she wanted to check on Micah, securing this jerk had to remain her top priority.

If he got the drop on her, she'd be of no use to Micah or anyone else.

Never removing her attention from his tense figure, she retrieved handcuffs from the small cedar box on top of her dresser and tossed them next to his head. "Pick them up."

He lifted his head and momentarily assessed her before reaching for them with his right hand.

Good. Now she knew which hand was most likely to be the dominant one.

"Cuff your right hand. Slowly."

"I can't do it in this bloody position."

"It'll be even harder with a bullet in your shoulder. Do it."

A rush of crimson flashed through his cheeks, spreading like wildfire across his forehead, the color a stark contrast to the white of his firmly clenched lips. Thin eyebrows pressed over eyes that were little more than lines on his face.

If looks had the power to kill, she would've been under at least ten feet of soil.

"Right wrist. Now."

A crash sounded from beyond the bedroom, followed by heavy steps tromping inside the house. Drawing closer.

He'd brought backup.

This was it. She couldn't keep more than two or three of them at bay.

Dang it! Why hadn't she called for help instead of focusing only on subduing this guy and checking Micah?

Now they were both sunk.

"Rawlings! Tanner!"

Praise God!

It wasn't *his* backup. It was hers.

"In here."

Footsteps pounded her direction. The door burst open, framing Monroe, the agent in charge of her surveillance. In less than a second, the gun that had been sighted on her face shifted to the man on the floor.

Monroe stepped closer. "I've got him covered if you'd like

to do the honors."

"Go for it." She didn't want to get anywhere near him.

Not to mention that if she got too close to him, he might take a chance and try to use her as a shield or hostage. Monroe, being closer to his size, wouldn't make nearly such an attractive target.

Monroe holstered his weapon. Another agent filled the space behind him as the lead agent moved toward her attacker.

Placing one knee in the man's back, he snapped the cuffs around the right wrist, wrestled both arms down, then snapped the other cuff around the left.

It was over. And she was safe.

A quiver traveled down her arm and visibly shook her gun.

Under the armed, watchful supervision of the second agent, Monroe hauled the suspect to his feet.

She lowered her gun. "Micah. Is he okay?"

More agents flooded the room. Monroe passed the handcuffed thug to someone else before turning to her. "He's gonna look like the loser of a boxing match, but he'll be fine."

Thank God.

Buzzing filled her ears and weak legs threatened to drop her to the floor. She didn't know what she would've done if Micah had died trying to help her.

"Tanner?" A slight frown creased Monroe's face. "You hear me? I said he was okay."

"He said… never mind. I expected the worst."

"I think maybe you better have a seat. Don't want you passing out on me here."

"I'm okay."

"You're bleeding."

She was? A glance at her arm confirmed Monroe's words.

Dang it. The stitches had ripped.

"Come on, have a seat." Monroe put a hand to her back and tried to guide her to the bed, but she shook him off.

This bedroom was the last place she wanted to be after what'd just happened. In fact, she might never sleep in here again.

She whirled and preceded him out of the room.

In the hallway, she spotted Micah sprawled face up on the floor, an agent kneeling beside him. Probably monitoring his condition until the ambulance arrived. Blood streaked across his face and crusted around his nose and mouth.

She fell beside him, her hand immediately going to his neck to feel for a pulse.

Strong and steady. Just like Monroe said.

Only then did she hear the approaching sirens.

"Come on, Tanner. EMTs are about here." A hand cradled her elbow and assisted her to her feet. "Why don't you have a seat out here and fill me in on what happened."

She'd been in law enforcement long enough to know the difference between a suggestion and an order. Collapsing into her favorite chair, she tried not to give in to the tremors threatening a hostile takeover of her body.

Monroe perched on the edge of the sofa across from her. Didn't say a word, just waited.

Several calming breaths later, she lifted her gaze to meet his. The sympathy she saw in his eyes almost shattered her control.

Almost. But not quite.

She released a shaky sigh. "What took you guys so long?"

Nice. Here he'd come to help and she was asking why he hadn't helped sooner.

The question didn't seem to bother him. "I was waiting for Rawlings to get back to me. My mistake. We should've stormed the place, but I was afraid of drawing attention if it turned out to be nothing."

Maybe it was her headache or the residual effects of the adrenaline that had dumped through her when she'd heard the intruder's accented voice, but Monroe's words didn't make sense. "If what turned out to be nothing?"

"The alarm company called us. Open window. I contacted Rawlings, he said he'd check it out and get back to me. Seemed like it was taking too long so I tried to follow up. When Rawlings didn't answer, we came running."

She gave the only response she could manage: a nod.

With his forearms resting across his knees and his fingers entwined, Monroe leaned forward. "I'm sorry. He never should've gotten that close. This mess is on me."

"It's not your fault. He's good at what he does, that's for sure." She tried to manage a smile, but doubted it came across as genuine. "At least we've got him."

"Dead to rights. Breaking and entering, assault, attempted murder. That guy ain't going anywhere."

He may not be, but that other guy was still out there. Until she knew he was securely locked away too, she'd never feel truly safe.

Twenty One

Pain pulsed behind her eyes. Between her shoulder blades. Down her spine.

In fact, Lana didn't think there was a single part of her that didn't hurt. At least the pain was solid confirmation that she was still alive.

She leaned against the wall next to the one-way glass and listened to the interrogation going on inside the other room.

It was not going well.

She doubted he'd said more than a dozen words since being brought in thirty minutes ago. He'd refused to give his name, wouldn't say why he'd come after her, and remained tight-lipped about his partner.

The only reason they had his name was because his prints were in the system from prior arrests.

Jimmy Smits. Arrested ten years ago for domestic violence, eight years ago for DUI, and four years ago for assault.

In spite of all that, no charges had ever officially been brought against him. The address on file, not to mention on his DMV records, led to a run-down apartment building where no one had ever heard of him.

Most interesting of all was that he had yet to request a lawyer. The man wasn't a genius, but with his priors it was the one thing she would've expected him to do.

She tuned back in as Barker leaned toward the suspect.

"You got any idea how big your problems are right now?

We've got you on multiple counts of assault and attempted murder, and that's just for starters. Add to that the fact that you targeted my deputies and sent two of them to the hospital–" Barker jabbed his finger at Smits, "–and I intend to see that you're prosecuted to the fullest extent of the law. You'll be lucky if you don't get the chair for this one."

If the threat fazed Smits at all, he didn't show it. Instead, he stared straight at the one-way glass.

Unblinking. Unmoving. Like a corpse in full rigor.

A chill stole through her body.

No, he couldn't see her. She knew that. But he knew she was watching. The cold I-hate-you-and-will-somehow-kill-you stare was for her benefit.

"This is your one chance to help yourself out here."

Smits finally blinked and dragged his gaze to rest on Barker. "You've got nothing on me."

"Really. You think a jury will overlook the fact that you attacked a woman in her own home – twice – were caught in that same home, and had knocked out the deputy guarding her?"

"We're involved. The guy I knocked out, see, I thought he was a bloody robber. I was protecting my girl."

His girl? Who did he think he was kidding?

Barker jerked back, crossed his arms over his chest, and glared down at Smits. "That's a far cry from her story."

The left side of Smits' mouth turned up in an arrogant smirk. "Well, it would be now, wouldn't it? Pastor's daughter and all that."

How did he know that?

A shiver danced down her back and she tried not to think about how much else he might know about her.

"What would dear old dad and mum think if they knew we were lovers?"

Fire roared across her face.

How dare he even suggest such a thing! Passivity was overrated; it was time to confront this monster.

She whirled. Fingernails bit into her palms as she stormed toward the hall.

A few well-placed kicks would have him eating those words. And possibly his tongue and cheek, too.

"You and I both know that's a dirty lie." Barker's voice, tight with rage, slowed her steps.

Calm.

With her hand on the edge of the doorframe, she turned back to the glass.

Neither Barker nor Smits had moved, although Smits' eyes were once again looking past Barker to the glass.

He'd been trying to get a rise from her.

And she'd almost given him precisely what he wanted.

Quakes attacked her legs so fiercely she had trouble standing. Everything in her wanted to go in there and put him in his place, but she couldn't do anything that might compromise the investigation. She forced herself to return to the glass.

Barker's tone was only slightly more controlled as he continued, "Seriously. Who do you think a jury would believe? A respected deputy without a single disciplinary mark on her record or you?"

Without a single disciplinary mark? What about her suspension earlier this week?

Hopefully that meant Barker had erased it. He should have, given that she'd done nothing wrong.

A slight shrug lifted Smits' shoulders. "It'll be enough to create reasonable doubt."

Could he be right? All it would take was one person on the jury who watched too many movies, one person who'd had a bad experience with a cop, or one person with a grudge against the church, and they'd buy Smits' story.

The church. His earlier words haunted her. Pastor's daughter.

If he knew that, he undoubtedly knew who her parents were. What church her father led. Where to find her family at any given time.

Pain jabbed her stomach.

They couldn't let him walk. There had to be something....

"What about all the damage? The bruises, stab wounds, it's all documented."

Smits rolled his head from side to side before looking at Barker. "She likes it rough."

"So you stab all your girlfriends?"

"That happened during a bloody break-in. I had nothin' to do with it."

He was cool. Too cool. Obviously one who'd been through all this before.

Unless they could dig beneath his calculated surface, they'd never get anything out of him.

"Good luck selling that one. She identified your voice as one of the intruders."

"Her word against mine."

"We know how much your word is worth. And with your record, the jury won't believe you either." Barker slid out a chair and sat down. "Look, I want your partner even more than I want to see you fry. Give him up and I'll get the DA down here to cut you a deal."

Seconds straggled as Smits didn't respond. Finally, he sighed. "It's been a long day. You gonna book me or am I free to go?"

Free to *go?* Who did he think he was fooling?

Barker snorted. "You'll be lucky to ever see the light of day again."

"I've heard that before. I'm ready to call my lawyer."

"You better hope he's a good one, because you're gonna need it."

"He'll have me out of this bloody place in no time."

"You think so, huh? You know it's the middle of the night, right? On a weekend, no less. You're not going anywhere until at least Monday. And to be quite honest, not even then."

"We'll see 'bout that."

Barker straightened, crossing his arms over his chest. "Let me tell you something. I don't know what happened in all those other cases, but I can guarantee you that these charges, they aren't going away. So go ahead. Call your lawyer. Let him tell you that the only play you've got is full cooperation."

Smits' attention shifted back to the window. Rested on her.

She knew it was impossible, but it felt like he could see her. Locking her knees did nothing to stop the tremors assaulting her.

Vaguely aware of Barker moving away from Smits, she couldn't seem to tear her eyes from him.

The door slammed behind Barker, the bang echoing down the hall.

Silence had never felt so menacing.

Smits licked his lips.

"Only play, huh?" Words drifted out slowly and softly. "I've heard that before, too."

It was good to be back on American soil. Even better now that she'd finally cleared customs.

Amanda glanced around the terminal, pulling her suitcase behind her. Someone should be here to meet her. Her gaze landed on Tim as he strode her direction. The serious expression on his face contained a grimness that was uncharacteristic, even for him.

No. She was too late!

Steps faltering, she stopped in the middle of the concourse as Tim advanced. A lump the size of her suitcase jammed in her throat.

"Jack. I–is he…?"

"He's fine." He grabbed her suitcase, but didn't move.

"Jimmy's missing. You know anything about that?"

Still?

Jacksonville wasn't that far away; he should've been back a while ago. Could he have run into trouble?

Not likely.

Knowing Jimmy, he'd stopped off for drinks somewhere and was passed out in some cheap motel. Or maybe even his car.

Traffic moved around them, but Tim seemed oblivious to it. Blue eyes locked on her.

Ugh. She hated it when he tried to read her. Mostly because she was pretty sure he normally saw more than she wanted him to.

"Amanda?"

"How should I know?" She started toward the exit, Tim falling into step beside her. "I have better things to do than keep track of Jimmy."

"You talked to him just before he went off grid."

She whirled to face him. "Are you monitoring my phone calls?"

"Don't be dumb. I pulled *his* phone records." The automatic doors whooshed open, a wall of heat slamming their faces as they stepped out into the midday sun. "Your number's the last one on there."

Great. Figured Tim would get all nosy on her.

Of course, if Jimmy had just done what he was supposed to do and hurried back after killing the girl, she wouldn't have to worry about explaining herself to Tim.

"Well, he certainly didn't run his plans by me. You couldn't track his GPS?"

He shoved her suitcase in the back of the Escalade and closed the rear door. "I tried, but he must've removed the battery or something because I got nothing."

Sliding into the passenger seat, she buckled her seat belt before turning to look at Tim. "Relax. You know Jimmy. He's probably with some girl."

"What concerns me is that it's not *some* girl, but a very specific one." Cursing, Tim slammed the car into drive and hit the gas pedal with enough force to squeal the tires. "I told him to leave it alone."

"Leave what alone?"

"Miller's girl. Jimmy wanted to go back and finish her off."

She fell against the door as he whipped around a corner too fast. "Calm down, will you?"

Easing off the pedal a little, he shot her a warning through narrowed eyes. "So help me, Amanda, if you had anything to do with this–"

"Seriously? You really think I can control Jimmy? If he went after her, it's because his massive ego couldn't let go of the fact that a girl beat him up."

Silence smothered the space between them for a few minutes before Tim switched on the radio.

She tuned out the country music, her mind straying to Jimmy. That stupid Brit better not have gotten caught. Not because she gave a flying leap what happened to him, but because Jimmy's loyalties resided solely with himself.

She had no doubt Jimmy would give up his own mother, not to mention her and Tim, just to save his hide.

"Ugh."

Lana jerked upright as the moan sliced the silence. What was that? Who was there?

The thoughts stilled as the hospital room came into focus.

That's right. She was in Micah's hospital room. Waiting for him to regain consciousness.

She must've dozed off.

At least the short nap had eased the pounding in her head.

Unfortunately, it had also allowed all her muscles to tighten. She'd never been one for pampering, but right now a full body massage sounded amazing.

Incoherent mumbling caught her attention.

Turning, she found Micah slowly blinking. Eyebrows scrunched together, confusion clouded his dark eyes.

His attention settled on her and he jerked. "The alarm!"

"Relax. We got him."

Silence lingered for several seconds as his gaze probed her face.

Probably looking for any trace of deception. Or further injury.

Good thing he couldn't see the fresh stitches that coated her arm. Or the plethora of bruises hidden beneath her clothes.

"You're okay?"

Yep. Definitely checking for fresh cuts and bruises. "I'm fine."

More or less. She had no intention of telling him that yesterday's encounter had exacerbated her prior injuries. Throbbing ribs, swelling, and an even greater number of stitches than before had her hurting in more places than she'd previously thought possible.

A sigh heaved from his body as he sagged against the pillows. "I'm sorry."

"For what? Not being invincible? I don't know if you saw that guy, but he was huge."

"I shouldn't have held off Monroe and his team. I didn't want them to blow their cover if it was nothing. I let you down."

"Hey. You put yourself on the line to help me. I'm more grateful than I can say."

"You shouldn't be. I practically let that guy into your house."

"Not even close." She gently touched his arm. "Don't sweat it. I would've made the same call if our positions were reversed."

"You could've been killed."

Or worse. No matter how hard she tried, she couldn't shake the dirty feeling of the man's eyes practically groping her body.

"I wasn't. And now we have him in custody and everyone's fine."

"Mostly." Micah gingerly touched his purple jaw. "Man, that dude packs a punch."

"Welcome to my world. For what it's worth, I've seen trucks smaller than that guy."

"Part of me really wants a chance to even the score." He rested his head back against the pillow, his eyes never leaving her face. "But it's over now, right? You're safe? The guy's locked up, not going anywhere…"

As much as she wanted to gloss it over and agree, she couldn't. "We only got the one guy. His partner's still out there."

"Then I better get out of here." He pushed back the blanket.

"Whoa, slow down. You just took a blow that would put a professional boxer out of the ring. What's the rush?"

"I can't watch your back from this bed. Not that I've done a great job so far, but I won't let anyone get by me a second time."

"Darn right because you aren't going anywhere."

"As long as that other guy's out there–"

"He's not coming back." The confidence in her tone conflicted with the doubt filling her mind. "We've got the more aggressive of the two. If their purpose in coming after me was what I think it was, a way to somehow manipulate Nate, then they don't have a reason to return."

"Yet this guy did."

Yeah, he had. While she had several suspicions as to the reason why, she refused to voice them. "Now that we have him, I'm sure it's only a matter of time before he gives up his partner. We'll get him to cut a deal."

Micah's frown told her he strongly disagreed, but he kept his concerns silent. "Who's Nate?"

Loaded question.

How did she explain that one? Somehow former-thief-turned-Christian-friend-for-whom-she-had-strong-feelings didn't seem like the best of answers.

Yet after all Micah had done for her, he deserved an honest answer.

Years protecting witnesses had taught her one valuable thing. When in doubt, keep it simple. "A friend. Reyes recruited him to infiltrate a militia group and evidently things have gotten a little personal."

"Your *friend* must possess some pretty special skills for them to go to all this trouble."

You have no idea. "I don't really know what's going on, but he called after the first, um, altercation, to make sure I was okay and to warn me. Evidently didn't think I took him seriously since he also called Reyes."

"Why would they come after you? Doesn't this Nate guy have family somewhere that they'd target first?"

"He has no family." Except his kids; praise God this group didn't seem to know anything about them.

"So. You and Nate?"

"There really isn't a me and Nate."

But she wished there was.

Wow. Where had that come from?

Of all the men she shouldn't fall for, a former thief and accomplice to a hit man should top the list. Maybe she needed another hit to the head to knock some sense into her. What was she thinking?

"I see."

She blinked and zeroed in on Micah. Even if she hadn't heard the disappointment in his words, there was no missing the look on his face.

She wanted to comfort him. Laugh it off. Say something,

anything to wipe the look away.

But she couldn't.

No matter how good her intentions, lying to Micah would only cause more harm than good.

"I should let you get some rest." She stood and offered a small smile. "I'll be praying for a speedy recovery."

She let herself out of the room, trying to forget the sadness in his eyes. The sigh that eased from her felt as heavy as her heart.

Micah was a great guy. A really great guy.

For someone else.

How it had happened was a mystery, but Nate held her heart solidly in his hands. And he probably didn't even know it.

In all the years she'd known Nate, he'd made no secret of his love for her. Given the chance, she'd make her own feelings clear to him.

All he had to do was come back alive.

Twenty Two

"Jimmy?" Tim's gaze strayed to the clock at the bottom of his computer monitor. Almost noon. On Sunday. The last time he'd seen or heard from Jimmy had been Friday night. When Jimmy had threatened to return to finish off Miller's chick.

That idiot better not have made good on his threat.

They were going to have to address this blatant disregard for protocol. "Where the heck have you been?"

"A bloody vacation in the Bahamas. Where do you think I've been?"

"You left without telling me a thing! How should I know?" Tim forcibly relaxed his grip on the phone. Anger and threats would get him nowhere with Jimmy. Years of experience had taught him that. "Where are you?"

"A bloody jail, that's where. Making my one phone call to my lawyer."

Jail. It could only mean one thing. But he wouldn't talk about it over the phone. "Where?"

Jimmy gave him the name of a jail in Jacksonville.

Yep. That idiot had gone after Miller's girl again. "Sit tight and keep your mouth shut. I'll be there as soon as I can."

"Tell me you weren't stupid enough to go after that U.S.

Marshal."

"No. I was thrown in jail for speeding."

Tim was tempted to strangle the man. Of course then they'd lock him in there. But still, how could Jimmy be so stupid? "I told you not to go after her."

Jimmy snorted. "Like it was all my idea. She's a master manipulator, she is, you know that?"

Were they still talking about Miller's girl? "Who is?"

"Amanda."

"What does she have to do with this?"

"She didn't tell you?" A humorless chuckle bounced off the bare walls. "No, course she didn't. She plays you, too. Lets you think she's all innocent when really–"

"What about Amanda?"

"She put me up to it. Convinced me to go after Miller's girl."

No. Amanda would've told him if she'd done something like that. "Jimmy, I swear, if you don't stop lying about her–"

"She ain't the angel you think she is. Not even close."

"You don't know her."

"I know her in ways you never will."

Pain radiated through Tim's jaw until he forced it to unclench.

Fine. Jimmy wanted to play it that way, he was out. And if he came around again, Tim would kill him personally. No one spoke that way about his family.

Even if a lot of what the man said was true.

"How soon can you get me out of this hole?"

After a comment like that, Jimmy had the nerve to ask for his help? Tim kept his voice even. "I told you not to go after her. You went anyway. You're on your own."

"You don't wanna be doing that. I won't go down alone. I'll drag you and her and everyone else at that bloody place down with me."

"Just try it. I have so many people on my side that you'll never even come close."

"You willing to bet Amanda's freedom on that?"

No, he wasn't. Something Jimmy not only knew, but was banking on.

Funny how in the space of five minutes, Jimmy could go from valuable asset to loose end. "What do you expect me to do? Break you out?"

"Do your lawyer thing and get me out."

What an idiot.

"Jimmy. I work for the prosecutor's office. You need a defense lawyer." He spoke slowly, hoping Jimmy would get it on the first time around.

Even if he could help, no way was he getting involved with this mess.

It was bad enough he'd show up on the visitation records. He intended to distance himself from this mess as much as humanly possible and once Jimmy was out, make sure no one ever heard from Jimmy again.

"Then I guess they'll hear all about your part in this. Maybe we'll share a cell."

Whether or not anything would stick was irrelevant. The last thing he needed was to have suspicion cast on him. He had too much to lose. "Look, I know a guy down here who works for a fancy firm. He's sympathetic to our cause. Let me get him on this."

"What if he says no?"

"I'll handle it. Just keep your mouth shut."

"I won't stay quiet for long. You better get me outta here fast."

Tim nodded and turned away from the table. It took all his focus to keep his expression impassive as he strode out of the building and to his car. He collapsed into the driver's seat and slammed the door.

Swell.

He'd known something was wrong, but hadn't thought things had gone so far south. Or maybe he just hadn't wanted to admit it.

But Amanda? Involved in something so reckless?

Never.

She was too smart for that. Besides, Jimmy wasn't exactly known for his honesty.

The doubts refused to be silenced. Why would Jimmy lie about something like that? What could he possibly think he would gain?

A tactic to get him to cooperate. Had to be.

Besides, why would Amanda care what happened to this woman? She had no motive, nothing to gain from Tanner's death.

Images of Amanda's flirtation collided with Miller's rejection of her. His sister was used to getting her own way, especially where men were concerned. And for some reason, she was infatuated with Miller.

Still, eliminating the competition was less infatuation and more obsession. And it seemed unlikely that Amanda was obsessed with Miller.

But what about the late night phone call she'd made to Jimmy?

He glanced at his watch. Okay. It'd be late by the time he got home. And Amanda was supposed to pick up Camo and Miller at the airport in the morning.

No matter. He needed time to cool off before talking to her anyway. But they would talk.

And one way or another, he'd get her to tell him the truth.

Nate watched the countryside streak by the window.

Finally, back in the states. Sardinia, with all of its drama and stress and near-death experiences, was behind him. Hopefully he'd never return.

They'd managed to catch a local news feed before

vacating the region; the explosion was big news.

Of course, they were calling it a botched breakout attempt rather than an attack on a top-secret lab that no one was supposed to know about, but that didn't surprise him too much.

Amanda didn't say a word as she navigated the rural back roads.

She'd been strangely silent since picking them up at the airport. In fact, other than telling them that Jack seemed to be responding to the antitoxin, she'd hardly spoken.

Weird.

The silence, which he normally didn't mind and certainly appreciated given the source, set his instincts on edge.

"Maybe I oughta drive."

Amanda sliced a look at Camo, who sat in the passenger seat. "Why?"

"You're obviously not paying attention."

"I'm fine."

"You missed our turn about a mile back."

Amanda glanced around, swore, and whipped the vehicle into a tight u-turn.

Bracing his hand on the dash, Camo waited for her to execute the maneuver before asking, "Sure you don't want me to take over?"

"Back off. I've got a lot on my mind."

Whatever it was, it had her stressed.

If her brother was improving, she should be happy. Ecstatic, even. Not irritable and preoccupied.

Was she plotting something? Maybe she already had.

The threat she'd leveled at Lana the other day flashed through his mind. Maybe this state of mind was the result of a guilty conscience.

No. Reyes was protecting Lana. Nothing would happen to her while under the FBI's care.

Somehow he wasn't convinced.

If only he could talk to Lana.

Soon. The test was over. He'd held up his end of the deal; if they held up theirs, he should be the newest member of White Fire. As soon as they got back to the house, he'd see if he couldn't get the information he needed so he could call Reyes and have the Feds move in.

Then he'd be headed home. To Lana. To his kids.

Of course, he didn't actually have a home to which he could return, but surely Dale and Annie would let him stay there. At least until he got a job and could get back on his feet.

Maybe he'd even be able to start a new group home. It probably wouldn't be soon, but maybe someday. These plantations they were passing would be great places for such a venture, although he'd want to find one a little closer to Lana.

He sat up a little straighter. Why hadn't he noticed all these plantations when Zoe had driven him here? Or when they'd driven to the airport?

Panic knifed his gut. He hadn't noticed because he'd been blindfolded.

They weren't concerned about him finding his way back to their place. In his experience, that meant one of two things.

Either he was in or they didn't expect him to leave alive.

Nausea pounded her like waves on sand during a storm. Lana tried her hardest to hide it as she listened to the conversation taking place inside the interrogation room.

Sitting on the other side of the glass, decked out in an orange jumpsuit that wouldn't look good on anyone, Smits sat shackled to a chair.

The DNA results had come back on the blood found in her home from the first attack. And with them, a wealth of information on the man who'd attacked her. The man who now sat opposite Barker in interrogation room one.

The man who didn't look nearly as confident as he had the last time she'd seen him.

And no wonder. The more Barker read, the more she realized just how lucky she was to have survived with nothing more than cuts, bruises, and an almost crushed windpipe.

Not lucky. Divinely protected.

The DNA they'd collected from him after his arrest hadn't yet finished being processed, but she knew without a doubt that once that process was complete, it would tie this man, Jimmy Smits, to the original break in at her home.

"Now how many was that? I've lost count." Barker made a show of flipping through the pages in the thick file on the table in front of him. "Huh. Ten."

Was it her imagination or was Smits noticeably paler than he had been a few minutes earlier?

Next to Smits sat his lawyer, a gangly man with reddish hair and a well-pressed pinstripe suit. In spite of the charges being leveled against Smits, the lawyer exuded arrogance like a peacock displaying his plumage.

"Ten women you raped and slaughtered in cold blood." Barker slapped the file closed. "That qualifies you as a serial offender."

"Not so fast. You have DNA, sure, but no hard evidence that it belongs to my client."

Barker drilled the lawyer with a glare. "Yet. We've sent samples to the lab and once they come back positive, the only decision your client will have left to make is the needle or the chair."

Silence descended. Whether it was because Barker awaited a response or simply for dramatic effect, she couldn't tell. Several seconds passed before Barker shifted his attention back to Smits.

"You know what they do to rapists in prison? Never mind how the guys would react if they learned one of your victims was only fifteen. Bottom of the totem pole, my friend."

A chair scraped across the concrete floor as the attorney

stood. "We're done here."

Barker glanced up at him before redirecting his attention to Smits. "If you're gonna try for a deal, this is your last shot. Once I walk out that door, you can take your chances with a jury."

"I said we're done!"

"What're you offering?" Smits' lips flattened out in a grim line.

"As your counsel, I'm advising you to not say another word."

Both Smits and Barker ignored the increasingly agitated lawyer.

"It's the prosecutor's call, not mine, but I'd guess life in prison with no possibility for parole."

"That's supposed to be an offer?"

"It gets the death penalty taken off the table."

The lawyer reclaimed the seat next to his client. "Jimmy, shut up."

Smits finally looked at his lawyer. "It's my *life* on the line here, you bloody fool!"

Swiveling to Barker, the lawyer cleared his throat. "I need a word with my client."

"No problem. Offer expires in thirty minutes."

"I'm telling you we can beat this."

Jimmy looked over at the serpentine lawyer Tim had hired to represent him. Nick something or other.

Panic shone in Nick's eyes. Knowing Tim, he'd probably told this guy he'd only get paid if he kept Jimmy from talking. The U.S. Marshal had moved them to a windowless room, presumably for confidentiality purposes, with a promise to return in a half hour.

"You need to keep quiet and let me do my job."

Jimmy snorted. "They've got DNA. We both know I'm screwed."

"DNA can be argued. Juries can be bought. Or confused."

"I'm done."

"You know Tim has contacts everywhere. He can make sure the evidence is compromised–"

"And what about the witness? He gonna make her disappear, too?"

"I–"

"Forget it." Jimmy slid his eyes closed. Life in prison wasn't his first choice, but it beat the death penalty.

"Jimmy."

Jimmy waited for Nick to continue, but nothing came. Opening his eyes, he found Nick surveying him.

Once he saw that Jimmy was paying attention, he continued, "I work for one of the biggest defense firms in town. I graduated in the top percentile of my class at Harvard. I'm good at what I do. Now let me do my job."

He didn't want to go to prison. Especially for the rest of his life. Maybe he should trust this joker.

But they were talking about his life. Not money or things or time. His life.

"I can't take that chance. He said the deal expires–"

"They always say that. Trust me, if it comes down to it, we can get it back. But we won't need to."

He wished he could share Nick's confidence. "Between the evidence and that little tramp–"

"I told you, don't worry about the evidence." Impatience tinged Nick's tone. "And as for Deputy Tanner, she'll be easy to discredit."

"I find that bloody hard to believe."

Nick leaned forward, elbows rested on the scarred table between them. "Did you know she was targeted by a serial killer about two years ago? The case made the front page all down the Florida coast. Some lunatic they called the Ripper.

She barely escaped with her life."

The Ripper. He vaguely recalled hearing something about that case.

"Then when her house was broken into recently – which, of course, you had nothing to do with – it brought back all these memories. Put her on edge."

Okay, he could buy that. "How're you gonna explain me being in her house?"

"You two met at a coffee shop near the courthouse and hit it off. She gave you her number, you guys talked on the phone several times–"

"You think they won't pull phone records?"

"Phone records can be fabricated. She called you, panicked because she saw someone outside her house, you showed up, encountered a jealous associate of hers, and things escalated. It was self-defense. After all, they're two highly trained, armed members of law enforcement and you're just a civilian. It'll work, trust me."

How he wanted to believe it. He couldn't remember the last time he'd wanted to believe anything so badly.

But the whole story sounded fishy, even to him. "She works for the Marshals and carries a gun. Nobody's gonna believe she panicked."

"You might be surprised." The doubt must've been scribbled across his face because Nick added, "Burden of proof is on them. All we have to do is create reasonable doubt. And believe me, I'm good at that."

Somehow he didn't doubt that.

So. Did he trust his future to this stranger or cover his own back?

If he covered his back, he'd have to admit guilt. No chance of getting off on a technicality or hung jury on that one.

But if he didn't deal, he could face the chair. Neither option presented a promising future.

"What do you say, Jimmy? You don't want to spend the rest of your life locked up, do you?"

A life behind bars wasn't much of a life at all. And if bad came to worse, he would bet that the feds would still cut a deal later on. Especially with everything he knew about White Fire's illegal activities. "If you're as good as you say you are, get me outta this bloody place."

The plastic smile never faltered. "No problem. Give it a day or two, they'll officially charge you, we'll plead not guilty, and the bail will be set. Soon as that happens, you're free until the trial."

"A day or two?"

"You can't rush these things. You'll be out in no time at all. Trust me."

Trust him? Yeah right.

Jimmy trusted him about as much as he liked him.

Twenty Three

The door hadn't even shut behind them when Tim appeared in the hallway by the base of the stairs. He barely gave Camo or Nate a cursory glance before his gaze locked on Amanda.

"Amanda, my office. Now."

Amanda paled and her eyes swallowed her face for a second before she masked the panic with forced indifference.

Nate glanced from her to Tim and back again.

Was she concerned because this kind of anger was out of character? Or because she knew she'd done something to deserve it?

Neither option offered much comfort.

She pushed her hair behind her ear and crossed her arms. "Geez, Tim, would you chill? Give me a minute–"

"Amanda. Now." The words came out as more of a growl.

Amanda thrust her chin forward. "I don't have to do what you say."

"Fine." Tim's eyes drifted to Nate and settled there for a moment. "Maybe you'd rather discuss Jimmy out here. In front of everyone."

The hands on the ancient grandfather clock against the wall seemed impossibly loud.

Not good.

Something about Amanda and Jimmy had Tim worked into a near rage. Amanda's comment about sending Jimmy after Lana repeated through his mind.

Everything in him wanted to demand to know what was going on. Not that they were likely to tell him anything.

Camo beat him to the question. "Where is Jimmy?"

An exaggerated sigh huffed from Amanda. "Never mind. The office is fine."

Without another word, Amanda strode across the room, brushed past Tim, and disappeared down the hall. Tim followed.

Seconds later, a door slammed.

Nate met Camo's eyes and attempted a nonchalant tone. "Wow. Tim get that upset often?"

"Nah. But if there's one person who can get under his skin, it's her. You have siblings?"

"No."

Camo smirked. "Lucky you. They know how to push your buttons better than anyone else."

Raised voices drifted down the hallway. While he could clearly make out Tim and Amanda's voices, he couldn't decipher any words. If only he could come up with a reasonable excuse to go down the hall, but Camo would see right through it.

Besides, the last thing he needed was to get caught eavesdropping.

Especially when Tim was in this kind of mood.

Camo picked up his bag. "This could take a while. I'm going upstairs to unpack. You should do the same."

A thinly veiled command if Nate had ever heard one. He nodded. "Might as well."

Following Camo upstairs, Nate entertained the idea that maybe their voices would carry through the forced air ducts, but quickly discarded the theory. That only happened in B-grade movies.

Still, once he was behind the closed door, he knelt next to the duct. Just to be sure.

No sound drifted through, only a blast of cold air from the air conditioner.

He wanted to force them to tell him what was going on.

He wanted to walk downstairs and straight out the front door.

Most of all, he wanted to get moving and not stop until he reached Jacksonville. But if the drive from the airport was any indication, they were miles from anything resembling a town.

Besides, with no transportation, no phone, and no resources, his options were beyond limited. Not to mention that he was still a wanted man. For now, it looked like he was stuck.

He just hoped this place didn't become his own private graveyard.

Amanda tried not to wince as the door slammed shut behind Tim. Leaning her hip against his desk, she waited. Big brother would let her know what was on his mind soon enough; no point in validating his temper tantrum by asking about it.

Stopping a full five feet away, Tim flexed his fingers and drew in several deep breaths.

Good. At least he was trying to calm down. There was no talking to him when he got so worked up.

"I got a call from Jimmy."

Okay, so that was good news, right? "See, I told you–"

"He's in jail."

Not good.

Still, Tim didn't necessarily know she had anything to do with it. "What'd the fool do? Drunk driving again?"

"He tried to kill Nate Miller's girlfriend." Each word came out terse, measured.

How should she play this off? Fake outrage over Jimmy's stupidity? Shrug it off as Jimmy being himself? Crack a joke about the delicate male ego?

Tim didn't give her time to consider other options. "He says you put him up to it."

Crud. She should've known Jimmy would sell her out.

Still, it was her word against his. Now to make sure Tim believed her version of the story. "Are you kidding me? Why would I do something like that?"

"You tell me. You're the one who's been acting weird ever since Miller arrived."

"Well, I had nothing to do with it."

He slammed his fist against the desk. "You think I can't tell when you're playing me? Stop lying!"

"I'm not–"

"You called him! The same day he went after her! Tell me why."

"Stop telling me what to do! I'm not one of your stupid lackeys so don't treat me like one."

"If you'd act your age, I wouldn't have to."

She pushed off the desk and stomped to within inches of him. "You have no idea what it's like to be me!"

"What, living in the moment? Acting on impulse without any thought to the consequences?"

"He wasn't supposed to get caught!"

Silence hung between them.

Dang it. She'd confirmed his suspicions. No amount of backtracking or denial would save her now.

"Why, Amanda? Why would you do something so stupid?"

She took a step backward and sagged into a leather armchair. "Jimmy's the stupid one. He's the one who got caught."

"That doesn't answer my question." Narrowed eyes regarded her from under furrowed eyebrows. Red singed almost every inch of his face and the set to his jaw told her that, while his voice was milder, he was far from calm.

"I was trying to get rid of the competition."

"So what, you thought if she was dead, he'd just naturally turn to you?"

It sounded ridiculous out in the open. "Something like that."

He swiveled the desk chair around and collapsed into it. "Why?"

"I don't know, okay? I'd had too much to drink and just acted." No point in mentioning that she'd slept off a lot of the alcohol by the time she called. "But seriously, Jimmy had already been planning to go after her."

"That's irrelevant. What's so special about Miller, anyway?"

"Hey, I don't question your choices in women!"

"*I've* never tried to have someone knocked off because of one. It's because he rejected you, isn't it?"

"Not even close." *It's because I want someone to love me the way he loves her.*

She swallowed the words. No way would she ever admit that to Tim – or anyone else.

"It's bad enough you sleep with half my men like some kind of cheap hooker, but now you try to have a U.S. Marshal killed to get the attention of a thief!" He swore. "Seriously. What were you thinking?"

This was pointless. She could talk until her voice was gone and he'd never understand. "Just forget it, okay?"

"I won't forget it. You tried to have someone killed!"

"You're one to talk. You've actually killed people, so get off your high horse."

"To further our cause. It's different. You made it personal." The chair spun as Tim pushed away and paced to the window. "Just like Jimmy. That's why he was caught. He let it get personal."

"And you've never killed someone for personal reasons?"

He whipped around to face her. "Never."

"It must be nice to be so perfect." Sarcasm saturated her words.

"I'm not perfect. I just use my head."

"And I'm stupid? Is that what you're trying to say?"

"What is wrong with you? If Jimmy tells them about your involvement, you could go to prison."

Prison.

The words "accessory to murder" sprung to her mind.

This wasn't supposed to happen. Jimmy was supposed to kill the girl, Nate was supposed to be heartbroken and turn to her, and she was finally supposed to be loved the way she'd always longed to be.

Tim's comment about her going to prison replayed in her mind.

What if she found herself locked in a small cell with some criminal who would strangle her with her own hair while she slept?

"Do... do you really think I could go to prison?"

"I won't let it happen. If Jimmy tells anyone about this, it's your word against his. The fact you were out of the country when this occurred will help your case."

"But I talked to him that day."

"We'll say that you and he were seeing each other. That you missed him and were calling to see how he was doing. But it won't come to that."

She wished she had his confidence.

But all she could think about was that people like her didn't go to prison. People like Jimmy, sure. She'd never survive there. She loved her freedom too much. And fresh air. Not to mention how horrible she'd look in an orange jumpsuit.

"We need to tell Miller what happened."

A gasp escaped her mouth.

How would he react when he heard? He was a criminal; he'd probably eliminate all of them with his bare hands. "We can't!"

"We have to. If he hears about this from the media or someone else, he'll assume we were involved and come after us. But if we get in front of this and make him think Jimmy acted independently, we might be able to secure his loyalty."

Or at least avoid his wrath.

She drew in a breath. "When do you want to tell him?"

"The sooner the better."

Lana wanted nothing more than to collapse. And not move for days, if at all possible.

But she didn't know where to go. For the second time in less than a week, her house was once again an active crime scene and inaccessible.

Not that she possessed even the faintest desire to go back. Too many bad memories had taken residence in that place.

Maybe she should consider selling. Find a place across town. Perhaps a condo in a highly secured facility. One with alarms, gates, and 24-hour security personnel.

She pushed the thought aside.

Now was not the time to make any serious decisions. Healing was needed in her mind as much as her body.

Maybe more so.

For now, she'd crash at her parents' house. It felt safer than anywhere else. And since her parents would be out of town for another four days, she wouldn't be putting them in danger should that second man actually decide to come after her.

She watched through the one-way glass as Smits was led from the interrogation room in handcuffs.

Why couldn't Smits have been reasonable and turned in his accomplice? Then this whole mess would be over.

Maybe she should talk to Smits herself. See if she couldn't trip him up.

Or at least talk some sense into him.

She'd catch him at the holding cell, before they took him back to the pod.

Ten minutes did nothing to prepare her to face him. While he looked better behind bars than he had in her home, she would've preferred to never see his face again. He slowly pushed himself off the bench and approached the bars.

"Missed me, did ya, luv? I'm touched."

"Don't flatter yourself. I just stopped by to tell you you're a fool."

Eyes narrowing, he clamped his lips together.

Fine. She really didn't care what he had to say anyway. "You're going to wish you'd taken that deal."

"Threats, luv? Sure sign of desperation, that is."

"Not threats. Fact." She realized that she'd crossed her arms over her chest at some point and mentally berated herself for the sign of weakness. "I don't know what your lawyer told you, but you will *not* get out of this one. You will go to prison. You may even go to death row."

"You'll have to convince the jury on that one."

"Don't count on it. Did you know that in Florida, the judge can override the jury? Oh yeah. The jury might recommend life in prison, but the judge can still sentence you to death. Face it, you're sunk."

"Not if they find me innocent."

A harsh laugh scraped her throat. "You? Innocent? With the evidence against you, they'll probably be back from deliberation within an hour. And this buddy you're protecting? Where will he be when they're strapping you into the chair?"

She didn't bother to wait for a response before turning to go.

As she strode down the corridor, his voice bounced off the walls behind her. "Think you're smart, don't ya, luv? We'll see how smart you are when they're fishing your friend's body from the water."

Half a step from the door, she froze. Her friend? Had to be

Nate, right?

No. He was just trying to get a rise from her. Acknowledging the comment would only provide him some sort of sick satisfaction.

But what if there was something to it?

Approaching the cell, she found that he hadn't moved from the spot she'd left him. "What are you talking about?"

"Nate Miller." His grin reminded her of a shark poised to strike. "You didn't really think they'd let him live, did you?"

"What do you know?"

"Don't know nothin' 'bout it. I'm just sayin'. He knows too much."

"You're lying." Her words argued with the truth ringing through her head. "He's helping them with something. They wouldn't kill him."

"He's outlived his usefulness." A low chuckle reverberated off the walls. "Face it, luv..."

She took a half step closer to hear his suddenly lowered voice.

"He's probably dead already."

No. He couldn't be dead. With his background, he could handle himself. Those guys wouldn't get the drop on him.

She couldn't convince herself. After all, they'd gotten the drop on her, hadn't they?

Smits' words replayed like a bad recording.

It made sense. Nate could identify them. Could probably lead the FBI to their location. He'd gone from asset to liability in less time than it would take her to turn and exit the room.

"You'd better pray you're wrong."

How'd she get so close to the bars? She didn't remember moving in–

His arm shot between the bars, his fingers closing around her lower arm and jerking her toward him. Before she fully realized what had happened, her cheek was pressed against the cold steel, his muggy breath tickling her skin.

Stupid! This wasn't her first time dealing with someone

behind bars.

She knew better than to get too close. How could she have made such a rookie mistake?

"And you better pray they make the deal a whole lot sweeter or that little tidbit is all you're gonna get."

She jerked free, stumbling slightly as he unexpectedly released her.

With her hands fisted at her sides to hide the trembling, she waited a few seconds for her breathing to normalize. "Life in prison is the best option you can hope for. You'd be wise to take it."

Whirling, she stalked toward the exit.

How could he still wield so much power from behind bars? For crying out loud, she wasn't some wimpy little kid.

Yet she shook like he could still get her.

His voice again bounced behind her. "Better hurry, luv. Might not be too late to save him."

The door slammed closed behind her, cutting off anything else he might say. If only it were that easy to banish that same voice from her nightmares.

Twenty Four

Nate jerked awake. Blinked hard and rubbed his stiff neck muscles.

A glance at the clock revealed he'd only been out for about ten minutes.

Dang jetlag. He hadn't meant to fall asleep. In fact, that was why he'd chosen to sit in the chair versus sprawling across the bed. One minute he'd been trying to figure out how to get in touch with Lana and the next, well, here he was.

Hard rapping sounded from his door. Must've been what woke him.

He opened the door and found Camo standing on the other side. "Tim wants us all down in the sitting room."

Great. He doubted they were getting together for an expression of gratitude. Falling into step beside Camo, he ran through the options in his head.

One. Mission over. Tim was going to kill him.

Two. Tim was going to make him an official member of White Fire.

Three. Tim was going to use Lana as leverage to get him to do something else.

Four. Tim was going to give him the money and have someone drive him into town.

He liked option four. But he wasn't nearly naïve enough to believe that would be the outcome of this situation.

No, something told him that if he wanted out of here, he was going to have to resort to force.

Or subterfuge.

But not yet. In order to get the clean slate promised by the FBI, he still had work to do.

Tim and Amanda glanced up as he walked in. For the first time he could remember, Amanda didn't smile or flirt; instead, she glanced away. Tim looked like he'd been pacing behind the sofa on which Amanda sat. The sober set to his lips promised trouble.

"Have a seat." Tim gestured at the chairs flanking the sofa.

Perching on the edge of one of the wingback chairs, he noticed that Tim waited until Camo took the other before clearing his throat. "First of all, thanks. My brother and the rest of the guys are on the rebound."

Nate nodded, but didn't reply.

"So, uh, I heard from Jimmy earlier."

This had the distinct ring of bad news. And with Jimmy involved...

Lana.

Nate struggled to draw air. If Jimmy had hurt her, there wasn't a force in the world strong enough to keep Nate from tracking him down.

"Uh, Jimmy called me from jail." Tim raked his fingers through his curls and finally settled his attention on Nate. "He went after your friend. Revenge."

Hearing it was even worse than having the idea run through his thoughts.

"She's fine–"

Nate shot to his feet. "You expect me to believe that? After what he did to her the last time?"

"It's true. I looked into it."

Interesting how Tim kept the sofa between them. Nate crossed his arms over his chest and waited.

The wait didn't last long before Tim continued, "It seems they expected him to return. They'd set up some kind of trap and when he entered the house, they caught him."

A trap.

With Lana as bait. Her idea, no doubt.

He didn't know who he wanted to throttle more: Tim for putting Lana on Jimmy's radar, Jimmy for going after her, SAC Reyes for agreeing to Lana's crazy scheme, or Lana for always putting herself in danger.

Of his options, only one was in the room.

"Look, I didn't know, okay?"

"Right. And I should just take your word on that one? You went after her before."

"Just to show you we were serious. But you did what we wanted. We have no reason to go after her now."

"You shouldn't have gone after her the first time. I told you I was in. You should've trusted me." Nate's hands throbbed from being clenched so tightly.

A brief hesitation, punctuated by a small nod. "You're right. If we'd left her alone, Jimmy's ego wouldn't have taken a beating and he wouldn't have felt this insane need to reclaim his honor."

"I need to talk to her."

"So they can trace the call back to us? Not a chance."

"You've gotta have a few burner phones around here, right? I'll keep it short."

"You're a fugitive, remember? Calling her is exactly what they expect you to do. Trust me. She's fine."

No matter how much he wanted to push it, something told him to let it go.

He'd just told Tim that they should've trusted him; didn't he owe them at least a pretense of the same courtesy? Especially if he wanted them to cut him in on the action?

He eased out a breath. "You're sure she's okay?"

"Not even in the hospital."

"Good." Nate glanced at the others in the room before returning his attention to Tim. "So what's next? You'd mentioned maybe having a place for me in your organization. The offer still stand?"

Tim stared at Nate. "You're good with that? After all this?"

"If she's okay, then yeah, as long as no one bothers her again."

"You'll have to cut all ties."

"No fooling." Nate did nothing to mask his sarcasm. "There's a bounty on my head, remember? Going back isn't an option."

Tim studied him. While his face gave nothing away, it didn't take a psychologist to figure out that Tim was trying to gauge his trustworthiness.

Nate maintained eye contact.

Finally, Tim nodded. "We could use a good hacker. If you're as good as they say you are, then there's a place for you here."

"It's been a few years, so I'm a bit rusty, but I can pick it back up again in no time." Assuming he could maneuver his way through all the latest security measures and firewalls, but with any luck it'd never go that far. "So what's the score?"

"Not so fast. I'll expect a demonstration before I tell you anything."

So much for wrapping this up today. "Name it."

"Let me confer with Zoe. I'll get back to you. For now, you can stay here."

Funny how he made it sound optional when they all knew it wasn't. Nate stuffed his hands in his pockets and tried to act casual. "Let me know when you figure it out."

If they figured it out. This could simply be a stall tactic while they decided how to kill him and dispose of the body.

If that were the plan, wouldn't Camo have done it in Sardinia? Why go to the trouble and expense of flying him back to the states if the plan was to kill him?

What he wouldn't give to get out of this place.

Did he have enough information to satisfy the FBI?

Probably not.

He could give them names and this place, but he still

didn't know White Fire's future plans. And that had been the deal.

So in spite of the danger, he was stuck.

Checking with the morgue regularly had paid off. Lana stared down at the blonde girl on the medical examiner's steel table.

It was her. No question.

The pale blonde hair with dark red tips and pink shirt banished any doubt. This was the girl she'd witnessed entering Richie Ochoa's house.

And now she was dead.

Swiveling her attention, she focused on the medical examiner standing a few feet away. "Cause of death?"

"We'll have to wait for toxicology reports to confirm, but my guess is overdose." The ME flipped through the pages trapped on his clipboard. "Found enough partially digested pills in her stomach to take down a sumo wrestler, plus traces of something consistent with a balloon."

Hmmm, Micah's drug mule theory was looking better all the time.

"And we don't have any idea who she is?"

"No ID or missing person report matching her description. Prints aren't in the system, either."

The information came as no surprise – after all, the girl was listed as a Jane Doe – but she'd hoped maybe some new information had come in.

"There was something else that you might find interesting."

Lana fixed her attention on the medical examiner. "What's that?"

"She was cut into. Postmortem. Not by someone with any

skill, either."

Looking down at the sheet draped body, Lana searched for signs of mutilation. "Where?"

"Her stomach."

If the girl had been smuggling drugs in her body, maybe Ochoa or one of his goons had tried to retrieve whatever might be salvageable. "Any idea why?"

"I don't speculate."

"You're into facts, I get that. But if you had to guess…?"

The ME hesitated. "Combined with the pills in her stomach, I would wonder if she was running drugs and maybe still had some balloons inside her that someone wanted to get out."

Good to know that someone else was thinking along the same lines.

After thanking the medical examiner and extracting a promise for him to keep her posted, Lana stepped out into the scorching Florida sun. She slowly removed the sunglasses perched atop her head and put them on.

Experience had already taught her the importance of avoiding sudden movements. While the pain wasn't as sharp as it had been, she ached all over.

Maybe she should've listened to Barker when he'd told her to take some time off.

But hiding out from the world would only make things worse. She had to reclaim her life.

Once she returned to the office, she'd pull the police reports. While she doubted the body had been found anywhere near Richie Ochoa's house, the timeline indicated that the girl died shortly after that midnight visit.

Ochoa was in this up to his soulless black eyes.

And once she proved it, Ochoa would never stand the slightest chance of seeing Maria again, much less gaining any kind of custody.

The trick lay in finding the evidence to support what she knew to be true. She had zero jurisdiction in this matter. And the last thing she wanted was to get into a jurisdictional boxing match with some cop because he felt his case was being threatened.

Not to mention that she had her own caseload to handle.

Barker would wring her neck for even thinking she could handle both. Especially after all that had happened the last few days.

But she didn't have a choice. Ochoa appeared intent on pursuing custody of Maria.

The evidence convinced her that Ochoa was already responsible for at least one young woman's death. He'd have to add a U.S. Marshal to the list before she allowed him to make Maria another of his statistics.

One way or another, she'd figure out what he was up to and bring him down.

"You've spent the most time with him. What's your take?" Tim leaned back in his desk chair and studied Camo, who sat across from him.

"Hard to say, but he seems like a decent enough guy. And before you ask, nothing happened with him and Amanda."

"That's something in his favor." Especially since, from everything he'd seen, it wasn't for lack of trying on Amanda's part.

"If anything, I have a hard time believing he killed those guards."

Alarms blared in Tim's head. "What makes you say that?"

"Gut feeling." Camo rubbed his chin. "He seems too soft. You know he saved my life down there. I was stuck and outta air and he put himself on the line to get me out. He coulda taken off and let me drown, but he didn't. Also watched out for Amanda without taking advantage."

"What do you mean?"

"Amanda got hammered the other night. He helped her to her room so she wouldn't get hurt or fall overboard. Beat a hasty retreat when she threw herself at him, though."

"You're sure about that?"

"Yeah. She kissed him but he broke it off and left her there."

Hmmm. Miller sounded almost too good.

What were the chances this whole thing was a setup and the guy was really an undercover agent for the FBI? "Think he could be a plant?"

Camo shook his head. "The guy was in prison for over two years. That'd be a really long undercover operation for an uncertain payout. And Eddie just went in six months ago. How would they know any of us would get caught?"

"Maybe we weren't the original target. Maybe they saw an opportunity and grabbed it."

"Still a long time to have an agent inside. Besides, he killed those guards."

"That could be faked."

"Eddie witnessed it."

"Maybe they got to Eddie, too." Now that he thought about it, Eddie had been awfully eager to get Miller on board.

Why? Because the FBI had promised him something if he did?

"Do you hear yourself? Eddie's been with us for years. You really think he'd turn that quickly?"

"Prison changes people. If he were desperate, he could do anything."

"Same thing applies to Miller. Yeah, I have a hard time seeing him kill three guards in cold blood, but you never know what someone is capable of."

"He's in love with a U.S. Marshal. What if they offered him some kind of deal?"

"He still would've had to fool Eddie into thinking he'd killed those guards. Eddie's not an idiot."

He wasn't the brightest color in the rainbow, either.

Camo rubbed his head and released a gusty breath. "Look, I'm not sayin' he's not a plant, but I just don't buy it. There're too many variables at play here for the FBI to be using him. And bottom line, if he is legit, we need him."

Camo was right. It'd be a shame to lose a good hacker just because there were some unanswered questions.

"Okay then. Let's make him earn our trust."

"What're you offering?" Jimmy stared at the woman from the prosecutor's office sitting directly across from him. Puffy blonde hair, lips painted so bright they could probably be seen in the dark, pinched features, expensive looking suit, all business.

"Jimmy, I really think–"

Jimmy slid his attention to his lawyer.

Not *his* lawyer, Tim's lawyer.

The man wouldn't even be here if the prosecutor hadn't insisted. "I don't bloody care what you think. I wanna know what they're offering."

No matter how he'd tried, he hadn't been able to get the words Miller's chick had said out of his mind.

Maybe she'd been lying.

Maybe not.

But what if the judge did sentence him to death?

He'd decided it was worth at least hearing the prosecutor out.

Folding her hands on the table in front of her, she cleared her throat. "We'll take the death penalty off the table."

He snorted. "That's it?" Shifting his attention, he honed in on the U.S. Marshal who'd interrogated him earlier. "Pathetic. You're wasting my time."

The prosecutor leaned in, her blonde hair bouncing around her face. "I don't think you understand. The evidence against you is tremendous. I've won cases with a fraction of what is stacked against you right now."

"You're the one who doesn't understand. The guy I can give you, he's the head of White Fire. We've already hit two places with a toxin. I can give you the rest of the targets."

"White Fire?" The U.S. Marshal planted his hands on the table and towered over Jimmy.

Yeah. He'd thought that would get their attention. "You've heard of us."

"What's the name of this toxin?"

"Jimmy." The warning in his lawyer's tone did nothing to still Jimmy's tongue.

"Shut up." He glared at the man before turning back to the U.S. Marshal. "I look like a bloody scientist to you? You should be more worried 'bout where he's gonna use it."

Silence.

Jimmy tried to smother his satisfaction.

He'd gotten 'em. Just a matter of time before they came back with a better offer. And he'd make 'em keep comin' back until the offer was good enough.

Maybe he'd ask for witness protection.

Yeah, that'd be a sweet deal. No prison, the government giving him a new name and place to live, money; he could handle that.

He was the one holding all the cards. They'd have to do whatever he wanted.

"I really need to confer with my client. Alone." Jimmy's lawyer leaned in, his tone firm.

He'd had enough of this guy. Only watching out for Tim's best interest, he was. "Forget it. You're fired."

"Jimmy, think about this. You don't want to do that."

"You got a hearin' problem? Get out."

Silence descended for several heartbeats. The lawyer's chair scraped the floor and his footsteps echoed off the bare walls as he walked to the door and exited the room.

"Life in prison is still the best I can do." The prosecutor pressed her bright pink lips together.

"Really, luv, don't insult my intelligence. I want zero time in prison and witness protection. Put me in some house on a beach somewhere."

A harsh laugh erupted from the U.S. Marshal. "Keep dreaming. You raped and murdered at least ten women, not to mention assaulting two of my people. You're not going anywhere."

"Then people are gonna die."

The blonde cocked her head. "Prove it and maybe we'll talk."

"How the heck am I gonna prove it from in here?"

"That's your problem."

Stupid little witch. Jimmy leaned back in his chair. "Guess I've got nothin' to say."

The Marshal straightened. "Good. Personally, I want to see you fry. We have other ways of tracking down your accomplice. Ways that don't require us to let you off easy."

Freakin' liar. If they had other ways, they wouldn't have offered a deal in the first place.

Unless something new had turned up.

He didn't know what that could be, but there were things that tied him to Tim and Camo. Phone records, for example. How hard would it be for the feds to get their hands on that? Probably not too tough.

Was he slitting his own throat by turning down this deal?

The idea of facing life in prison made him want to put his head through a wall. Already felt like he'd been inside for a week when it'd only been two days. Less, actually. They'd arrested him Saturday night and it was only Monday afternoon.

Was life in prison really any better than the death penalty?

Yeah, yeah it was. Being zapped by an electric current or having a needle jabbed into his arm didn't sound like fun either.

The prosecutor gathered up her papers and rose, preceding the U.S. Marshal to the door.

This was probably his last chance. Spill his guts or risk going to a jury?

"Wait."

Moving as one, they turned to look at him.

"No death penalty. In writing."

They returned to the table. A stack of papers slid across to rest in front of him.

He read every word. Or tried to. All the legal mumbo-jumbo was hard to follow. Probably should have a lawyer look it over, but he'd just fired his.

'Sides, he got the gist of it.

Grabbing the pen, he signed and dated in the indicated places before directing his attention to the Marshal. "You're lookin' for a bloke named Tim Williams and I can tell you where he lives."

Twenty Five

Nate pushed back from the computer and looked at the faces around him. "We're in."

"Really?" Zoe stepped closer to look over his shoulder. "That was fast."

And here he'd thought he was taking too long. "Five years ago I could've done it faster."

He looked back at the computer screen. Reyes had pretty much told him to do whatever it took, but had the Special Agent in Charge had any idea that would include hacking the Department of Defense's system?

Zoe snagged the mouse and clicked a few things before shaking her head slowly. "He really did it. We're in."

"Right on, man." Eddie slapped his shoulder. "See, I told you this dude was cool, yo."

"So what do you need me to look up?"

Tim smirked. "Right now, nothing. I just wanted to know if you could do it."

Great. He'd broken the law for no reason.

On the upside, he hadn't given Tim or his crew any sensitive information. Things could be a whole lot worse.

"Zoe, Eddie, I think we're done for now." Tim's tone was casual.

If Eddie and Zoe found the dismissal unusual, neither gave any indication. Eddie looked at Zoe. "Yo, wanna grab a beer?"

A limp shrug moved Zoe's shoulders as she preceded him

out of the room.

Nate tried to calm the snakes slithering in his gut. Clearly the dismissal didn't include him.

Why would he be singled out?

Unless Tim didn't trust him. Maybe he was going to have Camo take him down.

A second passed in silence before he couldn't take it any longer. "Now what?"

Tim studied him. "Now we move forward with our plan. I need the blueprints for Liberty Stadium and a way in."

"Don't you want Zoe in on this, too? She's a hacker, right?"

"We don't need two people on this. You're the better hacker. And I need this by tomorrow."

"What's going on there?"

Tim exchanged a look with Camo before answering. "NAACP conference. And we're going to steal the show."

Lana cleared the files from the top of her desk and locked them in the bottom drawer.

Activity still bustled around her, but she was so zapped she could hardly think straight. Even though she'd taken it easy yesterday, the events of the past week weighed her down, making today the longest Monday in history.

At least it'd been a good day.

A print had been lifted from the silver belt worn by the girl in the morgue. That print led to a low-level thug whose police record listed multiple tattoos, including a cobra encircling his neck. It'd been enough to get a warrant and the police had him in an interrogation room now, hopefully spilling all he knew about Ochoa and his operation.

Whether or not any evidence existed to make the charges

stick, it should create enough doubt in the mind of any judge to keep Ochoa from ever gaining custody of Maria.

At the very least, Ochoa would be too busy defending himself to be able to pursue the whole custody angle.

While she wanted him to go down for every dirty little thing he'd done, she'd be content as long as Maria remained safe and far away from that slimy punk.

As she powered down her computer, her cell rang. The caller ID flashed Barker's name.

She answered on the third ring.

"Reyes heard from his agent on the inside. This thing is wrapping up tonight."

"Tonight?" Paul would be coming home. She'd get to greet him with good news about Maria and hand him her own heart at the same time.

"Yeah. It's a joint task force now. We've got a location and are headed out. You coming?"

What kind of dumb question was that?

It'd take a restraining order and handcuffs to keep her away.

Fresh energy surged, fueled by adrenaline that she hoped would get her through whatever came next. "Where should I meet you?"

"The airport. We've got a plane en route to fly us to Charleston."

"I'm on my way."

He had what he needed. Now he had to find a way to get that information to Reyes.

No sign of an actual phone in this place. And Tim obviously didn't trust him enough to give him a cell phone.

Nate's fingers flew across the keyboard as he pulled up

the blueprints, but his mind worked through the bigger problem. Getting word to Reyes and getting out of here. Preferably before his cover was blown or he was forced past a point of no return.

If it weren't for Eddie sitting at the computer next to him, he'd try to access the FBI's website and send a message that way, but Eddie might see it.

Assuming Eddie could tear his eyes away from the porn on the screen in front of him, but it was a chance Nate couldn't afford to take.

He'd come too far to risk blowing it.

Maybe he could sneak out.

The garage was detached. He could steal a car and drive away without being heard by anyone inside the house.

If the car had a full tank, he could drive through the night and maybe make it out of the state before Tim even knew he was gone.

Of course Tim knew where he'd go. Worse than that, he knew where to find Lana.

He'd deal with all of that when and if he had to. Slipping away was still the best shot he had. Now he just had to get away from Eddie and make it to the garage without being seen.

A yawn snuck up on him.

That'd work. "Man, I think that jetlag's catching up with me."

"Uh-huh." Eddie didn't turn away from the screen.

"I'm gonna take a break. Grab a snack or something."

He exited the room, walking with purpose but not haste. Everything in him wanted to run, taking down anyone who got in his way, but he forced himself to maintain a normal pace.

Okay, hallway cleared. No sign of anyone in the main entry.

When they'd left the other day, they'd exited through the door in the kitchen. The garage wasn't far from that door.

From somewhere to his left, the murmur of the television. Camo? Amanda? Tim? With any luck, all three.

He went right. Down a darkened hallway. Past closed doors. Thin strips of light crept out from under several of them, but he heard no indicators that anyone was actually inside.

Almost there.

The kitchen was lit up brighter than a Christmas tree on December twenty-fifth. He blinked as he stepped inside.

Amanda leaned against the counter, a shiny green apple in her hand.

Dang. So much for sneaking out.

No matter. It was probably wisest to wait until everyone had gone to bed anyway. Of course that meant sneaking past Camo's room without waking the man, but he'd done it on the boat easily enough.

Wait. He couldn't sneak out. All the doors and windows chimed when opened. How could he have forgotten that very important detail?

Amanda swallowed the bite she'd been working since he'd entered the room.

"Whatcha doing?"

Oh, you know, thought I'd hotwire a car and get the heck out of here.

Probably not the wisest response.

He crossed to the fridge. "Needed something to drink."

Retrieving a bottle of water, he turned to find Amanda's gaze locked on him.

Crunch. Slowly chewing her bite of apple, she surveyed him in silence for several long seconds. "That's it?"

What did she expect him to say? That he came to see her? "Yeah."

Maybe he could take advantage of this situation to learn more about the grounds and their layout. That way he could give the FBI better information before they stormed the place.

"Where is everyone?"

She bit into the apple again, processed the bite, and pushed off the counter. "Tim's out in the stables. Last I saw, Camo was watching some stupid action movie. Jack and a few of the other guys are putting the final touches on the device so we're ready to go tomorrow night."

They'd be ready to go all right. To prison.

"They doing that in the garage?"

She shook her head. "No. There's a shed beyond the stables that they've converted into a workshop."

"You guys have horses?"

"Not just any horses. We breed champion race horses. It's a passion of Tim's."

Of course it was.

Ranked right up there with killing people because of something as superficial as skin.

That was his way out. "Sounds interesting. Maybe I'll pop outside and take a look."

"I'll show you." She tossed the apple core into the garbage and rinsed her hands in the sink.

Great. So much for sneaking away.

She opened the door, releasing a sticky wind that pushed her curls back from her face.

He followed her across the back lawn, purposely ignoring the garage that beckoned off to his left.

Directly in front of them loomed a stable larger than the average family's house. Light spilled onto the lawn from an open set of double doors.

"How many horses do you guys have?"

"Six mares and two studs. One of the mares injured her foot earlier today. I suspect that's where we'll find Tim, checking on her."

"Does Tim have some kind of medical training?"

"Tim?" She laughed. "No way. But one of our guys used to work at a vet clinic. He joined us and gets paid handsomely to take care of Tim's pets."

Ugh.

If this got ugly, Tim he could probably handle. Amanda definitely. But Tim, plus Amanda and another guy – maybe more, probably all armed – the odds were against him.

At one time, he'd been skilled at thinking on his feet. Looked like tonight he might find out if that was a skill he still possessed.

Twenty Six

The historic plantation rose out of the night in front of her. Light glowed from several windows on the first floor, as well as a few on the second.

With both the undercover agent and Nate inside the house, this was a rescue mission first, raid second.

A few feet away, the FBI agent leading this operation surveyed the scene in silence. Next to him stood another agent, maybe his partner, maybe just a second in command. At the very least, the two had worked together often and were likely friends, judging from the unspoken communication between them.

Kind of reminded her of when she and Alex worked side by side.

The second in command let out a low whistle. "We don't have the manpower to pull this off."

Regardless of the fact that the words had been spoken softly, Lana had no trouble discerning them.

What did he mean not enough people?

The joint task force that had been hastily constructed consisted of seven FBI agents, eight if she counted the man in charge, plus five U.S. Marshals' deputies. Seemed like plenty to her.

The agent in charge shook his head. "Manpower or not, we're gonna have to make it work. SAC Reyes made it very clear our primary objective is to recover our agent and the Bureau's asset."

Wow. Really?

While she didn't view Nate through the lens of his past, she couldn't believe Reyes had placed such a priority on getting a man with Nate's history out alive. And it didn't appear he'd even told his men with whom they were dealing.

Evidently miracles did still happen.

"Tactically, what are our options?"

The lead agent's gaze roved over the twelve agents and deputies surrounding him as he considered his friend's question. "We divide into teams. Most of us take the house, you guys," he pointed at Lana, a deputy she didn't know, and two FBI agents, "sweep the outbuildings."

The outbuildings, really?

Because, what, she couldn't handle herself in the house where the real threat lived?

It had to be the bruises.

She wasn't the only woman present, so she doubted it had anything to do with gender. No, the bruises had probably convinced this guy that she couldn't handle herself in a combat situation.

Satisfaction filtered across Barker's face. He'd set that up?

Of course he had.

Her connection to Nate, not to mention the fact that they suspected her second attacker was somewhere in the house, made the outbuildings infinitely safer on many levels. And given that she wasn't quite at a hundred percent yet, he'd probably requested that she be kept out of the house if at all possible.

She should be grateful that he was watching out for her.

But mostly she was irritated.

Irritated at being treated like a weak invalid. Irritated at the men who did this to her. Irritated at herself for getting hurt in the first place.

The lead agent checked his watch. "We go in hard and fast. At exactly 9:08. We'll take the front door." He gestured to his friend and one other agent, then assigned the remaining agents and deputies to breach via the house's other exterior entrances. "Keep an eye on the time. Come back alive."

Lana jogged behind one of the agents. The weight of the Kevlar vest slowed her down. Normally it wouldn't have given her much trouble, but the last few days had been draining. Keeping up was a challenge.

They skirted the edges of the lawn, approaching a detached garage.

The darkened windows made it unlikely that anyone lingered inside.

As she flattened herself against the side of the building, she caught a glimpse of another building, much larger, toward the back of the property. Previously hidden behind the house, it appeared to be a barn of some sort. A very big barn.

And judging from the light blazing inside, an occupied one.

In spite of Barker's efforts, she might see a little action tonight after all.

"It doesn't look too deep. We'll keep it clean and I'm sure she'll be fine."

Nate watched Tim gently stroke the mare's mane.

A full minute passed before Tim glanced up and noticed Nate and Amanda standing outside the stall. Surprise flickered in the brief widening of his eyes and he straightened.

"You'll keep tabs on her and call me if there's the slightest change?"

Nate suspected there was only one correct answer to that question. Fortunately, the vet seemed to know it. "Absolutely. Morning Star and I will be right here."

A tight nod and Tim moved away from the horse to approach them. "Why're you out here?"

"Relax, will you? Nate wanted to see the place and I told him I'd show him around."

Releasing the latch, Tim swung the gate open and stepped through, stopping a few feet away from Nate. "This area is off limits. And you have work to do."

"I'm working on it. I got the blueprints, but needed to get some air." He nodded at the injured mare. "What happened?"

"One of the guys left some debris on the ground and she got into it." A cell phone rang. Tim ignored it. "It'll never happen again."

The ominous tone in his voice brought to mind images of a shallow grave at the edge of the property. Somehow he didn't think Tim would hesitate to kill over a horse.

The phone stopped ringing. Only to begin again several seconds later.

Tim snatched it from his pocket, barely glanced at the display before accepting the call. "What?"

Seconds passed.

The color slid from Tim's cheeks and his jaw tensed. "Stall them as long as you can. Amanda and I will cover things out here."

Tim pocketed the phone and palmed a Ruger so quickly that Nate blinked. The business end of the gun was aimed at the center of his chest.

"Whoa, what-"

Tim took several large steps away, putting him out of Nate's arm reach. "Like you don't know."

"I have no-"

"Shut up! The FBI's at the house right now with a warrant. You're the only one who could've sold us out."

"When would I have done that, huh? It's not like I have access to a phone."

"How should I know? All I know is that out of all the people here, you're the one I trust the least. It's awfully suspicious that they show up about the same time you do."

Nate slowly exhaled. Stay calm. "Think about it. If I'd

tipped them off, would I have come out here? No way. I would've booked it on foot so they couldn't catch me, too. The law and I aren't exactly friends."

"Amanda, make sure the hatch is secure."

Amanda shot a glance at Nate before moving back the way they'd come.

The gun in Tim's hands shook. Rage or fear, Nate couldn't tell, but either way, emotion clouded Tim's judgment.

Which could be a good or bad thing.

Only one shot at this now. "If the feds are raiding the place, you're outmanned and outgunned. Give me a rifle. I can help."

Tim snorted. "And have you turn it on me and my men? Not a chance."

"You don't have many options."

The gun leveled as Tim settled into a shooter's stance. "You might be surprised."

"FBI. Drop it. Now."

A woman's voice, on his left.

Tim jerked his head toward the voice. "So. That's how it is, huh?"

Nate whipped around to find Zoe standing a dozen feet away, a small gun in her hands.

Funny how Tim didn't sound that surprised. Had he suspected?

Guess that explained how the FBI had gotten so much of their information. But how had they known to move in now? Zoe hadn't been around when Tim had told him the plan.

It wasn't important. For now, all that mattered was getting that gun away from Tim.

"It's over."

The gun wobbled slightly in Tim's hand, but he made no move to do as she'd directed. "Did Brody know? Did he figure out who you are? Is that why he's dead?"

"He's dead because he was driving too fast for the conditions and lost control."

"You killed him." Red flushed his face and his jaw clenched.

"He was trying to get away from us when he lost control, but we didn't force him off that road. He was careless and it got him killed. Nothing more." She paused. "Now drop. The. Gun."

Movement glimmered behind her. The vet! "Zoe–"

An arm curled around her throat and a hand enclosed her gun hand.

She struggled. The man drew his arm tighter until she made a small gagging noise.

Nate glanced away to find Tim staring at him with a gaze that plunged the room's temperature to below freezing.

The gun was still aimed at his chest.

Tim racked the slide.

The garage cleared in forty-five seconds.

Lana raced across the lawn on the heels of the agent leading the way, pushing through the pain ricocheting around her torso.

She could hear the labored breathing of the other agent and deputy behind her.

The four of them paused outside the doors to the barn.

The conversation on her earwig was little more than a whisper in the background as she strained to hear noises from inside.

Nothing. No voices, animal noises, or machinery.

The agent nodded and they rushed in, Lana and the lead agent taking the center, the other two sweeping in from the sides.

Hay mingled with the faint scent of manure. Dust particles hung in the air, illuminated by bright florescent lights suspended from the high ceiling.

Directly in front of them, an empty circular training ring took up most of the room.

Beyond it, a wall divided the training area from the stables. Two openings, one at either end of the wall, provided access to whatever was in the back of the barn.

Lana joined the agent on the left while the lead agent joined the deputy on the right.

Faint neighing drifted out from the doorway ahead.

Aside from the soft crunch of their shoes on the hay, the only sound she heard was her own heartbeat pounding inside her head.

She flexed her fingers on the grip of her gun, trying to ignore the dampness slickening her palms.

At the doorway, they paused long enough to receive a nod from the lead agent before proceeding through. Three closed doors to her left. Solid wall on her right. Ahead, that wall ended with the first of two hallways.

The agent jerked his head toward the closed doors.

Okay, he was taking those. She nodded at the hallways ahead, waited for his return nod, and edged forward.

A glance around the corner found the lead agent at the opposite end, checking stalls as he moved toward her.

No one else was in sight.

She stole past the first hallway. One down, one to go. She eased past the third and final door. Almost there.

Behind her, a soft click.

She whirled in time to see a flash of blonde hair. And a fist.

No escape route.

Good as dead.

The thoughts crashed into Nate's mind as Tim wrapped both hands around the grip.

He dove to the left, crashing against the ground as the gun went off.

The boom bounced between the stalls. Snorts accompanied the clacking of hooves, broken up by the occasional whinny.

To stop moving would be suicide.

Nate rolled, pushed to his feet, and lunged for the gun.

The fist slammed against Lana's temple. Her head bounced off the wood to her right.

Black rimmed her vision as she fell to the concrete beneath her. Bells echoed between her ears and amid them, something exploded.

Not an explosion, a gunshot. Nearby, but not aimed at her.

She blinked, pushed herself up.

Around her, the horses neighed, their cries drowning out the ringing in her head.

No sign of her attacker.

Her Glock rested at her feet. She hauled in a deep breath, retrieved it, took a shaky step forward.

Get it together! Someone could be dying.

Her next step was steadier.

Above the rumble from the horses, a second shot shattered the chaos.

Nate's hand wrapped around the gun's barrel. He forced the weapon up.

The recoil from the second shot traveled down his arm. The bang rang in his ears.

Tim tried to force the weapon down, but Nate was bigger and stronger.

Now to get the gun from Tim's grip. Nate slammed Tim's hand against the wood stall behind him with as much force as the awkward position allowed.

Curses spilled from Tim's mouth, almost drowned out by the noise from the horses.

The gun fell from his fingers.

Nate kicked the weapon away.

Hatred iced Tim's eyes. Tim's skull slammed into his forehead. Although he should've seen it coming, the head-butt took him by surprise. He staggered backward.

Tim jerked away.

The sound of another gunshot reached his ears at the same time that something smashed into his stomach.

Acid burned his core.

His thoughts stilled. Fog drifted across his mind and darkness edged his vision like a vignette.

The hand he put to his stomach came back red and sticky. He looked down.

Blood leaked through a hole in his shirt.

His legs quaked. His strength vanished. Then his knees buckled.

The pain faded.

He felt the concrete scratching his cheek, but didn't remember falling.

Thoughts drifted through his head like a slide show moving too quickly to make out the pictures.

He'd been shot.

He was dying.

Just like all the targets Matt had taken out so many years ago. Targets he'd helped Matt find.

Poetic justice.

Faces consumed his mind. Lana. His kids. The Webbers. Matt. His mother. People from church.

Lana's face returned. Had he ever told her how much she meant to him?

The noise surrounding him grew dim. Images faded into nothingness. He tried to fight it, but it was no use.

Darkness drowned him.

Twenty Seven

Noise behind her!

Lana glanced back to find the FBI agent darting out of one of the rooms. Good. Backup.

A third shot.

The sound dispersed the haze still lingering in Lana's mind.

The final row of stalls. It was the only place that her attacker could've gone. And the most likely source of all three gunshots.

She bolted toward it, paused, then glanced around the corner.

Five people, four standing, one on the ground.

She focused on those standing. A blond man and a woman who looked like she might be related, a redheaded man, and a dark-haired woman with blue streaked hair. The redheaded man had the dark-haired woman in a chokehold.

Blood pooled beneath the downed man.

He didn't look like one of theirs. Maybe he was the undercover agent. Or maybe the undercover agent was the woman in the chokehold.

Smoke drifted from the barrel of a gun clutched in the blonde woman's shaking hands.

Sensing the agent behind her, Lana burst around the corner, her own weapon up, leveled at the woman. "Drop it! Now!"

The woman started, the gun slipping from her fingers.

"Hands behind your head."

No one made a move to comply. The other agent and deputy approached from the opposite end of the row.

"Hands. Behind. Your. Head." Lana spoke slowly, her gaze locked on the blonde's glare.

The woman slowly raised her hands as both the agent and the deputy moved in. Cuffs dangled from the agent's fingers.

Lana turned her focus to the redheaded man. "Let her go."

The man lifted his arms and the woman jerked away.

For the first time, Lana noticed the gun in the dark-haired woman's hand. "Drop your weapon."

"It's okay." The agent behind Lana came forward to cuff the redheaded man. "She's one of ours."

Okay then. So if she was the undercover, who was the guy on the ground?

Lana transferred her attention to the victim. Still sprawled face down on the ground, blood saturated his once white t-shirt.

Tall. Muscular build. Auburn hair.

Relief trickled through her. Not Nate. His size looked about right, but the hair was all wrong.

The details clicked through her mind as she approached and knelt next to the body. Was he alive? Conscious? Her fingers went to his neck as she leaned over to look at his face.

No.

It couldn't be!

She jerked her hand away, stepped over him, brushed shaggy hair away from his closed eyes.

The noise around her faded. For several long seconds she forgot how to breathe.

Nate.

He wasn't moving.

Panic clawed at her stomach; pressure pricked her eyes. They were too late.

Had she felt a pulse earlier? Maybe he wasn't dead. The

blood pooling beneath him denied her hopes.

Still, she put her fingers to his neck again, prayed for the faintest...

There! Erratic and weak, but definitely a pulse.

"Call an ambulance!" She didn't remove her eyes from the pale face she knew so well.

"Already done." The deputy's voice sounded from behind her. "I called it in after the first shot."

No blood on his back; the bullet must still be inside. At least there was only one wound with which to contend.

She needed to get a look at that wound. Make a compress to stop the bleeding.

"Help me roll him."

The deputy crouched down beside her and gently helped her roll Nate to his back.

A grunt slid from his limp lips.

"Paul?" She shrugged out of her jacket and pressed it against the oozing wound. "Hey, look at me."

Aside from a faint fluttering of his lashes, he gave no indication he'd even heard her.

Water flooded her eyes. She blinked rapidly to clear her vision. A rebellious tear broke free and she wiped her cheek on her shoulder.

"Paul. You need to stay with me, got it? Help's coming."

They were way out in the sticks; how long would it take an ambulance to arrive?

She tried not to think about that.

Pray. She should pray.

Words refused to surface. All she could think was *please, God. Please.*

One of the agents stopped beside her. "You know this guy?"

"He's..." What had they called him? Oh, yeah. "The bureau's asset."

The agent swore softly.

Time lagged.

Sweat trickled down her neck, tickling its way between her shoulder blades. How long had it been? Five minutes? Ten?

More importantly, how long could he survive without help?

Fatigue shuddered down her arms. Where was that ambulance?

Wait. Was that a helicopter?

She strained to hear above the horses' protests, worked to drown out the chatter from her earwig.

The heavy thump-thump-thump carried in on a breeze.

Of course they'd send a helicopter. It'd take too long to get an ambulance out here. "Hold on. They're almost here."

She jumped as a hand landed on her shoulder. "How's he doing?"

The concern and familiarity of Barker's voice almost unhinged her control. Swallowing, she worked to separate her emotions from the situation. "Not good. Pulse is thready."

Over the earwig, someone directed the medics to the barn.

Please, God. Please.

Rattling. An approaching gurney.

She didn't remove her gaze from his face. Didn't release her pressure on the wound.

Please, God. Please.

"Tanner. Hey, kid, you gotta step aside."

An EMT appeared on the other side of Nate, his gloved hands going to the jacket she had pressed to the wound. Falling back, she let the second EMT take her place.

One cut away his shirt; the other listened to his heartbeat.

The whole thing felt surreal.

Nate's face blended with the stable floor. Cement gray wasn't a good look on anyone.

A rag was thrust into her crimson-coated hands. She glanced up to find sympathy in Barker's eyes.

It didn't look good.

They all knew it, even if no one would say it out loud.

But if God could raise people from the dead, surely He could keep one man from dying. *Please, God, please.*

"It was self defense! He was trying to kill my brother!"

Lana turned at the sound of the woman's voice. Only then did she realize that the horses had quieted.

The lead agent surveyed the blonde woman coolly. "That a fact?"

"Not even close." The undercover agent crossed her arms over her chest. "He was trying to get away."

"How were we supposed to know that?" The blond man's lips curled. "The man's a killer, after all."

That voice.

The words faded as she focused on the sound. She knew that voice. Even though she'd only been half conscious at the time, she had no trouble placing him as the second man from her home. The one who'd worn the blue mask.

"You." The small group turned to look at her as she strode closer. "You were in my home."

"You've got the wrong guy."

She stopped a few feet away and surveyed him. Right size and frame. Right voice.

But it was the smug satisfaction in his eyes that solidified her certainty. "Liar. You and your British scumbag friend broke into my home and tried to kill me."

A smirk twisted his mouth. "And why would I want to do that?"

"You tell me."

"It wasn't me. I don't know you."

"You know what? I don't care. Deny it all you want because we have your accomplice in custody right now. He's already told us all about you. You're Tim, right?"

The smirk faltered. Color slid from his face. "You're got nothing on me."

"We'll see about that."

Behind her, the gurney rattled across the floor. She

glanced back to see the EMTs rolling Nate toward the corridor.

This situation was contained. Without a word, she turned and joined Barker.

He jerked his head toward the door. "Go."

Forcing her legs to move, Lana jogged behind the gurney. Part of her wanted to be in on the FBI's raid and interrogation of the suspects, but a greater part of her wanted – no, needed – to keep an eye on Nate.

Like her presence would somehow keep him alive.

The EMTs loaded him into the helicopter and climbed inside. When she tried to follow, one of the EMTs held up a hand.

"Are you a relative?"

"No–"

"Immediate family only."

She pushed past him. "Try to stop me."

He wisely decided against it.

Slamming the doors closed, he directed her to a seat in the corner and hollered at his partner. "Let's go!"

The pilot lifted the chopper off the ground.

It might've been her imagination, but she thought Nate's color looked worse. How far was this hospital? And would they make it in time?

She was at the glass when he flat lined. The window separating her from the emergency room below prevented her from hearing the buzz, but the horizontal line on the monitor told her all she needed to know.

The nurses bustled around, supplying the doctor with a syringe and paddles. A jolt shook Nate's body.

No response.

Another jolt.

The line didn't waver. Tears pooled like acid around her eyes. She blinked, but otherwise didn't move, not even when they spilled down her face.

Please, God. Please.

The paddles connected with blood-stained skin again. And again.

Still nothing.

The doctor lowered the paddles and slowly shook his head.

No! Don't give up. Not yet.

The words stuck in Lana's throat. Not that the doctor would've heard her through the glass anyway.

The line jumped on the heart monitor.

That small blip flushed fresh life into the doctor and the whole room came to life with him. The nurses rushed around getting God only knew what and the doctor fussed over Nate's still body.

How long she stood there watching, she had no clue.

After what felt like years, Nate was wheeled out of the room via a door opposite the window from which she observed. The doctor, who'd more than earned his wages, spotted her and nodded at a large male nurse, who moved toward the door.

She crossed the observation room – which she guessed was primarily used by med students for training purposes – and hurried down the short flight of stairs. The nurse met her at the bottom step.

The pale blue of his scrubs served as a grim reminder of the stone colored countenance she'd witnessed earlier on Nate. She forced her eyes off the scrubs to the nurse's drawn face.

"I'm sure you saw how close we came to losing him in there." The nurse released a long breath.

"From what I could see, you did lose him." The words burned her throat as viciously as the tears had scorched her eyes.

"Momentarily." The nurse paused, probably in an effort to organize his thoughts, before continuing, "The doctor doesn't yet know the full extent of the damage. They're taking him into surgery now. In the meantime, we need as much information about your friend's medical history as possible."

Lana blinked several times. "I don't really know that much about it–"

"Is there any way for you to find out? It's very important. A family member you can check with?"

"No family." She didn't even know who his doctor had been back in Jacksonville. How could she hope to track down any sort of medical records?

Wait. The prison would have kept some sort of records, maybe would've even gotten his medical history from his previous doctor. It was worth a shot.

"Let me make some calls."

He nodded. "And there's the matter of paperwork."

"I'll do what I can."

"Good. Visit the admissions desk once you get the history and they'll get you started."

All she could manage was a small nod.

Sympathy crinkled the corners of his eyes. "Try not to worry. I think the worst is behind us."

She certainly hoped so.

"Any word?"

Lana jerked. Looking up, she found Barker striding toward her. Red webbed the whites of his eyes, giving evidence to an exhaustion she understood all too well.

"Not yet. Last I heard he was in surgery."

He nodded at the clipboard in her hands. "They've got

you filling out the paperwork?"

"Somebody has to." She glanced down at all the blank spaces. "Not that I have a clue about most of these things."

He sank into the chair beside her and glanced at the paperwork. "You're going to need a new admission form."

"Why?"

"You put Nate Miller. But Nate Miller died tonight."

What? But how? How could Barker have heard something she hadn't?

It didn't make any sense. The doctors knew she was out here; they would've told her if something had happened. And Barker just arrived. He'd asked her about Nate's status, which meant he couldn't know any more than she did.

"I–I don't understand."

"I just got off the phone with SAC Reyes. He made Miller a deal when he took this assignment. Successful completion of the mission and he'd give him a new life. With Miller's, uh, colorful past, the easiest way to accomplish that is to declare him dead. We'll leak the story to the media and let it go from there."

Wow. Not only was Reyes holding up his end of the bargain, he was making sure the door closed behind Nate's former life forever.

She set the pen down. "So what name should I be putting?"

Silence lingered as Barker appraised her. "Reyes didn't say, but I'm assuming Miller will probably stay in Jacksonville, right?"

Heat touched her ears. "Probably."

At least, she hoped he would.

"Then we'd better stick with Paul Van Horn, don't you think?"

Not the safest identity for Nate to assume. "Has that name ever been linked to Nate Miller?"

"No. There are no known aliases on file."

"What about address, Social Security number? Have

they established any official documentation for him?"

Barker hiked an eyebrow. "He lived with that identity for several years. You think he doesn't already have the documentation in place to validate it?"

True enough.

A doctor appeared in the doorway. She recognized him as the one who'd resuscitated Nate earlier. Blood smeared the front of his scrubs. She tried not to stare at it, but it beckoned her like a siren's call.

Nothing in his expression revealed the surgery's outcome. No relief, disappointment, sorrow, or satisfaction. Only a grimness that made her gut clench.

Crossing the room, the doctor stopped in front of them. "You're with the gunshot victim, right?"

No sound made it past her paralyzed throat. She managed a small nod.

"He's out of surgery. It'll be a long road getting back to where he used to be, but he's doing well. I expect he'll make a full recovery."

Full recovery. The words healed the wound in her heart.

Twenty Eight

Faint beeping pulled Nate from dreams filled with blood and death.

He cracked his eyes slowly against the bright light surrounding him. A veil shaded his mind and his blurred vision refused to clear. Where was he?

The last thing he remembered....

Reality hurtled through his brain. The stables. Tim and Amanda. Zoe. A gunshot.

Then nothing.

Was he dead?

His vision sharpened and the room came into focus. In front of him, a white wall with a TV mounted by the ceiling. To his left, an open door revealed a stark hallway with the same white walls and vinyl flooring.

Somehow he'd thought there would be more color in heaven.

The bed beneath him rivaled a slab of asphalt for comfort. A variety of monitors and tools sat next to the wall by his head. Tubes protruded from his arm.

Definitely not heaven. A hospital.

He'd survived.

He eased in a deep breath.

A fresh citrus scent assailed his senses. It was familiar, comforting. Intoxicating.

Lana.

Movements slow, he turned to find her head on the edge

of his bed. Her hair, contrasted against the white linens, looked even blacker than usual.

She'd pushed a chair flush against the side of his bed. Her legs were curled beneath her, her arms folded under her head, her eyes closed.

The position looked completely uncomfortable and he suspected she'd awaken with a crick in her neck, but he wouldn't wake her. No doubt she needed the rest, especially after what little he knew about the kind of week she'd had.

A small frown curled her lips downward and he wondered what plagued her dreams.

He absorbed the sight of her, enveloped the image with his mind.

Although her hair covered most of them, he caught a glimpse of some angry looking bruises on her neck. A bandage on her arm, more discoloration on her face.

All from that thug Jimmy, no doubt.

Given half a chance, he'd love to teach that jerk what it felt like to be someone's punching bag.

Even so, it was good to see her. No matter her condition, she looked beautiful.

A guy could get used to seeing this every morning.

Reality checked him. He wouldn't get used to it, so imagining it would only cause more pain.

"Convict" forever tagged his name. There was no way she'd be able to get past that, not now, probably not ever.

Almost of its own volition, his hand inched across the bedding to cover hers.

Her eyes snapped open, focused on him, and blinked twice. Straightening stiffly, she swung her legs down and stretched.

"Are you okay?" The words scratched from his throat.

"Me? I'm not the one who was shot. How are you feeling?"

All things considered, better than he should be. His arms and legs felt heavy, his thinking muddy, and he had a strange buzzing in his head.

But at least he was alive.

"Okay, I think." He twisted to see her better. Pain jolted up his side, sent alarms blaring through his brain, and stole the oxygen from his lungs. Black seeped into his vision.

"Paul? Paul." Her voice filtered through the agony. "Nate!"

The concern in her tone, the urgency, drew him back. Blinking, he found her leaning over him, lines etched across her forehead. He released a shaky breath. "Remind me not to do that again."

She slowly lowered herself back into the chair. "Be careful you don't tear the stitches, okay?"

"The doc tell you how bad it was?"

"Are you kidding? With all these privacy laws, they wouldn't tell me much of anything."

Silence overtook her for a few seconds.

Studying her face, he saw her chin twitch. And her eyes, did they look unusually damp? "What aren't you telling me?"

Her eyes slid shut. A tear broke free from her lids, hesitated on her lashes before trickling down her cheek.

Permanent internal damage.

Paralysis.

He tried wiggling his toes. The blanket covering his feet moved. Okay, so not that.

His mind flashed through one horrible option after another. Maybe something terminal had happened that couldn't be fixed. Maybe he only had hours to live.

"You flat lined."

The words were so soft that he couldn't be sure he'd heard her correctly. But there was no mistaking the anguish lining her face. "You were there?"

A jerky nod met his question.

A memory drifted through his mind. Lana leaning over him, telling him to open his eyes, to hold on.

She'd been at the stable. After he'd been shot.

Wait a minute.

He'd been outside Charleston, in the middle of nowhere, when he'd gotten shot. She should've been several states away, not watching him die.

"Where am I?" His voice seemed unusually hoarse.

"St. Bartholomew's Hospital."

That told him nothing. "Charleston?"

"Yeah."

"How... why're you here?"

Exhaling a shaky breath, she visibly worked to regain control. "There was a raid. Barker made sure I was included."

It seemed like there was more he should be asking, but at the moment he couldn't figure out what those questions should be. In fact, he couldn't seem to think of much of anything.

"You're awake." A man's voice came from somewhere behind him.

With movements slow and deliberate, Nate turned to find Reyes and Zoe standing in the doorway. They crossed to take up position by the side of Nate's bed.

"How are you doing?" Reyes' question sounded more like a formality than actual concern.

"Not bad, all things considered." He met Zoe's eyes. "So. Why didn't you tell me you were FBI?"

She pushed back hair that was no longer blue streaked. "Wasn't sure I could trust you. Audra Parker, by the way."

Even the Jersey accent was gone. Like she'd flipped a switch or something.

"Anyway." Reyes gave Lana a curt nod. "I was actually coming to give Tanner an update, but since you're awake, I'll tell you both."

Get on with it already.

"We found a storm cellar underneath the barn. It was packed with illegal weapons and explosives. Also found a guy tied up down there. Said he supplied the bio-toxin. The raid resulted in twenty arrests. None of them are talking, except

Smits, and he's given us several solid leads to pursue."

Nate felt his energy ebbing. With any luck, Reyes would leave soon. Maybe he could help the process along. "Thanks for the info."

"There is another matter we need to discuss."

For the first time, he noticed the briefcase in Reyes' hands. This couldn't be good.

The lab. In the law's eyes, it didn't matter that he'd been opposed to blowing up the lab. He'd been there, so he was an accessory whether he liked it or not.

One thing was clear. His freedom was history.

He should've known it was too good to be true.

"Look, I didn't have a choice. I tried to talk them out of blowing up that lab–"

Placing the briefcase on a chair, Reyes waved off his concern. "The lab is on foreign soil. We truly couldn't care less about it."

Nate sagged back against the mattress.

Phew. Maybe he wasn't going back to prison after all.

At the press of a button, the latches on the briefcase flipped open. Reyes removed a file folder and withdrew a single sheet of paper. "I thought you might like a copy of your death certificate."

What?

Nate stared at the certificate bearing his name. Dated yesterday.

At least he thought it was yesterday. In all honesty, he wasn't certain how long he'd been out.

"The official report will state that after being cornered by the FBI, you were gunned down in the crossfire."

Good. He'd made a number of enemies over the years and the last thing he needed was for one of them to get wind of his release and come hunting him down. If that happened, Lana or one of his kids could get caught in the middle.

Unfortunately, it wouldn't be the first time.

He looked up to find Reyes holding out another sheet of

paper. Also official looking.

"And a birth certificate for Paul Van Horn." Reyes held out the folder. "You'll find all the documents you need to officially become Paul Van Horn. Again."

Inside, he found a Social Security card and driver's license.

And a check. For fifty thousand dollars. Made out to Paul Van Horn.

A glance up found Reyes studying him closely. "Let's just say that there were monetary incentives being offered in a few of the cases that we've been able to link to White Fire."

While the money would come in handy, at the moment he was too tired to care.

He stuffed everything back into the envelope and set it aside.

"There is one more thing." When Nate looked his way, Reyes continued, "The bureau's always interested in people with your unique skill set. If the need for your talents should arise, would you be open to working with us again?"

"You want me to join the FBI?"

A faint smile thinned Reyes' lips. "Hardly. Think of yourself as more of an outside consultant brought in for special projects."

The only skill set he had involved breaking into secure places. Or hacking them.

The word "no" lingered on his tongue but went no further. What if the target was a group like White Fire and helping the FBI could save the lives of millions? Wouldn't it be worth it then?

Pain throbbed behind his eyes. He couldn't deal with this now.

"I guess it'd depend on what you needed from me."

"Fair enough. The issue may never arise, but we'll keep you in mind, just in case." With a glance at his watch, Reyes rose. "I can see you need your rest. Nice job on this case."

"Thanks." Audra smiled, probably the first real smile he'd

seen out of her. "You helped wrap up that case faster than I would've on my own."

Flashing a smile that felt about as genuine as a three-dollar bill, Reyes turned and strode from the room, Audra half a step behind him.

Nate turned to find Lana's eyes locked on him. "Free agent for the FBI. Who'd have guessed?"

"It's an interesting twist, that's for sure." Exhaustion beyond measure clung to every cell in his body, but he wouldn't give in to it, not yet. It'd been too long since he'd gotten to talk to Lana and he wasn't ready to let her go.

Especially not after coming so close to losing her.

Her voice cut through his thoughts. "I should go, too."

"No. Just don't hold me accountable if I fall asleep while you're talking."

Shaking her head slowly, she pushed herself up. "You're exhausted. I'll come back later. Promise."

Pushing past the pain, he snagged her hand. "Lana, please. Stay."

Her smile warmed him, even if it was filled with concern.

Lowering herself back into the chair, she didn't remove her hand from his. "So what's next?"

"I don't know. As soon as I'm better, I'd like to visit my kids, but then..." he tried to manage a shrug, but his body refused to cooperate.

"They'll be thrilled to see you."

"I hope so." He'd missed them so much. "Maria?"

"She's good. I think Richie will be dropping the custody issue, but if he doesn't, I promise you I'll make life incredibly difficult for him."

"Good." He couldn't wait to wrap that little girl in a hug again.

But after he saw his kids, then what?

Before he'd gone to prison, he'd always had work to do, something that needed to be fixed on the house or papers to file or bills to pay, but the house was no longer his. Neither were any of those responsibilities.

He knew what he wanted more than anything, but she was beyond his reach.

His gaze found Lana's. Eyes so dark they appeared almost black met his, and lurking in the depths, he thought he saw something.

No. It couldn't be.

But what could it hurt to ask? She knew how he felt, had probably always known, and when she turned him down, he could claim the painkillers had made him crazy.

"Lana."

His throat swelled shut and he swallowed hard. Man, this wasn't going to be easy.

"Is there any chance, I mean, do you think..." A frustrated breath vented from his lips. "Think you could ever forget my past?"

Black hair swished gently as she gave her head a small shake. "No."

Figured. He couldn't really blame her. Not even he could forget his past, how could he expect–

"But I'd like to try moving beyond it."

What?

He examined her face. Could he have misinterpreted her words?

Rising, she leaned forward and kissed his forehead before moving lower. All thoughts, all worries, all regrets, vanished as her lips met his. The kiss ended long before he was ready.

She eased back and settled in the chair.

This time her expression, if not the kiss itself, left no room for misunderstanding. Whether or not she'd be able to get over his past remained to be seen, but hope took root.

The Bible said that God worked in mysterious ways.

What it failed to mention was how much God also liked irony.

At one time, he'd embraced brotherhood with a man nicknamed The Shadow of Death. And now, in the shadow of death, he'd finally learned what it meant to be alive.

Dedication & Acknowledgments

Dedicated to the many wonderful people of strong faith that God has placed in my life throughout the years. My parents and grandparents (never underestimate the power of a godly heritage!), Pastor Marc and Michele, Pastor Del and Janet, and many others who are not named here; God has used your example, encouragement, and wisdom to influence me in profound ways. Thank you for being God's instruments.

Wow, God is good! Aren't you glad that He works all things together for our good? (Romans 8:28)

Thank you doesn't begin to cover the appreciation that is due to the many people who have supported this dream over the years. A very special thanks to my family, especially my Mom, who has read every word I've written – at least once, and to my special friends Janet and Del, who have helped mold this book into what you see here. I am so blessed to be surrounded by such a wonderful group of people.

A big thank you to Carissa and Grant for your help in getting the lab scenes "just right." I couldn't have done it without your expertise and I am so thankful for the time you both took to explain chemicals and protocols.

The greatest thanks, however, must go to the ultimate

Author and Lord of all. Thank you, God, for sparking within each of us a desire to create something of value. Anything we create shows the touch of the Creator. If you haven't read His book lately, I'd encourage you to do so. It's my favorite and worth reading every single day!

A note from the author

Thank you for joining me on Nate's road to redemption! Be sure to pick up the final book in the Deadly Alliances series, Deadly Deliverance. Deadly Deliverance circles back to Dimitrios, Lana's EMT brother from the first book in the series, and follows him as he tries to solve his friend's murder while protecting the people he loves from a group of killers.

I'm also excited for you to meet Stormy, a somewhat cynical woman with a past as dark as her name implies... if she can only remember what that past is! I hope you'll keep your eyes open for her story, Shadow of the Storm. I've included a sneak peek here so keep reading.

As I've written this series, I've grappled with the topic of honesty. It's such a hard thing to find in our society these days and yet, even the most dishonest of people will likely tell you that they value honesty from others.

While it seems like such a straightforward topic, in this world in which we live, it's anything but easy.

I've wrestled with the necessary deception that would come from someone living a life like Lana or Audra, a life where pretending to be someone else or hiding the truth about details of your life or work, seems to serve the greater good. Where telling the truth could endanger that person, their family or friends, or any number of other people. What would happen if Lana just told everyone about the witnesses she was protecting, the fugitives she was tracking, or people she'd helped place in WITSEC? Isn't dishonesty a good thing in a profession such as hers?

I must confess that I don't have the answer to that question and, frankly, am glad that it's not my dilemma to face. I have great respect for the countless men and women who work to protect others and must walk that line.

All I know for certain is that scripture tells us that God is truth (John 14:6, I John 5:6). So truth matters.

We're good at justifying little white lies, things that we say that aren't true but that make people feel better – short term anyway. We're also really good at avoiding the truth by telling half-truths or lies of omission, but those things are still lies.

Is there a situation you need to make right? Someone with whom you've been less than honest and you need to set things straight?

I'd challenge you to join me in pursuing absolute honesty in your day-to-day life, speaking the truth in love, with the other person's best interests at heart. How might your home, your workplace, your church – even the world – look differently if we actually tried to imitate Christ (as the term Christian implies) and lived lives of complete honesty and integrity? I think it'd change the world.

Thanks for reading. If you enjoyed this story, I hope you'll tell the other readers in your life about it... and maybe consider writing a brief review.

I'd love to hear from you; comments, suggestions, constructive criticism – they're all helpful. Feel free to email me at candle.sutton@outlook.com or message me on facebook (facebook.com/candlesutton).

May God bless you and remember to demonstrate an honesty that points the world to the One who IS truth!

Excerpt from

Shadow of the Storm

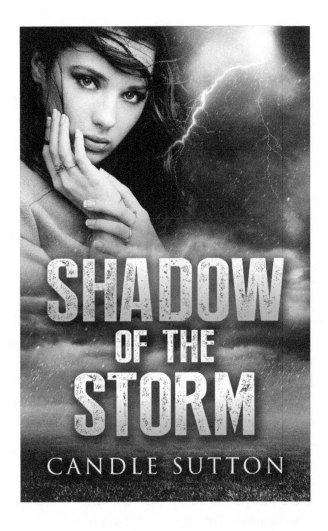

One

"You're gonna dump her off the bridge?"

The man's words penetrate the fog in my head. The ground beneath me bounces. I try to open my eyes, but they're heavy. Too heavy.

"You got a better idea? With any luck, they'll rule it a suicide."

A different voice, still male. This voice is deeper, more guttural, than the one that woke me.

"Why not just shoot her and be done with it?" It's the first voice. Slightly high-pitched and a little whiny.

"Because bullets can be traced, you fool!"

"Use her gun."

"I don't have it."

Somehow I know they're talking about me. And they're going to kill me if I don't do something to stop it.

Silence descends.

Pain stabs behind my eyes. Between that and the jackhammer pounding in my head, it's a miracle I can hear anything.

But I can hear things.

There's water. Rain, maybe.

Yes. Rain. And a rapid swish-swishing sound that I think is windshield wipers. Tires hum on pavement.

I'm in a car.

The fog slips away. Clarity sharpens my thoughts, which click through my head like a slide show.

Two men. Maybe more. Maybe not. Hopefully not. I don't know how many guys I can take on at once.

Why would they want to kill me?

I force my eyes open. At first, all I see is darkness, but then the darkness forms into shapes.

A few feet from my face is a small purse with rhinestones on it. A blue duffel bag rests beside it. Beyond them is the back of a seat.

I lift my head a few inches off the rough carpet scratching my cheek.

It looks like I'm in the back of some kind of vehicle. An SUV, I think.

Lightning flashes outside and I jerk.

A chunk of hair falls into my face.

I try to push it aside, but my hands are trapped behind my back.

Metal cuts into my wrists.

So I'm not just trapped. I'm handcuffed.

This night keeps getting better and better, doesn't it?

"What bridge?" Whiny voice breaks the silence.

A horn blares, preventing me from hearing the full response, but I catch the word "drum".

Instinct silences me. I don't know how I fit into this mess, why I'm handcuffed, or even if I'm really the one those guys intend to kill. The fact that I'm handcuffed in the back of a vehicle overhearing plans of murder doesn't bode well for my survival.

Okay, first problem. Get out of these handcuffs.

Simple, right?

I lay my head back on the carpet and ease my hands down my backside, around my hips, and toward my feet. My heels catch on the metal.

My fingers trace the shoes. Smooth finish. Long, pointy heel.

I got all dressed up for something tonight. And I'm betting it didn't include being kidnapped and murdered.

Pushing the shoes off my nylon-covered feet, I slide the handcuffs around my heels.

Huh. The slick surface of the nylons comes in handy for something.

Okay. So the handcuffs are in front of me. Now what?

They feel a little loose. Maybe I can slip free. I flex and twist my hands. The metal chafes the skin but I can't get the restraints over my thumbs.

Dislocate your thumbs.

The thought flashes through my mind like the lightning that occasionally illuminates the vehicle.

Dislocate my thumb? Who even thinks such a thing?

The crazier thing is that I know how to do it. Just like I know it'll work.

I clench my teeth and press my face against the carpet beneath me to muffle any noise I might make. Drawing a deep breath, I do it. Everything in me wants to cry out, but the only noise is the pop of the joint dislocating. As loud as it seems to me, I don't think there was any way that the men up front could have heard it.

Fire races through my hand. I force air in and out in measured breaths.

The pain fades to a dull throb and I slip my hands from the cuffs.

Turning my face back against the carpet, I push my thumbs back into the socket. This time, a small gasp does escape, but I doubt they heard me above the road and storm noise.

Now to find a way out of here.

Before we reach the bridge or the drum or wherever it is that these guys plan to kill me.

I twist to look at the rear door.

Good, it has a handle. So all I have to do is open the door and make a break for it. And hopefully not break my legs or neck in the process.

There's no telling how fast we're going. Having broken

bones will make me that much easier for these guys to subdue.

But I have to try.

I will not just sit here and let them kill me. If they want me dead, they're going to have to work for it.

The car jerks.

I slide forward several inches as the squeal of tires on soaked asphalt fills the vehicle. The horn blares and gruff voice releases a string of choice words questioning the intelligence of the driver who cut him off.

We're almost at a complete stop. It's now or never.

I scoop up my shoes, the purse, and the strap for the duffel bag in one hand and reach for the handle in the other.

Please don't be locked.

The latch releases and I thrust the door out. The dome light pops on.

Behind me, I hear the men yelling, which spurs me to move faster. I stumble out the back, my feet splashing in a puddle.

I need to get out of here.

Headlights approach.

A door slams.

Run, run!

I race across the street. A horn blasts from somewhere to my left, but I don't know if it's the guys who're after me or someone else.

Frankly, I don't care.

My feet hit the sidewalk and I angle for the closest alley. Little pieces of rock or glass, maybe both, prick the soles of my feet, but I can't put on my shoes. There's no way I can run in stilettos.

The blackness of the alley swallows me.

Rain pelts my face, the water running into my eyes. The deluge plasters my hair to my head and makes my dress cling to me.

Shivers rock my body. My limbs feel sluggish, but the

dumpsters flashing by tell me I'm moving quickly.

I drape the strap of the duffel bag across my body.

The action slows me down for a second, but it frees one of my hands. If those guys catch up to me, I need to be able to fight.

Footsteps echo behind me.

A sharp crack splits the night, followed a second later by an exploding brick a foot away from my head.

Not an explosion. A gunshot.

I don't know how I know, but I do. Those men are shooting at me!

Another gunshot. The bullet pings off the dumpster I just passed.

The dark of night is probably the only thing saving me right now. Even so, I'm an easy target.

I weave back and forth, trying to be as erratic as possible.

Are the footsteps getting closer? I risk a glance.

A dark shape lumbers closer. Only one. Where is the other guy?

Doesn't matter. I can't let him catch me.

I push myself to go faster. A cross street is up ahead. Maybe there will be someone there who can help me.

I burst out of the alley.

The street's deserted.

Where the heck am I? Shouldn't there be someone around? Someone other than these guys who want me dead?

I don't stop to consider the question.

I race across the street.

Another gunshot sounds as I enter the alley, another brick showers me in dust.

There's an intersection ahead. Looks like another alley. I make a sharp right into it.

Too sharp.

It occurs to me seconds too late. My feet slide out from under me and I go down, landing in a large puddle.

Pain vibrates up my arms but there's no time to dwell on

it.

I push myself to my feet and press forward.

Ragged breathing echoes between the buildings. Dang. That fall cost me valuable seconds. He's getting closer!

Tears blur my vision. I blink them away and they mingle with the rain running down my face.

This is pointless. He's going to catch me. Then he's going to kill me. So why fight it?

Because I don't want to die, that's why. I can't give up.

A meaty hand clamps on my shoulder and jerks me to a stop.

I scream.

Like what you see? Shadow of the Storm is available now in print and ebook format, available exclusively though Amazon.

Made in the USA
Coppell, TX
23 March 2021

52233491R00204